Also by Roxanne St. Claire

National bestselling author Roxanne St. Claire keeps danger and passion in high gear . . . in her acclaimed Bullet Catchers series

TAKE ME TONIGHT

"Sexy, smart, and suspenseful, *Take Me Tonight* is an absolute must-read. Roxanne St. Claire's Bullet Catchers series defines the very best in romantic suspense—if you haven't read one yet, what are you waiting for? *Take Me Tonight* proves that St. Claire really rocks."

—Mariah Stewart, *New York Times* bestselling author

THRILL ME TO DEATH

"Fast-paced, sexy romantic suspense. . . . A book that will keep the reader engrossed from cover to cover."

—*Booklist*

"Superior romantic suspense. . . . Sultry romance with enticing suspense."

—*Publishers Weekly*

"Suspenseful, exciting, and very hot. . . . Max and Cori have a chemistry that leaps off the page. . . . Be sure to turn your AC up to high when you read this book, because the action, the setting, and the romance are hot, hot, hot!"

—Fresh Fiction.com

"The plot never slows down until the final thrilling confrontation."

—The Best Reviews.com

TAKE ME TONIGHT

Roxanne St. Claire

POCKET STAR BOOKS

New York   London   Toronto   Sydney

An *Original* Publication of POCKET BOOKS

A Pocket Star Book published by
POCKET BOOKS, a division of Simon & Schuster, Inc.
1230 Avenue of the Americas, New York, NY 10020

This book is a work of fiction. Names, characters, places and incidents are products of the author's imagination or are used fictitiously. Any resemblance to actual events or locales or persons, living or dead, is entirely coincidental.

ISBN-13:   978-1-4165-2186-0
ISBN-10:   1-4165-2186-0

This Pocket Star Books paperback edition April 2007

10 9 8 7 6 5 4 3 2 1

POCKET STAR BOOKS and colophon are registered trademarks of Simon & Schuster, Inc.

Cover design by Min Choi

Manufactured in the United States of America

For information regarding special discounts for bulk purchases, please contact Simon & Schuster Special Sales at 1-800-456-6798 or businesss@simonandschuster.com.

*This one is for my stepsons, Rick and Marc Frisiello,
who are brilliant, gorgeous, funny, talented Renaissance men who can
whip up a mean fra diavolo with the same ease that they paint a picture or pen a poem. Through them, I see the past and the future,
and it all looks good.*

ACKNOWLEDGMENTS

Special thanks to a few individuals who helped me make this particular journey look so easy:

Marley Gibson, an amazing writer and dear friend, who generously provided photos, information, and suggestions on every
aspect of downtown Boston with lightning speed, dry wit, and
common sense. (Read her books—she's fabulous.)

Katie Wallis, of Arnold Worldwide Advertising, Boston,
Massachusetts, for being my eyes and ears in Beacon Hill and
many T stops along the way.

Janine Klem-Thomas, choreographer for the Orlando Magic
Dancers, who generously opened the locker room door and let me
into the life of an NBA dancer.

Tammy Strickland, one of the U.S. Top 100 Nurses, who made
sure I didn't inadvertently administer the wrong drugs to any
characters.

Henry Lee, President, Friends of the Public Garden, for kindly
walking me through this historic park, ensuring that every shade
under the willows is accurate.

Kim Whalen, Trident Media Group, who has repeatedly proven
herself to be a literary agent with endless energy, enthusiasm, and
spark.

As always, air kisses to my Pocket Books editor, the incompa-
rable Micki Nuding, who knew Johnny was The One even before
I did.

And, finally, all my love to Rich, Dante, and Mia (and Pepper!),
who think I'm chasing my dream without knowing that they've
already made my dreams come true.

Prologue

If tenacity had a face, Lucy Sharpe was looking at it.
A tornado of determination brewed in angry eyes. A
defiant jaw set against anything that got in its way. Even
her delicate nostrils flared as Sage Valentine leaned over
Lucy's desk and declared, "You owe me, Lucy. Big."

A hundred responses echoed through Lucy's mind,
a thousand ways to say hello for the first time in thirteen years, a million ways to reach out to her sister's
daughter and close the chasm that time and blame had
formed between them.

She remained as impassive as she would be with any
other potential client being turned away. "I'm sorry. I
can't help you."

"Can't or won't?" Sage crossed her arms and peered
down at her aunt, tilting her head. "Big difference."

Tenacity and attitude. Sage didn't look like Lydia
Sharpe, but she obviously had a few of her mother's
traits. "This job isn't right for the Bullet Catchers,"
Lucy said. "My company is a security firm."

"I thought you did investigations."

"Only as it relates to the security of our clients and the principals we protect."

"Come on, Lucy." Sage tapped the desk impatiently. "With all your contacts in government and law enforcement, after all those years in the CIA? You have to be able to get information I can't." She closed her eyes with a whisper-soft sigh. "I wouldn't ask you if it weren't important."

Lucy almost smiled. "I *did* check the temperature in hell when you called."

Sage dropped into the guest chair that she'd refused two minutes earlier, leaning elbows on the colossal writing table between them. "Proof that I am desperate."

Proof that she was resourceful. Another trait of Lydia's.

"Let me tell you what I have." Inches from Lucy's fingertips lay a file folder with details about www.takemetonite.com, a fantasy website run by computer nerds and supported by young women with more money than common sense. The file contained nothing that a dogged journalist like Sage couldn't have figured out on her own. For a Bullet Catcher file it was remarkably thin, but Lucy's sources had revealed enough to know that her niece was wasting her time seeking retribution and responsibility where there was none to be found.

"Takemetonite.com is a privately owned business set up to conduct mock kidnappings and subsequent fantasy rescues strictly for personal entertainment," Lucy said. "They check out and are, for lack of a better word, legitimate."

"So who owns it? Who does these kidnappings? Who polices this? How can it be legal? And who kidnapped my roommate the night she died?" Sage's frustration was clear in the last question.

"The site is owned by a company called Fantasy Adventures, a division of a large software gaming company in Southern California. FA has about forty employees who staff four operations in the U.S., including one in Boston, with plans to open about six more in the coming year. They are profitable and private about what they do."

Sage leaned back in the chair. "And what they do is kidnap women."

"Yes. No doubt you've heard of thrill sites, where people can arrange to do or experience just about anything for a price?"

"Anything," Sage said pointedly. "Including commit a murder."

"True. Those sites are hidden deep underground and are most definitely against the law. But takemetonite.com is much more mainstream, a company that will arrange for someone to have the experience and adrenaline rush of a nonviolent abduction, followed by a rescue performed by handsome young men. And what these young women do to . . . thank their rescuer is paid for on a sliding scale."

"So the men, the rescuers, they're like prostitutes?" Sage's expression was a mix of disgust and disbelief. "The last thing Keisha Kingston had to do was pay for sex."

"She didn't," Lucy said. "Your roommate was never kidnapped. Her suicide appears to have been unrelated to the fact that she'd registered with the site."

Those delicate nostrils flared again. Was that in response to this information, or the word 'suicide,' sitting between them like the proverbial thousand-pound elephant in the room, with all the same ability to crush them both?

Sage shook her head. "Keisha was one of the most intelligent, optimistic, and joyful people I've ever known. She'd be the last person to commit suicide."

"Her death was thoroughly investigated and the autopsy was unambiguous."

"Unambiguous as to *how* she died, not why. I want to know what happened while I was out of town for two months. I want to know what changed her life that much." She narrowed her determined eyes again. "Signing up for this thrill site was way out of character for her. As soon as I found it on her computer, it felt like a lead to me."

A *lead*. Sage was trained to sniff out a story, a cause, and a place to assign blame.

"Besides," Sage added, "she left our apartment precisely at the appointed time of her kidnapping. Two neighbors saw her."

"But she was found back in that apartment the next day," Lucy reminded her. "With a suicide note in her own handwriting and enough ephedra in her body to kill a cow."

"But she could have been kidnapped first," Sage pointed out.

"She never showed, which is very common. As many as one out of four registered participants bail before the abduction occurs. Apparently, fantasy abductions and rescues have become *the* surprise gift to give among more adventurous women, but not all of them want that type of surprise."

"But no one gave her this as a gift," Sage insisted. "She registered herself."

Lucy angled her head in agreement. "And the Boston operation of takemetonite.com confirmed that. However, she didn't show for her appointment. The abduction and rescue never took place and their records are rock solid. Believe me, I checked."

Sage released another frustrated sigh. "Lucy, you may not know this, but I'm an investigative journalist. If I could have just gotten past voice mail with that company, I could have figured out this much myself."

"I have no doubt of that." Lucy had followed her niece's every move in the last thirteen years. She'd read every story Sage had ever published in any magazine or newspaper, saving them in the same file drawer where she kept Lydia's work. But Sage didn't know that. Or care.

Lucy picked up the manila folder and set it in front of Sage. "But I *did* get past voice mail and I'm confident their records are accurate. You may have this."

Lucy resisted the urge to reach across the desk and touch her niece's hand. The gesture would not be appreciated or reciprocated. Instead, she cleared her throat and masked her sympathy with a cool tone. "I know that this kind of death is very difficult to accept, but your answers don't lie with that website. I suggest you let this go."

Sage stood up and slipped her handbag over her shoulder. "I didn't ask for your advice. I asked for your help. But never mind—I'll get what I need myself." Without bothering to take the file, she left the library. Lucy sat motionless while the voice of her new assistant floated down the hall, the front door to the estate closed, then a car motor revved and tires squealed out of the driveway.

Only then did Lucy take a deep and shuddering breath.

So that was it. Thirteen years of estrangement had come down to a six-minute meeting that ended with a thud. Well, there was no one to blame but . . .

Norman Valentine. And Sage's father was long past the point of shouldering blame.

She opened the file and leafed through the few pages. Takemetonite.com was legal and she had no doubt that the operation had nothing to do with Keisha Kingston's suicide, but she'd done a miserable job of convincing Sage of that.

Lucy closed her eyes. Her niece had grown to be as beautiful and spirited as her mother, even though she hadn't inherited Lydia's dark eyes and black hair, and her pale skin belied the Far Eastern coloring from previous generations. But she *had* inherited her mother's nose for news and trouble and a story, along with that terrierlike quality that made Lydia Sharpe one of the best reporters ever to write for the *Washington Post*.

Lucy had no doubt of what Sage would do next, and she was powerless to stop her . . . but not powerless to protect her.

Any Bullet Catcher could do that, but she needed someone who could be *believed* in the role. Someone who wouldn't demand to know who Sage Valentine was, and why she was receiving protection she didn't want; someone who never, ever questioned Lucy's judgment.

Johnny Christiano. Utterly trustworthy, blindly loyal, and every woman's fantasy. Sage would never know who really rescued her . . . and Johnny would never know why.

CHAPTER
One

Earbuds to block out any warning of approaching danger. *Check.*

Long flowing ponytail for an easy takedown. *Check.*

Low-slung runner's shorts to give even the clumsiest rapist easy entry. *Check.*

A midnight jog, a vacant park, not so much as a key in hand for self-defense. *Check. Check. Check.*

Didn't this woman have a mother to teach her any common sense?

Hey—not his problem. Johnny slipped deeper into the shadows of the Boston Public Garden and waited for Sage Valentine to make her next pass.

She approached at an impressive clip and he sank farther into a hedge thick with sickeningly sweet yellow flowers, gauging exactly how long it would take until Hot Legs got herself snatched. The first time she'd passed him he realized she was not only foolish, reckless, and irresponsible, but also fast. Following her at a safe distance, he matched her rhythm.

She rounded the pond, veered into the dim beam of a decorative lamp, then slowed down. Changing her mind? Rethinking her stupid plan? Just buying time? Johnny held back, waiting. She looked toward the footbridge to her right and the Charles Street gate to her left. Johnny, crouched under a low willow branch, saw her sports bra rise and fall with slow, even breaths. Fast, and not even winded.

A beam of headlights cut through the park and she whipped around, her posture suddenly transformed from clueless to alert. Then she wiped her mouth with the back of her hand, fiddled with her iPod, and started into an easy jog.

He stayed about fifty feet behind her, just close enough to get hypnotized by the pendulum swing of her ponytail and mesmerized by the hip-hugging shorts that barely covered her marathon-toned ass. If Lucy had told him she was a runner, he might have planned this differently. But his boss had been short on particulars and long on demands. He only knew what to do, no clue why.

How hard up could a woman be for a cheap thrill? Well, not so cheap. The cost of a plain vanilla fantasy kidnapping and quick release was a thousand bucks. Fifteen hundred if you added a simple rescue. Two Gs for the "deluxe," which he assumed included stud service from your white knight.

Evidently male strippers were *so* last millennium for today's fun-loving girls.

Not his problem, man. He'd just do the job Lucy had given him. That's what Bullet Catchers did. No judgments on the shortcomings of the principal.

She neared the gate and adjusted her earbuds, clearly back in her home state of oblivion. She now ambled slowly, bopping her head to the tunes, tightening her ponytail. Then she stopped, silhouetted against the pale beam that illuminated the swan-shaped boats moored in the pond. She bent over and stretched to touch her toes, her long, blond hair grazing the ground. On an exhale, she flattened her hands on the pavement, her body curled as gracefully as the swan boats behind her.

With a sudden jerk she straightened, squared her shoulders, clenched her fists, and walked directly to the open iron gate that led to Charles Street. Directly to her appointment with a kidnapper. Which either took the cake for stupidity or proved that somewhere in those sexy curves, she hid a set of titanium balls.

She lingered near the gate as a few cars passed the Beacon intersection, two blocks to the north. A white Audi zipped past on one-way Charles Street; otherwise it was as deserted as most of Boston's roads at midnight on a Monday. She walked slowly, drumming her fingers against her bare thigh.

Johnny waited just behind the open gate, stealthy and quiet, but he wasn't worried she'd spot him. Her focus was on the road. The muscles in her back tensed, though she was trying to act relaxed and unprepared. She glanced over her shoulder at the sound of a vehicle approaching. A van. Dark, older model. Parking lights only.

Showtime, baby doll.

She stepped to the curb, slowing near the crosswalk. Johnny counted to five, then broke into a light jog. The van veered into the left lane, dropped to about three miles per hour, then stopped just two feet from her.

She froze for a second, then broke into a light run, just fast enough to seem real. Johnny kicked up his speed as the van's back door opened.

"C'mere, honey," a man called. "I need some help."

She hesitated for a moment.

"C'mere," he repeated.

She took one step closer, then Johnny swooped in, grabbed her by the waist, and lifted her right off the ground, never missing a beat of his stride.

"Hey!" She squirmed in his arms and pounded him with one solid swat. "Not yet!"

He hoisted her higher and the man yelled from the van.

She whacked him again. "I haven't been kidnapped yet!" She punctuated that with a knee that barely missed his own titanium set.

"Come on, princess," he said as he charged toward the Camry he'd parked hours earlier. "This is how it works."

He reached the car in fewer than ten strides, held her immobile with one hand, yanked the back door open with the other, and shoved her in as the van screeched back into the street to catch up.

"Not . . ." He slammed the door and barely heard her muffled, "Yet!" She pounded the window in protest. *Yes, yet.*

The van approached just as he jerked open the Camry driver's door. "Hey, asshole, what are you doing?" The angry voice from the van was as Boston as baked beans and Johnny didn't take time to respond. He'd assumed that Lucy had prearranged this with the site, but even if there had been a communications breakdown, he knew what his job was. He slammed the car door and stabbed the keys into the ignition, but furious fingers seized a handful of his hair and pulled like hell.

"I can't believe you did that!" she shrieked.

Shaking her loose, he managed to start the car, threw it into drive, whipped it in front of the van, and flew across three lanes to turn right on Beacon. The van didn't follow. Still, the real rescuer could be close by with orders to find out who had just muscled in on the business. Just in case, he blew out of there.

She smacked her hand against the back of his seat so hard, he felt it in his chest. "That was too fast! I didn't even get kidnapped! I paid to get kidnapped, you son of a bitch!"

He managed to snag her furious gaze in the rearview mirror. "You're welcome."

She choked and threw herself back. "That's not what I paid for. I didn't get a *thing* out of that." She kicked his seat with a frustrated, "Ooh, *damn* it all!"

What the hell kind of buzz was she after? Climbing into a van with some creep for pretend danger? Was that really some kind of good time?

"You paid to get rescued," he said, looking at her in the mirror again. He hadn't seen a picture, like he usually did. On a normal job Lucy would have given him a dossier an inch thick, with every detail down to bra size. He adjusted the mirror slightly south. A decent—very decent—B-plus. "I am just doin' my job, miss. Where to?"

"Where to?" She sounded incredulous. "I didn't flag a cab to cruise Beacon Street. I paid to get *abducted,* thank you very much. And I did *not* get two thousand dollars' worth of abduction services."

"Two?" He coughed. "You bought the deluxe?"

Her eyes sharpened. "Don't you guys communicate at that company?"

"I was told it was a standard rescue operation," he said, hoping that would be the right term. "No deluxe."

She crossed her arms, her cheeks flushed with fury. "I was very clear in the application. I wanted the most amount of time I could possibly have before the rescue. My contact promised me at least an hour of kidnapping. An hour with the guy who's supposed to be the best there is."

"An hour? For what?" The question was out before he could stop himself. He backpedaled fast. "I mean, isn't the whole reason you sign up for this the rescue part? From a knight in shining . . ." He glanced at the dash and gave her his most endearing grin. "Toyota?"

She rolled her eyes. "I wanted the whole package." She turned to the window, lost for a moment, then back to the mirror. "How long have you been doing this?"

"Awhile."

"Do you do a lot of the rescues? Are you a regular?"

"Rescues? Oh, yeah, that's all I do, sweetheart." A bodyguard could certainly be considered a rescuer.

"And do you only work for takemetonite.com, or are you a freelancer for other operations?"

How many sites were there where chicks paid for fantasy adrenaline rushes? "Just this one."

"Do you talk to them much? The girls you save?"

"If they want." He had to give it more than this or she'd never believe he worked for the site. "I mean, I'll talk if they, you know, bought the deluxe package."

She leaned forward, pressing her fingers on his shoulders. "Let's be clear here, pal. Is that deluxe business straight sex or something kinky?"

He tapped the brakes at a light and shrugged. "Hey. It's your two grand, babe."

"You need to turn the car around."

"Huh-uh. No way. You're not going back to that park. You've been rescued. The first part is over, whether it lasted long enough for you or not. No do-overs."

"I know the rules," she said. "But you need to turn around anyway."

"Where do you want to go?"

She smoked him with a meaningful look. "I live off Chestnut Street in Beacon Hill. These are all one-way streets past the State House."

He zipped into the left lane to hang a U. "Home? You want to go home?"

"Yep. I want my money's worth." She reached back and whipped her hair out of the ponytail, shaking a thick blond mane around her shoulders, her expression fairly detached for a woman who'd just discussed straight or kinky with a perfect stranger.

Lucy had been uncharacteristically vague about this assignment, but it was a damn safe bet it didn't include gigolo services. All she'd said was don't let her go through with the kidnapping, and be sure she was safe. Nothing about the deluxe treatment.

"What did you say your name was?" she asked.

"My name?" He slipped into cover mode, like a trained actor. Tonight, he was a thrill specialist. He dropped a few extra dollops of sex and attitude into his voice. "It's whatever you want it to be, doll."

"Enough with the bogus endearments. What's your name?"

"Johnny. Johnny Christiano. What's yours?"

"Sage Valentine."

"Sage." He'd liked the name the minute Lucy had told him. "Tasty stuff, sage."

"I'm not named for the spice," she told him.

"Actually, it's an herb."

"Whatever. I'm named for wisdom."

Oh yeah? She sure wasn't demonstrating any of *that* tonight. He watched her closely, seeing the wary, worried look deepening her green eyes. Or maybe they were brown. Hard to tell in this light. But real pretty. Kind of tilted up at the sides and wide, with thick lashes and expressive eyebrows. Nice cheekbones, too. His mother always said you could tell a classy girl by her cheekbones.

Of course, Ma hadn't met a woman who paid a couple of grand to be kidnapped, rescued, and screwed for a good time. On second thought, with that family? Maybe she had.

Sage leaned her head against the glass and closed her eyes. "I still can't believe you wrecked my kidnapping."

"Was it your first time, Sage?"

"First, last, and only," she said with a sigh.

He couldn't believe it—he actually felt guilty for saving her ass. "Maybe I can make it up to you."

And he knew just the thing to put a smile on her face. It worked with every other woman he'd ever known. "Don't worry, angel. I have something special in mind for you."

At least one thing she'd read on the website had been true.

Guaranteed safe release courtesy of hot, handsome hunks specially trained to make your every rescue fantasy come true.

But she hadn't waltzed half-naked through the Public Garden, skipped down Charles Street, and behaved like a ditsy blonde just for a rescue fantasy. And forget about the money. That was half her fee if she managed to sell the idea to an editor—which, without the chance to interview the "master kidnapper," was probably moot anyway.

Worst of all, she hadn't had the chance to find out anything about the night Keisha had been kidnapped. Now all she had was a boy toy who used pet names and had screwed up her only chance at getting some facts straight. Her only hope was to keep up the charade and try to get something out of him.

She studied his broad shoulders, the way his black hair carelessly fell over a dark shirt. Strong neck, but not thick. Gorgeous eyes. Keisha's type? She'd liked them streetwise, but this guy was pushing that envelope to the breaking point. Still, had he met her roommate? Had he ever rescued her?

Would she actually have to sleep with him to find out? That last thought sent something scorching and unholy through her veins. She would do whatever it took, like she always did.

"You can park there, behind that Dumpster. You might get a ticket, but since the car's a rental, who cares?"

He shot a surprised glance in the rearview mirror. "How do you know that?"

She pulled the Hertz card from where it had peeked out of the back pocket when she'd kicked his seat, and waved it. "Dead giveaway. I don't own a car, either. If you're smart, you don't need one in Boston."

He barely shrugged one of those impressive shoulders and zipped into the spot, getting out of the car before she could even figure out where the handle was. He opened the door for her with the flair of a limo driver.

Half a step above a male prostitute, but a gentleman.

She climbed out and rocked back on her Nikes, finally having the opportunity to see what they'd sent her. Yep. Truth in advertising. About six feet, rock solid, and built to please the most demanding customer. Brooding dark eyes, silky black hair, a full mouth, and a nose with just enough of a bump to prove he'd been in a fight or two, but healed well.

Too bad his timing sucked.

"Whaddya think?" he asked, a sexy half-grin lifting his mouth. "Will I do?"

If she'd shelled out cash expecting quadruple orgasms at the hands of a blistering, dark, dangerous stranger, yeah. He'd do very nicely. "We'll see," she said.

But would he give her what *she* wanted? Answers, information, a lead? She'd have to butter him up to get him to talk, take down his defenses.

She *had* paid for the deluxe package.

She indicated the street that crossed in front of the alley where he'd parked. "It's just a few buildings down."

He put a protective hand on her shoulder and scanned the empty streets. "Nice neighborhood," he commented. "I like the gaslights and cobblestones."

"Have you been to Beacon Hill before?" Like the night her roommate died? "Ever have any other customers here?"

"Hard to remember," he said. "There are so many."

She stole a glance to see if he was kidding, but his expression gave nothing away.

"Who do you work for?" she asked pointedly.

That got the flash of response she wanted. "Takeme-tonite.com. You know that."

"I mean, at Fantasy Adventures. Who do you report to? Is there a hierarchy? Are you in, say, the customer relations department?"

He stifled a laugh. "It's sort of a loose corporate structure."

He wasn't going to make this easy. She pulled a key out from the hidden pocket of her running shorts and paused at the three stone steps leading to the apartment. "So how long has that website been in business?"

"I couldn't say."

Stepping up to the door, she slipped in the key and hesitated. Was this the right thing to do? What if she . . . did whatever . . . and he didn't answer her questions?

"You're still not sure, are you?" he said, leaning a little closer.

He smelled sweet, like the flowers blooming in the Garden. Like he'd . . . hidden in the honeysuckle.

"Were you waiting on Charles Street?" she asked.

"I've been fifty feet behind you since you left home, about an hour ago."

She sucked in a breath, her stomach flipping. "You followed me?"

"Down Chestnut, across Beacon—you shouldn't jaywalk, by the way—around the Common, past the little group of homeless people you said hi to, through the Public Garden, all the way to your last stretch by the swan boats. You were never alone."

She stared at him, unable to speak. He'd followed her, through the dark, through the shadows, through the night.

Damn, she hated the way her nerves tingled and her thighs tightened. Hated the way it *thrilled* her. Wasn't she smarter than the women who signed up for this kind of thing? Wasn't she smarter than Keisha, who'd ended up dead?

"What's the matter?" He brushed her chin with his knuckle, hot as a matchstick on her skin. "You're not having second thoughts, are you? 'Cause you don't have to do this."

"I'd just like to talk first. Is that okay?"

"Of course. Most women do." He put a hand over hers to help her turn the key, and electricity zapped every nerve in her body. "And I like to do something else, first."

Oh, God. "What's that?"

He dipped so close that his breath ruffled her hair, his warm, possessive hand searing the bare skin between her running top and shorts. "It's a surprise."

She turned the knob slowly. "I hate surprises."

"Really." He nudged the door open and guided her in. "Pretty strange way to spend a Monday night then, trolling for an abduction."

"I wasn't trolling. I'm not in this just for an adrenaline rush."

She'd left the apartment dark, and shadows ate up every corner. His hands closed around her waist, drawing her close enough to feel his chest, his stomach, his hips, and his thighs through her thin clothes.

"Then you're in luck," he whispered. " 'Cause I deliver way more than that."

She closed her eyes. She could do this, for Keisha. She could do whatever it took.

CHAPTER
Two

"I gotta know something before we go one step fur-ther." Johnny eased his grip on Sage's slender waist but didn't completely let go. He felt her gut tighten in anticipation. Or fear. Nah, not fear. Not a chick who buys stranger danger.

"No personal questions," she said.

Oh, so she had rules now. "Do you have any garlic?"

She eased away and turned on a lamp. "Garlic? Did I accidentally click the vampire box on the website?"

He laughed, checking her out in real light for the first time. "I'm just thinking through my options," he said, lingering for a moment on the glistening moisture beaded over her smooth skin, the taut nipples pointed through her runner's bra. An athlete, definitely, but curvy enough to make it difficult to look away.

She curled one hand on her hip and pulled his attention back to her face. "Shouldn't I be the one with options?"

"Absolutely. You're the customer, sweet face, and the customer is always right."

Behind her, a spacious living room seemed crammed with too much furniture in an array of muted colors. A carved marble mantel dominated one wall; on the other, a rounded bay of three windows opened to a clear view of the Common. He eased her aside and walked by her. "Where's the kitchen?"

"Why?"

He turned and dipped close to her, purposely invading her space, testing her and smelling the fruit of her shampoo. "That'd be where you keep the knives, right?"

She crossed her arms and didn't move an inch. "Are you trying to scare me?"

Someone should. Someone should teach a woman not to invite strange men into her apartment. Especially men who nabbed her on the street and threw her into a car.

But education wasn't his assignment. He was here to keep her out of whatever trouble she wasn't supposed to get into. He could think of two easy, appealing ways to do that. Only one would comply with the unwritten code of ethics of the Bullet Catchers. But the other might be what she was offering.

"Nope." He continued toward a doorway that, sure enough, opened to a darkened galley kitchen. "I'm trying to feed you."

He hit the fluorescents and cringed. "Whoa. I can't work in that light." He flipped them off, and she reached for an antique lamp in the corner of a tiny built-in desk area, illuminating paper clutter and a closed laptop computer.

"Work? What kind?"

The stove was ancient and, shit, electric. But there was decent counterspace and plenty of room. "No microwave? There's hope for you yet, blondie." He started opening cabinets. Dishes, glasses, coffee cups. "Pantry?"

She closed her hand over his forearm. "Are you serious?"

He slid his arm through her grip so that he could clasp her hand and pull it to his chest. "Tell me you have pasta, baby, and anything that resembles a tomato, and you'll see how serious I can get."

The corners of her very pretty mouth twitched. "In the fridge."

"Fresh parsley?"

She gave in to the smile that she'd been fighting. "Of all the rescuers on that site, I get Emeril Freaking Lagasse."

Dropping her hand, he relaxed into a cocky smile. "Not to put too fine a point on it, but I'm actually a little more creative than that guy."

She searched his face, obviously unsure what to make of him. And while a little bit of mystery was a good thing, he didn't want her asking a million questions, either.

"Let me ask you something," she said.

Maybe he should kiss her. There might not be time to distract her with a pasta puttanesca.

"No personal questions." He winked and touched her chin, tilting her face toward his in a provocative way. "Customer's rules."

She was having none of it. "Why did the guy in the van call you an asshole?"

So she'd heard that after all. "Because I . . . can be."

"Do you know him?"

"Of course. We go way back." In a quick move, he turned and tugged open the refrigerator door. "What do we have here? Red peppers? Oh, yes, darlin', I can—"

"You can explain something to me."

"Possibly. What do you want to know?"

"He didn't expect you to cut into the kidnapping so fast, did he? Were you even the one who was supposed to save me?"

Johnny stepped away from the refrigerator and closed the door. Everything he knew about undercover work, he'd learned from an FBI agent who'd infiltrated his family. One of the best suggestions Dan Gallagher had ever made was that when you're confronted with the *truth,* make it sound absurd.

He gave her a lazy, teasing grin. "Yep. You got it, hon. I was just strollin' Charles Street at midnight and decided to roll you into my car for the fun of it." When her eyes narrowed, he pointed playfully. "You're onto me. I just happened to know that you were going to get kidnapped at exactly that moment and wham, I screwed up the whole thing so I could have you all for my very self."

"Still," she said warily. "Something was weird."

He slowly slid his hand under her hair. A flurry of goose bumps rose over her flesh and the nipples he'd been admiring strained the thin cotton even more.

"What's weird is that we're still talking about it," he said softly, pulling her closer. "That part's over. Now comes your deluxe rescue. Mine happens to include a tasty little extra. Unless, of course . . ." His linen shirt grazed her breasts and her lips parted. "You want to skip the kitchen and go straight for the bedroom." He tunneled his fingers deeper into her silky thick hair. "You call the shots, doll."

She didn't move, still scrutinizing him, still unsure. If he didn't do something fast, she was going to put one and one together and come up with three. He lowered his hand, sliding over the bra strap and her skin, gliding to the luscious rise of her breast. Under his hand, her nipple pebbled and her heart slammed.

She put her hand over his, pressing him harder against her and molding his fingers over her entire breast.

"Don't even think about it." She removed his hand completely. "I'm starved."

Sage still felt the weight of Johnny's fingers on her breast and the wicked, wet tautness that it caused between her legs, when she locked Keisha's bedroom door behind her one minute later. She closed her eyes and put her hand precisely where his had been. Damn. No wonder he did what he did. The gourmet hooker was good at his job.

"God." She blew out the word with no small amount of self-disgust. What was the matter with her? Before he tried to mind-meld her with those eyes, she'd better do some checking on him. That van driver was pissed. *Why?*

She turned on Keisha's laptop, tucked into a Queen Anne desk in the corner.

Waiting for the machine to come to life, she tapped the desk impatiently, refusing to sit, refusing to inhale Keisha's perfume that still lingered a month after she'd died, right there, on that bed. Just being in this room gave her a creepy feeling. She hadn't come in here since the day she'd found the name of the website and launched this private, fruitless investigation.

Sage glanced at the dance-team poster that took up most of one wall. Twenty-three of the most beautiful women in Boston, clad in next to nothing, displaying a zillion dollars worth of bleached teeth and surgically enhanced boobs, a blinding array of beauty, good bones, and a lifetime of dance lessons. And there was Keisha Kingston, dead center.

And now, just dead.

The Internet access page lit up and Sage typed in www.takemetonite.com. The home page appeared as an innocuous dating site promising perfect personality matches and the love of your online life.

Sage slid the cursor over a heart-shaped icon bearing the question, "Want to be taken?" in reversed-out type. With one click, she had the password screen, entered hers, then the page dissolved to reveal the black and red slash of the real site.

She clicked on "Meet the Rescuers" and the screen flashed as images of dreamy, shirtless guys filled the left side, with hot-pink squares around the names next to them. Dusty. Thorpe. Coulter. Lincoln. Ellis. Blaine.

She clicked to the next screen. A highlighted blond named Leander. A drool-worthy black man who went by Samir. A rakish soldier in torn camos named Slade.

No toe-curling cook named Johnny.

Although he certainly fit the bill, with pecs from here to there and a face born to break hearts. Still, she clicked again, but there were no other rescuers.

Of course, it was possible that he just wasn't listed. It did say "some of our rescuers" on the first page. She flipped back and studied Dusty, Thorpe, and the gang. Instinctively she lifted her hand to graze the breast he'd just touched. Oh, yeah. Johnny Christiano could give any of those guys a run for their money.

But why wasn't he there? And why did he crash her kidnapping long before he should have? And why did that driver call him an asshole? And what, if anything, did he know about what happened the night Keisha was kidnapped?

He tapped on the door. "I found a bottle of merlot, princess. You want some?"

She almost closed the page of the website, but changed her mind. Instead, she unlocked the door and opened it in invitation. "Why aren't you on the website?"

He merely shrugged a shoulder. "Of course I am." He stepped into the room and raised a glass of red wine. "To fantasies."

She took the glass and set it on Keisha's dresser with enough force to splash a drop. "I can't find you there."

He stopped in front of the poster. Which made him human and male, but she watched for any reaction other than the typical "Holy shit, you know these girls?"

"So where are you?" he asked.

"Sorry to disappoint, but I'm not a Snow Bunny."

"No?" He gave her a sideways glance. "You into chicks?"

She almost laughed, but pointed to the stunning black woman with milk-chocolate skin and espresso eyes. "Keisha Kingston. My roommate." She kept her voice neutral. "Ever meet her?"

"Your roommate, huh?" He frowned, peering closer. "I thought you lived alone."

"Have you met her?" she asked again.

"Nope." He paused at various stunning faces and bodies. "These are the cheerleaders for the new NBA team? The New England Blizzard?"

As if any guy in Boston didn't know who the Snow Bunnies were. "Actually, they're a dance team, not cheerleaders." She indicated the laptop. "Why aren't you on that site?"

It probably wasn't easy to drag his attention from the wall of women, but he managed a casual glance at the screen. "Next page," he said, his focus pulled back to the poster.

She clicked, but got the same second page. "You're not there."

"Here." With strong hands he inched her aside and reached for the keyboard. His typing was fast, completed with long, steady fingers. She should have caught what he'd entered, but she was too busy admiring his hands, the dusting of a few dark hairs, the power in the breadth of his wrists. The man had exquisite hands. Exquisite everything, to be fair.

A fresh page flashed, and there he was. Bare chested, staring at some imaginary focal point, both arms above his head to showcase amazing biceps and the planes of a rock-hard chest. In the pink square, it said, "Johnny."

"Oh." She could hardly keep the disappointment out of her voice. She had no idea why, but she didn't want him to be one of them. And that was stupid, because he was her only link to what had happened to Keisha. But he had such an underlying sweetness to him. Like he was better than some loser model wannabe who sold himself for cash and a good time. But, he wasn't. "So you get your own page, huh?"

"Seniority has its privileges." He tilted his head toward the poster. "So where's your roommate tonight?"

The lie came easily: "She's out. You know any of the other girls?"

"Should I?" He returned to the poster, his brows furrowed in scrutiny as he read their names. "Vivian. Diana. Pamela. Claire. Nope, haven't had the pleasure." He paused as he studied the redhead who Sage knew had been a regular at takemetonite.com. She'd been the one to help Sage register.

"That's Ashley McCafferty," she said. The camera had easily captured Ashley's devilish smile, the dusting of freckles, the Irish-green eyes. It hadn't captured the underlying sadness that seemed to surround the girl, though. "Stunning, isn't she?"

His lifted a shoulder and an eyebrow in pure indifference. "Not my type."

Surely these rescuers e-mailed or drank beers together and exchanged stories. He had to know *something*.

She casually picked up the wine he'd brought her and took a sip. "So, have you rescued any of those girls? They're regulars on your site."

He turned to her, a twinkle in his eyes. "I don't kiss and tell."

"But you do kiss."

His lips curled up. "If that's what you want."

The throes-of-passion thing might work. Get him ready to burst at the seams, and he might at least lead her to the right guy. Not exactly what she'd learned in Journalism School, but it could work.

She put the drink down and beckoned him with one curled finger.

He looked a little surprised. "Yeah?"

"Yeah. Remember, I ordered de-luxe." She purposely infused the word with a power punch of implication.

He took one step closer to her, his jaw clenching a bit. "We've got all night, sweetheart. I thought you were starved."

"What I am is . . ." She wet her lips. "Out two thousand dollars for a kidnapping that never happened." She reached for him and, like the pro he was, he came right to her, wrapping those incredible arms around her. He smelled like the park, fresh and hot from running after her.

"Listen, baby," he whispered, putting his mouth over her ear. "You're making a big mistake."

She tipped her head back and stared at him. "I am?"

He traced her lower lip with a fingertip. His other

arm pulled her even closer, and the ridge of one unmistakable erection pressed against her stomach.

"You don't want to miss my puttanesca. It's award winning."

She drew back a little. "I paid for sex, not spaghetti."

"But why not have both? Come on." He tried to guide her to the door. "Let's eat. Then, we'll . . ."

"Now."

The word elicited the softest grunt in his chest and a quick flicker of surprise on his face. "Sage," he whispered. "We got all night."

She tightened her grip on his upper arms, and his steel muscles clenched under her fingertips. "You want to know what I think?"

"Maybe not," he said, half smiling.

"I think you're a phony."

"Yeah?" His long lashes brushed together as he squinted in disbelief.

"I think you're a fake. As pretend as the kidnapping itself. You're too nice to screw a woman you don't know."

"Is that what you think?"

She nodded. "It's what I know."

Before she could take one breath, he crushed her mouth with his, kissing her with so much force and competence that it actually felt like the floor was dropping out from under her.

"You don't know nothin', baby," he murmured against her lips. "Nothin'."

CHAPTER
Three

Instinct took over. The instinct that makes a man do whatever a man needs to do not to wreck his cover. And then another, more primal instinct fought for control. This one shot fire into his already hard cock at the first contact with this sexy, willing woman and just flared stronger when he tasted her mouth.

He took a step toward the bed and she murmured, "No," and pushed him to the door with one hand, the other already fingering his belt buckle in a way that most definitely did not match *no.* "My room."

Oh, this chick was serious about getting what she paid for. But he was getting paid to keep her safe . . . not satisfied. His body and brain braced for war, but she tipped the scales with another scorching kiss and eager, demanding fingers.

Without separating an inch or breaking the collision of tongues and lips and hands and bodies, she guided him across the hall to another room, this one dark and shadowy. He smelled the city's night air through the open windows, which sent the bodyguard in him on high alert.

But the man in him rocked into long, silky legs that wrapped around his. Round, firm, luscious breasts filled his hands. Blood surged through his body. Skin burned under his kiss. And two sex-charged bodies fell onto a bed that hadn't been made and was about to get messier.

Johnny had absolutely no doubt that Lucy did not have this in mind when she sent him to ruin some adventurous female's abduction fantasy. But his cover included stud service, and his customer expected the house special. Fast and furious, too.

She slipped her hand down his pants, closed a fist over his cock, and squeezed. He sucked in a breath, sliding into her hot fingers, as she finished the buckle with her other hand.

"Oh, look at you," she cooed appreciatively when he burst free.

Yeah, look at him. Some protector of the innocent. His gun was in an ankle holster and his dick was in her hand. "Sage—"

"Shhh." She kissed him quiet. "Let me. Let me." She lowered her head; her hair was so soft and sexy between his fingers, the scent of exotic fruit making his mouth water.

He had two choices. Blow his cover, or . . . She closed her mouth over him.

"Oh, *honey.*" Forget it. He had no choice now.

Her lips enveloped him, so tight and wet and insane he damn near howled. He slid his hands under her arms to pull her up, but her skin was creamy and warm and pliant, and he had to dip into the strappy top to touch her breasts. Had to squeeze them and tweak the hard buds between his fingers.

She moaned with pleasure and rewarded him by urging his cock deeper into her mouth. Droplets of sweat formed on his neck as blood raged through his ears with the same rhythm she sucked and stroked. His lungs seemed to burst from ragged, shallow breaths. His lower back prickled with heat, his balls throbbed, his brain went blank, and every cell in his body vibrated with the rush of pain and pleasure.

Did she want him to come? 'Cause things were headed straight that way, fast.

"Baby." He tried to pull her up but succeeded only in pulling the sports bra higher. She lifted her mouth off him and he almost growled with frustration and relief, but all she was doing was pulling off her top, giving him total access to her bare breasts as she went mercilessly back to work on his pounding erection.

She licked him once. Twice. Suckled his sac and flicked her tongue over his burning skin. He'd never . . . ever . . . last . . . another—

Wait a second. Who was the trick and who was the trick turner here?

He finally managed to draw her up, sliding her bare breasts across his shirt—which was still buttoned—lifting her so they were face-to-face.

"Listen, hot lips," he said, his voice as rough as her breathing. "You gotta give me a chance or I'm going to explode."

"You are?" Looking delighted, she cupped his balls

and started to stroke him again. "Let me know when."

He took her hand and forcefully removed it. "When." He softened the gruffness in his voice by bringing her fingers to his mouth for a gentle, erotic kiss. "Hey, angel, who's doin' who here?"

In the shadows, alarm flashed through her. "You don't like this?"

He snorted softly. "Yeah, I like it. But last time I checked, the de-*luxe* money flowed the other way." He eased her back on the bed, his night vision strong enough to make out the shape of her breasts. The dark targets of her nipples. The narrow waist and delicate dip of her midsection. Her stomach rose and fell with tight, strained breaths, strained from arousal.

He ran a finger along the stretchy waistband of her low-cut running shorts. "So," he managed with a soft, teasing laugh. "Deluxe . . ." He slid his hand inside, lower, down her flat belly to touch a tuft of glossy, feminine hair. "Means . . ." His middle finger stroked her mound. "This . . ." She was wet with moisture, slippery and ripe. "Is for you." He dipped inside her, closing his eyes at the erotic sensation of her muscle grip. Hot and tight and magical, this perfect woman's spot. "For you," he repeated with a kiss on her mouth.

She sucked in a breath, lifting her hips. "No," she whispered.

No? She wasn't moving like *no.* She wasn't breathing like *no.* She sure as hell wasn't kissing like *no.* He moved the nub gently from side to side and entered her with two fingers this time.

Her body quivered. He lowered his head and suckled her nipple, rolling his tongue and gently nibbling that sweet, sweet bud before moving to her throat, licking the sheen of perspiration, tasting salt and woman. If he pleasured her, satisfied her, he wouldn't break the unspoken code of ethics. The one that said you don't screw your principal.

But, son of a bitch, he sure was thinking about it.

"No," she murmured again. "Not me."

He fluttered his fingers, making her muscles spasm. "Yes, you."

Biting her lip, she breathed hard. "No," she repeated, pulling his hand out of her shorts. "I . . . want . . . you. I want . . . you. I . . ."

"I get the message." He laughed softly, thumbing her peaked breast with quick, tiny strokes. "You want me."

She rose on one elbow and stared him down. "I want you in my mouth."

How could he argue with that? "But don't you—"

"Hey," she said, tapping his chest. "The customer's always right."

She had him there. Her fingers closed over him again. She had him *there,* too. He swelled in her hand.

Once again, she disappeared below, covered his cock with her mouth, and vibrated it against her teeth with one long, slow moan.

He was going to be a goner.

He dropped back on the pillow in delicious defeat, shoving his hair off his face with two hands, inhaling deeply and getting a whiff of her tangy moisture still on his fingertips. The scent of her almost sent him over the edge.

She licked his head, stroked his shaft, and never let go of his balls. Closing his eyes, he let the pleasure kick in, let every drop of blood slam into one place, making him harder than he'd thought possible.

"Sage, honey. Please." He nestled his hands into her cornsilk hair as the intensity built. Low in his back. Deep in his stomach. Down to his toes he felt the explosion bubble and threaten. Twisting, out of control, out of this world. He was done. "I'm coming, honey. I'm—"

She released him so hard and fast, he lost his breath. "Not yet!" she insisted.

Oh, man. He clenched his whole body, focused every brain cell on one single concept. Stop. Stop. *Stop*.

It would have been easier to stop a freakin' train. But he dug down, found the strength, found the power, found one pathetic molecule of control. He stopped. He could barely swallow, move, or breathe, but at least he wasn't going to shoot a wad from here to the Boston Common.

She straddled him, her breasts glistening in the dim light, wet from his mouth, high and firm and hard with excitement. She tightened her hips around his, then closed her thighs over his erection, sliding him between her legs against the slippery material of her shorts.

He gave a low-throated growl.

Dropping her arms on either side of his head, she lowered her breasts inches from his mouth and rode him harder.

"I don't know what you think I'm made of," he

ground out. "But Superfuckingman couldn't take much more than this."

She smiled and sat up, stealing a beautiful nipple away as she wrapped her fist around him again and moved it up and down. "Johnny? I want something."

Anything. An-y-thing. He reached up to caress her breast. "Yeah?"

"I want to talk now." She pranced her fingers down his cock like he was the flippin' yellow pages. "Can we talk?" She fondled his balls. "Please?"

Okay. This was a test. A really hard, impossible, miserable endurance test. And he was seriously going to fail. "Whatever you want, doll." *Just don't stop.*

She climbed off him but didn't let go, didn't stop stroking and sliding her wet hands over his rock-hard dick.

Talk. Yeah. He could do that. He pushed himself deeper into her ruthless fingers. "What do you want to talk about?" he rasped.

"I want to talk about . . ." She circled the pulsing head of his cock with her thumb. Round and round, slow and sure and maddening. The pressure built again, agony, ecstasy, necessity. "The company you work for."

In an instant, the tidal wave of blood shifted north and his head cleared.

"What about it?" His voice was no longer strained, but totally guarded. The Bullet Catchers? She *knew*?

"Yeah." She curled her fingers, then grazed a nail down a pulsing vein. "You know, who works there. Who does what, who makes all the decisions, who are your clients. Just . . ." She squeezed. "Everything."

"Looks like you got me by the short hairs, princess."
His laugh was raw and forced, because absolutely nothing about this situation was funny.

Okay. Not so smooth, that transition. But Sage never
expected the equivalent of a male prostitute to short-
circuit her last working brain cell. And her utter lack
of finesse wasn't the only thing that bothered her.
She'd planned to seduce him, bring him to his knees,
while maintaining some semblance of her dignity.

Hah. She couldn't maintain some semblance of her
own *top*. And, just for the record, she hadn't faked a
single moan. Who would have dreamed that almost-
sex with a hooker hunk would have her humming
more than any man she'd ever been with? And she'd
paid for it.

Tamping down the mental lecture, she formulated
her interview strategy. Start with benign, open him
up, get him loose. She could do this. She'd gotten the
mistress of BankBoston's CEO to whisper the truth
about her lover's embezzling and gambling habit. She
had uncovered the real trauma in the ER at Mass
General, coercing information out of the head gyno
and bringing down a few arrogant doctors in the
process. Surely she could get the goods from this
wiseguy who cooked for fun and fantasy-fulfilled for
profit.

"Hey. Blondie." He tucked his hand into her waistband again, nudging the shorts lower, his body back in
his control, not hers. "Why don't you forget who sent
me here and just enjoy the fact that I am."

"Uh-uh." She shimmied her hips away from those wicked fingers. "Talk to me."

He chuckled again, his lips tipped up in a charming smile, moving the rejected hand back to her breast to rub his finger on the underside so lightly she thought she might scream. "You know, Sage, I'm really confused."

She didn't know what got her more. That little tender twist in his voice that really did sound like confusion, or the fact that he actually used her name instead of princess or angel or darling. Or maybe what got her was that touch that sent fireworks between her legs.

She gently removed his hand from her breast. "What are you confused about?"

"I wanted to talk. Before."

"You wanted to eat pasta."

"Part of eating is talking. But you . . ." He closed his hand over hers—the one that still held tight to a very hard, very masculine, very large erection—and eased her away with the same purposefulness she had used. "You seem to be bent on something else. What's going on?"

What was going on was that he was rapidly gaining his composure while hers was getting shakier by the second. "I really want to know more about takeme-tonite.com," she told him. "Before I, you know, finish you off."

She could have sworn she saw relief as his dark eyes shuttered for a moment. "You don't have to do that, sweetheart." He brushed some hair off her face and ran a knuckle over her jaw. "Surely you know that if I told you, I'd have to kill you."

She flinched at the words. Is that what had happened to Keisha? Had she found out too much about this bizarro operation?

"I'm kidding," he assured her, studying her expression. "It's a joke. Are you okay?"

No. She was not okay. And Keisha was dead. The thought steeled her, giving her the power to force a guileless smile and remember her plan.

"Yeah. I get it." She fingered the top button of his shirt. "But I don't think it's so much to ask. I just want to know who sent you. Who else you've . . . done."

She finished that button and started on another, her pulse spiking traitorously at the thought of seeing his chest.

"I told you, I don't kiss and tell."

She splayed her fingers over his chest. No hair. Silky smooth right down to the stone-hard muscle. She fumbled with the next button. "Yes, I know. The happy hooker has a moral code."

He didn't respond as she opened his shirt. Glorious. She flattened her hand over his breastbone and moved slowly from one pec to the other. Did he get told all the time how hot he was? Did other girls have to wipe their drool? Did he do this every single night?

Was she actually *jealous*?

She slammed that thought into a mental drawer. Maybe she could make him think he was so attractive, so special, so incredible, that she had to know all about the other women. How many, who they were, what they did. Then she could ask him. . . .

With a frustrated half snort, she fell back on the

pillow. Who was she kidding? She was half naked and about a thousand miles away from the original reason she'd signed up for a kidnapping in the first place.

"Hey," he said sweetly, cuddling her closer. "You're thinking too hard again, baby." He turned on his side and eased one leg over hers, pulling her lower half into him and dipping toward her mouth. "Let's just kiss for a while. You'll stop thinking, I promise."

That must be his specialty. Kiss his customers into relaxation. No, into oblivion.

His mouth covered hers again, open and warm and sensual and intimate. He fondled her breast, nibbled her lower lip, then rose above her, moving his legs in a way that she knew meant he was taking off his pants.

She'd never get what she wanted. He'd just touch her and tongue her and make her forget. She pushed at his amazing chest, but he just kissed deeper and burrowed his hand into the back of her shorts, searing her backside with a tender caress. She rocked up to meet his erection, punched by desire and the blood that surged through her body.

Dammit! This was the most pathetic attempt at eliciting information by using sex in the history of journalism.

Maybe if he knew part of the truth. Maybe if he understood she really hadn't signed up for this. She'd never mention Keisha, but maybe . . .

"Johnny." She reluctantly ended the kiss. "I have a confession to make."

He pulled back. "Your name's not really Sage."

"Yes, it is. But I'm not really . . . a customer."

He regarded her, then slowly, agonizingly withdrew his hand from her rear end, placing it on a much less intimate spot on her waist. "No?"

"No." She scooted up. "I'm a reporter."

His eyebrows shot up. "Really."

"And I swear everything you say is completely off the record. I won't use your name or quotes or anything. I'm just trying to get information."

His expression went flat. "A reporter."

"Don't worry. I promise." She actually put her hand over her heart. Her *bare* heart. The one he'd just been caressing. As though that would make her vow more valid. "I will not put your name in my story, even if it's not your real name. I'm trying to get information about these thrill sites. That's what I do. That's my job. I seek . . . the truth."

His gaze dropped to her chest, then zeroed back in on her eyes. "Quite an interview technique you've got."

She reached for her sports bra. "I thought . . . I thought if I got you . . ."

"I know what you thought." He took the top from her and opened the neck hole for her to slip it on. "Give the guy a blow job and he'll tell you whatever you want to know."

She never argued with the truth, no matter how ugly it sounded. She slid her arms through and smoothed the cups over her breasts. "I'm desperate."

He snorted softly and glanced at his still erect manhood. "So you're trying to get me the same way?"

"I really wanted to interview the guy in the van. That was my original plan."

"Now, is that an interview you do dressed or undressed? I'm curious how this works."

"No need to be sarcastic. I would have had an hour with the guy who is supposed to be their top kidnapper. But you prematurely rescued me."

"I didn't do *anything* prematurely."

"Please, will you just answer some questions?"

For a moment, he just looked at her, distrust and confusion in his expression. "So you did this whole thing because you're what, writing a story?"

"Yes." Sort of. She *had* tried to sell the idea as a story to one of the editors at *Boston Living,* hoping a press pass would give her the access to the website operations, but they'd been ice cold on the idea. "I haven't convinced an editor yet, but I string for a few different publications and I'm hoping somebody picks it up."

"String?"

"I'm a freelance writer. That's called a stringer."

He nodded, piecing her story together. "You're a writer and you registered for a kidnapping so you could do some undercover investigation? Do I have this right?"

"Yes."

"And what's your story angle?" he asked. "Are you trying to promote the product? To advertise the service and get more customers?"

She frowned at him. "That's not what reporters do. I'm not in marketing. I write the truth. I uncover things that are wrong or unethical. I find angles that are newsworthy."

"What's newsworthy about this? The fact that chicks are getting off on getting nabbed?"

She shrugged. "That's an interesting trend."

He snorted softly. "One way to put it." He started pulling his pants back up. "Let me ask you something, Sage." He gave her a sharp glance. "That is your real name, isn't it?"

She nodded. "Is Johnny yours?"

"Yeah." He buckled his belt. "Did you tell anyone that's why you signed up to be kidnapped? You know, the magazine or a boyfriend or anyone?"

"No. I didn't tell anyone."

He frowned. "You sure? No one knows why you're doing this? Even, maybe . . ." He pointed his thumb toward the hallway. "Your roommate the cheerleader."

Her gut squeezed, but she maintained a blank expression. "I didn't tell anyone." She straightened her back and lifted her chin. "But the site knows I've been rescued. So if you . . . if you do anything to hurt me . . ."

He looked insulted. "I'm not gonna hurt you, princess." He started rebuttoning his shirt.

"Listen, I won't use your name," she promised. "You'll be an unidentified source. Like . . . like . . ." She tried to think of one he'd know. "Deep Throat."

His laugh was bitter and low. "Cute. No, thanks."

She reached out. "Please. It's really, really important. I need the job. I need the money. Surely you understand that."

His eyes softened as he tucked his shirt into his pants. "Fine. Ask away. No promises you'll get anything quotable."

"Are you friends with any of the other rescuers at takemetonite.com?" she asked.

"No."

"Do you know and talk to the men who do the kid-napping?"

"No."

"Have you heard about anything unusual happen-ing in any of the kidnappings?"

That earned her another sharp look. "No."

She blew out a breath. "Are you going to answer no to every question I ask?"

He glanced at the messy bed. "I gotta tell you, I liked the first interview better."

"Please," she said. "This is very serious."

"I'm sure it is, honey, but let's be honest. I'm not going to tell you anything. And neither is anyone else who works for the company. You ought to find some other story to pursue." With a sigh of resignation and regret, he reached to touch her hair, smoothing a few strands in place. "If you don't mind, I'm going to take off now."

"I do mind," she said, her voice almost cracking in frustration. "I really, really mind a lot. I need this . . . story."

"Hey. Whoa." He sat on the bed, concern on his face. "I'm sure you have someone who can help you out of a financial jam. I mean, this place alone is probably worth a fortune."

It was. To the estate of Keisha Kingston, and Sage had about sixty days left to get out of there. "It's not just financial . . . it's personal."

"It always is." He kissed her forehead and tipped

her chin up. "Now, tell me one more thing. Are you going to sign up for another kidnapping?"

"Why?"

"I want to put in a request to be your rescuer."

The way he said it made her smile. Worse, it made her stomach flutter and her heart stutter while everything south of that just pooled into a big mess of female response. Under different circumstances—like, if he wasn't a *prostitute*—she could really like this guy.

"Are you?" he asked. "I need to know if you plan to do this again."

She shook her head. "I think you have to wait a certain amount of time before they let you register again, right? Plus, I don't have that kind of money without a—" She almost said *roommate*. "Regular job."

He seemed satisfied with that. "Well, good luck." He was still holding her chin when he lowered his face and kissed her so softly that she almost didn't feel it. "Next time, though, buy some tomatoes and I'll make puttanesca. You could use some comfort food."

She sat motionless until she heard the front door close. Then she fell back on the pillow, still warm from him, and sniffed the lingering scent of musk and man. Her first paid sexual encounter, and she'd lost him with the flash of a press badge.

She pulled herself up, drawn to the computer across the hall. The laptop was still running and the face of Johnny Christiano was still frozen there. She knew nothing about him. Nothing. Except that he liked to cook.

Pasta puttanesca. Didn't that mean "whore" in Italian?

Only one person would get the irony of that. Keisha.

She stared at Keisha's warm, dark eyes on the poster, and wished like hell she was still here. "Okay. I know. Complete disaster. Total flipping blowout from beginning to end."

Keisha's camera-ready smile beamed, frozen in time, forever happy. If only she were there, curled in her bed, ready for the postdate girl talk they'd shared since the day they'd both walked into a dorm room at Boston College and said hello. The frat boys had called them Salt and Pepper and they had been inseparable for years. Loneliness kicked Sage in the stomach.

"You know what's really funny, Keish? I actually liked that guy. There was something so damn sweet about him." She swallowed and touched the face that would never laugh or tease her again. "I'm so sorry I didn't find out what happened to you. I made a total mess of trying."

"What happened to her?"

Sage jumped at the voice, a gasp caught in her throat. She stared at the man who took up the width of the doorway and burned her with a look that was anything but sweet.

CHAPTER
Four

It couldn't be good news at this hour. But at least whoever was pounding on Ashley McCafferty's door distracted her from her nightly insomnia. She peered through the peephole and sucked in a breath.

Bad news for sure.

She whipped the door open and stared at her boss. "What's the matter?"

"Did you give Sage Valentine the password?" Glenda made the demand quietly in deference to the neighbors in the high-rise.

Ashley blinked, determined to hold her ground. "It's one o'clock in the morning. I have to dance tomorrow night. Couldn't you have called?"

Glenda glanced down the hall, as though communicating with someone at the elevator banks. One of her boys, no doubt.

Ashley involuntarily touched her face. One of Glenda's paid thugs could end her season with one crack of his knuckles.

"Did you give Sage Valentine the password?" Glenda repeated.

"So what if I did? She's had a rough time. She's looking for fun."

"She's looking for answers to why her roommate killed herself."

"So what if she is? I didn't think it would matter if she signed up. I didn't think—"

"Don't think!" Glenda pushed the door farther open with an angry *thwack*. "That's not what you get paid to do." She took a deep breath, fighting for control.

Swallowing hard, Ashley lifted her chin, her bravado rapidly disappearing. "It was a routine referral. If she didn't get it from me, she'd have gotten it from someone else."

Glenda's silvery eyes narrowed and her mouth constricted into a thin line, feathered from years of sneak smoking in parking lots behind auditorium doors. "Ashley, is it possible you don't understand the recriminations of your sloppiness?" The only thing Glenda hated more than whining and wimping out was sloppiness.

"What difference does it make?" Ashley asked, leaning against the doorjamb because her lower back was killing her after the military kicks they'd added into the "Funkytown" routine. They were just a tad out of her talent range. Like everything else the Snow Bunnies did.

"Using that particular password ensures a special experience," Glenda said. "She's not . . . one of us."

"I didn't see the harm in it." And she sure as hell didn't get why Glenda and company had to storm her apartment in the middle of the night. "So, what? Did something happen?"

"Yes, something happened," Glenda hissed. "You screwed up. How well do you know this girl?"

Ashley shrugged and crossed her arms over the thin T-shirt she'd slept in. "I knew her from Keisha. We went out a few times. I haven't seen her since Keisha's memorial service."

"Then you better get friendlier with her. I need you to talk to her about the kidnapping."

Ashley frowned. "Why?"

"I want to know if she got the special treatment because she used our password. Can you find that out? We have a deal with that site and I want to know if it's going south."

Ashley had to shake her head to be sure she was following this. "You showed up here at this hour just to ask me to talk to her about her fantasy kidnapping? Is there some reason you couldn't have told me tomorrow?"

"It's important to my program," Glenda said, her features drawn sharply, her skin sallow in the shadows. "And I won't see you tomorrow."

Oh, shit. "Why not?"

"Because I'm holding you responsible for the mistake."

Ashley closed her eyes. "Does that mean I don't get paid?"

"At the very least."

Oh, God. Misery shot through her lower back. She needed this job. If she wasn't an NBA dancer, she was nothing, nobody, a wannabe, the loser she'd always been told she was. And damn if Glenda didn't know that and use it against her. Her boss had pegged her as a pushover from the first tryout, and she'd taken advantage of it, using Ashley as her eyes and ears with the other girls.

"Hey, I'm sorry I gave her the password. I really had no idea that there was some special treatment involved, Ms. Hewitt. I thought it was okay. I thought I was doing the right thing."

Glenda glanced over her shoulder as though she needed a second opinion. "You just talk to that woman and find out exactly what happened to her. I don't care how you do it, but find out."

As Ashley nodded, Glenda leaned closer, her gaze as sharp as a knife blade. They called it "the look." And no one knew how to say no to whatever demand followed. "Victoria is ready. Get her this week."

"Victoria already refused. She's really not interested—"

One threatening eyebrow shot up. "Get her. Or else you're done for the season, and don't even bother to come to tryouts next year."

"Victoria is a hard-ass bitch who wants no part of a fantasy kidnapping. It's a waste of time to try."

"Then I'll be using an alternate until you succeed."

A burly man stepped out of the shadows and stood behind Glenda. With a smile that Satan could have painted, he rubbed his hands together while he studied

Ashley's face. One well-placed punch, and she would be out for the season, and they all knew it.

"All right," she agreed. "I'll do what I can."

"You left out the part about a dead body."

The silence on the other end of Johnny's cell phone was a little too long not to be calculated. But then, everything Lucy Sharpe did was calculated. That was her gift. Hell, that was her charm.

"I operate on a need-to-know basis," Lucy said. "You didn't need to know."

He adjusted the coffee cup so that the gold filigree handle was on the left and he could palm the delicate china cup. His index finger couldn't fit through the tiny hole, and the hint of hazelnut in the coffee was too delicious to lose a drop.

"Well, now I do," he said simply. Leaning forward as he sipped, he peeked over the rail of the tiny deck of the Beacon Hill Bistro, one story above the intersection of Charles and Chestnut, the early-morning sun warming the redbrick buildings and gilding the spring green buds on the trees. "You still there, Luce?"

"I'm here. So what did she tell you?"

More than you did. "That her roommate killed herself after she was allegedly involved in a fantasy kidnapping."

"Anything else?"

He frowned. "Isn't that enough? She wasn't trying to get kidnapped for fun and games." As if Lucy didn't know that. But the question was, why didn't she tell him? "She wanted to find out what happened to her friend that was bad enough to make her commit suicide."

"Whatever it was, it had nothing to do with takemetonite.com," Lucy said. "I've thoroughly checked the operation, they are legit. And this young woman did not show up for her appointment, so she was never kidnapped."

"At least not by them."

"I thought of that, and I've read the autopsy report." Of course she had. Why should that surprise him? "She was full of ephedra, enough to stop her heart."

Ephedra. What had Sage called it last night? The cheerleading drug of choice.

"I know that the abductions are little more than a playful scare," Lucy continued. "Followed by an encounter that may or may not be sexual with a rescuer. Whatever made Keisha Kingston take her life is really not our concern."

Then what the hell *was* their concern? But Lucy would tell him only what he needed to know, and if he hadn't been so damn attracted to Sage, he probably wouldn't care. It was his job.

He adjusted the tiny café chair to get a complete visual of Sage's building. Finding the bistro's second-story deck, which evidently remained empty during the cooler months, had been pure serendipity.

"I don't know, Luce," he said. "Something about this suicide is bothering me. According to Sage, the roommate was together, smart, ambitious, and seriously good-looking. No depression. No drugs. No money problems. No breakups with a psycho boyfriend. In fact, she was a health nut—"

"Ordinary women don't pay money to get kidnapped and rescued. Health nuts don't power down a substance like ephedra. She obviously had issues."

"Ephedra's in every vitamin store in America, and this whole kidnapping thing was something a bunch of her friends were doing." Why was he defending some cheerleader he'd never met? To Lucy? He never questioned Lucy's judgment. Ever. He softened the edge in his voice. "Anyway, Sage thinks there's some kind of connection."

"She wants somewhere to place blame."

"Then she's putting herself into some very tight spots to do that." He wasn't about to tell Lucy how tight, or that one of those spots was her bedroom.

He heard his boss sigh softly before she asked, "What else did she tell you?"

"Beyond her roommate's strange methods for getting kicks, nothing." But they had talked until four in the morning. He'd learned that she was twenty-seven, raised in D.C., a graduate of Boston College who wrote articles for magazines and dreamed of writing a mystery novel someday.

"And what did you tell her?" Was that nervousness in cool Lucy's voice? What was it about this assignment that had her wired so tight?

"The ingredient for a perfect risotto."

"Mushrooms?"

"Harmony. The cook has to be at peace with himself to do it right." Johnny smiled, remembering how Sage had laughed at that, though Lucy didn't.

"So you talked about cooking?"

He leaned to the far left when a city trash truck blocked his view of the apartment building. "Mostly we talked about her roommate. She's pretty torn up about it."

"Johnny, have you ever known anyone who committed suicide?"

He almost snorted. "In my family, usually someone was paid to do it for you."

"Well, I have. And, believe me, for the people left behind, murder would be easier to handle. At least you know the enemy you're after." Her voice grew sharper. "I just want to be sure you completely maintained your cover."

"No worries. She was totally convinced I'm part of the world's oldest profession."

"Good. I'm sure you've had tougher assignments."

There was an understatement. Of course, she was referring to his jobs with the Bullet Catchers, but he was thinking about the years before. He set the china cup in its saucer with just a little too much force. "Okay, so the job is done. Now what?"

"What do you think she'll do next?"

"Try and get herself kidnapped again. She writes these exposé feature stories for magazines. Did you know that?"

"Yes." Stupid question to ask a former CIA operative; she knew everything.

He waited for more, but when it didn't come, he couldn't stop himself. "So who's the client on this one, Luce?" Bullet Catchers didn't work for free and the principals they protected had big names or big money . . .

or a big benefactor footing the bill. Sage didn't seem to have fame or fortune, but she sure had someone's backing. "Is there a sugar daddy somewhere? A father, maybe? A lover?"

Lucy said nothing.

A lover, then. Or someone who wanted to be. Of course there would be. A woman who looked like Sage, with all that sizzle in the sack? No doubt somebody wanted to keep her out of the arms and bed of some fantasy rescuer and was willing to pay Bullet Catcher prices to do so. But Lucy wasn't saying, and Johnny knew the rules.

"Anyway," he said, his tone showing that he got the message, but didn't have to like it. "She's on a tear to find out why her roommate killed herself and I get the impression this is one chick who isn't deterred by road-blocks or rescuers."

He could have sworn he heard Lucy snort softly, but then she asked, "And how did you leave her?"

With a big, bad boner. "We talked until about three hours ago, then I went back to my hotel."

"Where are you now?" she asked.

"I'm on a restaurant balcony of some bed-and-breakfast with a bird's-eye view of her place, drinking excellent coffee, and awaiting my next assignment." He took a noisy sip as proof. "Now, gimme something good, Luce. A diplomat in Greece or an heiress in Rio."

"Max Roper had an heiress last summer and look what happened to him."

Married, expecting a baby, and running the Bullet Catcher's West Coast ops. "Good point."

"Thank you for doing this without a million questions," she said. "I know this is an unusual assignment."

Is? "No problem. You know you're my goddess."

She laughed softly. "All women are goddesses to you."

"But you're the greatest of them all." He kept his tone light, but they both knew it was no joke. He'd already gone to the ends of the earth for the woman who gave him his life back, and he would again. All she had to do was ask.

He finished the coffee, his focus still on the front door of that brownstone on the corner. He might never talk to Sage Valentine again, but he sure would like one last look.

"So, Johnny," Lucy finally said. "Did you like her?"

Every delectable inch. "Nothing not to like." Careful, man. Anything could be a trick question, regardless of her tone. "I try not to pass judgment on my principal, Luce. You taught me that a long time ago."

She just sighed again.

"So, give me the goods, boss lady. It's April. Tell me I'm headed for Paris."

There was another one of those calculated pauses and then: "I'd like you to stay there a little longer, Johnny."

He straightened in the seat, his gut tightening a little bit. "Sure. And . . . that would be . . . to . . ."

"Keep an eye on Sage."

"As her bodyguard?"

"Not officially."

A moving truck slowed and stopped in front of Sage's building and he got up without thinking, heading to the rail for an angle where he could still see the front door.

"I want you to stay in your cover and watch her for a little longer."

The truck turned and he had a clear shot of the door again. He gripped the cold metal rail with his free hand. "Under this cover, she thinks I'm a rescuer for the thrill site. Any ideas how I can arrange to watch her?"

"Figure out a way to stay around her."

"Uh, Luce, I don't know how amenable she's going to be to spending time with a male prostitute." Not to mention what her real boyfriend, the one with the money to pay for protection, might think of Johnny's diversionary tactics, or Sage's interrogation techniques.

"Then you'll have to be creative. And persuasive. And charming. Do whatever is necessary to keep her under your watch until she gives up this mission she's on."

The heavy glass and wood door of Sage's building swung open as a woman exited. She wore a long black sweater, a bright pink scarf, black pants, and black boots. Her honey-blond hair cascaded over her shoulders, and he remembered exactly the way it felt, the way it smelled like she washed it in mango juice.

"Creative, charming, and persuasive I can do, Luce," he said, surprised by the sudden kick of anticipation for his assignment.

She turned the corner onto Charles, heading away from the balcony where he stood. He scoped the entire scene in one sweep, counting pedestrians, taking note of a messenger on a bicycle and a delivery van pulling into a corner parking spot the moment it was vacated by a car.

"What exactly am I watching for?"

"Trouble. I want her completely safe. Do what you have to do."

He zeroed in on the dark van, specifically on the way the back bumper hung a few inches on the left side. He'd seen that before. Last night.

A man in a navy blue baseball cap and a shapeless coat emerged from the other side of the van. Had he gotten out or was he already on the street and Johnny had missed him?

"I'm on it, Luce." He snapped the phone shut and studied his target, now twenty feet behind Sage. The driver was still in the van.

Two seconds later, Johnny was tearing down the stairs to the street, feeling the comfortable weight of the weapon and hip holster he'd picked up when he'd returned to his Back Bay hotel to shower and change.

By the time he threw open the door and stepped onto the cobblestone sidewalk, he couldn't see Sage anymore. The guy in the navy cap was still visible, but the sunlight hit the dark windows of the van, making it hard to tell if the driver was still there.

Could she possibly have signed up for another kidnapping already? No. Not in four hours. Not possible.

As he passed the van, he shouldered himself deeper into his bomber jacket, keeping his face in the collar.

The engine was running and someone definitely sat in the driver's seat. Light glinted enough for him to make out the shape of a head, leaned forward, jaw moving. Fifty yards ahead of him, the blue baseball cap opened up a cell phone just as a splash of bright pink and black crossed the street.

When the baseball cap suddenly changed course and crossed the street, and the van pulled into the intersection headed in the same direction, he had no doubt they were in communication.

He'd worry about being creative, persuasive, and charming later. Right now he had a principal to protect, whether or not she knew it or wanted it.

CHAPTER
Five

Sage neared the Charles Street T station. With most commuters headed in the opposite direction at seven thirty in the morning, she should be waiting in the lobby of *Boston Living* magazine by eight thirty, when Eric Zellman arrived for work.

She hoped the busy editor didn't have a meeting and would indulge her latest story pitch. Now she had the "personality" he'd wanted when she'd suggested the takemetonite.com story.

And what a personality it was.

Funny, dry, cocky. A heartthrob's face, a Greek god's chest, and a . . . Oh, God, don't go down there. The man was built for every wicked pleasure.

Now all she had to do was persuade Zellman to let her do the story . . . and find Johnny. But she was resourceful; how hard could it be to find him again?

She jogged up the stairs to the train platform, pulling her scarf up against the chilly air. It might have been easier to grab a cab, but there was something comforting about the crowded, rumbling cars that snaked through the city, something about mindlessly staring out the darkened glass as they dipped underground, giving her time to zone out and think about last night.

Her body clutched at the memory of Johnny just seconds from losing it. The last thing she'd expected was to be so insanely excited by a guy who . . . She didn't even want to think about where he'd dipped that wick. About how many women had received his de-luxe treatment. And she *really* didn't want to think about the fact that she'd just have to settle for imagining what that treatment entailed.

She dug for her Charlie Ticket in the side pocket of her bag, slipping it into the turnstile before entering the platform. Someone bumped her from behind and she sent a look over her shoulder, but didn't make eye contact.

A train had just left and there weren't many people around, so she sat on the corner of a bench, near an older woman reading the *Boston Herald*.

They'd buy her takemetonite.com story, she thought bitterly.

Guaranteeing that her mother would roll over in her grave for loss of journalistic standards. But then, Mom had probably done a few 360s a week ago, when Sage had dropped in on Aunt Lucy.

After thirteen years, Lucy Sharpe was still the most mysterious, fascinating human on earth. Still the aunt who had moved in the shadows, showing up infrequently enough to make it an occasion when Sage was a young girl. The aunt who her father had turned away at her mother's funeral. The aunt who had refused to help Sage when she needed it.

The aunt responsible for the *first* suicide victim Sage had ever known.

A man paused next to the bench, close enough to pull Sage from her thoughts. She almost moved nearer to the *Herald* reader to make room for him, then glanced up and caught the intensity of his blue eyes peering out from under a ubiquitous Red Sox baseball cap. He held the eye contact a second too long, then the beginnings of a smile started. Sage averted her eyes and pulled her iPod earbuds from her sweater pocket, being sure he saw her insert one in each ear to deliver the Leave Me Alone message without ambiguity.

Even though she'd hardly left any room on the bench, he sat and let his shoulder brush hers. Stifling exasperation, Sage pointedly slid to the right, forcing the *Herald* reader to glare at both of them.

Sage stood and reached into her pocket to give the impression that she was turning up her music, despite the fact that she'd left her iPod at home. When a crowd of commuters poured through the turnstiles and filled the platform, Sage stepped closer to the tracks and peered into the distance, hearing the rumble of the rails as the Red Line hauled in at breakneck speed.

Someone bumped her from behind and she whipped around and met ice-blue eyes.

"Anxious for your train, huh?" he said.

She touched her ears as if to say *Can't hear you, don't want to.*

Surprising her, he reached up and tugged the wire, pulling the earbud out. "I said, are you anxious for your train?"

"And I said, 'I don't want to talk.' " She gave him a narrowed, threatening look, then lifted the earbud to reinsert it.

"But I do." He yanked the wire before she got it in.

She blinked at him, aware of the approaching train, the squeal of the brakes as it slowed, and the crush of people pushing toward the sunken tracks. Without responding, she turned away, her breath catching as she felt a strong grip on her upper arm.

His words brushed her hair: "Not very friendly, are you?"

She jerked her arm, but he just squeezed. "Let me go," she ground out.

"I . . ." The train roared closer. ". . . last night."

"What?" She couldn't have heard him right. She tried to free her arm again, but he pushed a little this time, toward the tracks.

"Hey!" She wrenched her arm again. "Stop it!" The train brakes let out a deafening, ear-splitting screech, drowning out her cry.

He pushed her toward the tracks again, a quick, nasty shove that made her stumble. Her boot scraped the concrete, her toe hit the open ledge of the track pit, and she turned to grab onto anything, a gasp catching in her throat just as a femine hand closed over her other arm.

"Buzz off, asshole. Can't you see she doesn't want to talk to you?"

Sage whipped around, blinking at the freckled nose and green eyes that had turned cold as they targeted the man.

"Ashley!" Sage exclaimed. "What are you doing here?"

Ashley McCafferty swooped her arm into the crook of Sage's elbow and possessively tugged her through the crowd. "Saving you from creeps."

Sage threw a look over her shoulder, saw he'd pulled the Red Sox cap way low and was looking in the opposite direction. Had he said something about last night?

The subway doors whooshed open and a crush of humanity pressed down on her, but Ashley muscled them inside and rushed toward an empty seat in the back of the car.

When they sat down, Ashley shoved an oversize duffle bag bearing the bright blue and white logo of the New England Blizzard under the seat. "So, where you goin', Sage?"

"I have a meeting in Cleveland Circle. How about you?"

"The arena."

Sage did a quick mental map and frowned. "You're headed in the wrong direction."

"Busted. I'm going home first. I spent the night, uh, elsewhere." She winked. "An investment banker with an MBA from Harvard. *Veddy* Brahmin."

Sage smiled. "Don't tell me—he saw you dance at a game and had to have your number."

"Something like that." Her face softened and she put her hand over Sage's. "So, how are you?"

"I'm okay." She squeezed Ashley's hand. "Thanks for asking. I miss her so bad."

"God, we all do. It's like there's a big hole in the squad. I'm kind of happy the season's going to end in a few weeks. I need a fun summer." She resettled into her seat, turning toward Sage. "Are you doing anything special this summer? Didn't you used to go to Newport with Keisha on the weekends?"

"I'll probably work this summer." The last thing she wanted to do was hang out at the beach in Rhode Island, constantly reminded of her lost friend. "And I'll have to move."

"That Beacon Hill place probably costs a fortune."

Keisha hadn't wanted any of the girls to know she owned the unit, so Sage just shrugged. "I can't stay without a roommate."

"Why don't you get one?"

"I don't want to stay," she said truthfully. "I'll get something smaller, out of town."

"Oh, sure." Ashley leaned closer and lowered her voice. "Did you ever sign up for that website? Did that special password I gave you help?"

"It did," Sage said, debating just how much to tell her.

"So what happened? How did it go?"

"Well, you know, I wasn't really in it for the thrill."

Ashley nodded knowingly. "I know, you told me. Did you find out anything about Keisha, then? What happened?"

"Actually, things got a little screwed up," Sage admitted. "The guy who's supposed to save you—"

"He's called the rescuer."

"Yeah, well, mine was a little overanxious, so I didn't get a chance to talk to anyone but him. And he didn't know her."

"Oh." Ashley drew the word out. "So did you get any, you know, special treatment?"

Sage cursed the warmth that rushed to her face. "Not really."

"Come on," Ashley said, nudging her with an elbow. "You can tell me."

"There's nothing to tell," she said. "I think it might have been a stupid way to try to get information. Anyway, I have another idea."

"Really?" Ashley's eyes widened in interest. "What's that?"

"I'm going to repitch the idea of a story about the website to the editor at *Boston Living*. I think a press badge can get me an insider's view. That's where I'm going now."

"To the company that runs the site?"

"No, the magazine headquarters. I can't get to a human being at the company." Though apparently her aunt had.

"Good idea. I hope it gets you what you need," Ashley said doubtfully.

"You know, except for you, none of the other girls

on the dance team will return my calls. Even Vivian, and she was good friends with Keisha. The only thing I know that changed in her life was this fantasy kidnapping, and I'm not even sure she went through with it."

The train pulled into Government Center and wrenched to a halt.

"What makes you think she didn't go through with it?" Ashley asked.

There was no way to explain that her aunt was a former spook who could find out anything about anybody. "Just a hunch," she said, gathering her purse. "I gotta transfer here. Thanks again for helping me ditch that guy."

"No problem. I'm an expert on creep evasion." She grinned and tucked her legs up so Sage could climb out of the seat. As she passed, Ashley squeezed her hand. "Let me know if you decide to give that site a shot again."

Sage nodded and then drew in a little breath when an idea took hold. "Do you know if you can request a specific rescuer for a second time?"

Ashley's green eyes lit with her teasing smile. "Liked him, did you?"

Let her think that. "I wouldn't mind finding him again. You know how?"

Ashley shrugged. "I guess you could just put in a request for . . ." She poked a playful finger at Sage's arm. "Don't tell me. Slade?"

Sage shook her head.

"Dusty?"

For some unfathomable reason, she couldn't bring herself to say his name and dump him in that group. Even though he belonged there.

Ashley playfully tugged the end of Sage's pink scarf. "Come on. Tell me. Was it Thorpe? Did he do the blindfold thing?"

Sage just smiled, but the little undercurrent of desperation in Ashley's tone made her heart hurt. Why were some girls so enchanted by this? The whole thing turned her stomach. "To be honest, my guy just cooked."

Ashley thudded back on the vinyl seat, screwing up her pretty features. "Really?"

"Yep." Sage gave her an exaggerated shrug. "Just my luck, huh?" She stepped through the door just before it suctioned closed.

Eric Zellman rushed into the conference room, whipped out a chair, and threw himself into it, his expression drawn with stress, his skin the pallor of most New Englanders' in early April: somewhere between pasty and gray.

"Sage, I got four minutes. I'm giving them to you."

"Then, I've got four words for you. The face of takemetonite.com." She frowned. "Does that count as four?"

He leaned forward. "Listen, I need a cover story that will shatter newsstand records, or we are living the last year of *Boston Living*. I need something better than some girlie website."

"The last year of the magazine? Seriously?"

He fell back on the chair with a drama queen sigh. "We are *so* going under. The Internet is killing us. *Vanity Fair* is killing us. Hell, the damned *Boston Globe* is killing us. We can't give a full-page ad away, even when we have Tom Brady wearing little more than his Patriots helmet on the cover." He waited a beat and grinned. "But the photo shoot was too much fun."

Eric would flip when he met Johnny. *If* he met Johnny. "Listen, about that website. I have one of their regular rescue guys lined up for a 'day in the life' sort of thing. You know, behind the scenes with—"

"A male hooker?" He made a face. "Not big enough, Sage."

"It's not just that, Eric. This is a huge trend. Women all over Boston, all over the country, are paying to be kidnapped and rescued. I'm telling you, this is the kind of story *Dateline* does."

"Let 'em." He shrugged. "I need a cover that people can't resist."

"They won't resist this guy. And I swear, this is a good story, Eric. Just like the Mass General feature. I could do that again."

"Not without a source as earth-shattering as Alonzo Garron. I still can't believe you got that doctor to talk like that."

"I'm good. What can I say? Trust me on this one."

He gave her a tight smile. "I'm sorry to tell you, Sage, but the powers that be don't want dirt anymore. Not unless it comes wrapped in state-of-the-art sex appeal."

"Perfect description of this guy."

"But he's nobody. I need a celebrity. Even if they're just a celebrity in Boston, but I need recognizable and I need hot. I need . . . never mind." He looked at his watch. "The kidnapping game is interesting, but not what I want." He pushed himself away from the table and stood. "Sorry, Sage."

She gripped her chair. "What about the Snow Bunnies?"

"You mean the cheerleaders for the new basketball team?" For the first time she saw a glimmer of interest. "Maybe."

"They've used this site," she said quickly. "Could I use that angle to get into takemetonite.com?"

"No." He leaned on the table and shook his head firmly. "The fantasy-site story doesn't do it for me. What's your in with the Bunnies?"

She took a deep breath. "My roommate was one."

"Oh yeah," he said slowly as recognition dawned. "I forgot that. The girl who committed suicide, right?" He chewed on his thin lower lip, thinking. "Okay. Maybe. The day in the life of a professional NBA cheerleader."

Roll over now, Mom, because journalistic integrity is taking a backseat today. "Actually, they're dancers."

"Whatever. Do they fuck any of the basketball players? That might be interesting. Could we get Paula Abdul for a quote? Wasn't she one of those girls once?"

"I don't know. Maybe." Her heart squeezed. She was selling herself, and Keisha, down the river—but for the right reasons.

Eric pulled at the goatee that trimmed his chin. "The Blizzard might be the second-class team in town now, but the Celtics are getting boring and who knows? Then they could be advertisers. I don't want to alienate their marketing people."

"Mass General didn't blacklist us," she shot back.

"They aren't the potential advertisers that the New England Blizzard is." He checked his watch again. "You want to do some research and get me a proposal?"

"Just give me a contract, Eric," she said. "You know my work. I'll do whatever it takes to get you something great."

"You don't do fluff."

"I could." She didn't have to like it, but she could do it. "I could get behind the scenes. . . ." She saw him wavering. "In the locker room." One eyebrow lifted and hope took flight in her stomach, and she went for the jugular: "Or I could take the idea to the *Boston Herald* weekly magazine."

He smirked at her. "Brat. Okay. Pick up a press pass on your way out, and Jennifer will mail you a contract. Get me a draft in three weeks and some courtside seats to the play-offs if they make it in."

"You got it." She beamed in appreciation.

She was still feeling victorious in the elevator, holding the laminated pass she'd just earned. This would give her access to lots of people who had known Keisha very well. People who had been close to Keisha when she died, during a month when Sage was in Texas trying to track down dirt on the former governor of Massachusetts, which she never even got.

The lobby bell rang, and when the elevator doors opened, every coherent thought evaporated at the sight of a man in blistering black leather, leaning against a marble post.

He'd followed her there. He'd followed her *again*.

Somewhere in her brain, a warning bell rang. She ignored it.

Johnny levered off the column and approached her. "Hey, hot stuff."

"You've turned tailing me into an art form."

He tipped her chin with his knuckle. "I just used my powers of deduction." He turned her face to the building directory on the wall. "*Boston Living,* fourth floor."

Either he was the world's best listener or he'd bugged her apartment. "And here I thought you were just another pretty face."

He laughed and slipped his arm around her shoulder. "I'm the whole package, baby. So, what was the meeting about?"

"I got a story contract."

"A story on the website?"

She shook her head. "I couldn't sell him that one. But I'm going to do a story on the New England Blizzard dance team."

He held open the door, a rush of chilly air mixed with a blast of Cleveland Circle traffic. "So, since you couldn't get the story you wanted, you're using this as a back door."

Definitely not just a pretty face. "I want to find out why my perfectly happy, sane, confident friend would kill herself. I'm going to do whatever I have the power to do to find out." She held up the press pass. "This gives me a little power."

"You have me, too. More power."

"More distraction, you mean."

"Don't do this alone, Sage. Let me help you."

She should say no. She should run from the male prostitute.

"You'll need a car, right?" He held out the keys with the Hertz tag dangling.

"Don't you have to work? Aren't there women to rescue and . . ."

He tucked her arm under his, pulling her close. "I'm all yours." He dipped his head low and whispered in her ear, "If you want me."

The problem was . . . she did.

CHAPTER *Six*

"Kelley's!" Johnny hit the steering wheel with a victorious tap as the name came back to him. "That's the place up here I like."

"The seafood shack in Revere Beach?" Amusement and the late-morning light made Sage's pretty eyes look more green than brown as they twinkled at him. "Seriously?"

"There's a bunch of those shacks up here, but that one has unbelievable fried clams. I remember the last time I was here. . . ." He'd been on a security detail with an ex-CEO of General Electric who'd been, happily and coincidentally, a true foodie. "The clams were really good," he finished.

"It's always crowded there."

"I know," he said with the air of a regular. "A couple of years ago, it was the highest-grossing restaurant in the country. That's a lot of clams, baby." He glanced at her to see if she got his joke, but she was looking strangely at him.

"How long have you lived here?" she asked.

He could hear the undercover master's voice. *Stay as close to the truth as you can*, Danny G would say. "Not that long."

"Did you move here from New York?"

Before he arrived in Boston, he'd been in L.A. on an assignment. Before that, Vancouver, and before that . . . he had to think. Oh, of course, that fun month in Jakarta. Before that, a couple of gigs in California. Then . . . "Yeah. New York."

"Where? In the city?"

"All over," he said vaguely, frowning at the traffic. "I guess I have to stay on Route One to get to the arena, huh?"

"It's just past Revere. Where do you live? Or . . ." She repositioned herself to face the front again. "Don't you want anyone to know?"

"I like to keep a low profile."

After a few seconds, she asked, "Were you in the same line of work in New York?"

"Similar." He put a hand on her arm. "Let's talk about you."

"Why? Are you embarrassed that you get paid for sex?"

"Guess it depends on what I get paid."

"Ba-dum-bum." She crossed her arms, slipping out of his touch. "You make jokes when you're uncomfortable."

"I'm not uncomfortable. I'm just funny. And good-looking. And handy with a Crock-Pot. Keep me around." He found her hand and threaded his fingers through hers. "You won't regret it."

She settled a little farther away, leaning against the door.

"Hey." He skimmed the silky fabric of her trousers, following the line of her taut runner's legs. "Admit it, you like me. Regardless of my career choice."

"Career choice?" She shot one perfect eyebrow in the air. "That's an interesting way of putting it."

"I'm a fulfiller of fantasies, baby doll. Believe me, there are worse things I could be."

"True," she said, her voice rich with sarcasm. "Like a killer. A thief. A liar."

He'd been damn near all three in another life. "Or a reporter," he said with a quick smile.

"See? You make jokes when you're uncomfortable."

"Who said I was joking?"

She tapped his hand playfully and didn't move away from him again. "You mean you put journalists in the same league with killers, thieves, and liars?"

"Not all journalists. Not you." He squeezed her thigh, congratulating himself on the smooth change of subject. "So how long have you been writing?"

"I've freelanced since I graduated from B.C., almost six years ago. I always wanted to be an investigative reporter. My mother worked for the *Washington Post* and she was my role model."

He glanced at her. "Was? Is she retired now?"

Under his fingertips, her thigh muscle tensed. "She's dead."

"Oh, I'm sorry. And your dad? Brothers and sisters?"

She blew out a sigh and turned to the window. "No

siblings. My dad lives in Vermont. Alone." She waited a beat, then added, "He has Alzheimer's. Doesn't really know what day it is, I'm afraid."

"That's a shame."

"Yeah, it is. And what about your parents? Are they in New York?"

He opted for the truth, since it didn't seem to matter with this cover story. "My parents were killed in an accident in Tuscany when I was a kid."

"In Tuscany? Were they on vacation?"

"No, they lived there."

"You lived in Italy? You grew up there?" At his nod, she added, "You don't even have an accent. I mean, not an Italian one."

"My mother married an Italian businessman and moved there before I was born. I was sent back to the States when they died. I was young enough to lose the accent and barely remember the language." His true reasons for turning his back on Italy were way too complicated for this conversation. For any conversation.

"And who did you live with? When your parents died?"

"Family in New York, but I went on my own pretty young." Time for a subject change. "So, Sage, you have a boyfriend?"

"No."

He winked at her. "Want one?"

She laughed lightly. "No, thanks."

"Why? Because of my 'career choice'?"

Her smile faded. "If you're asking seriously, I don't think I'd be able to get past what you do."

Or what he used to do. "It's all right, sugar. We'll just have fun. No strings. No promises."

"No sex."

He punched his hand over his heart and grunted like she'd shot him.

"But I'll let you cook for me."

"Chicks. They only want one thing." He shook his head, his teasing smile belying the victory he felt inside.

He was still smiling when they parked at the Manzi Arena and headed to the business offices. As they walked down a long, narrow hallway toward the wing to the dance team's management offices, Sage put her hand on his arm. "This will be boring for you. Why don't you go see if you can watch the basketball team practice or something?"

"Oh, let's see. What'll be more interesting? The nine-foot guys slam-dunking or the twenty-some beauty queens doing backbends and splits? Hmmm. I don't know."

"The girls won't be here. And anyway, who am I supposed to say you are?"

"Personal assistant, chef, chauffeur, bodyguard." He nudged her forward. "Boyfriend."

She continued toward the office. "Well, maybe you'll recognize one of the girls and then I'll know who to talk to. Ashley's the only one who's admitted to being kidnapped, but a lot of them have done it."

"Maybe I will," he said.

"But you heard me on the cell phone on the way here. It wasn't easy to convince Julian Hewitt's assistant to give me this interview so quickly, and I want to do it alone. I get people to talk more, one on one."

"Sure," he agreed as they entered a tiny front office. She'd push back if he was too insistent. "I'll wait for you here."

When the receptionist disappeared in the back to get the manager of the New England Snow Bunnies, Sage stayed standing, studying the wall of eight-by-ten autographed beauty shots of the Bunnies.

"Keisha's gone," she said softly, indicating an empty slot. "You'd think they'd at least leave her picture up."

She said it more to herself, so he didn't answer, instead dropping into one of the chairs and scooping up a copy of *Boston Living*. "You write anything in here?" he asked, showing her the cover.

"Oh, yeah. Big story. It's called 'The Real Tragedy in the ER.' "

He flipped to the table of contents. "Cool."

The door opened and he looked up, expecting a man. Instead, a hard-looking woman in her early forties came out, her eyes sharp, her blond hair short, flat, and unstyled.

"Are you the reporter?" she asked without preamble.

Sage extended her hand. "I'm Sage Valentine with *Boston Living* magazine. I have an interview scheduled with the dance-team manager."

The woman shook Sage's hand briskly. "Julian's been called away for a meeting. I'm the choreographer and I'll do the interview."

"All right," Sage agreed. "But I'm planning a fairly in-depth feature and will eventually need to talk to everyone, including Mr. Hewitt."

"You can start with me," she said, her tone as unattractive as her face.

Johnny held up the magazine. "I'll wait right here."

Sage nodded and turned to the woman. "I'm sorry, I didn't get your name."

As they walked through the door, Johnny only caught part of her answer: "I'm Julian's wife, Glenda."

Perfect. A witch's name.

Glenda Hewitt's office had about as much style and personality as the plain gray sweat suit that clung to her protruding bones and sinewy muscles. Keisha had hated the woman, as all the Snow Bunnies did, but she was supposed to be a good choreographer and rumored to have a gooey center, if you could find it. At the moment, she was all crust.

"So, Ms. Hewitt." Sage opened a worn reporter's notebook to the first empty page, zipping through a mental file of what she knew about Glenda Hewitt, other than the fact that she was punctual as hell and would not allow soda or chocolate on the premises, Keisha's favorite two food groups. "I understand you and your husband came to the Blizzard after stints with the Dallas Mavericks and the Phoenix Suns."

Glenda leaned across her metal desk with a glower that probably struck terror in the hearts of her entire dance team. "Let's get this right out in the open, Miss Valentine. I know why you're here."

Sage blinked. "You do?"

"I know Keisha Kingston was your roommate. If you're digging for dirt, you won't find it."

So much for a *secret* investigation. "I'm not digging for dirt," Sage replied. "I'm here to do what we in the magazine business call a puff piece. As far as Keisha's concerned, I only hope to honor the dance team that she loved."

Glenda steepled her fingers and rested her chin on them, staring at Sage.

"I work very, very hard to create cohesion and synchronicity on this team. There is much more to dancing than kicking and jumping," Glenda said. "I will not, under any circumstances, let the media undermine that."

"I have no intention of undermining anything," Sage assured her. "All I want is a few interviews, some access to the young ladies, a day for photos, maybe a chance to see one of the games."

Glenda nodded. "Fine. But please be aware that we are moving into play-off season, and we have a tight schedule. I control the girls' time and I will control all of your access to them."

"I didn't realize that was your function," Sage said, bristling at the woman's arrogance. "I thought you created their dances and your husband managed their schedules. Has that changed?"

Glenda's blue eyes turned to hard, cold steel as she held out a single typed page. "Here's a list of girls you can talk to. These are the only dancers cleared to do media interviews. The *only* ones. If you attempt to interview any others, I will rescind all access."

No wonder Keisha had hated this bitch. "That's not a problem," Sage said. "But, Glenda, I guarantee you that—"

"You can call me Ms. Hewitt and I know what you're about to say. You are doing a positive feature. And that's wonderful."

Sage opened her mouth to speak, but got the universal symbol for Halt in the form of one raised palm. "You will do it my way or not at all. That's the way this operation works, and if you don't believe me, you can ask any of the dancers."

"Well," Sage waved the paper, "I can ask nine of them."

The desk phone beeped and Glenda rewarded Sage's sarcasm with a smirk as she answered it.

Waiting, Sage skimmed the list of interview candidates. She recognized the names but didn't know any of the women personally. There were a few different cliques within the Snow Bunnies; this list didn't include any of Keisha's closer friends, none of the dancers who'd been around last season.

When Glenda hung up, Sage raised the paper. "These are all rookies, Ms. Hewitt."

"The season's nearly over; they've been around. And the team is only two years old. No one is a veteran here."

Sage nodded as twenty possible questions bounced around in her head and were quickly discarded. The kind of questions an investigative journalist was trained to ask, not what this woman would readily answer.

"So why did you and your husband leave the Suns?"

"We joined this organization for the opportunity to

make a mark in the very competitive world of NBA dance teams."

Sage picked up her pen and jotted down the well-rehearsed, and useless, quote. "And do you do all of the choreography?"

She nodded. "Of course."

"And select the songs?" Somewhere, there might be a reader who cared. Maybe.

"The girls get some input on the song selections."

"And how often do you practice?" Yeah, this would be one helluva piece of cutting-edge journalism.

"We practice almost every night that there isn't a game."

Sage knew that, and felt foolish for asking. "What makes the Snow Bunnies different from any other NBA dance squad?"

"Spirit, talent, warmth, and tremendous love for the city of Boston."

More drivel. She couldn't think of a single other meaningless question. Sage put her notebook on the table and purposely lowered her voice. "Did you know that some of your dancers like to pay for the privilege of being professionally kidnapped and rescued?"

Glenda met her stare, but said nothing.

"Are you aware of this, Ms. Hewitt?" Sage asked.

"Not only am I aware of it, I am, in fact, in charge of it."

Sage dropped back in her chair, her mouth loose with surprise. "What do you mean?"

"The fantasy kidnapping is a key part of my bonding program, Ms. Valentine." She stood like a professor about to give a lecture, crossing her arms. "The most important element of a dance team is not, as you may think, the talent of the dancers."

"No?" Sage didn't need to lift her notebook or pen. She was trained to memorize good quotes, and her reporter's instinct was buzzing in anticipation that she might get one. "What is?"

"Unity." Glenda smiled for the first time, but her eyes remained cold. "They dance better, they look better, they attract more attention, and they do their job of enthralling the men in the audience who buy tickets if they are a unified, well-oiled team, just like the basketball players."

"And what does this have to do with fantasy kidnapping on a thrill site?"

"Shared experiences, especially exciting ones, create a bond. We do many activities that get them to connect with one another. It's not easy to get twenty-two highly competitive women to form friendships. I find creative ways that force them to appreciate each other."

"Do they talk about it with each other afterward?" she asked.

"Yes. And with me. But they won't talk about it to you."

Oh yes they will. "Why not?"

She pointed to the paper. "None of those girls has participated in that program yet. And if you mention it to them, they won't know what you're talking about." She waited a beat and curled a shapeless lip. "So don't."

Sage folded the paper. "I'd like to talk to someone who has participated. I think this is a fascinating aspect of their training. I'd like to include your team-building efforts in the story."

"I hope you will." She made a point of checking her watch. "But if you include the fantasy kidnapping in the story, I will not give my approval to run it."

"Your approval?" Sage suppressed a choke.

"When I heard you were coming in, I called Mr. Zellman at *Boston Living* magazine. My stipulation is that I have final editorial approval or there is no story. That was his assistant who just called, giving me that approval."

Sage opened her mouth to argue, then stopped. Who cared? She wanted access and information; this story was just a means to an end. And she could bypass this pesky choreographer in her sleep. There was nothing to be gained from arguing with her. "Fine."

"And I will be present for every interview or you will not talk to a single member of the New England Blizzard organization."

"That's—"

"Not up for debate. Every interview will be scheduled through my office, and you will have exactly one week to conduct those interviews. You will not need to do a photo session; we will provide pictures of the dancers for your article. And, what else did you want? Oh yes." She opened her drawer and pulled out a small white envelope and handed it to Sage. "Tickets to tonight's game. You can bring your boyfriend."

"He's . . ." Not worth it. "Thank you."

"Goodbye, Ms. Valentine."

So much for access. So much for a press pass. So much for getting information. Sage slipped her notebook, pen, and the tickets into her bag, then leveled a hard look at the other woman.

"Did you arrange for all of the kidnappings?" she asked. "Or do some of the Snow Bunnies go to the site on their own?"

"I assisted in the arrangements."

Sage's pulse jumped. "Then do you know what happened to Keisha that night? Who kidnapped her and who rescued her?"

She shook her head. "She never showed. Her kidnapping never took place."

Exactly what Lucy Sharpe had said. "How do you know?"

"Because she called me that night and told me she'd changed her mind."

Blood rushed in Sage's ears. Could this woman know the answer to the question? "Why? Did she say why?"

Her look was one of genuine sympathy. "Because she was despondent and depressed. Surely you read her suicide note."

Sometimes I think I'll never be good enough.

Keisha's words, and her handwriting, were still burned in Sage's mind. "Yes, I did."

"Then you know that she was a desperately unhappy woman, riddled with self-doubt and crippled by the competitive nature of this business."

"No, she wasn't," Sage replied, her back straightening with indignation. "She was very happy, brimming with self-confidence, and thrilled to be a Snow Bunny. You didn't know her at all."

"On the contrary, Ms. Valentine. You're the one who didn't know her at all."

Resentment rocked through her. "I most certainly did. She was my closest friend."

"Then why were you in Texas when she had to have an abortion?"

Sage stared, openmouthed. "An abortion?"

Glenda tilted her head. "Evidently you didn't know her that well after all."

Glenda waited five minutes before taking out her cell phone. How had he known this was going to happen? The man was brilliant. Utterly brilliant. She dialed the number he'd given her with shaky fingers.

"We have a problem," she said when he answered the phone. "Her name is Sage Valentine and she was Keisha Kingston's roommate."

"Why is that a problem, Glen?"

Because the whole thing could blow up in their faces? She managed to keep her voice steady. "Because she's an—"

"Investigative journalist. I know that."

She closed her eyes. Sometimes he was too brilliant. "She's supposed to do a puff piece on the dance team, but she couldn't make it through the first interview without mentioning the kidnappings. She has an agenda." And they were on it.

He just laughed softly, a dry, baritone chuckle. "I bet she does."

"You're not worried about her? She's not going to give up. I could refuse to do the story and close every door in her face."

"Please don't. I like tenacious, resourceful, beautiful women. You know that."

Envy spurted in her stomach. "She's not *that* beautiful," Glenda said sharply. "Not like *my* girls." Sage's flowing blond hair and mysterious dark green eyes were striking and unusual, true. But she was not the all-American purebred that he liked. Glenda's trained eye could see there was something in that blood that gave her eyes a hint of an exotic tilt, and her lips were too full to be considered perfect.

"Manage her," he said simply. "You're very good at that."

"I plan to. I am limiting and monitoring her interviews. She won't find anything."

He snorted softly. "I've always said you can control anything."

Anything but time, and she had less and less of that every day. The only thing that could extend her time was money . . . and a miracle. He could offer her one of those.

"I can control twenty-two egotistical cheerleaders. I can surely control one nosy reporter," she assured him. "I'll keep you posted."

"That's not the only reason you called, I hope."

She swallowed hard. "Yes. For now."

"But I've been expecting a call with a date and time." He waited, drawing out the silence. "When and who, Glenda? I'm ready."

And when he was ready, she had to provide. If she didn't, he'd go somewhere else. To someone else. If that happened too many times, she'd be out of the picture altogether.

"I thought I would have someone this week, but we've hit a snag." She closed her eyes and braced for the response.

"I don't like snags."

"I know. We're very close. You of all people know that there's an element of nature involved that can't be controlled."

The phone rumbled with his low laughter again. "I thought you can control everything, Glen."

"I should have someone soon."

"Tomorrow night is as long as I can wait." He ended the call with a swift click.

She dropped the phone onto the desk with a thud, replaying the conversation to capture just what caused her stomach to burn. It wasn't his demands; he always demanded. It wasn't the little dig about her need to control. It was . . .

"Oh." She frowned and whispered to herself, "How does he know she's beautiful?"

Controlling Sage Valentine and her story might not be good enough. She could be all sorts of trouble for Glenda.

But she still had control. Because she had twenty-two gorgeous, athletic specimens of female humanity out there ripe for the picking, and he couldn't get to them without her.

*   *   *

Sage held an eggplant in each hand and looked at Johnny. "They look exactly the same to me," she said, the blank expression that she'd worn all the way back from Revere still in place. "Same weight, same color, same size. Eggplants."

He tsked lightly, turning one over. "See that indentation, like a belly button? That's a female." He set the eggplant in the bin and dropped the other into the cloth grocery bag he'd bought so he didn't scream "tourist" at every market in Boston's North End. "Males are less bitter, just like their human counterparts."

She didn't react. In fact, she hadn't laughed at a single joke in the past two hours. Whatever that Hewitt woman had said to her in that interview had sent her into such a silent, dark mood that he ditched fried clams at Kelley's to cook the girl some real comfort food.

"I think that covers it, sweetheart," he said, mentally reviewing his menu. "Unless you want to stop for Limoncello. You look like you could use a shot."

"I can't drink in the afternoon. I'll get a headache."

"Not from the good stuff," he assured her, as he paid in cash for the produce. He thanked the owner in Italian and guided Sage onto the narrow, cobbled street, keeping one arm on her back, the groceries in the other.

But she didn't say a word. All the way back to the car—including a stop at Maria's for the cannoli shells that he'd fill himself after dinner—and for the drive back to Beacon Hill, she didn't talk. When he parked the car near the Dumpster, she stayed in the passenger seat, still lost in her thoughts.

"Sage," he said as he opened the door for her. "It might help to talk about it."

"I can't."

"It's about Keisha, isn't it? You found something out."

She nodded, and climbed out of the car. "It's personal. You wouldn't understand." She started down the alley toward the street, leaving him to kick the car door closed with frustration.

Easy, Johnny. He could practically hear Lucy's calm voice: Don't get personally involved. Don't *care*.

But he couldn't help wanting to share whatever it was that hurt her. He wanted to pull her close, touch the sad expression on her face, and kiss her until she told him and he made her forget. He'd get it out of her eventually. In the meantime, he was "watching" her, which was all Lucy had asked him to do. Which someone, somewhere was paying for him to do.

He caught up with her in a few strides. "You'll like my soup," he promised, dipping close to her from behind as she pulled keys from her bag. "I got everything we need for the best comfort food of all. *Pappa al pomodoro.*"

She laughed softly. "Sounds beauti—"

He walked right into her as she froze in place, her hand on the doorknob. "It's not locked," she muttered, turning it as she pushed the door open.

He dropped the bag of groceries and pulled her back. "Don't go in." Stepping in front of her, he eased the door open. "Don't move," he instructed over his shoulder, his eyes scanning the room.

He loosened his shoulders as he walked, slowly moving his hand to the Glock hidden under his jacket. The living room was empty, untouched. The kitchen looked precisely as he'd last seen it, but for a coffee cup in the dish drainer. The laptop and papers on the built-in desk were just as he remembered them.

He glanced back to make sure Sage stayed where he'd left her, but she was already in the living room.

"Don't touch anything." He mouthed the order, inching toward the hall. The first door, to her room, was partially open. Moving silently, he pulled out his gun and flattened the door to the wall, scanning the room. Her iPod was charging in a wall socket, a jewelry box remained closed on the dresser. There was no evidence that someone had been in there.

He yanked open the closet door, used the gun to move clothes, then checked the bathroom. Nothing. Still on guard, he returned to the hall.

He closed the door until it latched and stepped into the hall.

Sage stood at the entrance to the kitchen, her eyes widening as she saw the gun he held. "What is *that*?"

He shook his head to keep her quiet, holding up one finger for her to stay and wait—which she ignored—and walked to Keisha's room.

The door was wide open and the bureau, nightstands, and a small chest at the foot of the bed had been ransacked. The little antique desk where her laptop had been was empty.

He spun around at Sage's gasp; she stood open-mouthed, staring at the wall.

The poster of twenty-some cover girls hung torn in half, ripped right down the middle, tearing Keisha Kingston's smiling face in two. On the wall behind it, words were scrawled in thick black marker:

Whores must die.

CHAPTER
Seven

"Let me in there!" Sage yanked her elbow out of Johnny's grip and tried again to shove him out of her way. He'd pushed her right back into the hall, a gun—a gun!—in one hand, the other holding her back.

"No can do, princess." He'd become a human wall, six feet of heat-carrying muscle and brawn that refused to budge. "First of all, it's just going to upset you. Second, it's a crime scene and we're calling the police."

"I'm not upset," she insisted. "I want to go back in that room."

"Not upset? You're shaking."

She inhaled hard in frustration, slicing him with a glare and steadying her voice. "I am going back in that room and—" She held her hand up to stop the argument before it started. "And I am going to see what's missing, examine the scene, and then maybe we'll call the police."

"Maybe?" He slid the gun somewhere on his hip in a well-practiced move.

"Why are you carrying that thing?"

"I'm licensed," he replied.

"I didn't ask if you were licensed. I asked why."

He half shrugged. "In my line of work, I run into some loonies."

"And you *shoot* them?"

"I scare them."

She didn't even want to think about the fact that last night she'd dragged, undressed, and practically raped a man packing a pistol. "Let me go in there." She put both hands on his chest and softened her voice. "Please. I have to see."

He closed his eyes, obviously torn. "All right." His sigh said it was anything but. "Let's do an inventory. But this wasn't your garden-variety B and E."

She didn't know what a garden-variety break and enter looked like, but she didn't argue his point.

"That . . ." he cocked his head toward Keisha's room, "is a crime of violence."

"I realize that. And I'd like to see if I can figure out who did it." She pressed harder against the stone of his muscular chest.

Reluctantly, he stepped aside and let her go. A memory of the day she'd entered the room—two days after Keisha's body had been found by one of the Snow Bunnies and had been taken to the coroner—hit her like a punch. That day, sadness had flattened her. Today, anger had her stomach roiling.

She stared at the poster, at the vicious slash of a black Sharpie, then scanned the floor with the wild hope that whoever had done this had left a mark, a clue, the pen cap, or a distinctive footprint on the hardwood floor. There was none. She took a step forward and immediately his hand closed over her shoulder.

"Don't touch."

"You think there's a fingerprint?" she asked.

"Maybe. Laptop's gone."

"So they did steal something." She gave a dry laugh. "That actually makes me feel better—like they didn't come in here just to slap hate mail on the wall."

"If that were the case, they'd have taken the laptop you keep in the kitchen. And your jewelry case is untouched."

"You're starting to sound like a cop."

He didn't answer, and she moved to the bureau, to Keisha's exquisite collection of porcelain boxes. Under the dozen or so hand-painted lids, she'd kept an array of bling—gifts from boyfriends, some she'd bought herself.

Sage reached for one box and Johnny was beside her in an instant. "Here." He pulled out a white linen handkerchief from his pocket and gingerly lifted the lid. "Anything missing?" he asked, holding the lid of a tiny box, painted to replicate the famous Tiffany blue with a white porcelain ribbon.

Two-carat diamond earrings glinted in platinum settings. A gift from Keisha's father, a partner at one of the largest investment firms in the world.

"No, that's all that's ever been in that Tiffany's box. Try another one," she said.

He replaced that lid and slid one decorated with delicate roses to the side. There was the Chanel Star

Watch that the entire dance team had received as a gift from the owner of the New England Blizzard at the end of their first season.

"You're right about one thing," Sage said softly. "This wasn't a standard burglary—unless he was dumb as dirt."

"But he took the computer," Johnny said.

"I know." She peered into one last box that he revealed. "And this tennis bracelet is worth a lot more than a laptop."

He set the lid down exactly as they had found it, then tucked the handkerchief back into his pocket as he walked to the poster. He stood very close and scrutinized the tear in the paper. He'd taken off his black leather jacket, and now she could easily see the menacing pistol stuck into a small leather holster attached to his belt. Who was this man, who carried a loaded gun and a freshly ironed hankie?

"Did Keisha have any crazed fans?" he asked.

"Not more than the usual. Sometimes guys would call who'd dug up her number on the Internet. Or they'd hang out near the exit to the arena, but the girls had a secret way of leaving, and plenty of security."

"A boyfriend?"

Sage closed her eyes as she remembered what Glenda Hewitt had told her.

An abortion. She still couldn't fathom that Keisha would have endured that and not shared the fact with her roommate and closest friend.

"She wasn't seeing anyone when I left for Texas," she said quietly. "But I was gone a month. We didn't talk every day, or even every week. She . . . might have." She sat on the edge of the bed, nibbling on her lip. "I've tried to remember who she was seeing, but in the midst of the basketball season, she had so many games and commitments, she didn't have a lot of time to date. But there must have been someone."

He turned to her. "What do you mean?"

Why hide it from him? "Glenda told me that Keisha had an abortion while I was gone. She implied that might be why she committed suicide."

"An abortion?" He glanced at the wall, thinking. "Wonder if this is just some whacko antiabortionist who got her name from a clinic."

She considered that. "That's possible, I guess. But I'm not sure I believe Glenda. Keisha was too smart to get pregnant."

"Nothing's foolproof. Maybe having to make that decision was enough to put her over the edge. You weren't here. You don't know what—oh, hey." He was next to her in two steps, his face sympathetic, his hands strong on her arms. "I didn't mean to take you on a guilt trip."

"It's okay. I wasn't here, you're right. But still . . ." Surprised by his tenderness and how much it touched her, she shifted her gaze back to the wall. "Would things have ended differently if I had been?"

Whores must die.

And suddenly the world tilted sideways and she closed her hands over his arms, holding on to him, but staring at the wall. *Whores must die.*

"What?" he asked. "What's wrong?"

"Maybe she didn't commit suicide," she said, her voice strained. "Maybe whoever did this . . . killed her. Because he thought she was . . ." She couldn't say it. "Bad."

His nod was nearly imperceptible. "That would be the literal translation of the writing on the wall."

She closed her eyes and whispered, "I think I'll have that drink now."

She had to talk coherently to the police, so Johnny brewed peppermint tea while Sage quietly tried to come to grips with the revelation she'd just had.

"You're a nurturer," she mused as she plucked the tea bag from the cup and let it drip. "You know that?"

Johnny sat across from her at the table in the portion of the living area that she called a dining room. "I've been called worse," he said with a smile. "By you, as a matter of fact."

A glimmer of amusement lit her eyes, turning them the deep green color of the herb that matched her name. "And," she said, training that sage gaze right on him, "you seem to know a lot about crime and investigation."

"Common sense." Not to mention a few years with the mob and a few more with the Bullet Catchers. "And, of course, lots of TV."

The look on her face said she didn't buy it, but she swirled her tea without comment. After a minute, she said, "The only thing more preposterous than Keisha killing herself is the possibility that it was murder. She didn't have any enemies, she didn't have a violent boyfriend, she didn't ever hang with anyone remotely questionable. She was squeaky clean."

"Except a little sideline of getting kidnapped and rescued for fun."

"That doesn't make her suicidal. Maybe she was just going along with Glenda's bonding games. I have to look at everything differently now."

"You don't have to do anything," he said. "The police are coming. You give them a report, and then you stay behind locked doors and out of harm's way."

She scowled at him. "Are you nuts? Not that I want to go in harm's way, and I won't, but my story on the Snow Bunnies is more important than ever." She snapped her finger and pointed at him. "And the computer! Whoever took it now has the links and passwords to takemetonite.com. There could still be a connection."

"There isn't." That was one thing he knew without a doubt, because if Lucy had checked the operation out, she'd done it thoroughly. Although he was dying to call her and throw this new monkey wrench her way. She—and whoever was the client on this job—needed to know what had happened.

"You have to do something for me, Johnny."

"Anything."

That made her smile. "You have to get me in to interview everyone who works at that company. I want to talk to whoever kidnapped—"

"She didn't show."

"Then whoever *didn't* kidnap her," she shot back. "Whoever was supposed to take her. Whoever set it up. I don't want to be stonewalled; I want to know. Before, I thought there could be a clue to why she killed herself. Now this could be a murder investigation."

In point of fact, she was right. "I'll do my best," he promised. Maybe he could drop the cover, come clean with Sage, and really do what he was meant to do: protect her from the whacko who sliced the poster, and figure out what had happened the night her roommate died. He wanted to know almost as much as Sage did.

And he couldn't forget about the van he'd seen that morning. He'd tracked Sage and her follower to the train platform, and witnessed their exchange, and the interruption by the cheerleader. All that time, someone was still in that van . . . or in her apartment leaving love letters.

"Did they let you see the suicide note Keisha left?" he asked. "I assume there was a standard investigation."

She nodded slowly. "Yes, I did see it. I wasn't here when they did the investigation, because there was a big snowstorm and I couldn't get into Boston for a while. By the time I got home, they were finished and the medical examiner confirmed that it was suicide. Someone from the Boston PD did talk to me briefly, but by then they had closed the investigation."

"Did the note look legitimate?"

"It was Keisha's handwriting, if that's what you mean. It was very short. She'd written it on a green index card that had sticky on the back, like a Post-it note."

"What did it say?"

She released a slow sigh. " 'Sometimes I think I'll never be good enough.' "

He leaned the chair back, locking his arms behind his neck. "That's it?"

She nodded, her brows drawn. "In all the years I knew her, since our freshman year in college, I never heard a syllable of self-doubt come from that woman's mouth. She believed she rocked the world."

"She didn't leave a message to her parents or family or friends? No apology to people she loved? No rationalization?" He slammed down on the front two legs of the chair. "That's not a suicide note."

"It was hers. At least it's what she decided to write before she swallowed enough ephedra to kill herself."

Or someone made her. "What was listed as her cause of death?"

"Suffocation."

"A side effect of the drug," he said.

A hard rap came on the front door.

"That's the police," Sage said, pushing away from the table. "Maybe they'll tell us there's been a rash of break-ins along the flats of Beacon Hill and they caught the guy."

"Don't count on it," he murmured.

"Believe me, I'm not."

Detective Steven Cervaris had obviously done quite a few B and Es in Beacon Hill, Back Bay, and South End. He was patient, seasoned, and bored. While Johnny stayed in the kitchen, Sage showed the officer the front door, which had no sign of forced entry, described the missing computer, explained that many valuable items had been left behind, then dropped the bomb.

"The burglar left a calling card in one of the bedrooms," she said.

Bushy eyebrows rose; startling blue eyes blinked with interest. "What's that?"

She indicated for him to follow her, explaining that her roommate, a dancer for the Blizzard, had died a month earlier.

"Oh, yeah, I read about that," he said, his New England accent drawing out his vowels. "Didn't realize this was the building."

Sage opened the door, steeling herself to see it again. "This burglar certainly did."

He studied the handiwork, leaning closer to examine the rip in the poster, carefully dabbing the tiniest edge of the *W* in *Whores* with the tip of his finger.

"The computer that was stolen was in here." Sage indicated the Queen Anne desk. "But nothing else was touched. And she had plenty of good jewelry and expensive clothes."

Detective Cervaris scanned the room slowly. "When did she die, again?"

"About a month ago. March fourth."

"Who handled the investigation?"

"I talked to an Officer McGraw when I finally got into town. He said it was a standard suicide investigation."

"Where were you when it happened?"

"On business in Texas."

He nodded. "I'll get the file."

"Detective," she said, sensing a too-quick dismissal. "My roommate had absolutely no reason to commit suicide. She was very happy and stable and successful."

"Happy, stable, successful people are sometimes not really so happy or stable."

"I realize that, but I think that this"—she indicated the wall—"could be proof that it was murder."

He shot one of those thick brows north. "I wouldn't call it a signed confession."

"No, but it shows that maybe someone had an ax to grind."

"That doesn't mean whoever broke in here today is a murderer," he said. "Could just mean that your apartment was burgled by someone who isn't a Blizzard fan."

"That's a little more radical than 'Boo Blizzard,' wouldn't you say?"

He lifted one shoulder as if to say, Boston fans are tough. In the background, she heard the soft digital tones of a cell phone ringing, but not hers.

"Who's the guy in the kitchen?" the detective asked.

"He was with me all day. Since morning."

"I didn't ask for his alibi. I asked who he was."

"He's—"

"John Christiano." Johnny stood in the doorway and extended one hand. "I'm her friend." He held up his cell phone. "I'm going to take this call outside."

"Did he know your roommate?" Detective Cervaris asked when Johnny left.

"No. We just met recently."

He opened the closet door with a handkerchief. "How'd you meet?"

"A blind date," she said.

"Is this her stuff?" He eased some of the clothes aside, but there was very little room to move a hanger.

"Yes. I'm waiting for her parents to come and collect all her things. I imagine they'll put the apartment on the market, since it belonged to her. Are you going to dust for prints?"

"Yeah, but don't get your hopes up." He glanced at the bed. "Didn't I read that she OD'd?"

"Not on illegal drugs. She ingested a massive quantity of an herb called ephedra. They don't consider that a technical overdose."

"Ma huang," he said. "Chinese stuff."

"Yes, a derivative of that. It's taken for weight loss." Not that Keisha needed to lose an ounce, but all the dancers were obsessive about their Monday morning weigh-ins. Keisha spent most Sundays starving and drinking water to avoid Glenda's wrath. They slavishly drank her carb-free weight-loss drinks and even reported their menstrual cycles to account for water-weight gain. Keisha had hated all that, but had been smart enough to cooperate to keep the bosses happy.

"Not very easy to commit suicide with that stuff," the detective commented. "Of course, combined with enough caffeine and an energy drink or six, you could pretty much suffocate yourself, or induce a heart attack and stroke." He gave her a questioning look. "Is that how she did it?"

"According to the medical examiner, yes. But she wasn't unhappy," Sage said again. "And she wasn't . . ." Her gaze drifted to the wall. "A whore."

His expression softened. "I'll have some prints taken and we'll run tests for hairs, trace evidence. I take it you've cleaned this room since the original crime scene investigation?"

"Yes. When will you take the evidence?"

"Today. Soon. Don't leave," he said, folding the paper she'd given him earlier with the information about Keisha's computer she'd taken off the system disks in the drawer. "I'll start running the serial number of the computer and see if it shows up in pawnshops. Are you sure nothing else is missing?"

"Her jewelry's all there." Sage pointed to the bureau. "And it's expensive."

"That was a twelve-hundred-dollar computer," he said.

"True, but the Chanel watch is worth more."

"What's on the computer is sometimes more valuable. Credit card information, private e-mails." He gave her a pointed look. "Compromising photography."

"I've been through every inch of her computer and there were no naked pictures, if that's what you're implying. But there was something interesting."

He tucked a hand into his trouser pocket. "I like interesting. What was it?"

She explained about takemetonite.com and the fact that Keisha had never shown up for her appointment. She gave him the information she had, and prayed like hell he wouldn't track Johnny to the site.

"There could be a connection," she said after he'd written it all down. "But I haven't been able to find one."

"I'll check that out, and the investigation that took place when your roommate died," he said. "In the meantime, please let me know if anything else is missing."

Thanking him and taking his card, Sage showed him to the door, and saw Johnny standing about twenty feet away on the sidewalk, talking into a cell phone. Setting up a rescue for later tonight? Her stomach tightened just a little, but she pushed the thought out of her head. Back in Keisha's room, she stared at the wall. The bed. The empty desk.

She'd never considered that it hadn't been a suicide but she'd been focused on finding out why. Now she had to consider a whole host of possibilities.

Did this break-in mean anything? Maybe someone was looking for evidence he'd left behind? But then why write all over the wall?

Unless the message was directed at Sage.

With a shiver, she gave the room one more scan, then opened the closet door with her toe. Keisha's closet was tiny, a remnant from the old building that had never been updated as the apartment had been over the years. She'd often complained about how she had to cram her clothes in there, and had to keep all her dozens of shoes, belts, and handbags under the bed.

Sage got on her knees and lifted the dust ruffle around the platform of the queen-size bed. The shoe boxes and storage containers were all out of order, as though they'd been rifled, although some were still stacked in twos. Stuart Weitzman. Manolo Blahnik. Prada. She hadn't studied Keisha's purchases and wouldn't know if a Louis Vuitton bag was missing or not.

Sage reached under to push two shoe boxes to the side and the movement caused the top one to tumble, and the lid fell off. Paper fluttered to the floor.

No, not paper. Index cards. Poking her head farther under the bed, she lifted one, surprised that it adhered slightly to the hardwood floor. Like a . . .

Like a Post-it note, only the size and shape of an index card, all brightly colored. Exactly what Keisha had written her suicide note on.

She stretched her fingertips to grasp as many of the fallen cards as she could. She pulled out a handful and emerged from under the bed, dust tickling her nose.

Keisha's distinctive handwriting was on every one. One sentence, no more:

Behind my face, there is nothing.
I'm scared of losing everything.
I sleep with rich men to boost my confidence.

Barely able to breathe, Sage read another one:

Sometimes I can't go on.

"What are you doin' down there, princess?"

Sage jumped at the sound of Johnny's voice, and looked up to see him standing in the doorway. "Reading." The word came out in a croak.

He took a step into the room, peering over her shoulder. "Reading what?"

"I'm not sure." She held up one of the cards. "It's like a whole stash of . . . suicide notes."

Johnny crouched down next to her. "You mean, she wrote more of them? What were they, practice?"

Sage fanned the cards. "I don't know. I just had no idea she was this unhappy." Sighing, she leaned around him to look at the poster. "But I'm going to figure out what happened or die trying."

"Not if I have anything to do with it, you're not."

She half smiled at the protective note in his voice. "It's a figure of speech."

She hoped.

CHAPTER
Eight

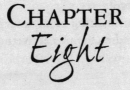

Without warning, everything was bathed in darkness. Followed by a split second of surprised silence. Then a pinpoint of electric blue laser light bounced over the high gloss wood floor, then another and another, all moving rhythmically to a rumbling bass so deep, it had to be from a subwoofer the size of a small building.

Tha-bumba. Tha-bumba. Tha-bumba bumba bumba.

Someone screamed. Someone whistled.

Johnny slipped his hand into Sage's and glanced at her, but her focus was straight ahead, her intensity palpable.

"Ladies and gentlemen!" bellowed an omniscient voice, through so many speakers the whole arena vibrated with every word. "Welcome to the Manzi Arena, home of the one and only, your New England Blizzaaaaaard!"

At the deafening cheer in response, Johnny squeezed

her fingers and leaned close to whisper in her ear, "I'm a Knicks guy myself."

She shot him a look, reminding him that although they held hands, and although they sat pressed next to each other in very expensive courtside seats, this was not a fun sports date.

This was a continuation of a quest that had started shortly after the crime technician left, after delivering the news that there were no fingerprints in Keisha's room but that he'd taken what he could. Sage had jumped right to her computer, compiling lists of every single person her roommate had known, surprising Johnny with the fact that she'd already downloaded Keisha's address book and had saved all of her e-mail from the month before she'd died.

The only thing that had surprised him more was her demand that they trade his fantastic dinner plans for a hot dog at Manzi Arena. He'd thought she was kidding, but then she'd produced a white envelope and he had no doubt that if he didn't agree to go along, she'd be here alone.

The bass beat increased and the first notes of a familiar disco song shook the house into another frenzied cheer.

"Are you ready?" the announcer hollered. When the response wasn't deafening enough, he screamed again, "Boston, Massachusetts, are you ready?"

Eighteen thousand or so gave him the hoot he wanted.

"Because there's a snowstorm on the way!"

That elicited more madness and screaming.

"And this storm is smokin' hot!" His voice rose to a crescendo. "They are twenty-two of the most beautiful, most talented, most mind-blowing women in the world, each and every one ready to melt . . . some . . . ice!"

Two sets of double doors burst open and a blast of steam and dry-ice vapor pervaded the basketball court. The music blared and the house rocked as the spectators stood, clapped, and stomped in approval.

Over the loudspeaker, a high-pitched voice whined, "Won't you take me to . . ."

The shout was unified, and earshattering: " 'Funkytown!' "

Sage stood, like everyone else, pulling Johnny's hand so they could see over the one row in front of them. Through the smoke and fog, two lines of glittery girls in sprayed-on white leather hot pants and silver halter tops fanned out like liquid mercury across the floor.

Legs kicked in unison, long hair in every shade ever invented swung left to right in a synchronized wave. Twenty-two dazzling smiles lit the arena as a shower of blue and white spotlights sparkled over whipcord-toned thighs, cantaloupe-shaped asses, and an endless display of nature's finest creations—helped by a few plastic surgeons.

Johnny barely saw the array of female flesh. In his mind's eye, he was still examining nearly two dozen neon-colored sticky-backed index cards, each bearing a one-liner rich with self-doubt, misery, and personal anguish.

Evidently, being one of the most beautiful, most talented, most *mind-blowing women* in the world wasn't enough to make Keisha Kingston a happy cheerleader. And no matter how much Sage had stared at the bleak message left by the intruder, and how hard she clung to the belief that the words *Whores must die* somehow proved that Keisha hadn't taken her own life, those index cards told a very different story.

He hadn't had a chance to tell Lucy about the suicide notes. While Sage had talked to the detective, he'd checked in with the home office. After hearing about the break-in, his boss's edict had been clear: Stay with Sage, protect her, and maintain your cover. No timeline, no explanation, and no room for a single question. And no word on the identity of her benefactor.

"I wonder where Ashley is," Sage whispered. "She's usually the third to the left."

In that spot, a dark-haired girl kicked and shook and smiled so hard, he thought her face might break each time the vocals pleaded they "talk about it, talk about it."

"I saw her this morning," Sage told him. "She wasn't sick."

"Who else do you want to talk to?" he asked.

"Vivian Masters." Sage pointed to a tall, breathtaking girl in the second row. "She's one of the few other women of color on the squad, and I know she and Keisha were close, but she's never called me and didn't come to the memorial service."

He recognized Vivian from the poster, a stunning

Beyoncé type, a magnificent blend of the best of several races, with slanted golden eyes and skin the color of creamy latte. "Is she on the list that Glenda gave you?"

She shook her head. "We'll have to catch her at the exit, when they leave."

"They walk out of here at night alone?"

"They have security and a private exit, but I know where it is."

"Funkytown" hit the big finale. The front row of girls bent back in a gymnastic spine-twisting pose, and the back row kicked over them, then turned and touched their toes, wiggled their rear ends, and finished with over-the-shoulder looks of invitation.

"What do these women get paid?" he asked Sage as they sat down.

"Not much." She reached for her soda and sipped through the straw. "I think it's ninety a game," she said after swallowing. "They don't do this for money."

"Fame?"

She shrugged. "More like notoriety. And access to hot clubs, opportunities to model, make special appearances. They all have day jobs."

The Snow Bunnies bounded off the court and the lights dimmed again, and this time the crowd got even louder. As the starting lineups for the Chicago Bulls and the New England Blizzard were introduced, Johnny studied the sidelines.

In the first row behind the women he saw the hawk-eyed face of Glenda Hewitt and, beside her, a tall, lanky man who split his attention between a handheld electronic device and the backsides of the cheerleaders.

"What was Keisha's day job?" he asked.

"She had a trust fund from a very rich father, but she worked for a florist as a cover."

He turned to her. "A cover for what?"

"All the Snow Bunnies are required to have a job, so she worked part-time for a florist in Boston. Very part-time." She smiled humorlessly. "Like she showed up once a month and picked a free bouquet for the apartment."

"What did she do the rest of the time? Shop?"

"She mentored underprivileged girls in Jamaica Plain. And, yeah, she hit the malls regularly."

At the quarter break, the girls danced and Sage pulled out a piece of paper with names typed on it. "This is the list Glenda gave me. The ones I'm officially allowed to talk to." She was pointing out who was who to him when Johnny sensed someone coming toward them.

In the aisle, he met intense gray eyes set deep in a tanned, lined face, a shaved head, and a barrel chest that advertised a commitment to bench-pressing. The guy looked like he was in his fifties or more, but he exuded confidence, money, and authority.

In a move most people would have missed, he checked out Johnny, then shifted his attention to Sage and broke into a wide smile. "There's the best reporter in Boston."

She turned and beamed, extending both arms and stepping past Johnny to get into the aisle for a warm hug. "Oh, hello!"

The man held her close, then pulled back to look at her. "It's wonderful to see you, dear."

"You, too." She held both hands and leaned toward him, affection in her body language. "Johnny, this is Dr. Garron, a good friend and one of my best sources."

Johnny instantly recognized the name from the story he'd read in *Boston Living* magazine. There hadn't been a picture, because he would certainly have remembered Alonzo Garron, the former head of obstetrics and gynecology at Mass General and the key source for Sage's story about insurance fraud at the hospital.

"I'm John Christiano," he said, shaking the other man's hand.

"I see you have better seats than I do," the doctor said to Sage, a tease buried in a slightly Hispanic lilt. "I guess I don't know the right people."

"They're buttering me up," she said, tilting her head toward the court. "I'm doing a story on the Snow Bunnies."

The doctor drew back. "I shudder to think what evil you will expose there." His lips twisted into a half smile. "But it should make for very provocative reading."

"This will be a fluffier piece than I usually do," she said apologetically. "How is your new practice going?"

"Fantastic." He held up a clenched fist to underscore his exuberance. "If I invite you in for a tour, will you write nice things about it?"

"As you know, I don't usually write nice things," she said, laughing lightly. "But I can send you some business."

He reached forward and took her hand again, sending Johnny to sharp attention. "I may take you up on that, Sage," the man said softly. "And tell me, how's everything? Are you coping?"

Sage shrugged. "Every day gets a little better."

"I worry about you," he said, his eyes warm and sympathetic.

Who was this guy? A source? A friend? Johnny watched the extended eye contact between them. He was something, that was for sure.

Oh. Oh, of *course.* Johnny could have smacked his forehead. This man was the secret Bullet Catcher client. He had the money, the clout, and, clearly, the interest.

"And what do you do, Mr. Christiano?"

As if he didn't know. "I'm a—"

"Chef," Sage said quickly. "He's a phenomenal chef."

"Really?" Garron looked interested, and amused. Like he was in on the secret. "Where do you work?"

"I'm between gigs now," Johnny said coolly. "On the hunt for something new."

"Are you trained?" Garron asked.

"CIA." Would Garron get the double entendre?

"Ah, the Culinary Institute," Garron said, nodding in approval. "You should talk to Hendrick Kane at the Ritz-Carlton. I believe they're looking for someone."

"Thanks," Johnny said. Was this an order from a client or just a clever way to keep his cover? "I've heard good things about Kane's work. I'll check into that."

"You should," Sage agreed, her eyes bright.

"Call me." Garron handed him a business card. "I'll put you in touch with Hendrick. We go way back."

"Thank you." Johnny pocketed the card without looking at it. He would later, after he talked to Lucy and impressed her with how quickly he had sniffed out the client.

The second-quarter buzzer sounded, and Garron kissed Sage on both cheeks, whispering something in her ear that Johnny didn't catch.

When they sat back down, he could have sworn she was glowing.

"Nice guy," he said vaguely.

"He is," she agreed. "A great doctor who took a huge risk."

"Didn't he lose his job because of that article?"

She shook her head and reached for her drink. "He quit and started his own practice."

"He likes you," he said quietly. "Was his interview as pleasant as my first one?"

She almost choked on her sip of Coke, but managed to swallow and glare at him.

"What? He likes you." Johnny pulled out the card. Dr. Alonzo Garron, General Obstetrics and Gynecology. "Is he your gynecologist?" he asked.

"No, I go to a woman." She glanced at the card. "But I'll refer some friends to him, if I can."

He repocketed the card and buried a smart-ass comment about who the good doctor really wanted in his stirrups. After all, he might be the good *client*, too.

"You know, Johnny, maybe you ought to call him. Maybe you should talk to the guy at the Ritz."

"Oh, honey." He took her hand and smiled. "You want me to waste all my talent in the kitchen of some hotel?"

"It's a good company, a great hotel, and it's—"

"Respectable."

"Beats rescuing." She notched an eyebrow in challenge.

"So, what are you saying?" he asked, laying a possessive hand on her thigh, the denim warm, her muscle tight. "Would you like me better if I had a different job?"

She looked him right in the eyes. "Yes."

It would be so easy. So easy to tell her the truth, explain that he was a Bullet Catcher, here to protect her. Then they could act on this electricity and finish what they'd started in bed the night before.

He glanced over his shoulder just in time to catch gray eyes staring down at him from ten rows back. As much as he wanted to return a nonverbal message, he resisted. The client wanted to remain anonymous and wanted the protection to be covert, for whatever reason. Johnny's job was to find ways to stick around and offer that protection.

"I'll call the Ritz tomorrow," he promised.

Ashley stuffed her hands into the warm pockets of her satin Snow Bunnies jacket, tucking herself into the shadows of the arena exit, listening to the pattern of cheers reverberating from inside.

How dare that bitch punish her by putting in an alternate? After all the extra work she'd done for those damn *team-building* exercises? And what good did it do? They each wanted what the other one had. All this fake bonding and unification, fantasy kidnapping and stupid word games, all the sharing and baring of souls—did it help? Hell no. Every girl on that squad hated the next one.

Half of them were happy that Keisha was out of the picture because she was the best-looking one on the team, and everyone knew it. And now she had to get Victoria Brandt signed up. That wasn't going to be easy. About a month ago, when Glenda had said Vicky was "ready" for her turn, the little bitch had practically clawed Ashey's eyes out when she had suggested she go for it.

But Ashley knew better than to question her boss. Plus she liked the extra money Glenda paid her under the table and she liked the job security. Sort-of job security. Face it, her dancing sure as hell wasn't good enough to suit the perfectionist choreographer.

A cheer erupted so loudly, it could only mean one thing. The game was over. This door would open in a few minutes and some hired muscle would escort the girls in groups to their cars. That would be her opportunity to snag Victoria and convince her that if she didn't do the fantasy kidnapping, she'd be the next one with an alternate dancing in her slot.

Bonding by intimidation, that's what Glenda did.

At the sound of footsteps around the side of the building, Ashley tensed. No one ever came back here.

The players left on the other side of the arena, so that's where the fans lined up for autographs. No one knew the Snow Bunnies slipped out this way after the game, and keeping that secret was in their contract. She had to hand it to Glenda and Julian on that account: they were freakish about security.

A woman's voice drifted closer, followed by a man's response. Was that Sage Valentine? She popped out from behind the wall to see Keisha's former roommate and a tall, well-built guy who instantly put a protective arm around Sage.

"Ashley? Is that you?" Sage stepped toward the doors, and the man, Ashley noticed, put his free hand behind his back.

"It's me. What are you doing back here?"

Sage paused in the shadows. "Why didn't you dance tonight?"

The guy stayed a half a step behind Sage, but Ashley felt his intense, hooded eyes locked on her, and took a peek at his chiseled, handsome face. His lips were full, his cheeks darkened by a hint of beard.

"I hurt my back," she lied, wishing like hell she could have impressed this hottie by having danced tonight. "Are you looking for one of the girls?"

"I am," Sage said. "They come out back here, don't they?"

"Usually." Ashley looked at the guy, waiting for an introduction. When one didn't come, she asked, "Who are you?"

"I'm Johnny."

Ashley tugged down the bill of her ball cap. Too

bad she hadn't bothered to straighten her hair or put on stage makeup.

"Johnny," she repeated. And he was . . . a boyfriend? A brother? A fan? She looked expectantly at Sage, but Sage seemed to be watching *her* watching *him*.

After an awkward pause, Ashley tilted her head to the door. "I forgot something in the locker room, and I'm technically not allowed into the building if I'm not dancing."

"Really?" Johnny asked, giving her a suspicious look. "Why's that?"

"Glenda's weird like that," she said with a quick laugh. "But she's the boss. So who you waiting for, Sage?"

"Remember when I saw you on the train and told you I was pitching a story to *Boston Living*?" Sage asked. "Well, they want a feature on the Snow Bunnies."

"Really? That is so cool." She reached for Sage to squeeze her arm, and the guy immediately stepped closer. "Oh, please tell me I can be in it."

Sage pulled out a piece of paper and unfolded it. "Glenda only wants me to talk to certain dancers. Here's the list."

"Surprise, surprise." Ashley held the list toward the moonlight to read the names. "She must have control of everything." Of course, her name wasn't on the list. "So why do you have to come here, now? Can't you interview the girls before practice or something?"

Sage gave her a sneaky smile. "You know me, Ashley. I'm not going to just talk to these girls." She took the paper and refolded it. "I want to talk to the ones who aren't preapproved to quote the company line."

Ashley laughed dryly. "Like me."

"Yes, like you. And like Vivian."

"Scratch that. She does no media, ever."

Security lights flickered above the doors, then came on full strength.

"They'll be out in a second," Ashley said, using the enhanced light to take a good long look at Sage's friend. Who was staring at her like she had grown a second head. Did she look that different without stage makeup?

"Do I know you or something?" she asked pointedly.

He shook his head. "I think I'd remember."

Next to her, she sensed Sage tighten up. Well, who wouldn't be jealous with a guy like that?

"Maybe you've seen me dance," she said, uncomfortable under his scrutiny.

"Maybe you've met him somewhere else?" Sage suggested, her voice heavy with implication.

"I think *I'd* remember," Ashley echoed.

"It's okay, Ashley," Sage assured her. "You can admit it. I don't have any claims on him."

"Oh, I'd admit it," she laughed, wishing he'd just smile a tiny bit. "Honestly."

The back door clunked open and three of the girls stepped out with chatter and laughter. Two arena security guards were right behind them.

"Ashley!" one of the girls said. It was Holly, the alternate. "We missed you!"

Right—if she'd been there, Holly would have been at home. "Bad back," she said glumly. "How was the game?"

"We won." Jacquie Howard flashed a victorious smile, then elbowed the woman next to her. "It was perfect except that Gabrielle totally screwed up the spin on 'I Want You.' "

"I did not," the third woman denied. "You missed the count."

"Is Vivian around?" Ashley asked the girls. "There's somebody here who wants to talk to her."

"She's going out with the players," Jacquie said. "She's scheduled to sign tonight."

Sage stepped forward like she wanted to talk to Jacquie or Gabrielle, but the guard stepped between them. "Sorry, gotta get these ladies to their car." He shot a menacing look at Sage's friend Johnny. "No autographs back here."

"It's okay," Sage said. "I'll go around front and see if I can get Vivian."

Ashley nodded, then leaned very close to Sage to whisper in her ear, "He's hot. Were you serious about not having any claims on him?"

Sage glanced at Johnny where he stood just out of hearing distance. "He's the guy from the website. The rescuer."

Ashley frowned, drinking in every detail of his face as she studied him from under the brim of her hat. "Honey, I know every man on that site. I've met almost all of them and slept with half. That guy is not a rescuer for takemetonite.com."

Sage's jaw dropped in surpise. "Yes, he is."

"Is his picture on the site?"

She nodded. "On page three of 'Meet the Rescuers.' "

Ashley just shook her head. "There is no page three."

"You can't know them all."

"I can and I do." Ashley tapered her eyes and checked Johnny out again. "Is he the guy you got the other night? The one that cooked?"

When Sage nodded, Ashley just shook her head. "Sorry to break it to you, but he's a total poser who has nothing to do with that website."

CHAPTER
Nine

As they hustled to the front of the arena, Sage wanted to demand to know what Ashley meant, but couldn't quite form the right question. And in her business, if you wanted the right answer, you had to ask the right question.

Anyway, she'd asked him questions the night before. He'd dodged them all already as adeptly as he did the postgame revelers pouring into the parking lot, the whole time wearing a tight, focused expression.

"So what's the matter with you?" she asked.

"How well do you know that girl Ashley?"

"Why?"

With his arm on her back, he guided her past a group of men, all the while studying everyone who passed them. "Does she normally wear a blue baseball cap?"

"What difference does it make?"

"It matters."

"I don't know. Half the city wears Red Sox hats. They're blue, right?"

His grip tightened as they reached the sizable crowd surrounding some of the players, and several more security guards. "Is this where you're expecting to find Vivian?"

Sage stood on tiptoe to see if she could find the woman in the middle of the crowd. "Yeah, there she is. Signing."

"You want to wait for her?"

She gauged the line. There were at least forty people in the crowd, but most of them were there for the players. Still, it could be ten or twenty minutes, and there was no guarantee Vivian would talk to her anyway. "I don't know," she said. "I didn't want to get her in this situation. I wanted privacy. But we're here now."

"Let's wait over here," he suggested, indicating a brick planter.

She walked with him to it, scooting up on the ledge and burying herself deeper into the jacket.

"You cold?" he asked.

"Are you for real?" So much for her interview finesse.

He half laughed, sliding up next to her, but drawing back in surprise. "What kind of question is that?"

"I mean, are you who you say you are?"

He blinked, that sublime mouth lifting in a half smile. "I told you, I'll be whoever you want me to be."

His favorite line. "Ashley didn't think you were really a rescuer with takemetonite.com. And you don't seem to be too sure of her, either. So, what gives?"

He leaned back on his hands, looking at the crowd and thinking before he slid a sideways glance at her. "I shouldn't do this," he said slowly. "I really, really shouldn't do this. But I'm going to."

He turned to her, his knee brushing her thigh as he took one of her hands in his. "This morning, after I left you," he said, rubbing her knuckles with his thumb, sending warm pulses up her arm, "I went home. And then I came back to your apartment."

The pleasure pulses stopped. "You did?"

"I saw you leave and go to the Charles Street station."

"You followed me again." She refused to let that thrill her. This was getting a little scary. "So that was why your car was still in Beacon Hill and you were in Cleveland Circle. You followed me. Why?"

"I wasn't the only one who followed you," he said, notably not answering the question, but his response hit hard anyway.

"What do you mean?"

"I thought it was a guy in a baseball cap. He got out of a van—the same van that tried to pick you up last night—and followed you. Only, I realize now that it wasn't a guy. It was her. Ashley. The cap has a distinctive rounded bill."

Sage frowned at him, trying to reconcile all this. "Are you sure?"

"You saw her on the train, didn't you?"

"Yeah, but she said . . ." Her voice faded.

"I was on the balcony of the hotel on the corner when I spotted her, but then I—"

Sage practically choked as she stopped him with a

flat palm. "Wait just a second, here. You were up at the Beacon Hill Bistro balcony, spying on me?"

He lifted a shoulder. "Just making sure you were okay. And that van pulled up and one person—Ashley—got out and followed you to the T station. And someone else stayed in the van."

"Maybe the person who broke into my apartment."

He nodded like that was exactly what he thought.

"And you saw Ashley, in her baseball cap, follow me to the T stop?"

"I didn't see someone follow you, but by the time I got a ticket I saw her get on the train with you."

She leaned back, thinking. "There was another guy in a blue baseball cap," she said. "He was pestering me."

"I saw him," Johnny said. "Different cap."

"Ashley actually stepped in and got rid of him for me." She pulled herself back to something he'd said earlier. "Why did you think I wouldn't be okay?"

He took her hand again, his eyes soft and sweet. "It was a rough night."

No, no. Not sweet. She had to remember what she was dealing with here. "So, do you do that for all the women you rescue? Go back for seconds the next day?"

She could have sworn a little color drained from his face, but it was impossible to tell in the light. "No."

"Or is it because you're not really a rescuer for that site?"

He put his hands on her cheeks, his fingers unbelievably strong and warm. "It's because I like you, sweetheart."

She didn't flinch. He was so close she could feel his breath. "Then why would Ashley tell me you're a poser?"

"You tell me." He covered her mouth with his, holding her face like it was the most precious thing he'd ever touched. His tongue parted her lips with expert precision and teased its way inside with a move he'd obviously perfected with years of practice. His fingers threaded her hair as he tilted her head, deepened the kiss, and flicked his tongue swiftly, lightly over the roof of her mouth. He ended the exchange with the quickest, tiniest nibble of her lower lip and a soft caress of his thumbs over her earlobes and down her neck.

Shivers ran up her spine and heat lightning bolted in the opposite direction.

"Poser or pro?" he asked.

"You're a pro," she murmured, barely able to open her eyes.

"Yes, I am." He closed his hands around the back of her neck and pulled her closer to whisper in her ear, "And, I like you."

Oh, hell. She liked him, too. Ashley could be wrong. "The crowd is breaking up over there," she said. "Let's find Vivian."

"Okay." He gave her a look so erotic and promising, it took her breath away as effectively as the kiss had done. "Then I'm going home with you tonight, honey."

If she said no, he'd just follow her anyway.

Johnny held Sage's hand in his jacket pocket and led her toward the dissipating crowd, the taste of her still making his blood spike. Deflect accusations, Dan Gallagher would say. Use the truth. Change the subject. Do something that proves you are what you say you are.

And Dan, of all people, would support the kiss-the-holy-hell-out-of-your-principal-if-necessary approach. Anyway, it worked. She dropped the poser issue and didn't argue the suggestion that he stay with her tonight. Which beat the hell out of casing her apartment from his car all night.

"Vivian?" Sage eased her hand out of Johnny's pocket and quickened her step as they approached a woman wearing a white satin jacket and full stage makeup. Flat out one of the most exquisite females he'd ever seen, except for the scowl that crossed her face when she realized who had called her.

"I'm done signing," she said abruptly to the security guard, handing a program back to one of her fans.

"Vivian, wait." Sage hustled forward and Johnny recognized the wide-chested, protective response from a bodyguard.

The dancer held up a hand to stop Sage, and gave her muscle a visual plea Johnny had seen a hundred times: *Help.*

"No more autographs," the guard said to Sage brusquely, putting his body between her and Vivian and at the same time sizing up Johnny.

Vivian scooped up a duffle bag and started for the door of the arena.

"Vivian! Please!" Sage demanded.

The other woman hesitated, then turned. "Sage, I'm sorry about Keisha. I don't know what was going on in her life. But I can't help you."

"That's not why I'm here," Sage said. "I'm doing an article for *Boston Living* magazine. I want to interview you."

Vivian's amber-gold eyes flickered in doubt. "I heard. I'm not interested. Talk to the other girls." She held up her hand again and nodded toward her bodyguard. "I have protection now, and I'll use it. Nobody can scare me."

She powerwalked into the building. Sage just stared, then turned to Johnny. "What was that all about?"

"That," he said, "was self-preservation."

"But why?" Sage wondered. "I thought she was close to Keisha. Is she that terrified of Glenda? Of fans? Of the media?"

"She's scared of something."

"It's just weird." She shrugged and sighed. "She was my best hope."

He put his arm around her and started toward the parking lot. One more person to talk to Lucy about, one more name for a background check. Too bad Raquel had left her job as Lucy's right hand to travel with that Russian spy. She'd have the 411 on every single person he'd met, with that magical computer of hers.

"Let's go. Are you hungry?"

She laughed. "Don't tell me. You want to cook tonight."

"*Pappa al pomodoro,* baby. It's waitin' for you at home." Maybe he could deflect more questions with cooking. If that failed, there was always more kissing.

"You know," she said, leaning into him. "You really ought to call my friend Dr. Garron. I'm serious. You could work at the Ritz."

"Of course I could."

"Did you really train at the Culinary Institute?"

He laughed. "The Culinary Institute of Nona Cardinale." The moment the name came out of his mouth, he almost choked. What was he *thinking*?

"Nona? Is that your grandmother?"

"*Nona* is Italian for 'grandmother', yes." Please God, let her focus on the title and not the name. She was so damn curious. By tomorrow morning, she'd have googled Cardinale from here to Sunday, and found a reference to him. Oh, yeah. That mob boss, Achilles Cardinale, the one in jail for every crime ever committed? *Yep, sweetheart, that's my Uncle Arkie.*

"And she taught you how to cook?"

Go with it, Johnny. "She taught me everything," he told her. "From what to do with porcini, to how to take the eyes and tentacles out of a squid."

"Ewww."

"Not ewww. *Calamari alla ripieni alla fiorentina.* Like you died and went to heaven with a bottle of olive oil and a lemon wedge."

"You have a beautiful accent," she said, laughing. "Even if you don't speak the language anymore."

"It's in the blood." And so was a lot of other bad shit. He quickened their pace toward the dim back parking lot where she'd told him the dancers parked. The back exit was abandoned now, the security lights off for the night. "And I promise you won't say *ewww* when I make my—" He froze and jerked her to a standstill.

"What?"

He just shook his head, his body on alert, his ears like radar listening for the sound he thought he'd heard. The *thwumpf* of a landed punch.

"What is it?" Sage demanded.

He put one finger up to his mouth, moving away from her as he scanned the lot and reached for his weapon. A few cars dotted the open space, a few clumps of trees and bushes blocked a complete view.

But there it was again. Followed by a grunt and a moan. A silent shit-kicking. He'd recognize that sound anywhere. He put one hand over her lips and pulled out his Glock, tilting his head in the direction of the noise. There was a cluster of cars, including some SUVs and a small truck creating a barrier, but he was fairly certain it came from there.

His rented Toyota was on the other side of the lot. He had two choices. Race to his car, armed, and get Sage to safety and out of there. Or go find out who was getting the beating and save a perfect stranger, and probably give up his cover in return.

The wallop of fist against flesh was loud enough for Sage to hear, and powerful enough to reach into every cell of his body and fill him with disgust and hate and pity. He'd been on the giving and the receiving end of that, and neither one was pretty.

A woman whimpered in pain. *Shit*.

"I'm taking you to the car," he said, pinning Sage with a look that allowed no argument. "Stay low and keep the doors shut. Then I'll see what's going on over there."

Her eyes widened when an engine revved and rubber squealed as a car pulled out from behind the SUV and screamed off. In the shadows, someone stumbled, then yanked open a car door, falling into the driver's seat.

Johnny covered Sage with his body and hustled them both toward the injured woman, recognizing her even without the baseball cap. He reached the sports car and whipped open the door, to be greeted by the bloody face of what had been a passably pretty redhead.

He dropped to his knees and reached for her.

Her head wobbled like she was drunk, then she pushed him with way more force than he'd expected, knocking him back just enough for her to reach the car door and tug it closed.

"Hey!" He shot up just as she managed to turn the ignition, slam on the accelerator, and fly out at the same speed as whoever had beaten the crap out of her. The only thing she left behind was a dark blue baseball cap.

Picking it up from the ground, he held it out to Sage. "Jealous boyfriend? Lunatic fan?"

She took the hat, then peered in the other direction, where the taillights of the first car had disappeared.

Sage twisted the hat, her scowl deepening. "I don't know."

"Come on," he said gruffly, pulling her to him, fighting the waves of anger, and remembering his purpose was to protect her. "Let's get out of here."

"You okay?"

He ratcheted up his chin in a nonchalant nod but, in his head, all he could see was the angry red welt on the pretty, freckled face, the dribble of blood down her chin. He'd seen too much of that in his life. "Yeah, sure." Nothing a little cooking and kissing couldn't make him forget. "I'm fine."

He *was*.

"Fine" would be an excellent way to describe the man in front of her stove. Sage sat at the open counter that separated the kitchen from the living area, studying the fine shape of him, the fine movements of an artist at work, the fine beauty of a man built for every imaginable pleasure.

All very *fine*.

She sipped her red wine, nearly draining the glass. It was her second since they'd gotten back, when he'd produced a small duffle bag from the trunk of his car, taken a shower, and changed into jeans and a T-shirt. All she'd done was drink the wine he'd uncorked and then watch him prepare his feast.

Since he entered the kitchen, he'd done a running commentary on olive oil, and how the heel of a hand and a sharp knife were the only garlic press needed by any man or woman. All the while, he'd sliced and diced and soaked half a loaf of bread in broth, and sautéed tomatoes until the pungent scent filled the apartment.

He went way past fine. He slid right into exquisite, extraordinary and exceptional. Wouldn't it be wonderful if he was . . . something else? Like, not a prostitute?

"Would you seriously consider calling my friend Dr. Garron about the job at the Ritz?" she asked, lifting her glass.

"I told you, I'll call tomorrow." He glanced over his shoulder. "Can I be your boyfriend then?"

She choked so hard the chianti went up her nose.

"I'm gonna take that as a no."

Wiping her mouth, she laughed. "I don't want a boyfriend."

"You sure? I cook."

"I see that. I *smell* that."

"Wait'll you taste that."

She smiled, wrapping her fingers around the stem and setting her chin on the wide rim of the goblet. "But woman cannot live by food alone."

"I do other stuff."

A shudder twisted through her. "Yeah."

His shoulders dropped just a little, a gesture she couldn't miss in the fitted black T-shirt. She let her eyes roam over the V shape of his back, the perfect male roundness of his rear, the long, muscular legs. Her boyfriend. Now there was a thought. "Wouldn't you like to have a different job?"

He set a spoon on the counter and turned from the sizzling pan, his look as intense as the aroma of bay leaves and basil. "What a person does or did in his profession doesn't dictate who they are."

His eyes were dark with something she couldn't name. Oh, yeah she could. Shame. The impact wrenched her heart, and she pushed her response way back down. He was salvageable, this fine man. Redeemable.

Oh, what was she doing? "You know, I have way too much to think about," she said quickly, "to worry about your business."

"Yep, you do."

She closed her eyes for a moment, thinking of the fear in Vivian's face and the sound of someone hitting Ashley.

Whores must die.

"Let's start figuring it out," he suggested. "Together."

She leaned back on the stool, surprised by how much she wanted him to help her, and believed that he could. "Okay. Square one. The suicide. If it *was* a suicide."

"You don't think those index cards full of insecurities sort of confirm that?" he asked, finally picking up his glass of wine for a sip. He turned from the stove, the drink suspended. "Or the fact that she had an abortion."

"Maybe Glenda just said that to torture me."

He frowned over the glass as he drank. "She's a sicko, then. But you need to find out if Keisha really had an abortion. It's a starting place."

"I don't think information like that is readily available to the public."

He regarded her for a minute, then turned back to the sizzling tomatoes. "I might be able to pull some strings and get some information."

He didn't see her dubious look. The guy was so sweet. Helpful, nurturing, except for that gun he whipped out on special occasions. She didn't want to tell him she doubted that he could get the information. For all she knew, he could. "And what about Vivian? Why do you think she's so defensive?"

A cell phone beeped from his belt and something indefinable changed in his body language. "I'm going to take this," he said quickly. "Outside."

She popped off the bar stool. "No need to leave. I'm going to take a shower."

He gave her an appreciative nod, then answered the phone with a simple "Yo."

Yo? She slowed her step into the hall, her ears trained on the kitchen. He said nothing for a moment, then, "Can't really talk now."

Who was it? A woman? A job? She forced herself to hurry into her room and close the door loudly enough for him to hear, fighting the unfamiliar sensation of jealousy. Was that really what was making her stomach burn? Jealousy over a male prostitute?

Oh, *please*.

She made the shower extra hot, clipping up her hair so she could let the stream pound her back. She still tingled from the heat when she dressed in a cropped tank top and jeans, wet tendrils dripping water down her nape. She brushed on a coat of mascara and followed her nose back to the kitchen, where indescribable aromas wafted, along with Johnny's low-pitched voice. Her bare feet made no sound on the hardwood floor, so she cleared her throat to announce herself.

"Don't worry, Lu—" He froze at the sight of her, then gave her a wide, sexy grin. "Except for the electric stove, I could be in love. Catch you later, hon."

She smiled. It would have been impossible not to. "Who was that?"

"My boss." At her look, he reached out and curled his fingers around her wrist, drawing her close. "Look how pretty you are, all squeaky clean."

"You call your boss *hon*?"

"I call lots of women that." With his left hand, he tucked the phone into his pocket.

"So you work for a woman? A woman runs that company, Fantasy Adventures?" She couldn't keep the skepticism out of her voice.

"One runs my area," he said, leaning in and taking a whiff of her hair. "Mmmm. It's mango season."

"Did you ask any questions? About Keisha?"

"I did, and I even have them checking on Vivian Masters. I want to know if she was ever a client." Like it was the most natural thing in the world, he pressed a kiss on her damp neck. "Maybe give us a clue to why she acted so weird."

For a minute, she couldn't speak. She just felt the air slide out of her lungs. "You know, you are so nice."

He nibbled his way to her ear and tickled her lobe with his tongue when he got there. "Does that mean I can be your boyfriend?"

She laughed, sliding one hand around him, letting her breasts press against his chest. "You can be my friend, how's that?"

His tongue dipped into her ear, sending shock waves down her body. He pulled her tighter, his chest was like carved marble pressing against her. She closed her eyes, tilted her head, and tried to remember to breathe.

"Okay, my friend." His voice was raspy, close. "Taste this."

She parted her lips, ready to taste his tongue and temptation again.

Something hot and tangy and juicy slid between her lips. She moaned at the flavor of spice and sweet, the incredible softness that oozed through her mouth. Her eyes popped open. "Oh, what *is* that?"

"Comfort." A drop dribbled down her chin. He licked it off. "You need some."

God, did she ever. The fiery tip of his tongue touched the corner of her mouth. She managed to swallow, the mix of flavors and textures dancing in her mouth. She wanted more. More comfort. More taste. More Johnny.

She tipped her head and kissed him like a starving woman.

CHAPTER
Ten

"Whoa, easy, hot stuff." Johnny chuckled into their kiss, tasting the *pomodoro* mixed with a trace of peppery chianti in her mouth. "Comfort food. Not comfort . . . comfort."

Her fingers curled around his neck and she molded her body to his, the heat from the stove paling in comparison to what he felt through the achingly thin tank top that boasted of nothing but nipple underneath.

He finally broke the kiss, but not until his hands had found a home on the dip between her lower back and her sweet rear end, and his lower half rose to the occasion.

She opened her eyes wide, her pupils nice and big from arousal. She looked so pretty, he just wanted to kiss her some more. And that was exactly what she expected. Only he'd just hung up the phone with his boss, who had said "protect her," not "seduce her," and definitely not "screw her stupid."

The same boss who had met his question about Alonzo Garron with a long silence and a simple statement: "Johnny, you need to stop asking questions about this assignment and just do it. For me."

He had to remember where his loyalties lay—with the woman who had saved him from hell. Whatever her reasons, she wanted the client to remain a secret.

He eased away from Sage. "It's dinnertime, puddin'."

"Then feed me, *sugarbear*."

He laughed softly and reluctantly let go of her, but she stayed very close as he grabbed a soup bowl and started to ladle crushed tomatoes, broth, and soaked bread into it.

"I know why you call me those things," she said, pulling open a drawer. "You can't remember a woman's name because there are so many."

He set the ladle in the pot and closed his hand over her wrist. "No spoons."

"We drink from the bowls?"

"We use bread. Metal ruins the taste of this soup." He nodded toward the dining area. "I put a loaf out there."

She peered over the counter to her little dining-room table. Surprise opened her mouth into a little circle, drawing his attention to the feminine, round, enticing O. "Wow. Place mats, napkins, fresh wine, and candles."

"And no pesky spoons." He took the two bowls and jutted his chin toward the kitchen door. "After you." He deliberately waited a beat before adding, "Sage."

She gave him a sly smile and led the way to the table. As she spread a napkin on her lap, he put the bowls next to each other, as close to her as he could get.

He broke off a hunk of the crusty bread and handed it to her, then lifted the pepper mill and ground some over hers, then his.

"In Tuscany, foreigners think the locals are sort of classless, scooping their soup up with bread. It's like seeing someone eat asparagus with their fingers. It's proper, but seems wrong. Okay, pick out the center of the bread and make a scoop, like this."

She did, then held the bread poised over the soup. "I'm sure most of this will miss my mouth."

"That's half the fun." He dipped the cup of bread into a chunk of perfectly cooked tomato, enjoying the soft mew of pleasure that accompanied her first bite.

"God, this is really good," she said, eagerly digging down for another bite. "So who did you say taught you to cook? Your nona? What was her last name?"

Tomato-soaked bread caught in his throat and he worked to swallow. "My grandmother, yeah. Some skills just get passed to the next generation. Like I bet your mother was the one who taught you to write."

"In a way."

"You're very good," he said with another mental pat for seamless conversation shifting. "I really got into that article about the hospital and all those smarmy docs taking payola from the insurance companies."

She wiped her mouth with the napkin and reached for more bread. "That's what my mother taught me to do. Hunt down bad guys and expose them for what they are."

He felt a little blood drain from his head. "Bad guys? She covered crime?"

"Her beat was business, actually. But she loved nothing more than finding politicians on the take and companies with evil CEOs."

"Like mother, like daughter, huh?" He sipped the wine and watched the way the candle flickered green glints in her hazel eyes. She didn't wear any makeup that he could tell, but her skin had an ethereal glow to it . . . or maybe that kiss had sizzled her blood as much as his. "How old were you when she passed away?"

She studied her soup. "Fourteen."

"That's how old I was when my parents were killed."

"Well," she said quietly. "Then you know how hard it is."

He touched her hand. "I didn't think I could live," he admitted, giving in to the little black hole in his stomach that always accompanied the memory of having to leave Italy. "What happened to your mother?"

She averted her eyes, studying the soup. "She committed suicide."

It was his turn to open his mouth into an O of surprise. "Suicide?" he asked with a rasp.

She nodded, and casually reached for another piece of bread. "It was a long time ago. Thirteen years."

He ached to know what had happened, but all he could process was how she was dealing with her friend's suicide after thirteen years of living with her mother's. "You should have told me."

She tore her bread, obviously struggling to look indifferent. "It doesn't matter anymore. And if you're saying that because of Keisha, well—"

"Of course I am. That's made this really hard on you."

Her smile was wry. "You sound like my aunt. Only she wasn't so sympathetic. She basically said, Get over it. Like . . . like . . ." She dug the bread into the soup so hard that droplets of sauce splattered on the place mat. "Like that's possible."

"Your aunt. Is this your mother's sister?"

Wiping her mouth, she held up her napkin. "Last person I want to talk about, ever. Let's get back to the situation at hand, okay?"

"Okay," he agreed, taking a bite. He certainly had no desire to discuss family.

"Suicide or not, Keisha's dead," she said, her voice taking on a calculating quality. "Ashley McCafferty got beaten up after the game, and didn't want anyone to know about it or help her. Vivian Masters is scared of something, everything. Somebody broke in here and defaced the dancers' poster, took her computer—"

"But left her bling."

She nodded. "We found a stash of suicide notes. And Keisha might have had an abortion before she died." She tapped the table impatiently. "Did I forget anything?"

Just that she had a bodyguard and didn't know it. Oh, and she thought he worked as a male prostitute. But, if she found out what he'd done in his previous life, prostitution would seem like a ticket to sainthood.

She toyed with the bread, tearing a tiny bit off as she stared into space. "What should I do tomorrow? Start meeting the girls on the list?"

"Why don't we visit Ashley and see what happened to her yesterday?"

"Good idea. Why don't *we*?"

"I'd like to go with you. *Sage*."

She rolled her eyes. "I'm sure you mean 'hot stuff.' "

He grinned and leaned closer. "You are hot stuff, you know that?"

She inched forward, her gaze steady. He was starting to recognize that look; she wanted something. Information, usually.

"Now tell me about your nona," she said. "Didn't you say she had a different last name? Was this your mother's mother? Is that who raised you after your parents died?"

He had a couple of choices. Lie. Accidentally knock his wineglass over. Go for another subject change. Or . . .

"I'm done eating," he said, moving closer. "Done talking. Kiss me, baby."

Sage was getting used to these unexpected lip-locks when he wanted to change the subject. With any other guy, she'd call him on it. With Johnny, she just kissed him back.

His lips were warm from the soup, soft and pliant and incredibly competent. Well, they would be; he was a professional. He cupped her cheek with one hand and tilted her face to get into the kiss. God, she loved that move. His fingers were so commanding and sexy, as in control of the kiss as his mouth and tongue.

"So, who's dessert?" she whispered against his mouth.

"I have cannolis," he said. "Only we have to fill them with cream."

"Oh." She slipped her tongue into his mouth, traced his lips, and gave in to the shivers of arousal that cascaded from her lips down her breasts through her tummy and landed right between her legs. "Cream."

"It can get kind of messy, but . . ." He pushed his chair back slowly, standing up and dragging her with him. "It's worth it. Come with me."

There was no thought of arguing. Her body pretty much waved the white flag at *cream* and *messy.* "Let's go."

She half expected him to head straight down the hall to her bedroom, but he stopped at the kitchen and finally broke the kiss. She leaned against the doorjamb because her legs were getting more and more useless with each minute.

"Where do you keep the mixing bowls?" he asked.

"Mixing bowls?" Was he serious about cannolis? "Um, in that cabinet. What are you mixing again?"

"The filling," he said, opening the door and pulling out a blue ceramic bowl. "This is perfect." He opened the refrigerator and started lining the counter with a package of cheese and some oranges. "Damn, I forgot curaçao. You don't happen to . . ." He glanced at her. "Never mind. It's optional."

"You're making this from scratch?"

"Well, yeah. I mean, if you're in a huge hurry . . ." His lips curled in a smile like he knew exactly how depraved she was. And liked it. "I could use an electric mixer to speed things up, I guess."

"You say that as though I suggested we get Happy Meals at McDonalds."

He laughed. "I like to work with my hands, that's all."

"And you do it so well."

He gave her a sexy, knowing wink as she scooted up onto the counter and watched him smash ricotta cheese with a sure hand and her wooden spoon. He placed the bowl next to her, then opened the bag of confectioners' sugar he'd bought earlier.

Powdered sugar sprinkled on his fingers as he worked, whitening the fine black hairs near his wrist. He squeezed the life out of an orange, and a lock of hair fell toward his eye. He lifted the remnants of the orange to her mouth and she sucked, practically melting off the counter as he whipped up a concoction of cheese and sugar and fruit.

She closed her fingers over his wrist. "Hey, Johnny-cakes."

He chuckled at that. "Yeah?"

"Thanks."

"For dessert?"

"For the company. And for the comfort."

"My pleasure." He kissed her nose. "Sugar."

He found a small plastic bag, filled it with the sweet-smelling cream, then made a makeshift pastry bag by cutting a little hole in the bottom corner. Mesmerized, she just watched, getting hungrier and achier and weaker by the second.

"Here you go." He twisted the end and held the bag out to her.

"Me?" She inched back. "I don't know how."

"It's easy. Italian kids can do this before they're three. My sister could do ten to my one and she . . ." His voice trailed off as if something strangled him.

"You have a sister?"

He offered the bag again. "Yeah. Here."

"Are you close? Is she older or younger?"

She saw the roped muscles in his neck grow taut, then relax. It happened so fast, she almost missed it as he turned to open the oven and pulled out a tray of curled, golden pasty shells.

"Younger," he finally said, staring at the pastries as though he'd never seen one before. As though he'd completely lost track of what he was doing.

"What's her name?" Sage asked.

She got a blank look in response.

"Your sister?" she prodded. "What's her name?"

Without answering, he reached for a pastry shell from the tray, picked it up, then dropped it, swearing softly and brushing his fingers as though he'd burned them. He gingerly grasped the edge of a shell, lifted, and blew on it a few times. "Here you go."

The reporter in her went on alert. Why was he being so damn evasive? "What's her name?" she asked again.

The playfulness evaporated from those near-black eyes. "Bella."

Oh, of course. Her heart dipped in disappointment. He didn't want to get personal. It was like the hooker in *Pretty Woman*, who wouldn't kiss on the lips. He had his limits. Fun, games, food, and sex. No talking about family.

For some reason, that made her ache in a whole different way.

He positioned himself in front of her, holding the shell out. With one touch of his hip to her knee, he nudged her legs wider so he could get closer to her on the counter. "So, blondie, you want to interview me some more, or cream some cannolis?"

She didn't want to interview him. She didn't want to pry into his private life, or know his sister's name, or need his brand of comfort so damn much. She didn't want this ache in her chest. The only ache she wanted from him was much farther south and far less vulnerable. She didn't want anything, but what he offered.

"Cream."

"Good choice," he said, coming in closer. "Just slide that tip right there in the hole."

She managed not to roll her eyes at the obvious double entendre, and got the corner of the bag into the cannoli he held.

"Now squeeze. Not too hard, baby, just slow and gentle and easy. There you go." A steady stream of sweet, white goo seeped from the half-inch hole he'd cut, oozing into the cannoli and wafting scents of vanilla and orange and cinnamon.

"That smells so good," she said.

"Mmm. Wait'll you taste it." He gave her a smoldering look. "It's like a little orgasm for the mouth."

Her whole body sort of . . . liquefied. "Oh."

With the sexiest half smile she'd ever seen, he lifted the filled cannoli toward her lips. "Here, sweetheart. The squeezer gets to lick the extra. Nona's rules."

She could slide right off the counter, she was so boneless and weak. He inched the pastry closer. She opened her mouth, and he stared at it, placing the creamy end to her lips. She licked a hunk of filling, groaning slowly as the mind-numbing sweetness and indescribable smoothness spread through her.

"If that's what you can do to my mouth . . ." She opened her eyes. "I don't even want to *think* about what you can do to the rest of me."

He slipped closer, heat and sex emanating from his body. "Then don't think."

With remarkably steady hands, she set the bag down and gripped the countertop. This was crazy. She couldn't just get down and dirty and have sex with this paid gigolo—a man who wouldn't even talk about his family.

Could she?

"You're thinking again, princess."

"I want to know about your nona."

His eyebrow flicked a little upward. His wide shoulders dropped ever so slightly, as if he'd secretly exhaled in resignation. With just as steady a hand, he laid the pastry on the counter.

Hope wrapped stupidly around her heart. Maybe she'd be the one. The one *babe* or *angel* or *sweetheart* he would confide in. Hating the fact that the very thought thrilled her, and *really* hating how much she wanted him to, she tightened her grip on the counter and waited for whatever personal revelation he would share.

She'd take anything. Any little thing would assuage her guilt for being so turned on, so hungry, so willing to take this further.

With maddening deliberation, he dipped two fingers into the bowl, scooping up a dollop of creamy filling. With his other hand, he lifted the bottom of her tank top right over her bare breasts.

He slathered the cream over her nipple, making her gasp.

"The first one was for your mouth, angel." He closed his eyes and lowered his head. "And this one's for the rest of you."

As much as she liked her cozy fifth-floor apartment, Ashley had really picked the building for its roof. There were prettier places in Brookline, quaint Victorians in the hills and hip brownstones tucked into tree-lined streets. But Ashley had chosen to live in a fifteen-story square box filled with little old ladies and wannabe yuppies because of the glorious roof that looked out over Boston's innermost suburb.

Up here, usually alone, she could escape. It was as close to flying as possible. She loved it most in the dead of night when she couldn't sleep. Something that now happened with way too much frequency.

Taking a few steps to the metal railing that lined the rooftop, she reached down to brush off some gravel that dug into the dancer's calluses on her bare feet. Just bending over made her head hurt. She swore softly as she sidled up to the rail and leaned over to soak up her favorite view—the gray stones of the hundred-year-old cathedral next door, surrounded by ancient willows and lush green grass.

A light flickered through the church's huge rose window, sparking the deep blues and reds of the stained glass. Was somebody in there at this hour, praying? What were they praying for? Were they in worse shape than she was?

She touched her swollen jaw and closed her eyes, inhaling a whiff of cabbage or onions or whatever some insomniac old lady was cooking that wafted through the roof fans.

That bastard had ruined the season for her. She knew she'd never get Victoria to go along with the kidnapping, but she hadn't expected to take the rap for it. Especially after that bitch Victoria had hissed in Ashley's face and stomped off like freakin' royalty. She stared at the window, at the tiny light, feeling something . . . achy in her heart. She wanted to go in there. She wanted to walk down the cool slate aisle and slide into a pew and pray for a way out of the mess she'd gotten into.

The light flared, as if another had been lit behind the stained glass. Who had told her that the round stained-glass window was called a rosette? Oh, it was Keisha. She'd learned that in an art-history class at Boston College.

Keisha must have felt the same kind of hollowness. Other girls had said that, after the whole kidnapping experience. They felt empty and used, and couldn't explain why. She'd never felt that way. She got a kick out of it and, if she was lucky, some hot sex. Why did that make other girls feel empty?

She jerked around at a noise across the roof—not the clunk of a heating duct or the echo of someone using the noisy trash chute. She squinted into the shadows, seeing nothing but the outlines of a few grills, some chairs, the little structure that covered electrical equipment. Behind that was the door to the stairwell, but she couldn't see it from where she stood.

She listened again, hoping some other sleepless fool wasn't coming up there for a cigarette or to contemplate the universe. She didn't want to talk to anyone.

But everything was quiet again.

Letting out a breath, she leaned farther and stared at the cement below. She could jump. It wouldn't really be so hard. She'd be dead in an instant, and then she'd be done.

Is that what went through Keisha's mind? Like when you have that crazy moment driving down a two-lane street, that if you just jerk your wheel to the left, *wham*! Into that big truck and it's all over.

If she were splattered on the concrete below, no one would see that she'd had her face bashed for her stupidity. They'd remember her as a cute dancer, a girl who had tried hard and almost made it. Not too bright, that Ashley McCafferty, but cute as a button.

At another sound, she glanced over her shoulder. Was that the stairwell door? Automatically, she lifted her hands to cover the bruises. How would she explain this to Mrs. Rosengarten? And, God, how could she stand the sympathy of pregnant, gorgeous Hallie Clifton? They were both members of the rooftop insomniacs club.

She slid farther down the edge. If she walked all the way around the perimeter, she could avoid whoever it was and slip back down the stairwell. She'd need to hide in her apartment for days. Stepping gingerly, she saw someone move in the shadows. Too big to be Hallie, too quiet to be Rosengarten.

She heard something scuff, then the soft clearing of a throat.

Someone was definitely out there.

She reached the corner that the three guys who lived in 901 had turned into a makeshift cigar bar, the pungent smell of their old butts almost as bad as the cabbage. She stepped on something squishy and let out a little gasp, imagining a dead mouse, but only a half-smoked stogie stuck to her bare feet.

"Assholes," she muttered, brushing it off.

"Ashley?"

She stood straight and stared in the direction of the voice. A man's voice. And not Vick French, that wannabe screenwriter who lived on the fourteenth floor and came up here to clear his writer's block.

Whoever it was, she didn't want to face him. Didn't want to talk to anyone and explain that she had walked into a wall or fell off a cheerleading pyramid or whatever. She tiptoed in the shadows, the door in sight now.

"Ashley. I know you're here."

She froze as the first stirring of dread numbed her fingertips. But that was ridiculous. She knew every person in the building, especially the ones who didn't sleep well. She just had to say hello and good night and then go to bed. "Who's there?"

Nothing. No breathing, no sound.

"Did someone call me?" she asked again, hearing an unnatural tightness in her voice.

Nothing. Was it the wind? The air duct? Her imagination? She picked up her pace across the rooftop. Screw hiding. Whoever it was didn't matter in her life.

"It's your turn, Ashley."

She froze, fear suddenly kicking in her belly. "Who's there?" she demanded.

Nothing. "Where are you?" she asked again, pivoting on her bare foot.

Not a sound. Swearing under her breath, she headed toward the stairwell door. Somebody was screwing with her, or maybe her imagination had gone haywire, or maybe it was Vick French acting out one of his mystery plots.

Half expecting someone to jump out of the shadows, she reached the metal door, turned the knob, and whipped it open. A blast of warm air hit her and she stepped inside.

She must have imagined it. She headed down one flight and turned the corner for the next.

Then she heard the door upstairs. Someone had come into the stairwell behind her.

She started to run. She had to get all the way to the fifth floor. Ten stories. It didn't matter who it was or what he wanted, terror propelled her home and blood raged in her ears.

She rounded the thirteenth floor, grabbed the chipped yellow railing, and literally pushed herself, but one leg of her long sleep pants folded under her bare foot and she stumbled. Only her grip on the railing kept her from going face-first into gritty concrete.

Behind her, above her, she heard footsteps, as fast as hers. Making no effort to be quiet.

"Why are you running?" he called, the weird, low voice echoing through the darkened stairwell. "It's your turn."

For what? Her turn for fucking *what*? She didn't want to stop and ask.

A wave of déjà vu swamped her as she spun past the doorway to the eleventh floor. She'd felt this way before . . . sort of.

When she'd been kidnapped the first time. The searing terror, the lump in her throat, the wild, insane thump of her heart. But that was supposed to be a rush—like a roller coaster. You knew it was safe. You knew you wouldn't die. It was the dangerous, scary, edge of *fun*. This wasn't.

She scrambled faster, the ninth and eighth floors a blur. Thank God she was an athlete; she might not be able to remember every dance step as well as she should, but she was fast as lightning.

"Ashley!"

God almighty, he was closer. No more than one flight of stairs behind her now. "Go the fuck away!" she screamed, her voice sounding shrill. Should she just jam on into the seventh floor and scream in the hall? Of course. Of *course*. Why was she trying to—

A hand clamped so hard over her mouth and jerked her head backward, she was blinded for a minute. His other arm wrapped like a vise around her waist, pulling her into a hard, muscular, big body.

"This is the thrill, Ashley." His voice was a menacing whisper in her ear. "This is the ride. Do you like it?"

She groaned into his hand, shook her head, and tried to elbow him.

"You can fight. That's okay."

Had someone signed her up again? It had never been like this. It was always sort of gentle, sort of playful. Like a kidnapping in an old romance novel when the heroine was in a coach riding toward the castle. This was like a horror movie in a dark stairwell.

She flailed again, but he yanked her head, her poor, bruised head, and she heard tendons in her neck crack. Trying to turn, she managed to see that he wore a black ski mask, like they all did.

Why was he being so mean and rough? She'd been through this five or six times. It had never hurt.

"Let's go." He kicked her forward, buckling her knees and making her sink into him.

She shook her head violently and tried to bite his hand but her teeth sunk into bitter, wet leather. He managed to drag her down the next flight of stairs. Six. Where was he taking her?

She tried to scream, fight, kick and thrash, but he was so strong. His chest felt massive, his arms like a bodybuilder's. All she was doing was blasting out her vocal cords and making herself exhausted.

They passed five. Her floor. He pushed her down, she stumbled, but he held firm, lifting her like she was nothing. They passed three, two, the lobby, and with one fierce kick he opened the security door to the garage.

Ashley thrust against his arm and hand, her head nearly bursting with the effort. But it was like fighting granite and steel. None of the kidnappers had ever been vicious or scary. None had ever hurt her.

He dragged her to a dark blue car and kicked the back, and the trunk silently rose. He was putting her in *there*?

Think, Ashley. Think.

But she couldn't think. She couldn't see the make of the car or a license plate or his face or anything as he flipped her on her side and threw her into the trunk, something hard and metal jabbing her hip. Instantly, she opened her mouth to scream and thrust her hand up to tear off his mask.

He swatted her arm away and slammed something cold and wet and stinky over her mouth and nose. She gasped in horror, tasting bitter, disgusting liquid as pain stung her nose and exploded in her head.

"It's your turn, Ashley."

The trunk slammed and everything was over.

CHAPTER
Eleven

The first whiff of coffee floated into the living room like a siren call to Johnny. He'd heard Sage moving about, listened to the pipes clunk during her shower and the water run while she puttered in the kitchen, but he remained on the living room sofa, where he'd slept. Well, where he'd spent the night nursing a hard-on and guarding the front door against anyone coming in or out.

He needed coffee almost as much as he needed to go to the bathroom.

He took care of that first, noticing that Sage's door was closed, but the hall bathroom was open, the black-and-white tile floor still warm and damp from her shower. A few minutes later, he found her in the kitchen, at her computer.

"How'd you sleep, buttercup?"

Over her shoulder, she tried for a disinterested look, but it turned into a slow pass over his bare chest. "'Buttercup'? Are you serious?"

"A term of endearment." He opened the cabinet where he remembered seeing coffee mugs and pulled one down.

"A placeholder."

Okay, she was still mad. Not at him, per se, but at *this.* She hadn't been angry when he'd initiated sex on the kitchen counter, but he hadn't gotten past the first cream-filled lick when she'd called a halt to the action and disappeared behind closed doors. So, not mad. Scared. Frustrated. Confused. And judging by that full-body inspection, maybe still a little hot and bothered.

"I'll call you Sage, if you prefer." He took a sip of strong black coffee, leaning against the counter where they'd nearly done the deed the night before.

She kept her attention riveted on the screen, reading what appeared to be a list of e-mails. "I'd prefer that you . . ."

Here it comes: *I'd prefer that you disappear.*

"Tell me the truth." She faced him. "Is that so hard to do?"

Could be impossible. "The truth about what?"

"You."

He grinned over the cup rim. "I'm so dull it hurts, honey."

"Don't *do* that."

"Sorry. I'm so dull it hurts, *Sage.*"

She shook her head. "Not that. Call me monkeyface if you want, but don't be so evasive."

"Monkeyface—that's cute. I'll add that to the repetoire."

"I'm serious, Johnny. Why are you so secretive? What are you hiding from me?"

He sucked so bad at undercover work. "I'm not—"

"I know who you are, what you are." She leaned back in the kitchen chair, a pained expression in her eyes.

"You do." He said it as a statement, sipping coffee and resisting the urge to see exactly what was on that computer screen. Just how good an investigative reporter was she?

"Yes. And we both know that how you make a living is distasteful to me."

It said so much about her, that she used that word. "Uh-huh."

"But what happened last night . . . I was ready. . . ."

"Me, too." He took half a step forward, but she pinned him with a look.

"I didn't want to say no."

"But you don't want to sleep with a guy who does it for a living." He shrugged. "I can't blame you, ba— Sage. It's okay. We can be friends." Exactly what the client wanted, no doubt. "Don't sweat it."

A little smile lifted the corners of her mouth. "As a matter of fact, I sweat it all night," she admitted, pushing herself out of the chair and walking toward him. "I just about soaked my sheets in sweat."

The image of her writhing around, naked and fantasizing about him, shot way too much juice to the erection he'd finally gotten under control. "Well, that's—"

"Did you sweat?" she demanded.

A lone drop of coffee hit the burner with a hiss, but he didn't speak. Her attention drifted over him again, lingering below the belt as though she could merely eyeball him into a hard-on. Which, come on, she could.

"Then there's a simple solution," she said when he didn't answer, pushing a lock of hair over her shoulder like she was clearing the way to take what she wanted.

"I don't get it, Sage. What happened to *distasteful?*"

She stepped closer. "I find your *work* distasteful. Not you."

"Thanks. Ditto." He held up his coffee mug, as if that could hold off a woman who'd spent the night sweating over him. "But you're right, we should keep this platonic."

Was that disappointment that darkened her eyes? "We don't have to."

He lifted one shoulder. "It ain't gonna change my history, baby." A history that went way past *distasteful*.

"I don't want to change history," she insisted. "I just want to know it."

He rubbed the stubble of last night's beard growth. "What do you want to know? How many? How often? How come?"

Something flickered in her eyes. "I want to know about your sister."

No way. He'd never told anyone, and he never would. The truth was hidden in a little frame house on the shores of Lake Como, and there the truth would stay, safe and sound. He'd never tell anyone, never take that risk. "What's so important about my sister?"

"I mean, I want to know something personal. Something revealing and private. Something you don't tell other wom—clients. That's what I want."

"Chicks." He grinned. "You always want that personal stuff."

She moved closer, undeterred. "This chick wants a connection, yes."

"And if you don't get one?"

She shrugged. "I don't sleep with someone just because they're hot and available. Call me old-fashioned, but I just need more than physical attraction."

So as long as he held out on the personal goods, he could probably get through this assignment without screwing the principal, infuriating the client, and blowing his cover.

He took a long gulp of coffee and finished it, moving away from her to put his mug in the sink. "Well, I don't have any issues with hot and available. I guess we're just different, then."

"I'll start," she said. "Then you'll see how easy it can be."

She leaned against the counter and took a little breath like she'd been practicing a speech and was about to deliver it.

"Here's something personal," she said. "The last time I talked to my father, he thought I was my mother. He called me Lydia, and I cried all the way home from Vermont."

His heart twisted. "I'm sorry, Sage."

"Me, too. Your turn."

He choked a laugh. Where would he start? *About*

my sister . . . "I gotta think about it. And anyway, I need to know the rules here. Like, what happens? I tell you my childhood secret and you jump my bones?"

She grinned. "If the secret's good enough." Behind her, the computer beeped.

"Saved by the bell," he joked. "Better see who's dinging you, doll."

Her look told him he was not off the hook, but she checked the screen to see who'd sent her an instant message. "Oh," she said softly, magnetically drawn to the computer.

Behind her, he read the words on the screen, sent from yellowbird1. *R U still looking for info about KK?*

"KK," she whispered. "Keisha Kingston." She dropped into the chair and instantly typed back, *Yes. Who are you?*

A friend. I can help u.

She glanced at Johnny, her eyes bright. Then she typed, *Who are you?* again.

Mt me today? was the response.

"Not until you know who it is," he said, putting a hand on her shoulder and reading the exchange.

She ignored the comment and typed *when and where?* into her response box.

No wonder Lucy had sent a bodyguard for her.

BPL. Courtyard. 9:00 AM.

"What's BPL?" he asked.

"Boston Public Library." She thought for a minute before typing, *Who do I look for?*

You'll know. Mt me at fountain. 9 sharp.

"That's in forty minutes," she said, then typed, *OK.*

But her two-letter response was met with a message that yellowbird1 had signed off. She stared at the screen for a minute, then stood, grabbed her handbag, and started to the living room.

He had her by the elbow before she made it halfway across the room. "You can let me sit next to you or behind you, but either way, I'm gonna follow you."

She wrested her arm from his grip. "Then hurry up and get dressed."

He scooped his T-shirt from the back of a chair and pulled it on, watching her mildly amused expression when he checked the clip on his weapon, racked the slide, and stuffed it into the back of his waistband. "Now I'm dressed," he told her.

"And to think I go to most interviews armed only with my pad and pen."

"That's why you need me," he said, slipping into his jacket to cover the Glock.

"Where was the gun the night I met you?" she asked as she turned and let him help her into her jacket. "When I undressed you?"

"On my ankle, and you never really got my pants off."

She opened the door and turned to face him. "Tell me a secret and I will."

"Here's one." He dipped his head and brushed her lips as he spoke. "I sweated all night, too." He flicked her lip with his tongue, then deepened the contact to a full, hungry kiss that tasted like coffee and toothpaste and shot lead into his cock.

After a good ten seconds of tongue war, she pulled away. "You want more of that?" she asked.

He stayed close to her face, his breath already too tight, his blood already too hot. "For a good reporter, you ask a lot of dumb questions."

She inched back. "Then tell me something personal, Johnny. Confess some secret that you never, ever told any other *babe* or *sweetheart* you took to bed. Just one thing." She touched her lips to his, teasing, breathing. "Come on. Spill something on me."

"Okay." He closed his eyes so he didn't have to see her face when he wrecked her little game of foreplay. "My sister's dead."

He jogged down the steps to the street without waiting for her reaction. Hey, she asked for it.

Copley Square was packed with commuters and students, tourists, and the usual aggressive panhandlers. Navigating their way from the T station to the Dartmouth Street entrance of the library, Sage held Johnny's hand; her heart still hurt a little from his confession.

My sister's dead.

And she'd been such a smart-ass last night, demanding to know his sister's name and if he was close to her. If he'd dropped that little bomb to shut her up, he'd hit his target. Neither of them had said much on the train ride over, but they had kept their hands entwined.

"If you had to make one guess who yellowbird1 is, who would it be?" he asked as they approached the stone steps flanked by massive marble and iron sculptures.

"One of the girls. Probably Vivian." At the ornate, arched doorways, Sage paused. "You have your license for that hardware you're carrying? 'Cause there's a metal detector. Otherwise, you'll have to wait here for me or give it up."

He opened the door. "I have it."

"Massachusetts?"

"Yep."

"Good, you show it to the guard and talk guns for a while. I'm going to the courtyard."

"Not alone, you're not."

She released a breath of pure exasperation. "Johnny, whoever wants to meet me wants to meet me alone."

"Precisely."

"I can't interview someone with you breathing down my back, brandishing your firearm."

He bit back a laugh. "I'm not brandishing anything. Listen. I'll stay nearby, but not with you. Whoever you're meeting won't have any idea I'm watching. Don't leave my sight, and I'll stay completely in the background." He punctuated that by placing his hands on her shoulders. "I promise I know how to do this."

Something about his confidence in the situation struck a chord. "Okay. But don't interrupt me for any reason. Sometimes it takes a few minutes to get a source to loosen up and talk. She might want to go somewhere else. No questions, okay?"

"Okay."

When they reached the security guard, he spoke privately to the older man, showing him something Sage assumed was his carry license. While he did, Sage studied the glorious staircase that led up to the main reading room.

Who was she about to meet and what would that person tell her? It wasn't the first time she'd gone off to meet an anonymous source in an unusual location; that went with her job. But this story was personal, and that made her clench her fists in the pockets of her jeans jacket and send a little buzz of anxiety through her.

"Let's go, sweetheart." Johnny's touch on her arm sent a little buzz of something through her, too.

"You stay back. Far back. The courtyard is down there, to the right." She started to walk away and he reached for her.

"Whoa. Wait a second. If we get separated, we need a plan."

This was getting way too cloak-and-dagger for her. "Here's the plan." She pulled out her cell phone. "Call me." She recited her number, turned, and left him.

In the courtyard, she zeroed in on the fountain in the middle, but not a single face among the morning readers and coffee drinkers looked familiar. She glanced at the wrought-iron tables scattered around the patio and behind columns that lined the perimeter of the bricks. She walked from one side to the other, but no one said anything or showed any interest in her.

She turned around and didn't even see Johnny.

You'll know. Mt me at fountain. 9 sharp. She glanced at her watch: 9:02.

You'll know. Who would she know?

A man working on a laptop glanced up at her, then back at his screen. A woman feeding a baby in a carriage gave her a meaningless smile. An older couple sat side by side on the stone ledge surrounding the fountain, sipping coffee and eating pastries.

Everything was quiet but for a child's laughter from one of the tables in the back, and the gurgling fountain spray.

Sage started to circle the fountain. Past a few college students in a cluster and a woman reading a paperback. Then, on the last side of the fountain, she saw it.

A neon-green index card, faceup. Her heartbeat ratcheted up as she took a step closer, instinctively glancing over her shoulder to see who watched her. No one. Not even the man who'd promised he would. Where was he?

She lifted the card that had the same sticky back as Keisha's, riveted by the tiny printing on it.

Take the elevator to Level B.

What was this, a flipping scavenger hunt? She'd have ignored the order, except for the mode of delivery. This was precisely the type of card Keisha had written her suicide notes on. *That* message couldn't be ignored.

She set off for the main entrance, remembering she'd used an ancient elevator once to cart a lot of books she'd needed for a story. She reached the main entrance quickly, glanced at the guard, and passed by the massive staircase, her attention on a little corridor to the left that peeled off to a narrow hallway. There, the brown and gold chipped paint of a very old Otis elevator awaited her.

She peeked around again for the man who'd promised he'd never have her out of his sight, but either he was exceedingly good at following undetected, or she'd lost him to the alluring smell of paninis coming from the Novel Café.

Half expecting the elevator to be out of order, she pressed the button and the rickety doors slid right open. She stepped inside the dimly lit car. When she hit the button for the basement level, the doors wobbled to a close.

Still no sign of Johnny.

"Paninis," she whispered to herself. He was probably talking to the cooks right now to get the recipe. It took a minute until she realized the elevator wasn't moving. She pressed B again. And again. Nothing.

Maybe there were stairs to the basement? She pressed Door Open, and the old trap rattled, then shook and started upward.

"Oh, come on," she said, perspiring in the airless little car. "I don't want to go up." But the car continued, dinging and passing the second floor, then stopping at the third.

But the doors didn't open. She pressed every button, each tap against the ancient plastic keys and their worn white numbers becoming a little more frantic. Nothing. No movement, no air, no sound.

She stepped away from the doors, wondering if the car was weight activated like some elevators. Probably not, since it was built in the nineteenth century. She hit every button twice, punched a nonworking emergency call with the heel of her hand, and grunted in frustration. Whoever had sent her there could be gone by the time she got out of this thing.

"Hey!" she hollered, hitting the doors. "I'm stuck!"

When no one answered, she jumped just in case the car did need to feel the weight of a person. A little, then harder. A *clunk* jerked the whole car, making it drop a foot so suddenly, she almost screamed and lost her balance. Then darkness descended.

"Oh!" This couldn't be happening. The lights were out, the doors were stuck, and, as far as she could tell, she was between floors.

She pounded violently on the doors again, the darkness creeping her out and turning her light coat of perspiration into a hair-raising chill.

"Help!" she called again. "I'm stuck in the elevator!" Fueled by frustration and a growing fear, she slammed her hands against the call buttons so hard, she heard one pop off and hit the floor.

One more solid whack on the doors and the car thudded and groaned. Oh, God, was she going to free fall? Bracing herself against the wall, she held her breath and squeezed her eyes shut.

The groaning started again, but now she could see a sliver of light as the doors started to part. "Oh, thank God." Slowly, they creaked open, revealing the solid wall of the cement elevator shaft in front of her and the flat opening of the floor about a foot over her head.

Could she hoist herself into that two-foot opening and escape? Or should she wait for someone to decide to use the elevator and help her? That could take hours.

Her appointment was probably long gone. Swearing at her luck, she backed up to figure out a way to climb to the opening. She jumped again and the car fell another foot, closing off the opening completely.

She gasped, thrown to the floor with the impact. Her stomach dipped, then flew up to her throat as the car fell again, with the doors still open. Her scream echoed in the tiny car, reverberating around the darkness.

With a thunk, the car stopped as suddenly as it had fallen, and this time the shaft opening was much easier to reach through the open doors. Trying to slow her galloping heart, she took a deep breath, wiped her palms on her pants, and stood on very shaky legs.

"Hold still, you bastard," she whispered to the car, reaching to the platform of what must have been the second-floor corridor. On tiptoe, she stretched up, got a grip on the rubber strip along the floorboards above her and hoisted herself, using every ounce of upper-body strength she had.

With a solid grunt, she got herself partway through the opening. With one more mighty pull, she'd be out. She locked her arms just as the doors groaned in motion.

Not now. Not now! The car creaked, starting a noisy climb on its deadly cables. The doors slammed against her ribs, trapping her. And, unbelievably, the car kept going. Higher and higher. In ten seconds when the car reached the next floor she would be sliced in half.

She opened her mouth to scream, but terror froze every muscle.

"Sage!"

"Hurry!" she screamed.

With his own grunt of power, Johnny fell to the hall floor, stuck both hands between the doors, and flung them wide open, then yanked her from the car as it disappeared up into the shaft.

"Oh, my God," she whimpered, dropping against him. "I can't believe that. I can't. . . ." She pulled back. "How did you know where I was?"

His eyes were furious, his jaw clenched in anger. "I saw you get on the elevator. But it's the only one in the building and . . ." He shook his head, perspiration on his upper lip, his whole body taut with anxiety. "Jesus, Sage."

"Sorry," she said. "I didn't know the damn thing was an accident waiting to happen."

Behind her, the cursed elevator rumbled to a stop and the doors had the audacity to open. "Don't even think about getting in there," she said.

But Johnny's attention was locked on the inside of the car. As the hair on the back of her neck rose, she turned to follow his gaze.

"That was no accident," he whispered.

Stuck to the back wall was a chartreuse index card. *Stop or you'll be next.*

CHAPTER
Twelve

She was wet. Sticky. Sore.

Before Ashley opened her eyes, she felt the familiar ache of having ridden someone long and hard. Who had she fucked the night before?

She'd been kidnapped. Her eyes popped open and she pulled her hand up, rustling sheets and blinking into dim light. Who'd arranged this? Which of the Snow Bunnies had gotten her the mean guy who threw her into a freaking trunk and knocked her out? She swallowed, but could only taste the vile, bitter flavor of some serious drug.

And now where the hell was she? This wasn't a hotel.

She gripped the edge of the bed—more like a cot with rough, cheap linens—and tried to make something out in the darkened room. There was no window, no dresser, nothing but another flimsy cot, an empty bookshelf, and a door. Where was she?

"Hello?" she called out. Who'd rescued her last night? She couldn't remember. She sat up, a sharp, stabbing pain in her abdomen. Sucking in another breath, she pressed on her stomach. What was she wearing? Something white, blue, baggy. A man's T-shirt? Pajamas?

Where were the sleep pants she'd been in? She closed her eyes and tried to remember the kidnapping. It hadn't been like the others. For one thing, it had been a total and complete surprise. No one had even hinted that they'd signed her up. But that happened. Not a lot, but it happened.

And who had rescued her? She couldn't remember. Had they smoked weed, like that one time with Samir? That stuff had been laced with something, but at least she remembered the sex. But this time . . .

"Hey!" she called again. "I wanna go home now."

The rescuers never took the girls to their own homes. They always went somewhere cool—a hotel, an apartment set up for wild sex—it all depended on how much cash someone was willing to slide across the Internet.

She plucked at the Motel 6–quality sheets on the metal cot. Whoever had set this one up was a cheap shit.

The little cot creaked as she got up and took small steps toward the door. God, her pussy hurt. How could she have forgotten something like this? Was she really as stupid as Glenda had said? As everyone had always said?

Use your face, Ash, her father would say. *'Cause there isn't much else worthwhile in that empty head.* She hated when that bastard was right.

She put her hand on the doorknob, fear wrapping around her stomach as she imagined being locked in the windowless cell. But the knob turned easily and she opened the door to a hallway, as dark and creepy and windowless as the room she was in. Her bare feet touched cold linoleum and she smelled something vinegary, or pungent like bleach.

"Is anyone here?" she called again. "Samir?"

The hall ended with two matching doors facing each other. She turned the cool, silver knob on the one on the left, but it was locked.

"All right, kiddies, let's see what's behind door number three." The knob turned easily, but the door was hard to open. Metal and thick, it moved like a vacuum was holding it closed.

She'd pushed the institutional-style door about eight inches when it jammed. Swearing, she eased her head into the opening to see into the room. "Is anybody—"

From the other side, someone shoved the door back at her, pinning her head between the solid steel and the door frame.

"Ohhh!" Her cry of pain caught in her throat as white pinpricks of agony blinded her momentarily. She jerked the door with both hands, trying to free her head, but someone just crushed the vise harder, smashing her skull.

She grunted, pushing harder with every ounce of strength, tears of pain blurring her vision, her heart thumping so hard against her chest, she couldn't breathe.

"You're supposed to be asleep, Ashley."

From a million miles away, she heard the voice. The same voice from last night. The man who had kidnapped her.

"Stop!" she managed to say, using her knee to try to

push the door open and free herself from the pain. "Please."

"You shouldn't have come in here."

In where? She felt the metal denting her head, crushing her skull, but she somehow got her head deeper into the doorway, peering through her tears into the room.

She slammed her hip and shoulder against the door, twisting her neck and hearing something snap. It gave enough for her to yank her bruised and battered head free and she almost collapsed with relief.

The door swung open and a man loomed over her, a silhouette against a dim light. "You shouldn't have done that, Ashley."

"Please!" she begged in a strangled sob. "You could have killed me!"

"As a matter of fact, I'm about to." He grabbed her by the hair and yanked her into the room, into the light.

She squeezed her eyes open and closed, trying to breathe, trying to survive. But someone grabbed her from behind and the rough terry of a washcloth slammed over her mouth. The acidic, nasty smell and taste burned her lips and nose.

Her knees buckled, her head fell back, and she saw what was on the wall.

She had one last thought.

The girls. They were all going to die. Every one of them.

"I can't stop."

Sage made the pronouncement as she walked into the living room, the morning light spilling over

Johnny's bare torso, the blanket she'd given him for a makeshift bed long ago fallen to the floor. She took a minute to drink in the way he looked, half undressed and so achingly masculine, her mouth actually watered at the sight of him. It had been so tempting to drag that gorgeous flesh into her bed last night.

She could have used the comfort after the episode in the library, but she settled for letting him feed her stomach. She'd crashed shortly after dinner, exhausted and scared from her brush with death.

But this morning she woke as determined as ever, marching into the living room with the telltale index card in her hand.

He lifted his head, his clear eyes telling her he hadn't been sleeping, either. "You can't stop what?"

She waved the card at him. "I know this is a warning, but that's like a billboard that says DON'T STOP NOW."

With a smile as sexy as his chiseled, smooth chest, he scooted up on the sofa. "So where do you want to search for truth today, baby?"

She'd expected a fight, a warning to stay home and be a good girl.

"You're all right, you know that?" she said, pointing the card at him. "I shall reward that thinking with coffee."

She turned and headed to the kitchen.

"I've been trying to think of ways to verify what Glenda told me about Keisha having an abortion," she said as she turned on the water. "There has to be a way to find that out."

"I might be able to."

She startled at the sound of him in the kitchen

doorway, not expecting him there. He filled up the whole thing, all bare chested and sleepy eyed and delicious. "You're very kind, but I don't think you can just pick up the phone and call the local abortion clinic and—oh!" She snapped her fingers and pointed at him. "Alonzo! He could tell me. He might have access to that information."

"The doctor?"

"Yes. He was head of obstetrics at Mass General; he'd have access to every database they have." She reached for the cordless phone, but he grasped her wrist before she'd lifted the receiver.

"You don't have to involve him, Sage. Really, I might be able to help."

"I doubt that, but you're . . ." His expression was a strange mixture of concern and determination. "Oh," she said, as realization dawned. "You don't want me to call him because of that job at the Ritz. Then you'll have to follow up."

He forced a smile. "That's right. And, really, I might be able to pull a few strings and get some information. Just leave him out of it, okay?"

"Oh, my God. Am I . . ." She scrutinized his expression of disdain. "Am I reading the vibe right here? Are you jealous of him?"

His eyes flashed. "Yeah, you sure are reading the vibe. The guy has the hots for you."

"Are you serious?" She snapped the top off the coffee can. "You, of all people, could be jealous?"

"What if I am?" he said, cocking his head to the side. "I told you, I like you."

"If you do," she said slowly, ignoring the insane little thrill that his statement sent through her, "then you'll consider a new job."

He jutted his chin toward her phone. "Fine. Call your friend. We'll take it from there." He disappeared into the hall without even waiting for a cup of coffee.

Johnny wasn't ready to abandon his theory that Alonzo Garron was the secret patron paying for Bullet Catcher protection of Sage Valentine. He knew what Lucy had said, but it made perfect sense. Including the fact that the doctor dropped whatever appointments he had in order to have lunch with Sage at the Ritz-Carlton in Back Bay. Making it ever so convenient for Johnny to have an impromptu interview with Hendrick Kane in the kitchen of the Ritz Café.

Part of him didn't want to leave Sage for one minute—especially when the client, if he was, would take note that the Bullet Catcher hadn't done what he was being paid to do. But since Garron had arranged the kitchen interview, Johnny assumed he wanted to see Sage alone.

"I'll wait for him," Sage said when they arrived at the restaurant. "You don't want to be late. Go, please."

"All right," he agreed. "And what if I get the job?"

She reached up and touched his lip with her fingertip. "Then you can be my boyfriend."

He closed his hand over her finger and kissed it. "Now that's incentive." Not that he'd get the job or take it, but he was playing Garron's game.

In the hotel lobby, he stopped just long enough to

call Lucy for information. He wasn't sure how he'd tell Sage he got it; let her think he was Superman.

"I need to know if Keisha Kingston had an abortion," he told Lucy after they'd exchanged greetings.

"We'll find out," she assured him. Lucy Sharpe's network of contacts and information was legendary and one of the reasons why the Bullet Catchers were the best security firm in the business. "Anything else?"

"Yep, easy one. An address for Ashley McCafferty."

"Hold on. I'll turn you over to Nancy."

He settled on a wingback chair in the lobby facing the entrance. He didn't mind waiting. The longer he could put off his "interview" with Hendrick Kane, the better.

Just as Lucy's assistant clicked on the line, a red Mercedes pulled up to the valet and Garron climbed out, a cell phone pressed to his ear. Johnny dropped back into the wings of the chair, not wanting to talk to the guy he suspected was footing Sage's Bullet Catcher bill.

"Ashley McCafferty lives on Beacon Street in Brookline," Lucy's assistant announced.

"Hang on a sec," Johnny said, turning his head to the side and covering his face with the phone while he listened to Garron's end of a cell phone conversation as he walked by.

"I'm sorry, honey," the doctor said in a hushed whisper. "I did want to see you, but this meeting came up unexpectedly and I've been wanting to get together with this drug rep for a long time."

Honey? A drug rep?

"One more thing," Johnny said after the doctor was out of earshot. "Can you check on the marital status of Dr. Alonzo Garron of Boston, former head of obstetrics at Massachusetts General Hospital?"

"Sure. McCafferty lives at 1876 Beacon Street, apartment 520. Hold on another minute for the Garron info." In the background, fingers tapped a keyboard as Nancy accessed the unparalleled Bullet Catcher database.

Would Lucy have agreed to provide service to a guy who was watching a woman just because he wanted to get her in the sack, and he was already—

"Married," Nancy said. "To Alicia Garron, age thirty-three, second wife. No children. Anything else?"

"Nope. That's it, sweetheart. Thanks."

He could tell Sage where Ashley lived, he could probably even tell her whether or not her roommate had had an abortion, and he could undoubtedly think of some clever way to explain away all that knowledge. But he knew better than to tell her that her friend Alonzo was married and trying to get in her pants. She would just tell him he was jealous.

And son of a bitch. He was.

"Are you looking for someone in particular out there?"

Sage turned from the wide open view of Newberry Street to see the gleam in Alonzo Garron's eyes as he leaned over the table.

"Just people-watching," she said, matching his smile and standing to accept his friendly embrace and a Euro air kiss on both cheeks. "Nothing like spring in Back Bay."

He waited for her to sit back down before pulling out his chair and taking a cursory glance out the curved window that faced the restaurant. "It's still cold. We'll have our one day of spring sometime at the end of the month, then we'll be sticky until September. I like to spend the summer at our home in Marblehead Neck."

"On the water?"

"Directly. I'll have to have you up sometime. It's an extraordinary place."

"I'd like that." She wasn't here to make light social plans, but some small talk was necessary. "How's the practice going?"

He nodded, giving his napkin a fluff so that it floated onto his lap in one easy move. "I have found Nirvana, my friend."

"Weren't you in private practice years ago, before you ran the department at the hospital?"

He waved his hand as though it didn't count. "I delivered babies and took Pap smears and doled out birth control pills and tied the occasional tube."

She laughed a little. "And now, no babies, no Pap smears, no pills or tubes?"

"Different tubes," he said. "Test tubes."

The waiter delivered two menus and she opened hers. "Infertility treatment?" she guessed.

He lifted salt-and-pepper eyebrows, wrinkling his dome in a way that only a handsome bald man can pull off. "I hate to be crass, but there's a lot of money to be made from rich forty-somethings who forgot to have children."

She nodded, a little black hole of guilt burning in her gut. Here he was making dreams come true for women who couldn't have children, and she was about to ask him to do something he might consider—he *should* consider—highly unethical.

"It isn't about money with you," she said to delay the discomfort of her topic, but her comment obviously warmed him.

"I get great joy out of giving the good news to ladies who are aching to be mothers." He reached across the table and placed his hand over hers. "And when are you going to settle down and have yourself a baby?"

She pretended to choke and he laughed, picking up a cobalt-blue tumbler of water to sip.

"I'll call you when I'm ready, Doc. Prepare to wait awhile."

"Not even with that nice-looking young man? The chef?"

"We're just friends."

This time, his laugh was wry, not hearty. "If you think that, you're blind. Or you believe that I am."

"No, seriously," she insisted. "We just met."

"That didn't stop him from checking me out like one threatened male to another."

Sage smiled. "He's a little protective."

"As he should be. You are a beautiful, intelligent, talented woman with a lot to offer a man. He should be protective, possessive, and . . . employed."

Her cheeks warmed. Let him think it was the compliment and not the fact that Johnny *was* employed— as a boy toy for fantasy-starved women. "Thanks, Dr.

Garron. For your kind words and the interview opportunity for him."

"Please, Sage, I'm Alonzo to you." He opened his menu and pulled out a thin pair of reading glasses. "Now, let me order for you. I know the chef." He winked as he slid the frames on. "And, if all goes well in the kitchen today, you will, too."

After he ordered and the waiter left with their menus, he leaned forward and lowered his voice. "If you're really not interested in the Italian boy, you might want to give a Latin man a try."

Was he serious? She laughed in surprise. "Are you flirting with me?"

He plucked a toast tip from the basket, never taking his eyes off her. "From the moment I met you, Sage, I knew you were the kind of woman I wanted—"

Her jaw dropped, but he laughed and finished, "For a daughter. The kind of woman I would want for a daughter."

"Oh." She couldn't begin to decipher where he was going with the conversation, but decided to give him the benefit of the doubt. "Well, thank you." She took a sip of her water, suddenly thinking of her father tucked into the darkened corners of his own diseased mind, living in a home in Vermont, calling her "Lydia" when she visited and insisting the year was 1990. "And you're the kind of man I would like for a father."

He frowned. "You're not close to him?"

"He's ill. And my mother passed away when I was a teenager."

"What's wrong with your father?"

"Alzheimer's."

His face fell. "Oh. I'm sorry." He looked thought-fully at her. "Are you much like him, Sage?"

She lifted one shoulder. "In some ways." She needed to steer the conversation to her original objective. "I have to ask you a question, Dr. Garron. It might be a little uncomfortable, I'll warn you."

"A medical question?"

"In a sense. I need some information and I'm not sure it's absolutely kosher to ask for it."

He tilted his head. "Try me."

"You remember my roommate, Keisha Kingston?"

He gave her an appropriately sympathetic nod. "I never met her, as you know. What is your question?"

She took a sip of water. What was the worst that could happen? He'd be insulted because she'd asked and he'd been unable to help. "Is there any way, with your connections, you can possibly determine whether or not she had an abortion before she died?"

To his credit, he didn't flinch. "Perhaps."

As their server brought salads, Sage waited. When he picked up his fork to eat, she asked, "Would you?"

He plucked at a crumble of blue cheese, then slowly set his fork down and dabbed the corner of his mouth with a deep blue linen napkin. "Have you ever been pregnant, Sage?"

"Are you asking if I could sympathize with Keisha's situation? I'm not indicting her for having an abor-tion, I'm just trying to find out—"

He silenced her with a hand. "I'm merely asking if you've been pregnant."

"No."

He nodded slowly. "Have you ever tried?"

"Uh, no. I've never been in that committed a relationship."

"You don't have to be committed. You're young."

Where was he going with this? "I'd like to be married before I have a family."

"That's normal. But, what are you? Twenty-six?"

"Twenty-seven." She wanted to squirm in her seat. He wasn't her father. He wasn't her doctor. Was this necessary? "Can you help me find out about Keisha, Dr. Garron?"

"Sage, what will that information change? If Keisha had an abortion, or if she did not, will that bring her back?" His voice was soft, his eyes back to gentle gray.

"Of course not. But I need to know why she died."

"She died because she was either scared or stupid or both." He reached for her hand again. "Do you have to know?"

Sage glanced out the window. "I'm not so sure of that anymore," she said softly. Her attention shifted to the man in the leather jacket standing on the bustling corner of Arlington and Newberry Street. "That was a fast interview."

"Or maybe your friend is a liar."

She blinked at him. "Why would you say that?"

He sighed as if he didn't want to deliver this news, but had to. "No one by the name of John Christiano ever attended the Culinary Institute."

I attended the Culinary Institute of Nona Cardinale.

"I know that," she admitted, somehow not surprised that he'd checked into Johnny's background. How much did he know about what her "friend" did for a living? He was thorough, and smart. "But he's a very good cook."

"He also doesn't maintain a residence anywhere in Boston. Did you know that?"

No, but how did *he* know? "He recently moved here from New York."

"He doesn't maintain a residence in the state of New York." He lifted the fork to his mouth and added, "Or anywhere else in the United States."

Irritation boiled up. "Why the thorough background check? Because you recommended him for an interview?"

"I'm doing what any father would." His tone softened. "Since it sounds like you really don't have one watching out for you anymore."

"Alonzo, I'm not sleeping with him, and if I were, it's not your business."

"Someone needs to tell you that the young man out there"—he shifted his glance to Johnny—"is not whoever he says he is."

Somewhere, deep down inside, she knew that was true. And she never ignored the truth. *Never.*

"I'll do my best to help you get that other information," he added.

CHAPTER
Thirteen

Whatever the doctor had told Sage, it left her uncharacteristically quiet on the way to Brookline. Johnny asked her a few questions, but she kept her answers short.

Even more troubling was that she didn't ask him a million questions about his interview. Which had been so brief, hurried, and uncomfortable, he was fairly certain that Hendrick Kane was not hiring and had been strong-armed by Garron into the meeting.

No matter. Sage was quiet, and Johnny didn't like it.

"What did you eat?" he asked, resisting the urge to slide his hand into hers or put his arm around her.

She looked up at him, her hazel eyes leaning toward the ivy green of her sweater. "Is that all you care about?"

"Whoa. Harsh."

"I don't know what we ate," she said. "Food."

Whatever she'd eaten didn't agree with her. "I'm

going to take a wild guess and say that you didn't get what you wanted out of Sean Connery in there."

"I got what I wanted. He's going to help me."

"Good." Johnny watched dry cleaners and florists and appealing little delis roll by. "Did he tell you that he's married?"

He felt her glare. "What is it with you two? Are you doing counterresearch on each other? How do you know anything about him at all?"

"So he checked me out, huh?"

"Enough to know you lied about attending the Culinary Institute."

And still set up the interview. Why? Just to be alone with her? "What else did you talk about?" Like why was he paying to protect her without her knowing about it?

"His new business."

Johnny nodded knowingly. "Gynecology." He must have left just enough skepticism in his voice to get her defensive.

"He's specializing in infertility treatment now," she said quickly. "Helping women have babies and realize lifelong dreams."

"Big money in that." Enough to pay for round-the-clock supervision, at least. "Hey, next stop is Washington Square," he said. "Her building—".

"You know, Johnny." It was clear she was a million miles away, thinking. "I still want to talk to those people at the website."

"Well, I can't help you there, sugar."

"Why not?"

"I quit." At her look of surprise, he added, "I thought that would make you happy."

"Happy? I don't care where you work or what you do. But you are—*were*—my only connection to that place, and I still think someone there might know something about the night Keisha was, or wasn't, kidnapped."

"Well, I quit."

"Why?"

He patted her hand. "I knew you hated it."

She choked softly. "You're not my boyfriend, Johnny."

"Hey, a guy can hope."

They reached Washington Square, and he followed her out the back door of the subway car, right in front of the fifteen-story gray and white box where Ashley lived. They waited for the light to cross Beacon. When a couple of heavily tattooed punks passed them, and one gave Sage a good, hard eye sweep, Johnny instinctively positioned himself next to her and behind one step, where he could assess and stop every threat.

At the high-rise, no one answered the buzzer for A. McCafferty. There was no guard, no doorman, and Johnny didn't have an entrance code. But the first person who came out, a preppie on the phone, held the glass door for them without so much as a glance at their faces. So much for security in the high-rise.

"Apartment 520," he said, guiding her to the elevator.

"How do you know?" she asked, pressing the call button. "They don't put apartment numbers in the phone book."

"I got on the Internet at the Ritz while I was waiting for you. It's all there, if you know where to look."

"When did you do that?" She poked the button again, as if that could hurry the process. "You were standing on the corner before we got our main course, waiting for me."

A man joined them, and two older ladies came out of a rec room, wrapped in towels and smelling like chlorine, saving him from another lie. He was really getting sick of lying to her. He officially hated undercover work and didn't want another job like this.

They got off the elevator on the fifth floor, which featured gray indoor-outdoor carpeting, beige walls, brown doors, and a long hallway in either direction.

At 520, near the stairwell at the end of the hall, they struck out again. Sage shifted from foot to foot, her impatience mounting with each unanswered knock. She gave the door one more pounding with her fist.

"Ashley! It's Sage Valentine. Are you there? Please?" With the frustrated plea, she grabbed the doorknob to shake the door, then let out a little gasp when it turned all the way. "It's unlocked."

Stupid. Way, way too stupid.

He automatically reached to his hip, closed his fingers over his weapon, and eased her to the side. "Ashley?" he called, inching the door open. He glanced at Sage as he slowly pulled out his Glock, his look telling her to stay back. "Anybody home?"

Glass crunched under his boot. It was everywhere. The entire entryway to the small, modern unit was covered in clear, broken glass. He raised the gun with both hands and took one step forward, his focus on the empty living room, the stream of sunlight that poured in through a window that ran the length of the living room, a much darker bedroom to the right.

"Oh my God," Sage whispered behind him. "Look at that."

On the wall next to the door, a framed poster hung askew, the glass exploded. Black marker was scrawled right over the pretty faces this time.

Whores must die.

"It's technically not a crime scene," Detective Cervaris said as they closed the door to Ashley's apartment, so many hours later that Sage battled hunger and fatigue. "No one has reported her missing."

Sage almost reached up to grab his weathered skin and rattle his head. "Then where is she?"

He gave her a patient nod. "I understand your concern, Miss Valentine, and don't think I'm saying that . . ." he pointed a thumb over his shoulder at the apartment door, "is a form of modern art in there. I see the pattern. Like I said, I'm going to talk to the right people at the New England Blizzard—"

"The Snow Bunnies," she said urgently. "It's actually a separate organization."

He held up his hand and shuttered his eyes as though his world-class patience was coming to an end with each interruption. Well, too damn bad. This was the second "nonstandard break-in" in three days. And this experienced Boston cop had to see the pattern, even if no one had reported Ashley missing and her calendar had a dark line and "pick up at 8:45" written on today's date. He suggested that this meant she had left town. But Sage insisted it could be a reminder to pick up her dry cleaning.

Other than the smashed glass over her poster and the "Whores must die," it appeared that nothing had been touched in the apartment. There was no evidence of any crime except vandalism.

"We'll find her, we'll get in touch with people who know her," the detective said to Johnny. "We'll handle this from here."

"You have our cell phone numbers," Johnny said. "Please call us if you find anything at all. We'll be ready to help you however we can."

Our, us, *we*. When did they become a unit? Still, Sage knew that arguing in the hall with the old detective and the young self-appointed boyfriend was a waste of time. She'd get rid of him when they got home.

Or maybe she'd let him cook for her and make jokes and spread sweet cream on her nipples. Comfort food, comfort talk, comfort sex.

She was still thinking about that, and the defaced poster in Ashley's apartment, when they walked out of the building and Johnny guided her to a yellow taxi at the corner. You couldn't flag one in Brookline.

"You called a cab?" she asked.

He opened the back door. "You're in no shape to take the T."

Part of her wanted to argue, but the smart part closed her mouth and climbed across the cracked seat and stared at the gray stone of All Saints Cathedral.

"The Eliot Hotel," he said to the driver. "In Back Bay."

She turned from the church. "We're going to a hotel?"

"I don't want you to be home. You're more secure away from the apartment."

"Excuse me?" She nearly choked on the question. "Don't I get consulted? And since when are you my personal security officer?"

He gave her an endearing, lopsided smile and touched her cheek with a fingertip. "Baby, let me just take care of you tonight." The kiss on her temple was so tender, she hardly felt it. "That's what I do."

Confusion and unanswered questions shuddered through her, along with Alonzo's warning about Johnny, the image of vicious, hateful words over beautiful faces, and the neon-green index card in the back of a deadly elevator. But all she could do was close her eyes and inhale the smell of his leather jacket, mixed with evergreen air freshener and the fruit shampoo he must have used at her house.

She didn't speak, didn't open her eyes, and sure as hell didn't feel like arguing. Instead, she listened to the rumble of the train running parallel to the road, and to the first few drops of rain that spattered on the roof of the cab. Johnny's fingers found her nape and gently massaged the taut muscles there.

That's what I do.

Comfort. Security. Sensuality.

She could feel herself slipping into the safety net he offered. She studied the strong lines of his chin, the thick lashes, the intensity in the eyes that met hers. He wrapped his other arm around her and kissed her so sweetly that for that moment, she didn't care if this was "what he did."

He did it so damn *nice.*

A soft groan pulled from her throat as he traced his tongue over her lips, then dipped it into her mouth. Instinctively she lifted herself toward him, nestling her hands around his neck, combing her fingers into his hair as she pulled his head to her. He spread open her jeans jacket and kissed down her neck to the rise of her breasts. He closed his palm over one breast, sending an instant shock wave through her angora sweater and straight into her stomach. Thumbing her gently, he lifted his head, his eyes black with the same arousal that had her heart pounding and her hips aching to move.

Oh, yeah. This is what he did. A professional lover.

He didn't say a word. Didn't smile. Didn't breathe. He just moved his thumb back and forth over the fuzzy material, hardening her nipple, torturing her.

She'd never done it in a cab. But he probably had, a dozen times. So what? Surely he had a condom, and she wanted him. Really wanted him. All the way. Why not here? Why not now?

She glanced over his shoulder. Through the steady rain, she recognized Kendall Square. They had ten minutes, fifteen if there was traffic around Boston University, until they got to Back Bay. With the rain and luck, twenty. Enough time. She dropped her head back, inviting a more intimate touch.

He repositioned his hand, warming the skin of her breastbone and inching his fingers into the V of her sweater. "C'mere, honey," he whispered. "Let me kiss you. Let me touch."

Oh, Lord, he was so good. She parted her lips and closed her eyes and his mouth burned her exactly at the second his fingers touched her swollen flesh. He flicked her nipple, flicked her tongue, and flicked her switch to *on*.

Moisture pooled between her legs where an ache, painful and powerful, tightened her muscles. She dug one hand deeper into his thick hair and flattened the other on his chest, sliding it down because she wanted to touch the erection she knew he had. Proof that the desire was mutual.

And it was. Stiff and substantial and really, really mutual. He grunted softly as she rubbed him once, then she just moved on pure instinct, sliding one leg over his lap, wanting nothing but the chance to rub against him until the fire flared.

Rain sluiced down the windows, cars and stores and buildings zoomed by, and the driver was long forgotten. Sage kissed him while he caressed over and under her sweater, she rolled over him while he grew even harder and bigger against her crotch. Sweat and heat emanated from him, along with gentle moans, whispered words, and wet, wet kisses. No clothes came off, no barriers were breached, but they imitated the act and she was too far gone to do anything but try not to scream as an orgasm started to clutch her.

She gripped his hair, yanking his face closer, his mouth to hers. She just wanted to take and ride and roll and rock and touch and release all this pressure against him.

"No, no, baby." He eased her back on the seat. "Wait."

"What? Why?" The words were little more than strangled vowels.

"Because I don't . . ."

She pushed a damp hair off her face, the muscles in her lower half twitching and tightening, frustration replacing the reckless abandon she'd just given into. "What do you mean 'you don't'? You don't mess around in cabs? It's not part of your *job*?"

"Stop it."

The heat turned to icy disappointment and then morphed into anger. She hit his arm a little harder than necessary. "Do I need to pay you?" The unfinished climax threw extra venom in her voice.

He glared at her, his jaw clenching, his neck muscles flexing. "Stop it, Sage."

She didn't *want* to stop. She practically punched the seat, turning to the window just as the cab whipped to the curb where a charcoal overhang protected the elegant, understated entrance of the Eliot Hotel. The cabbie called out the fare, but Johnny didn't move.

Instead, his expression turned hard and demanding. "Do you really think this is work? Is that what you think?"

"I decided not to *think* about fifteen minutes ago. See where that got me."

He blew out a disgusted breath. "Come on, Sage."

"Oh, now I'm Sage. What happened to babycakes and sugarplum?"

"You're too good for this," he said, his voice so strained it was barely above a whisper. "For . . . that."

"Oh, please," she said, using disdain to hide her disappointment. "What a complete crock. I wasn't too good the other night."

Wordlessly, he put his index finger on her lower lip, slid it into her mouth, curled it around her tongue. What was he trying to do, kill her? "It's different now. I know you. I really like you."

What? He could only do it with strangers for cash? Fine. She'd stuff a hundred-dollar bill in his pants, if he'd just let her *finish*.

Before he said another word, she reached between his legs and grabbed him. At the same instant, she sucked his finger into her mouth with a noisy squeak. His jaw went slack, and his eyelids half closed as he watched her lips, watched her devour his finger while his erection grew like a tree trunk in her grasp.

"I said that's twelve fifty," the driver repeated with an edge in his voice.

"Okay," Johnny whispered. He flung a twenty through the plastic opening, then closed his fingers over hers, pressing her hand down on his erection. "Let's go."

He got out first and reached for her, and before two raindrops had hit her head, a heavyset doorman had an umbrella over both of them and pulled open the brass-trimmed entrance to the dimly lit marble and mahogany of one of Boston's best-kept secrets. Oh, God. How long would it take to get a room at the Eliot?

From behind an old-fashioned registration desk, complete with "keyhole" cubbies, a man smiled. "Evening, Mr. Christiano." He glanced at Sage. "Miss."

He was staying there?

She glanced up to question him, but he kept her tightly under his arm, and practically swirled her around to a curved staircase trimmed with gleaming brass rails. "I'm on the second floor," he said, hustling her up.

She almost tripped on the plush, oriental carpeting. "You have a room here?"

"Actually, a suite."

A *suite*? At the Eliot? That slowed her, but he urged her on, his step as eager as her humming body, his focus dead ahead, presumably in the direction of his room. Suite. But the questions started to buzz louder than the sexual pull.

"How—how can you afford this?" The suites had to be three hundred a night. "How long have you been here? Is this part of the gig—like where you bring women after you rescue them? Do you—"

He pushed her against a door. "Shut up, Sage."

He made sure she did, kissing her so long and so thoroughly, she could barely breathe, let alone talk. Behind her, she sensed him fumbling with a key, then the door gave way and he backed her into a pitch-black room.

It smelled like wood and silk, all dark shadows and heavy furniture.

How did he manage *this*?

She threw the nagging questions into the back of her mind and let the sensation of his mouth, his clever, talented mouth, take over. He opened her jacket, sucking her tongue while he slid the sleeves down her arms. She responded by thrusting his coat open and shoving it to the floor.

Their heavy breaths echoed in the room, the only sounds the swoosh of clothing and her moan of frustration when he pulled away to flip the dead bolt and the privacy lock.

"C'mere," he demanded the minute they were locked in, yanking the bottom of her sweater up. The angora stuck to her wet lips as she raised her arms, desperate for what would come next.

The sweater disappeared and he reached around for her bra clasp, but she tugged at his T-shirt. He let her rip it over his head, then went back to work on her bra. He moved her backward through the shadowed room, through a set of open French doors just as he released her bra and she shimmied out of it. A bed hit the backs of her knees and she collapsed onto it, pulling him on top of her. Brocade and silk and soft mounds of pillows met her back as his sleek, hard body pressed down on her.

"Wait," he whispered, reaching to the nightstand. "Now, baby," he murmured as he climbed back on top of her. "Now. Here. *Now*." The hint of franticness in his voice almost put her away. Then he closed both hands over her breasts, kissing her cheek, her ears, grinding his hips against hers. "You're so damn perfect."

She wasn't, but maybe that was his line. No, no, don't think about that. Don't think about his lines or his women or his job. Don't *think*. Feel. Enjoy.

He pressed her breasts together and licked her cleavage, then one nipple, then the other, in quick, desperate succession like he couldn't get enough.

Maybe that was a trick, too.

His hands were shaking when he popped the button of her low-rise jeans; they were actually trembling as he scraped the zipper and thrust his fingers into her panties. His quick, helpless breaths mingled with a low, slow growl so real that it couldn't be practiced, it couldn't be something he learned at *work*.

Could it?

He palmed her mound, slid one, then two fingers into her, and sucked so furiously on her nipple, she knew he'd leave his mark on her flesh. She rocked into his hand and fumbled with his pants, struggling to undress him as he pushed at her jeans and managed to get only one leg out. His desperation was so sexy, she almost came in his hand.

She unzipped and released him, grabbing the hard, hot shaft and stroking it furiously, feeling his whole body quiver. "You're not faking this."

He managed a rough laugh. "No, I'm not." The last word was strangled as he thrust himself into her hand, all size and man and blood engorged. One more twist got rid of his pants, and he produced a condom. Oh, God, so many tricks, so many moves.

She had to stop imagining he practiced this, used this. She had to *stop*.

"Stop?" he asked. "Now?"

"Did I say that?"

He nodded, a little terror darkening his eyes. "I will. I can."

Oh, God. That was his very best trick of all. The sweet, kind, protective prostitute who could stop the madness whenever his client wanted to.

"No, no," she assured him. "I just don't want to think about . . ." She touched his cheeks, his mouth, his jaw. "Please. Inside me."

He shoved his boxers down, stabbed himself into the condom, and in one swift move spread her knees with his, one panty leg still hooked to her calf.

"I know what you're thinking, Sage," he said as he slid against the wet slickness between her legs, his erection massive and threatening now.

"No, you don't." She lifted her hips to take him in. "And I don't care."

"Yes, I do," he said, his tip entering her, opening her. "And yes, you do care."

He plunged into her with a long, low grunt of satisfaction, the width of him shocking her muscles, the tip of him touching her womb. Pleasure and pain collided and crashed; their hips met violently with each thrust. He kissed her and held her and filled her so much, she couldn't do anything but take it.

She didn't care what he did, who he was, how he lived. She squeezed his shoulders, his hips, his shaft, and let the first wave wash over her, dragging her higher, higher, higher to the peak, then slamming her over the edge into a spiral of pure ecstasy.

He came seconds later, his face contorted, his eyes closed, the powerful tendons in his neck strained as he lost the fight for control. Then he collapsed on her, sweat-soaked and spent.

For a long time, the only sounds were labored breathing and pounding hearts. Finally, he managed to push back a strand of hair and press his lips against her cheek.

"Hey," he breathed.

"Hey yourself." She didn't care that just looking at him was like a kick in her stomach, because he was so damn gorgeous with damp black hair kissing his eyebrows. She didn't care that his first question would be *Was it good for you, sugar?*

He shifted to take some of his weight off her, but remained very much inside her, still hard. "You know what?" he whispered.

"What?" *You're really something, baby doll. That was amazing, honey.*

"Now I'm your boyfriend, Sage."

CHAPTER
Fourteen

"My boyfriend? Are you kidding?" Sage laughed, making him slide partway out of her, so Johnny deliberately gave a push to let her know he could go again without a break.

"Does this feel like kidding?"

"Why do you want to be my boyfriend so bad?"

Tell the truth when you can, no matter how sticky the situation. He lifted himself and heard the suction of their skin separating. This definitely qualified as *sticky.* "So I can be around you twenty-four/seven."

In the moonlight streaming through the sheer curtains, he drank in her creamy complexion, all rosy from coming so hard, with a few blond hairs stuck to those incredible cheekbones. Man, who wouldn't want to be her boyfriend? And that was just her face. The rest of her was just as delectable. Narrow, with a few choice curves. Tight. Hot. Sweet.

His cock stirred in agreement. "Twenty-four/seven," he said again. "That's what I want."

She shifted to separate them, taking away her silky, warm envelope.

"I don't believe half of what you say. You work for some fantasy company, or you used to, doing God knows what. You keep a suite at a tony hotel but drive a rented Toyota. You lie about where you went to culinary school, you carry a freaking revolver—"

"It's a pistol, actually."

"Whatever—it shoots. You go through a crime scene like NYPD blue, for God's sake, and you . . . you . . ."

"I have a black belt in shaolin. And I make a cheesecake that would bring you to another orgasm." He propped himself on his elbow. "Haven't you ever heard of a Renaissance man?"

She laughed again. "Or a con man."

Or just the lousiest undercover professional in the history of the Bullet Catchers. "Hey, I know I'm a little slick for you. But I'm a good guy, honestly." He trailed a finger over her jaw and grazed her lower lip, swollen from kissing him. "Good at a lot of things that make you happy."

"And you want to be my boyfriend."

"Let me ask you something. Do you give every schmuck such a hard time when they like you, or am I special?"

She reached out to touch his face again. "You're special."

With a loud sigh of relief, he dropped off his elbow and let his head hit the pillow next to her. "Thank you, God."

"But I don't really want a boyfriend. They tend to get in my way."

He reached for her, turning her on her side to face him. "Then let's just be lovers and friends. I don't care what you call me, I want to stay with you. And I won't get in your way."

"You're always in my way," she said, closing her eyes with a smile that said she didn't mind. "So, boyfriend. What's your middle name?"

"Anthony. My name is John Anthony Christiano. I'm thirty-one, six feet tall, never been married, and I love . . ." He leaned close to her ear. "Big secret now, one I would only tell my girlfriend. This is it, my intimate revelation. You ready?"

She nodded, with a grin. "Tell me."

"I listen to Dean Martin music."

"Dean Martin? Isn't he dead?"

"Good music lives forever."

She laughed softly and turned to him, sympathy softening her expression. "Johnny, I'm really sorry I pushed you about your sister."

Where did that come from? "It's all right." He levered himself from the bed to start flipping the decorative pillows onto the floor. "Why don't you finish getting undressed and get under the covers with me?"

She didn't move. "You don't want to talk about it, do you?"

No, he sure as shit didn't. "Come on, angel." He pulled the spread down to where she lay, and tugged. "The sheets are incredible here and I want to see you completely naked."

"And that's another thing." She rolled over. "How can you afford this hotel?"

"I'm loaded. Come on." He hauled the spread down hard enough to move her. "Don't make me pick you up and strip you down."

Reluctantly, she climbed off the bed and he swept the heavy spread right off and let it fall to the floor. As he did, she stepped out of her pants, kicked off her one remaining shoe, and walked straight to the window, making an exquisite silhouette. And an exquisite target.

"Get away from the window, Sage."

She turned. "Nobody can see into a dark room two stories up."

He wouldn't tell her how wrong she was; she'd just want to know where he'd gotten the surveillance experience. Instead, he walked up behind her, wrapped his arms around her narrow frame, and shimmied his cock against her taut little backside. "I'm not done with you."

She turned around, her eyes glistening. "Would you like to know why I chose investigative reporting as a career?"

He'd *like* to get under the covers and take a slow trip over every inch of her naked body with his tongue, his fingers, and a few other appendages. "Because that's what your mother did?"

"Not really." She let him lead her to the bed, where she propped up a pillow, slid under the covers, and patted the bed in invitation. Oh, boy. Time to *talk*. "Because I'm obsessed with finding out the truth."

Just his luck for an undercover assignment—a fact finder with a body that brought him to his knees, and a mouth that could suck the truth out of a black hole. "That's a noble cause," he said, getting in next to her and making sure his whole body touched her whole body, praying for a distraction from her search for the truth.

"So was my mother, and that's actually what killed her. But—"

"How?" He ran one finger over the silky skin of her shoulder. Much better to examine her past than his.

She let out a deep sigh. "It's really a long story, but, bottom line, she was going to write a story that would have exposed some very nasty stuff about a government organization." She closed her eyes. "But her sister put a stop to that."

"Is this the aunt you mentioned before?"

She nodded. "She found out about the story and managed to stop it, but not before she made my mother look like a fool and a liar. She lost her job at the *Washington Post,* and about three months later . . ." She shook her head. "She lost her identity, I guess. And had nothing to live for."

"No? What about you?"

The moment he asked the question, he felt her body tense.

"Evidently," she finally said, "I wasn't enough to make her want to live. But I blame my aunt. She killed my mother as sure as if she tied the noose herself."

He'd seen a guy die from hanging once. Only it wasn't a suicide and he hadn't stopped it. Revulsion rolled through him, and he curled his leg over her and pulled her closer, knowing that physical contact couldn't take the pain away but that it might help.

"I believe," he said softly, "that betrayal is the worst crime you can commit."

She looked at him for a long moment. "Have you ever been betrayed?"

Had he ever. And he'd betrayed. He closed his eyes and saw Bella's face. "Everyone has, kiddo." He rubbed his leg over hers. "But why would your aunt do a thing like that? What did it matter to her?"

"Oh, please." She pulled the covers up and tucked her chin down. "Don't get me started on Lucy Sharpe."

The words hit his gut, sharp and shocking. *"Who?"*

"My aunt, Lucy. I hate that control freak."

His head literally buzzed with the stun. Lucy was her *aunt?* No, it couldn't be true. It couldn't be.

Though . . . with Lucy? Of course it could be true. He sat up slowly, fighting every natural reaction. *Hang on, man. Do this right.* "You . . . hate her." He dug deep for the cool that he'd learned from observing Dan Gallagher, Alex Romero, and all the other Bullet Catchers. And of course their boss, Lucy Sharpe.

"Yes."

"That's . . . that's a shame." Whoa. Points for massive understatement.

"No, it's not." She shot him a sidelong glance from under thick lashes. "She's manipulative and cunning and ruthless."

Not ruthless. Well, sometimes ruthless. "When's the last time you saw her?"

She snorted softly. "About two weeks ago."

"Why?" He had to work to keep the surprise out of his voice.

"Because I thought she could help me with the takemetonite.com website." She closed her eyes. "She

made me think she could help, too. Instead of just answering my questions, she summoned me to her estate
in New York, only to give me nothing. Nothing at all."

Now it all made sense. There was no benefactor.
There was no client. There was Lucy—manipulating
and controlling like always. Not telling Johnny the
whole story . . . and now he had one more layer of secret to hide from the woman he'd just slept with.

"What did you expect her to tell you?" he asked.

"I expected her to find something out, because she
knows people," Sage said. "She was in the CIA. She has
this elaborate security firm she runs with a bunch of
black-ops types, doing who knows what."

He knew what. And they weren't all black ops.
Some were just ex-wiseguys who Lucy had saved from
the life. One was a former astronaut, another had been
in the Secret Service. Dan had been FBI, Max had been
DEA. And there were a couple of spooks in there, too.
"Did she help you?"

"No, all she told me was what you've said. Keisha
never showed. And takemetonite.com is a legitimate,
profitable, mainstream business not doing anything
technically illegal."

And yet, she still wanted Sage protected. "Did you
tell her you were going to sign up to be kidnapped?"
he asked.

"Absolutely not."

But Lucy knew, of course.

"I hate to talk about my aunt," she said, snuggling
closer, her long legs warm against him. "Just like you
hate to talk about your sister."

He used the excuse to cuddle her, to tuck her head against his chest to hide his expression as he swallowed the urge to punch the bed. *Dammit, Lucy! Why didn't you tell me?*

But then, what difference would it have made? Would knowing who Sage was have stopped him tonight? He closed his eyes and remembered how control had evaporated and desire had taken over in the cab. Yeah, he'd have slept with her.

Sage skimmed her fingers over his chest, over his stomach, dangerously low. And he would sleep with her again. Soon.

But all he could think about now was Lucy.

What would Sage think if . . . when . . . she found out? Worse than the male prostitute she worried about, he was there at the bidding of the woman she hated. A woman he would never betray.

Oh, man, he didn't even want to think about this mess.

Sage gave him a smile as she closed her fingers over him. "What's going on?"

"What do you mean?"

"You were rock hard when we got in this bed. What happened?"

Lucy happened. "You hang on to that, doll face, you'll get me hard."

"Don't call me that." She withdrew her hand and inched away. "Don't call me those names."

He let out an exasperated breath. This job had just turned into a freakin' land mine. "Sorry. I won't call you anything but Sage." He kissed her forehead, her cheeks, her lips. She opened her mouth and invited more.

He obliged, his head was spinning with questions and denial.

Lucy's *niece*. How could this be? She had none of Lucy's exotic Micronesian blood—she was blond and about ten years younger than Lucy. He abruptly pulled away. "Didn't you say you were twenty-seven?"

Her mouth was still open as she frowned at him. "You're worried about my age? Now?"

"I just wondered because, well . . ." How could he explain that he knew her aunt wasn't even forty years old? Was it possible they were just eleven years apart? "I just want to know more about you."

"I'm twenty-seven, five foot five, never been married, and I've never heard Dean Martin sing, but I'm a big Elton John fan." She arched her body against his. "Do you still like me?"

Tipping her chin, he kissed her softly. "Very much, Sage. I like you very much." And the bitch of it was, he really did.

What would his boss think of that?

And when Sage found out . . . *No, don't go there, man.* She wouldn't find out. Or at least when she did, he'd be long gone.

"Good," she whispered, her fingers already working magic. "Because I like you, too."

The bodyguard was gone.

Vivian Masters sensed it the moment she woke up, and tangled her fingers in Taz's soft fur. The cat mewed, stretched, and curled into her owner's warm body, not the least bit interested in whether the man Vivian had paid to stand guard at the bottom of the stairs was gone.

The quiet was total. The birds hadn't started chirping outside the clapboard-covered house. No neighbors walked a barking dog or slammed a car door on the Wellesley cul-de-sac. Not even a trash-can lid rattled, even though it was pickup day. She'd rented the two-story Cape house long enough to know every sound, and when one was absent.

She inched one leg along the sheets, the out-of-her-price-range thread count silky against her bare skin. The bedside clock said seven twenty, but it was half an hour fast so that she could avoid her perennial lateness.

She had nothing to get up for this morning, however. No radio interviews, no local talk shows, no grand openings of new stores or photo shoots. Vivian maintained a very low profile now. And Vivian maintained a very high-profile bodyguard just in case. . . .

But he was gone. She knew it like she knew how the bare floor would feel against her feet, how Taz would follow her with her green eyes, and act like she wasn't interested in the effort it took to mew for breakfast. Vivian knew she was alone in her house. And she was scared.

Pulling a worn Patriots sweatshirt over her head, she stepped to the window and looked at the little lawn and garden she worked so hard to keep pretty. Her grandmother would call it a "white folks' yard," just like Gammy would call the round table with a flouncy tablecloth and white lace doily a "white folks' table." Once she'd told Keisha that, and they'd laughed until they'd choked.

Keisha understood that stuff. Keisha knew.

Her heart clenched, as it always did when she thought about her friend. No matter how she tried to rationalize it, she knew in her deepest gut that she'd sent Keisha to her maker, just as if she'd given the sister the fatal dose of E with her own two hands. Guilt mixed with fear in her churning stomach.

No matter how many times she tried to tell herself that she'd misunderstood Keisha's message the night she died, another voice—Gammy's?—said, *Girl, you are lyin' to yourself and that's the worst form of deception.*

God, she'd been lying for so long, she couldn't remember what the truth was anymore.

Maybe Keisha really had come home from her appointment, juiced up, and exploded her generous heart out of insecurity or stupidity.

Or maybe not. Which was why David the Goliath was supposed to be downstairs with a big honkin' gun to take down anyone who figured out what Vivian knew.

She opened her bedroom door, the squeak echoing across the tiny hall to the second bedroom, which she used as an office. The bathroom between the two rooms was dark and empty. She looked down the steps to the landing. Maybe he was asleep. She wouldn't be able to see him until she got halfway down.

"David?" she called. "Are you there?"

She jumped at the sound of Taz hitting the floor with a soft meow, then took a few steps farther. She would have heard the alarm if he'd left the house, or if anyone had come in. It was never disarmed. Ever.

"David?"

Nothing. She stared at the steps. Should she go down there and look for him? In the kitchen? Watching TV? Grounds for dismissal, but still, a girl could hope.

Then she remembered her little pistol. She hadn't thought about using it, because he'd been there. Turning, she stepped over Taz and found the tiny gun in her underwear drawer. Following everything she'd learned when she bought it, she clicked the safety, cocked it. Lord, that sound echoed through the house—wouldn't a bodyguard worth his salt come barreling up the stairs at the sound of a pistol being cocked?

She pointed it at an angle toward the ground, like she learned in the firearms safety class, her arms trembling. At the landing she stopped, surveying the entryway, the formal living room to her right, the dining room, and the cozy den beyond. There wasn't much more to the house. Around the corner to the back was the kitchen, with a tiny sunroom where she nursed flowers back to health and kept her exercise equipment. Maybe he was there. She let him use her weights and elliptical machine.

"David!" she called, her voice sharp with frustration, but made stronger by the confidence of having a gun.

The kitchen was empty, cold. As was the sunroom, although it caught a little of the eastern morning sky and beamed a yellow band of light right across the faces of her New England Blizzard Snow Bunnies poster above the weight bench. Where was he?

At the kitchen door, she moved the blinds she'd recently installed. The garage was a separate, small building, about forty steps over a gravel driveway from her kitchen door. Forty long steps with heavy groceries or a couple of inches of snow. Now, the single, windowless door was closed tight to protect her little yellow VW punchbuggy.

The bodyguard drove a small SUV, always parked to one side of the gravel drive since he'd started the job. She stared at the empty driveway.

The bastard had bolted.

She glanced at the alarm pad. READY TO ARM. He'd disarmed the alarm! Some freaking bodyguard. Angry, she set the gun down and yanked the cordless phone from the charger on the counter, stabbing in the number for Wentworth Securities. For God's sake, David was a partner in the company that provided security for the Blizzard.

She slammed the phone on the counter on the tenth ring, turning to see Taz staring hungrily at her.

"Come on, little sister, let's get you some food."

She popped open a can of cat food, and simply dropped it on the floor when she remembered that the bodyguard had kept his duffle bag and phone charger in the den.

She hustled in there but he'd cleaned out, without even getting paid for the last week. Probably got a better job, a better client. Why else would he just *leave*?

The sound of a car pulled her attention to the window. Through the sheer curtains she saw a dark van drive by at about ten miles per hour. It wasn't the lack of speed that bothered her—no one drove fast on the cul-de-sac. It was the familiarity of the vehicle.

Oh, God. Her gut tightened as the van turned around at the end of the road and headed back up the street. Less than a minute later, it cruised by again, dark windows, rusted paint, a fender that could fall off at any moment.

Flying up the stairs, she dived into sweatpants, stuck her feet in Adidas flip-flops, grabbed her handbag, and raced back downstairs. She paused just long enough to peek through one of the three rectangular windows in the front door. No sign of the van. She had a minute. Maybe. In the kitchen, she scooped up Taz midbite and charged for the door.

"Shit," she mumbled, shaking. "The gun." She grabbed the little pistol from the table, flung open the door, and ran to the garage. She swore again as she nearly dropped the cat when her handbag slid down to her elbow with a *thud*. Somehow, she managed to reach down and twist the handle of the garage door with the hand that held the pistol. Why hadn't she ever installed an automatic opener and a door that rolled up instead of tilting out so awkwardly?

Certain that she'd drop the gun and shoot her foot off, she managed to get the door high enough to dive under. As she did, she heard an approaching engine. The van would have to get past her house for the driver to see the garage. He'd have to pull into her driveway to actually see her go inside. She had less than ten seconds to get that door down.

With a grunt of effort, she slammed the door like a thundercrack on the cement floor. Instantly, darkness and the dank smell of dirt and her own fear washed over her.

Taz mewed hard in anger, but she just clutched the cat tighter. "Ssh. Please, for God's sake, don't make a sound." She was petrified to move, terrified of knocking over the snow shovel or the rake. She could see nothing.

Her mouth dry, Vivian stood stone still, the weight of her bag, the wiggling cat, the cocked gun she had no idea how to handle all bearing down on her.

Then she heard the tires on gravel.

Taz stopped squirming for a moment, probably sensing the fear that skyrocketed Vivian's pulse. She'd been warned. Keisha had left the message and, without realizing it, had warned her.

A heavy door slammed and a man's footsteps crunched in the driveway. Even if he went into the house—and she was certain the latch hadn't caught and, of course, she hadn't turned on the alarm—she couldn't drive away because he was blocking the driveway.

How long until he went through the house and discovered her missing? How long until he pulled open the garage door—which locked only from the outside? There was no side door. No escape.

She still didn't move, trying to hear . . . anything. Somewhere in a corner an animal skittered and Taz almost jumped out of her arms, no doubt at the scent.

Could she take the chance of opening the garage door and running? Could she get help? Of course! She could call the police! In the darkness, she reached into her handbag. She didn't dare put Taz down; she'd mew so loudly to get that mouse, she might give them away. And maybe he wouldn't come into the garage. Maybe he'd assume she had left with her bodyguard.

Unless he knew . . . Oh, Lord, of *course* he knew the bodyguard was gone.

"The rat bastard got bought off," she hissed as she rummaged through her bag.

The first thing her fingers touched were her keys, which gave her an idea. She could hide in the car, and use her cell phone. Gingerly, she made her way to the driver's side of her car and pulled open the door. She cringed at the squeak, but blessed the light, climbing inside with a prayer of relief when she set Taz on the passenger seat.

The cat instantly cried and scratched, but Vivian set the gun on the console between the seats and opened her bag again, peering in for the phone. *Please, God in heaven, don't let it be in the house.*

There it was, at the bottom of the mess. She yanked it out and looked at the screen. One measly bar of battery. Just as she dialed the 9 of 911, she heard the house door slam close. Terror froze her fingers before she hit Talk. Shoes ground against the gravel in swift, determined steps. He was coming in! She dropped the phone and seized the gun at the very second Taz jumped on it.

She sucked in a gasp, bracing for the deafening sound of a shot. But the weapon slipped over the console to the back and hit the carpet with a soft *thump*. The first crack of the garage door opening echoed inside.

Could she get to the gun and fire it before he got to her? But the door didn't open. It snapped, it rattled, then nothing. He'd locked her in there.

With each breath as loud as her thundering heart, Vivian twisted to see the floor in the dim light. She grabbed the gun just as she heard an engine start and tires chew up her gravel driveway, then disappear up the hill.

Climbing out of the car and using the interior dome light to guide her steps, she walked to the garage door and tried to lift it. Locked. Well, what the hell did that prove? Why wouldn't he come after her?

She peered at the lock mechanism, aimed the gun at it, and prayed that what she saw in the movies worked in real life. The shot sent a wicked vibration up her arm and nearly burst her eardrums, but power and resolve surged through her. Feeling Lara Croft–invincible, Vivian hauled the door up. Whoever was out there, she'd shoot his ass!

But thank God, there was no one. The driveway was empty. She ran back to the car and shoved her key into the ignition.

It was time to quit hiding her secret, to quit lying. More than anything, it was time to avenge Keisha's death. With the gun hot on her lap, Vivian stomped on the accelerator, backed out of her garage, and drove like hell on wheels.

CHAPTER
Fifteen

The change in Johnny was subtle, and a woman less experienced at interviewing reluctant sources might have attributed it to the four—five?—orgasms they'd given each other last night and this morning. But Sage knew it was something other than great sex. Whatever was on his mind that morning was deep, important, and profound. What else would account for the fact that he hadn't eaten, cooked, or even mentioned food in, what, fifteen hours?

He tapped the bathroom door open just as she spit out a mouthful of Scope she'd found in the hotel basket of toiletries.

"I'm starved," he said.

So much for that theory. She looked into the mirror, capturing his gaze over her shoulder, then taking in the broad, bare chest and the drawstring pants that hung perilously low on his narrow hips, which she remembered licking that morning in the shower.

"I was wondering if your problem was related to food."

A sneaky smile threatened on his lips. "I don't have a problem, sweetheart."

She decided to ignore the *sweetheart*, and the lie. Turning, she leaned against the sink and locked her hands on her hips. Like she just had done, he gave her a full-body visual, dallying on the bra and underpants she wore. His chest rose just enough for her to know he was drawing a silent, tight breath.

"Well, I have a problem," she told him.

He took one step into the bathroom. "Let me fix it."

Before he even touched her, little sparks of sexual anticipation exploded on her skin. She shook her head. "Don't. We'll never get out of here."

His hands slipped around her waist and slid right up to unfasten her bra. "And your point is . . ."

She dipped away. "That you are starved and I have no clothes or a toothbrush."

"This is a full-service joint, toots. We can have food, clothes, whatever, in a heartbeat. What do you want?" He pulled her back, dropping a kiss on that spot he'd found last night, the one between her shoulder and her neck. The one that weakened her knees and turned her brain to Jell-O.

She flattened her hands on the planes of his chest, already familiar to her palms, and resisted the urge to trace the dips and muscles and taste his taut, dark nipples. *Oh, Sage, you got it bad.* "What I want is to go home."

"Let's do my home today."

She pointed to the Dopp kit that held his razor, toothbrush, and a number of shampoos—from other hotels, all high-end. "This isn't a home. You live out of a suitcase."

He shrugged. "I move around a lot."

A little shiver crept up her spine. "And you stay at pretty nice places."

"I told you, I'm—"

"Loaded. I got that. Then why do you . . ." She dropped back against the counter, focusing on his magnetic eyes, trimmed with long lashes and trained on her. "You're a snake, you know that?"

He grinned. "Yeah. And now I'm your snake." He nestled into her, warm lips going for that spot again. "And I haven't ever met a woman who could make me skip dinner *and* breakfast."

Was it possible the subtle change in him was because of . . . her?

Think again, Sage. He was a liar, a bad boy who did things to her body that were undoubtedly illegal in some states.

And he was so damn sweet he made her heart roll like a tumbleweed in the wind.

"Hey," he said, tipping her face up to his. "Why the big sigh, doll face?"

She narrowed one eye in a silent threat.

"Oh, I mean Sage. Why the big sigh, Sage?"

It was worse when he used her name, it was more intimate. She tried to wriggle out of his grasp, but he had a solid grip. "Because I want to go home."

"Seriously, what's at home that you can't have here?"

"My laptop, for one thing. This is a workday. I have a story due. I have to interview more dancers. I have to talk to people and find out who the hell is leaving his autograph on Snow Bunny posters." She inched out from between him and the sink. "I have to find Ashley McCafferty."

He held up one hand. "Stop. Replace every *I* with *we* and let's go."

She regarded him warily. "Why are you doing this?"

He managed to go from snake to hurt puppy with one quick blink. "How many times do I have to tell you? I like you. Plus, I'm your boyfriend now."

"Is that the only reason?"

His expression changed again, so lightning quick, she almost missed it.

"That's the only reason," he said, pulling her face toward his to kiss her. "Plus, I can make you a brunch so good, you'll never forget me."

As if she could. "Okay. I guess I could use an egg."

"What kind?"

"Uh, scrambled?"

He scowled. "So pedestrian. How about a smoked salmon frittata with dill and just a scooch of sun-dried tomatoes?" He wiggled his eyebrows. "Or I can make you my spicy breakfast sausage, which will guarantee you are mine forever."

He was kidding, wasn't he? He was just a flirtatious, playful, sexy, nurturing . . . body for hire. Wasn't he?

He was still extolling the glories of breakfast sausage when they crossed Charles Street to Sage's apartment building, laden with plastic bags of groceries. Spring was pushing hard for an early arrival and the warmer temperatures brought Bostonians out in droves, crowding the already busy streets of Beacon Hill.

There were so many people milling in front of the cozy brick storefronts that Sage almost didn't notice the woman sitting on the steps into her building. She was hunched over, as though she would roll right into herself and hide if she could. Her hair was caramel colored, falling over her face, her legs folded into her sweatshirt because, despite the weather, she looked cold.

For a moment Sage thought it was a panhandler, but then she leveled a gaze the color of cut topaz directly at Sage.

"Vivian?" Sage slowed her step.

It was Vivian, in a football shirt, old sweatpants, beach shoes, and not a speck of makeup. Still, she was stunning. Sage rushed closer, a million questions running through her head. "What are you doing here?"

Vivian bent over to pick up a fat, white cat, burying her face in the fur as she whispered, "Keisha was murdered."

Sage dropped one of her bags, and tomatoes rolled over the cobblestones.

Looking directly at Sage, she added, "And since I'm pretty sure I'm next, we gotta stop the freak."

Johnny draped his arms around both of the women, guided them up the stairs, then handed Sage his bags.

"Don't move. Either one of you." Before he unlocked her door, he reached under his jacket.

"He has a gun," Vivian whispered. "That's good."

It was? "Vivian, what are you—"

She stopped Sage's question with a tilt of her head

over her shoulder. "Let's get inside first. I'm feeling way vulnerable right now and I don't like it."

A minute later, Johnny widened the door to let them enter. "It's secure in here."

Vivian pointed a finger at him. "You're good," she said, her streetwise tone one of pure admiration. "My muscle never does that."

"Then you should fire him." Johnny took all the bags from Sage and headed to the kitchen.

"No need," Vivian said dryly. "He quit."

"What's going on?" Sage insisted, drawing the other woman into the living room. "What do you mean, Keisha was murdered? What do you mean, you're next?"

With a sigh, Vivian fell onto the sofa and put the cat on the floor. "Hope you're not allergic or anything. I had to run out fast."

"No, it's fine," Sage said, crouching down to pet the animal and look up at Vivian. Tiny lines of stress feathered from the corners of her remarkable eyes, and her skin, always glowing, was a little sallow. Something was taking a toll on her.

"I was the last person to talk to Keisha," Vivian said, then she held up a hand to correct herself. "I was the last person to *hear* from Keisha. She left me a voice mail the night she died."

Hope curled deep inside Sage. Did Vivian have the answers she longed for? "What did she say?" she asked.

Vivian tugged a handbag off her shoulder and pulled it on her lap. "If my battery held out, you can hear it. I saved the message and pretty much have it memorized by now."

Sage thunked to the floor on her butt, staring at her guest. "Why didn't you tell me?"

"She was scared," Johnny said, suddenly appearing from the kitchen and parking his hip on the back of the sofa. He looked down at Vivian. "That's why you hired a bodyguard, right?"

She nodded. "And I gotta wonder how much it took to make that thug disappear at exactly the right time this morning." She pulled out the phone and started pressing buttons, then gave Johnny a questioning glance. "Who are you, by the way?"

"Oh, I'm sorry," Sage said. "This is Johnny, my—"

"Friend," Johnny finished.

Vivian shot her a "yeah, right" raised eyebrow, then lifted her phone. "I put it on speaker. Listen."

"Viv, oh my God, you were so right."

Keisha's voice hit Sage like a slap across the face. She let out a little "oh" but managed to swallow "my God," and listen.

"There is some bad shit goin' down," Keisha continued, her voice taut and strained, as if she were running and talking at the same time. Then, for about ten seconds, there were no words, only her labored breathing and a steady, rhythmic clicking—high heels on concrete, maybe? The eerie sound sent a chill up Sage's spine.

"I don't know what the hell just happened to me . . ." Keisha fought for another breath, then added, "but it was no fucking fantasy, that's for sure."

With each word, she grew more winded. Not just a little panting, but like she was . . . dying. *Asphyxiating.*

"Listen, I'm almost home. Some prick just dumped

me on Boylston and it's the middle of the night and
I . . ."

The recording scratched, thumped, and went silent.

"Is that it?" Sage had risen to her knees and leaned
her whole body toward the phone, as if she could actually reach Keisha.

"No, wait," Vivian said. "It takes a second. She
must have dropped the phone."

A muffled cry filled the speaker and Sage held her
hand up to her mouth to stifle a gasp.

"You fucking whore!" The man's voice was crystal
clear, and loud. "You're gonna get it, whore!"

Whore. *Whores must die.*

Johnny's eyes were narrowed, his attention rapt on
the phone.

"You're gonna get it now," the man warned. "You and
your whore friend, the other one. All of you are whores!"

"Oh my God," Sage whispered, her hand still
pressed hard against her mouth.

"There's more," Vivian said, quieting her with a
hand.

"Hey!" A woman's voice bellowed on the recording.
"Let her go! I said let her go!"

Then the recording went dead. Vivian stabbed the
phone. "That's it."

"Did you give this to the police when they investigated her death?" Johnny asked.

"Of course I played it for them. I found her, you
know. I came over here the next day and—"

"How'd you get in?" he asked.

"I have a key."

"Then why didn't you use it today?"

She scorched him with a look of disgust. "The locks have been changed. You want to hear me out or ask questions, brother?"

Why *was* he interrogating Vivian? "What did the police say about the message?" Sage asked Vivian.

"They said some jerk was probably needling her on the street when she was walking home, and the message actually supported a suicide theory." Vivian dropped back on the sofa, clearly disgusted. "There was no sign of a struggle, she had straight ephedra capsules next to her, and they found a suicide note under her pillow. And no one ever reported an assault or seeing anything in this neighborhood that night."

"Why do you think you're next?" Johnny asked, a little more softly this time.

"Because I'm the other one."

"The other what?"

"The only other black dancer."

Johnny looked dubious. "That's kind of a stretch, don't you think? He could be talking about anyone." He glanced at Sage, and she was certain he was thinking of the "Whores must die" message they'd seen in two different places.

"What about Ashley?" Sage asked.

"She's not black," Vivian said.

"What makes you think this has anything to do with race?" Johnny asked.

Vivian sighed, obviously weighing what she had to say. As if sensing her owner's misery, the cat jumped up onto her lap. "I did the kidnapping thing first," she said, stroking the cat absently. "But something weird happened."

"What?" Sage and Johnny asked at the same time.

"Well, for one thing, it wasn't anything like they promised."

"Like who promised?" Johnny asked.

"Like the girls who'd done it already. Ashley. Rebecca. Briana. They said it was cool, fun, sexy. Not like those other stupid games Glenda makes us play."

"What stupid games?" Sage asked.

"Oh, she makes us do all sorts of bonding nonsense." Vivian waved her hand dismissively. "Dumb shit like writing down your secret insecurities, and trying to identify each other blindfolded using your thumbs. The takemetonite.com thing—that was just another bonding activity so we could all have the same experience, but we weren't allowed to discuss it. That was part of the game. No one could tell anyone what they did, if they had fun, if they screwed the guy who rescued them. But some did. Some, not all."

If they screwed the guy who rescued them. Sage tamped down discomfort. "So what happened when you got kidnapped?" she prodded.

"I got tossed into the back of this big, industrial van, right in the spot where I was supposed to be, in that creepy garage under the Common. I didn't see anybody's face or talk to anyone. They covered my eyes and tied my hands—tight, too, it hurt like hell. Then we drove for a few minutes. The next thing I knew I was in this room. Alone. On a cot or something." She took a deep breath and tunneled her fingers into the cat's long hair, eliciting a mew of pleasure. "Some guy came in the room and I felt a light shine on me, but I was blindfolded. He took off the blindfold and stuck a flashlight in my face so close, I couldn't see anything. Nothing, you know?"

Sage nodded, her heart pounding.

"And then he swears, says like 'fuck this' or something, and yanks the thing back over my eyes and leaves. I'm just sitting there, tied up and blindfolded like I'm in some badass movie. The next thing I know, someone is dragging me out of there and throws me back in the van. And I heard this same guy saying, 'Next time you bring me a mutt, someone's gonna be in big trouble. They're no good to me.'"

"A mutt?" Sage stared at her. "Like a dog?" Vivian was so breathtakingly beautiful that the phrase was just laughable.

"I think he was referring to a mixed breed," she said quietly. "Anyway, next thing I know, the van doors open and I'm back in the garage, near my car. Kidnapping over."

"Did you talk to anyone about this? Did you tell Glenda about it, even? Or Keisha?"

"Keisha," she said softly. "I was mad. Insulted and just mad about the mutt comment. I thought it was racist and she did, too. So, she decided . . ." She closed her eyes. "*We* decided that she should sign up, too, and see what happened to her."

For a moment, no one spoke. They knew what had happened to her. Keisha had died.

"So, after she . . . Well, I got a bodyguard," Vivian said. "Because I got freaked out. And today, he disappeared and that goddamn van came up and down my street and somebody went into my house."

"Where were you?" Sage asked.

"Hiding in my garage. Then I came here, because you're the only person I know who loved Keisha like I did."

That was true. But Keisha had never socialized with them together. She kept them separate and Sage never knew why.

Without a word, Johnny left the room. Sage decided to use the opportunity to talk privately. "Vivian, do you think it's possible Keisha had an abortion?"

Vivian looked up from the cat. "Well, then, that's the other thing."

"What other thing?"

"She was pregnant."

Blood drained from Sage's head. "She was? Why wouldn't she tell me?"

Vivian closed her eyes. "It was over, but she wasn't sure what to do."

"What was over?"

"Her affair with LeTroy Burgess."

Sage recognized the name of the high-profile Blizzard instantly. "I thought they were just good friends. I know Keisha thought he was all that, but he's happily married."

"He's *married*," Vivian corrected. "I don't know if 'happy' plays into that. And if it weren't for that message she left, I would have directed the police to talk to that sorry excuse for a tree with root rot."

"Do you think he killed her?"

She lifted one shoulder. "The brother is a madman, and if Keisha went public, there goes half his eight mil' a year to the wife and kid."

Keisha had had an affair with *LeTroy*? Could he be the one warning her with messages? Was he afraid Sage would take that story public? Or was she looking too hard for nefarious motivations where there were none? "Maybe he forced her to have an abortion and she was so miserable about it that she killed herself?"

"I don't know. But out of respect for her, I've kept the information to myself. Why ruin her reputation? She's dead and I think somebody killed her, and somebody might do it again."

"You sure about that?" Johnny entered the room, something bright in his hand. Sage recognized the neon colors of the sticky-backed index cards. " 'Cause here are some suicide notes. A lot of them."

Vivian sat up straight and stared at the cards he held. "That's no suicide note, bro. That's from the game of *Exposure*." She air quoted for emphasis, and injected plenty of disgust into the word. "Which is Glenda's idea of twenty women sitting in a room giving each other ammunition for Olympic-quality backstabbing." She glanced at Sage. "We all make that shit up to keep Glenda happy. Is *that* what the police called a suicide note?"

"Yes," she said. "They showed me the one they found that night. It said, 'Sometimes I think I'll never be good enough.' Didn't they show you, when they interviewed you?"

"After I talked to them, I took about a month's worth of sedatives," Vivian admitted with a sigh. "You may recall I didn't make the memorial service."

"We should tell Detective Cervaris about this game," she said to Johnny. "And the voice mail."

"Yeah. I just put a call into him. And I got a good friend who's a reliable bodyguard for you, Vivian. He'll be here this afternoon. Now, I'm going to make some breakfast."

He went into the kitchen and Vivian's eyes widened in surprise. "Ain't he a handy tool to have around?"

"Yeah," Sage said, standing slowly and walking to the stack of cards Johnny had set on the back of the sofa. "He's handy, all right."

"Seriously sweet on the eyes, comes equipped with a sidearm, and knows his way around a kitchen. Where'd you find that man?"

She picked up the top card, debating how to answer. "He found me, actually."

"You must have yourself a guardian angel, sister."

"Mmm." Sage barely heard the comment, her focus shifted to the words Keisha had written. "Are you sure everything she wrote on these cards was a lie?" she asked Vivian.

"Trust me, those Bunnies are wicked competitive," Vivian said. "No one is stupid enough to reveal their insecurities to someone who could use that knowledge against you. Every single statement was made up."

"Really?" Sage handed the card to Vivian and watched her read it. "Even this one?"

Vivian Masters is a pathological liar.

CHAPTER
Sixteen

"Tits out, Briana! And would it kill you to kick above your waist for a change?"

Briana arched her back, bit her lip, and kicked so high her knee touched her nose.

"Better. Taylor! Did you forget you have arms? Or are those wings flopping like a seagull?"

Taylor dutifully locked her elbows and pointed her fingertips, but something else caught Glenda's eye in the back row. Pamela Brayden's pained expression as she pressed her fingers into her belly. Glenda marched through the formation and stopped in front of the normally spunky young woman, debating exactly how to confirm what she already knew. Some questions were simply more effective than others.

"Have you looked at yourself in the mirror today, Miss Brayden?"

Pamela met Glenda's disapproving look with one laced with intimidation. "Is there a problem, Ms. Hewitt?"

"Cat-ravaged hair on your head, grocery bags under your eyes, and your second chin is threatening to hit your cleavage, which could use a little more support today. How do you think that's going to play on national television tomorrow?"

"I just feel lousy, okay? I have a stomach virus or something."

"A stomach virus?" Glenda asked sharply.

"Or something." Pam leaned forward and lowered her voice. "I know you hate this as an excuse, but I'm totally getting my period."

"Yes, you are," Glenda said quickly. "By my calculations, you're due tomorrow."

Out of the corner of her eye, she caught a look passing between two of the girls, accompanied by an eye roll.

"Go ahead and roll your eyes, Miss Doyle. But it is my job to know everything about every one of you, including when you bleed. I also know that you're trying to hide that strained ankle tendon and that you changed the color of self-tanner you use. It is my business to know everything about every *body* in this room."

She turned back to Pamela. "See me after practice and I'll give you something for the symptoms. You can't be doubled over in pain and running off the court to change your tampon tomorrow night." She zipped to the back of the group. "All right now, ladies, into the H formation. Let's start 'I Want You to Want Me.' " Her double clap was interrupted by a question from the front.

"Who do you want in the middle, Glenda?"

"Vivian."

"She's not here."

She whipped her head in the direction of Vivian's warm-up spot. "Where is she?"

The daytime practices were not mandatory, of course, only evenings. But this was the start of play-offs and the Blizzard would be on ESPN tomorrow night.

So where was she? A pinch of worry nipped at her gut. "Julia, you take the center of the H for the first ten run-throughs."

A low groan traveled over the room.

"One more sound and you'll do twenty." She clapped again and the girls scurried into position. "Cue the music!" she called to her assistant. When the bass started, and a rocker screamed "I want you . . ." Glenda pushed the studio doors open just as the girls shouted a rigidly unified, "To want *me*!" in response.

Would he want to try Vivian again? Behind her back? Was he getting that desperate? There was no telling what he'd do lately. He had taken Ashley on his own with no warning, leaving Glenda to clean up his dirty work when the girl got too curious. Sighing, she pushed open the door to the office next to hers. It was empty. So where was Julian?

She dug out her cell phone, dialed, and he answered on the first ring. "Yes, Glen."

"Where are you?" she asked.

"I'm very busy. What do you want?"

His voice, even gruff and impatient, always made her reel. He was godlike to her. What he could do, the magic he could work, never ceased to amaze her. At first, she'd just been enamored of his talent. Then, he was the answer to her prayers. But now, her admiration had moved to something more difficult to control. And, God, she hated losing control. "Do you happen to know where Vivian Masters is?"

"The mulatto?" he snorted. "Why would I care?"

"I thought maybe you got . . . desperate."

"No, Glen. I'm not that desperate. But while I have you on the phone, I've been thinking you could help me with something."

Anything. She'd do anything. "Name it."

"Sage Valentine."

"The writer? Keisha's roommate?" The heat of jealousy burned again. What did he see in that girl?

"I think she's perfect."

So he had seen her somewhere. When? Where? "I think you'll be very disappointed," she said.

"I'll be the judge of that."

"She's not what you're looking for, I assure you. She has none of the qualifications and . . ." Glenda dug for something, anything. "I don't think she's pure."

"Her imperfections, in this case, make her more attractive to me," he said. "And you have the ideal opportunity with that story she's doing. Get her."

"I'll have to get her ready. It could take a little time."

"Do it quickly—unless you prefer I use someone else. You're not the only game in town, you know. And I know you need the money, Glen. I understand your time is running out."

She gripped the phone. She hated when he reminded her of why they'd first started this. "This goes beyond money now. I believe in you. You know that."

"Still, money buys Emily time, doesn't it?"

Anger rocked her when he used her daughter's name. He always had to have the power in this relationship. "I'll get Sage. In the meantime, do you need someone else? Tomorrow night after the game?"

He cleared his throat, thinking. "That would be good. And don't tell me who. I want to guess who it will be while I watch."

"Of course."

As soon as she hung up, she went to Julian's computer and logged on. In a flash, she entered www.takemetonite.com. She bypassed the fake first screen, entered the password he'd taught her and a white square box flashed a warning and asked for another code.

This is where it got tricky. She entered her code, holding her breath until the firewall came down. In ten seconds, it fell, and Glenda was logged in and able to change anything on anyone's itinerary page. She scanned the database of names, zeroing in on one of her girls. So many of them were signed up. Some got a real kidnapping, enough to seed the team with the idea. And some . . . didn't.

Like Susannah Gray. She closed her eyes to think about where the girl was in the cycle. Yep. Perfect. And she had the requisite blond hair, blue eyes, excellent figure, sharp wit, and, oh-so-important to him, perfect teeth.

She typed in a few more passwords and, like magic, was able to change the information on a page that only Susannah Gray would see when she logged in. At takemetonite.com, they would simply get a message that Ms. Gray had canceled her appointment.

Before she logged out, she switched to another itinerary page. Sage Valentine. There was no change on her page, no follow-up to that last mess up, no date for another appointment. Why did he want her so much? What was so special about her?

Irritation itched her. She wanted her girls, and only her girls, to be his choice.

When she returned to the rehearsal studio, they were on the last riff of "I Want You to Want Me." On the far right, Susannah Gray beamed her flawless smile. When the music stopped she was still smiling, pleased with her performance.

"Susannah!" Glenda called.

She snapped to attention, the joy disappearing from her face. "Yes, ma'am?"

"I need to see you in my office. It's urgent."

She saw the girl flash a worried glance to one of her friends, then she turned to Glenda, her smile in full force, if a bit strained. "Of course, Ms. Hewitt."

Susannah should do the trick nicely until she could get Sage Valentine. The problem was, Sage couldn't be controlled the way her girls could. If anything went wrong . . .

There'd be another resident at the bottom of the Charles River.

"Psst. C'mere. I got something for you."

The fussy feline waltzed across the kitchen with her nose lifted in disdain.

"Don't give me that 'tude, puss. You want what I got and you want it bad."

Taz inched toward the piece of sausage Johnny balanced on his fingertip. She sniffed, then allowed a glimmer of interest in her pretty green eyes.

"Yeah, that's right. Homemade. No Jimmy Deans for my girls."

He heard Sage's soft laugh before she appeared in the kitchen doorway. He looked up from his crouched position and, as he did, the cat snapped the food with a swift tongue, then purred.

"You like to have women eating out of your hand, don't you?" Sage's smile was as warm and real as the night before.

"Of course I do," he said, standing to brush the bits of food from his hands into the sink. He had no right playing games with Lucy's niece. And now that Vivian Masters had stirred things up with her creepy message, he should concentrate on the job at hand. Not the temptation to turn up the heat again.

"How's she doin' back there?" he asked.

Sage shrugged. "She's resting on my bed. The poster upset her, and so did that card claiming she's a liar. She says it was Keisha's idea of a joke."

"What do you think?"

"I think," she said, picking up a sponge and wiping a counter he'd already cleaned, "that somebody should stay with her—"

"I told you, I got that covered."

In spades, actually. His phone call had landed him a surprise chat with Dan Gallagher, who had just arrived from Sydney with the legendary Australian spook-turned-Bullet Catcher, Adrien Fletcher, who'd come to the States for some special training.

Johnny hadn't talked to Lucy directly—a blessing, considering what he had to say to her—but he'd briefed Dan, and in a matter of minutes he had Lucy's approval to send in another bodyguard. Dan was coming to Boston, too. Johnny knew how close Dan and Lucy were; she was probably sending him in to check on her niece.

"So, this friend of yours who's going to protect Vivian. Is he another rescuer?"

"No, just some gym rats I met when I first moved here."

"Was that a plural? How many rats are coming over?"

"A couple." At her surprised look, he shrugged. "Hey. I called in the cavalry, babe."

She seemed to accept that, going over to her computer. With a sigh, she carried it to the dining room, a quiet *ding* letting him know she'd turned it on.

He followed her out there—and Taz followed him—and sat across from her. "You going to work now?"

"I'm going to organize my thoughts," she said. "I'm going to make a list of people involved. I'm going to google all the dancers who I'm allowed to interview and get some background on them before I set up meetings, then I'm going to outline all my questions. So yes," she said, tapping a few keys. "This is work." She hit another one. "You ought to try it sometime."

He slapped a hand over his heart. "Ouch."

She raised her eyebrows and half smiled. "Truth hurts, big guy."

He propped both elbows on the table and dropped his chin on his knuckles, staring at her, seeking a genetic link to Lucy, but she was so fair and different. She had high cheekbones, but not the chiseled, sharp angles that made Lucy's face so distinctive. Sage's were more . . . lovely, more feminine. And though her hair was salon-streaked blond, the underlying shades were light brown, nothing like the raven black of his boss's. Black except for the mysterious white streak down the front. For a moment, he wondered if Sage knew what trauma in Lucy's life had caused the much-talked-about streak.

She looked up at him, giving him a perfect shot of the tilt in her eyes, which could be a hint of Pacific Islands, but the slant wasn't as dramatic as Lucy's.

"Do you mind not scrutinizing me while I work?" she asked.

"Can't help it. You're beautiful."

Her expression changed to a smile. "You're nuts."

"What are you, anyway?" he asked. "Irish? English? German?"

"I'm a mix of a bunch of stuff. My father has English and Scottish and maybe some Scandinavian on his great-grandmother's side, but no one has ever done his tree." She typed some more, and frowned, reading. "My mother's father was French, and her mother was . . ." She paused, clicked, then shook her head a little. "Micronesian."

Bingo.

"Whoa. Exotic."

"I guess. I've never been there. My grandmother was born in the middle of the Pacific a million miles from nowhere."

Her grandmother had been born in Pohnpei and he knew exactly where it was; Lucy had a detailed map of the little island on her library wall. "Don't you want to go and meet your island relatives?"

She peered over the laptop. "I think we covered how I feel about my relatives."

Careful, Johnny boy. Dangerous territory ahead. "That's right, your aunt." He couldn't help it. He had to say it. "Lucy Sharpe."

She nodded absently, rubbing her chin, her focus intent on the screen. "Uh-huh." She clicked some more, her eyes narrowing with interest as she read.

"So is she your mother's older or younger sister?" Had to be younger.

"Much younger. She was eleven when I was born. My mother was nineteen."

Yep, the math worked. There was no way he could deny it: Lucy had sent him on a private assignment and she needed his blind loyalty to make it happen. All the Bullet Catchers were loyal, but he was . . . indebted. And Lucy knew that meant he would do this without asking questions, and would never reveal to the principal who was behind her protection.

Ms. Machiavelli does her thang.

But why the secrecy? If Sage found out, what was the worst that could happen? Couldn't she understand that her aunt had her best interests in mind, forgive him, have wildly awesome sex with him a few hundred times to thank him. . . .

No, that was the *best* that could happen. Bullet Catchers were trained to figure out the absolute worst possible scenario, and plan on it. So . . . she'd find out the truth, hate him forever, and kick his ass on the street without a kiss goodbye.

No, that was still optimistic.

The worst that could happen was . . . she'd find out the truth, forgive him, admit she was crazy about him, have wildly awesome sex to thank him, and then she'd find out the *real* truth about him.

That he was Achilles Cardinale's nephew, who had spent way too many years on the streets of New York City as a wiseguy. And then, she'd find out about Bella.

His heart took a dive down to his shoes. *That* would be the worst case scenario.

She clicked again. "You're really making me uncomfortable, staring like that."

"Forget I'm here."

"Like you can be ignored."

He chuckled. "Then put your computer away and talk to me."

"No." She shifted in her seat and read something. Twice. Three times. Then she tilted the screen down to see over it. "I appreciate your quest to be my boyfriend and all, but am I ever going to get a night free? Maybe to go out to a bar with my friends or . . . or go see a movie?"

He'd watch her from across the bar, from the last row of the theater. "Sure, if you really want to."

"I might." She tapped a few keys and he heard the little sound of a bookmark being set. "Sometime. Now, who should we google first?"

His phone beeped the melody of "Danny Boy." "Cavalry's here," he said. "I'll go show them where to park." Dan probably had a car and driver, but he wanted to give them a final briefing. Johnny stood and pushed back his chair. "Sage?"

She looked up, obviously surprised he'd used her given name.

"Don't leave this apartment and don't let anyone in. Do you understand?"

She saluted. "Yes, sir."

"I'm serious. And don't let her leave." He pointed to the bedroom.

"Okay."

He started toward the door, grabbing his jacket from the chair.

"Johnny?"

He turned to find her staring at him.

"You'd actually make a helluva good boyfriend."

"You think?" He grinned. "Even if I don't work?"

She tilted her head to the side. "I shouldn't have made that crack."

"No sweat, sugar."

She still looked at him as he took one more step toward the door, no smile now. Just all that intensity directed at him. The way it had been the night before. And the way it would be tonight.

"What is it?" he asked.

"I like you," she admitted. "That's all."

His return smile was tight, like the band that had just squeezed his chest. "That's enough." Too much, actually. He blew her a kiss. "More on that later, babe."

He purposely didn't call her Sage. He purposely didn't let his gut flip over at her heartfelt admission. He purposely didn't even let himself think about the fact that he liked her, too. A lot.

Because that took worst case scenario to a whole new level.

As soon as Johnny left, Sage returned to the bookmarked page at www.takemetonite.com. They'd invited her back for another kidnapping, this one on the house. Did Johnny know that? Maybe he hadn't quit. Maybe he got fired and they were just making it up to his customers.

If Vivian was telling the truth, there was a connection between the kidnapping and Keisha's death. Something she still couldn't quite put her finger on kept her from sharing this information with Johnny. Her e-mail beeped with a new message from ghewitt@nesnowbunnies.com.

Glenda was e-mailing her? She opened it quickly.

Would like to expedite your story with some behind-the-scenes access to the girls. Can you come to tomorrow night's game? Arrive early, I'll take you into the locker room. Two tickets at Will Call. (Sorry, no men allowed in the locker room.)

Sage didn't reply right away. She clicked back to the search engine and typed in "LeTroy Burgess," and got back a long list of press coverage and fan sites. Lots of biographical material about his stellar high-school basketball career, his draft into the NBA, his various trades, including the one to the start-up New England Blizzard. Scrolling through, she opened and closed a dozen websites until she found pictures of LeTroy and Desirée Burgess, and their two-year-old daughter, Ava Blue. According to the media, LeTroy had a happy life, a good marriage, a rock-solid career, and a mountain of money.

Why would he have an affair with Keisha? Why would *she*?

Sage had to talk to LeTroy. She returned to Glenda's e-mail and hit Reply, then took a moment to consider how to ask for what she wanted.

> *Thank you, Glenda. I'll be there. Would love to chat with some of the dancers before the game. My editor has asked to add some player quotes. Think I could get a postinterview game? LeTroy Burgess would sell the most magazines—any chance? Thanks, Sage*

The response was almost instantaneous:

> *No interviews with players during play-offs. Will look into something at a later date. G*

She was still considering detours around this roadblock when the front door opened and Johnny peeked in.

"Brace yourself, baby doll. My backup's here." He stepped in, followed by two men who pretty much sucked out whatever air Johnny had left in the room.

"Hi." Green eyes danced, a lock of burnished-gold hair fell, and well over six feet of muscle and charm beamed at her. "I'm Dan Gallagher."

Behind him, another man, broader and even more imposing, stepped in. He shook his head like a lion, throwing off waves of long, tawny hair, revealing a tiny gold hoop glinting in his ear. "G'day, Sage." The Australian accent was as thick as his mane, and just as attractive. "Adrien Fletcher."

She closed the laptop and stood. These were gym rats? Maybe she should quit running and start lifting.

"Hi," she greeted them. "Nice of you guys to come over."

"I can't stay," Dan said. "I just wanted to meet you."

"Oh, well, hello." She glanced at Johnny, who rolled his eyes.

"He's nosy like that," Johnny said, shrugging out of his leather jacket. "Fletch is going to hang with Vivian. He'll take her home when she's ready."

Dan warmed her with another heartbreaking smile that revealed the tiniest overlap of his front teeth. "So you're Sage Valentine."

"In the flesh."

"He's given to hyperbole, our Johnny boy." Dan dropped onto the sofa, crossed his long legs, and draped his arms over the back. "But in this case he didn't exaggerate. You are stunning."

She rolled her eyes, but couldn't fight a grin. "Thank you."

Johnny winked at her. "Nothing this man says is to be taken seriously," he warned. "He's a gifted liar."

Dan just laughed, giving her a sense that the two knew each other very well. Didn't Johnny say he'd just moved to Boston? This friendship had subtle overtones of longevity. The other man had moved to the bay window and pushed the curtain aside for a slow, thorough scan of Chestnut and Charles streets.

"Nice place," he said. "Bet it costs the earth to live here."

"It's not cheap," she conceded. "Where are you from?"

"Canberra." He looked over his shoulder, a dimpled smile turning him from gruff to gorgeous. "Ever been down?"

She shook her head. "I'd love to go, though. How long have you lived here?"

"Not that long," he said, turning away from the window, but the light silhouetted his substantial breadth. She normally didn't like facial hair, but on him, the triangular tuft under his lip was perfect. As was the earring, and the windblown hair.

"Is the bar from *Cheers* near here?" he asked, his dimples making another appeareance. "I loved that show."

"It's right down on Beacon, just a few blocks from here."

"It's a tourist trap, Fletch," Dan said.

A million reporter's questions screamed in Sage's

head, starting with how long had they known Johnny. But he suddenly entered the living room and held up a very small gun.

"Whatever happened to pom-poms for cheerleaders?"

"Where did you find that?" Sage asked.

"In Vivian's handbag."

Her jaw dropped. "You went through her bag?"

"And found a gun. Don't question my process, honey." He turned it in his hand. "One bullet's missing."

"Maybe her bodyguard didn't take a buyout," Dan said. "Maybe he took a bullet."

Sage gasped in a little breath, and the Australian man stepped forward and took the gun out of Johnny's hand, smelled the tip and examined it. "Fairly recently, I'd say." He spun the weapon like it was a toy. "Cute li'l thing, isn't it?"

"Not very effective, though," Johnny said. "I doubt it could do much damage."

"It damaged the hell out of my garage-door lock and saved my freaking life." Vivian bounded into the room, wearing only a T-shirt that barely skimmed her endless thighs. Her long hair was tossled, her golden eyes blazing as she grabbed for her gun. "Give it."

Fletch whipped it right out of her reach. "Sorry, pet. You need a license to carry this bit o' lead."

"I've got one, and who the hell are you—Crocodile Dundee?"

Dan coughed a laugh.

"I'm Fletch." He slipped the gun into the pocket of his trousers and extended a hand toward Vivian. "Evidently I won the lotto, eh?"

She glanced sideways at Sage. "You know these guys?"

"I do," Johnny said, stepping forward. "Adrien Fletcher, meet Vivian Masters. And that," he indicated the sofa with a nod of his head, "is Dan Gallagher. You can trust these men with your life."

"I need two?"

Dan stood. "Regretfully, I just stopped by to meet Johnny's new friends. Believe me, you are in excellent hands with Dundee here." He gave her a sweet smile that almost covered the quick trip his eyes took over her.

Vivian put her hands on her hips and swiped them all with a tough look. "Listen, I'm not lying about anything. Keep the gun if you want; it just makes me nervous. But don't second-guess what's going on here. I need protection." She checked out Fletch's broad torso. "You'll do. And let's go soon, because I've already missed practice today and I have to dance on national TV tomorrow. Got it?"

Fletch turned stone serious. "I'll die before you do, sheila. Now, you want to dress or go like that?"

Vivian stared him down, then pivoted like the dancer she was and headed back down the hall. "Follow me," she called. "I want you to know what you're getting into, so you better see something."

He notched up a brow as if he weren't at all used to being told what to do, but then followed her. To see the poster, Sage assumed.

A low digital tone sounded, prompting Dan to check the readout on his cell phone.

"I'm real sorry I can't stick around for the show, but my ride's here." He walked over to Sage, put one hand on her shoulder, and tipped her chin toward him, looking at her like . . . well, like Johnny had, a few minutes earlier. Far too closely. "You be careful, Sage Valentine." Then he kissed her forehead.

As he headed to the door, Johnny followed. "I'll be right back, Sage."

When the door shut, Sage just stared at it. Why had that man kissed her? They'd never met before, yet he almost seemed to know her. She touched her forehead, unable to shake the feeling that Dan Gallagher was trying to tell her something.

Curious, she went to the window. Across the street was a dark sedan with black windows, parked but running. In a moment Johnny and Dan approached it, and Dan opened the passenger door and climbed in. Johnny leaned on the side of the car, talking into the window, laughing once, then looking back at her apartment.

Sage ducked behind the curtain, not wanting to get caught. But she couldn't resist another peek. That was no ordinary sedan. That was a Town Car, chauffeur driven.

What the hell kind of gym did these rats crawl out of?

CHAPTER
Seventeen

The place was like a meat market. Thighs, hips, buttocks, waists, and oh so many sets of perfect, round, medically manufactured breasts. The smell of hair spray, self-tanning cream, and deodorant hung in the dressing-room air, as thick as the undercurrent of tension and excitement. High female voices rose, punctuated by laughter and the occasional shriek of frustration or coo of delight.

"I'm sorry." Sage leaned forward to hear what the soft-spoken Pamela had just said. "Did you say three times a week?"

Pam nodded. And smiled. She did that a lot, revealing teeth like a row of Chiclets chewing gum. "Every week. No matter what. It's a full-time . . ." The rest was garbled by the sudden outburst of two hair dryers.

"Uh, do you think we could step outside, Pam?" Sage asked.

Pam glanced to her left, where Glenda Hewitt appeared to be reading a music list but was clearly taking in every word of the conversation. Glenda immediately held out a hand. "Stay here, Pam. No one is allowed to leave the dressing area."

With a little shrug, Pam moved closer to Sage. "I'm sorry, I can't yell. I'm saving my voice for the game."

"I understand," Sage assured her, wishing she had a place to set down the "complimentary energy drink" Glenda had given her the minute she arrived. But there were no more pertinent questions. Who cared how many times these girls danced a week or how many lessons they took or what commercials they were on? Pam wasn't going to answer the questions Sage really wanted to ask; certainly not with Hawkeye two feet away.

"Have you seen Ashley McCafferty?" Sage asked. "I'd really like to talk to her."

That got Glenda's attention. "She's gone to see her family in Indiana," Glenda said. "She left on Thursday morning. I had a car pick her up and take her to the airport."

Pickup at 8:45. Sage could still see the words on Ashley's calendar.

"Why would she leave before the basketball season is over?" Sage asked Glenda.

"She'd been moved to alternate status," Glenda explained. "She wasn't dancing up to par."

Pamela's expression of sympathy confirmed that. "It's tough," she said. "Very competitive."

Sage glanced over Pamela's shoulder and caught Vivian's eyes in a long vanity mirror trimmed with classic dressing-room makeup lights. Sage sent a silent "please, help" to Vivian, who tilted her head to her right, indicating a young woman with long dark hair who sat next to her. Sage recognized Claudia Larkin immediately. Vivian made a tiny gesture as though she were typing.

Claudia must have done the takemetonite.com kidnapping. Could Sage get to her without Glenda Hewitt following and controlling the interview?

Another hair dryer kicked in and a woman approached Glenda. Seizing the opportunity, Sage said to Pamela, "Could you excuse me a quick sec?"

Without waiting for a response, she dodged a couple of half-dressed women and slipped across the dressing room. She didn't speak to Vivian, but crouched down next to Claudia, setting her plastic cup on the vanity. Claudia gave Sage a very off-balance look, her left eye fluffy with fake lashes, her right eye unadorned.

"Claudia, I'm Sage Valentine."

Claudia nodded, and glanced over her shoulder to where Glenda was still in conversation with another dancer. "Sorry, I'm not on the list. I can't talk to the media."

"And why is that, do you think?" Sage asked.

"Could be a million reasons. Because I didn't shake my ass hard enough against the Miami Heat? Because I am not one of Glenda's chosen few? Because I wore the wrong eye shadow for the last game? Who the hell knows why some of us get selected for extra benes and some don't."

"Maybe it's because you participated in a takemetonite.com kidnapping. You know, no one on my list has done it. I'd like to talk to you about it. Off the record, if you prefer."

Her eyes shuddered and the fake lash lifted at the corner. Claudia turned to the mirror, swearing softly.

Sage touched Claudia's wrist. "What happened when you were kidnapped?"

In the mirror, Claudia checked Glenda's position again. God, they were all so terrified of the woman. What power did she really have over them? "Nothing."

"Nothing? You didn't have a thrill? A scare? A rescue? A good time?"

Claudia ripped the lash off in frustration and tossed it onto the vanity before she grabbed a tiny tube of glue. "I don't remember."

"You don't remember anything?"

She rolled her eyes. "There might have been some drugs involved, you know? This, I'm sure, is why I'm not on the short list for a *Boston Living* interview." She squeezed a line of glue onto the lash and gave Sage a fake smile. "Ask Briana. She said it was like the Second Coming. And Third. Now, if you don't go away, I'll be the only one out there with invisible eyes."

"What *do* you remember?" Sage prodded. "The car? The man who kidnapped you?"

She dropped her hands to the table. "I know why you're doing this. You want to know what happened to Keisha. I know she was your roommate and she was scheduled the night she died. Right?"

"Right." Sage squeezed her hand. "Please help me."

"Then you need to talk to one person." Claudia

took one last look over her shoulder and whispered, "Shit, here she comes."

"Who, Claudia?" Sage begged. "Who?"

"Her lover," she said in a low whisper. Then she started blinking wildly, fluttering the lash in front of her eye. "Sorry, Sage," she said loudly. "I can't talk to you now. Glenda, are any of the makeup artists free to help me with these lashes? The new ones don't work nearly as well as what we had before."

"They're busy now, Claudia. Some of us have to do without professional assistance." Blue eyes glared at Sage. "Bring your drink, dear; I have your next interview lined up."

If it wasn't LeTroy Burgess, she didn't want it. How could she get to him? Here, tonight? Once he disappeared behind some gated house, she'd never get to him. She glanced at Vivian, who carefully applied lip liner and didn't acknowledge Sage.

"Glenda," Sage said, standing up. "I absolutely have to talk to one of the players after the game tonight. If you can't help me, I'm going to wait outside their locker room and use my press pass to get an interview." She wouldn't like that, Sage hoped. She might want control, which could give Sage access.

Glenda frowned with concern. "I didn't know it was that important, dear. Who do you want to talk to?"

"LeTroy."

"Of course you do." Glenda's lips rose in a gentle smile. "He's one of my favorites and so delightful with the media. I can arrange that for you."

She could?

"With one caveat. No photography. He has very strict limits in his contract."

"Fine. Great. When and where?"

"Find me as soon as the final buzzer sounds and you will have a few minutes alone with him after the game. Will that be enough?"

"Perfect. We'll find you, where, right here?"

"Not *we*, dear." She underscored that with a finger pointed directly at Sage. "You. Alone. Don't bring your starstruck boyfriend."

"He's not—"

"Alone." Glenda masked the sharp tone with a fake smile, taking her cup and handing it to her. "Now you better let these girls concentrate on doing what they do best: being dazzling and breaking hearts and firing up our fans."

In the mirror, over Glenda's shoulder, she saw Vivian roll her eyes.

Glenda grasped Sage's arm and maneuvered her toward the door. "I'll see you after the game." They passed Pamela, who still wore her smile, and sipped water.

"Did you take two of them?" Glenda asked her.

Pamela nodded and sipped again.

"Good girl, you'll feel better in no time." Glenda continued whisking Sage toward the door, past bodies and booties. "Susannah!" she called to one of the girls shimmying into hot pants. "Good luck tonight, dear! My money's on you!"

The young woman beamed back. "I'm excited and nervous, Glenda. Thank you!"

Could Sage have misjudged the tough-talking

choreographer? Here, in her element, with her girls, she seemed . . . almost soft. Caring. And cooperative.

"Remember now, Sage," Glenda said as she opened the door to a long hallway leading to the arena. "Meet me outside, at that door." She pointed to another exit, on the opposite side of the hallway where she and Johnny had waited the other night. That must be the secret exit for the players who don't want to be mobbed by fans. "I'll be sure you talk to LeTroy, if you're alone."

Johnny wouldn't like it, but that's the way it was going to be. Hell, he had plenty of secrets of his own. She wasn't going to feel the least bit guilty about ditching him after the game. She sensed that she was getting closer to an answer, and she'd do whatever it took. This time, it might take deception.

"It's good to be undercover again."

Dan laughed softly, propping his sneakered feet on the back of the empty arena chair in front of him. "Spoken like a true spook."

"No, seriously." Lucy Sharpe matched his position, placing her bright pink Skechers next to his high-end size 12 Nikes. She'd never owned a pair of pink shoes, which made the cover—New England basketball fans stuck in the nosebleed section—all the more satisfying. Kind of like the time she had to pretend to be a geisha to steal some military secrets from a Japanese diplomat. "I miss the field, sometimes."

"Not enough to join us," he said dryly. "Which is too bad, since we'd make an awesome team, Juice."

She smiled. He'd dubbed her Juicy Miss Lucy when he first came to work for her and, unfortunately, it stuck. Few other Bullet Catchers had the nerve to call her that or any of their other pet names, like Ms. Machiavelli, to her face. But Dan had nerve. Steely nerves, lightning reflexes, and a sense of humor that could make even the hardest heart laugh. No matter how much pain it had endured.

Lucy trained her eyes on the two men who stood a few feet from courtside. They talked like casual friends, but she could see them casing the arena. Johnny said something that made Fletch chuckle, but Lucy noticed that the bulky Aussie never stopped checking out the crowd.

"Fletch wasn't happy about leaving Australia for training," Lucy mused. "But I think he likes this unexpected action in the field."

"Who wouldn't? Wait until you see this unexpected action." At Lucy's sideways glance, he added, "Not that it matters, but she is ridiculously hot."

"She's not technically an assignment," Lucy corrected. "File this one under favors."

Dan leaned much closer than any other employee would dare get to her. "File this one under Juicy's pet projects."

She brushed back a strand of her blond, shoulder-length wig. "She's family, Dan."

"Vivian Masters? She's not."

Lucy met those appealing eyes that always seemed to see through her. "Sage Valentine is."

"How long you gonna keep Johnny boy here?" he

asked. "I could use him on the detail in Mexico City next week. Then Alex heads back to Cuba for a while, and I thought Johnny could pick up the work he and Jazz are doing in Miami. Chase is—"

"The last time I checked, I ran this company." She made no effort to soften her tone or the look she gave him. Blond wig, tinted shades, and pink sneakers aside, she was still the sole proprietor of the Bullet Catchers. Dan was the specialist she trusted most, but not her partner. She would never have a partner, in work or in life. Not again.

He gave her a half nod, tempered by a glint in his grass-green eyes. "I'm just asking, ma'am. You run the company, you make the assignments, you call the shots."

"And you rein me in when I let family ties threaten to bind the organization."

He put a familiar, warm hand over hers. "I suspect the financial viability of the Bullet Catchers is not in any danger of hitting red for a long, long time."

"You would be quite correct." The organization was wildly profitable.

"So, you're entitled to use the resources to help anyone you want."

She was. Part of her resented the fact that anyone, especially one of her employees, felt it necessary to tell her that. The other part, the soft part that had laughed for the first time in a long while the day she met Dan Gallagher, wanted to lay her head on his shoulder and thank him for all his support. But that was her problem. If he ever had any inkling that she had moments of weakness like that, she might lose the best security specialist she had.

"There she is," she said, lowering her feet to the floor, her full attention shifting to the silky blond hair and confident gait of Lydia's only child. She entered the arena at the far end, a long way from Johnny and Fletch. "God, she's pretty." She barely realized that she'd whispered the words, or that Dan had threaded his fingers through hers.

"She is," he agreed. "Spunky and smart and . . ."

"And what?"

"Quite taken with her new boyfriend."

Lucy processed that. "Well, Johnny's good, Dan. Initiating a romance made perfect sense so that he could stick around and keep her out of trouble." If it went beyond the casual kiss, she'd chalk that up to Johnny maintaining his cover. It was too important to protect Sage while she dug around for answers. They might be estranged for all the wrong reasons, but Lucy loved that girl like she was her own child.

Sage had slowed her step, smiled and waved at someone in the stands.

"Johnny's pissed at you for not telling him who she is, Lucy," Dan said softly.

It wasn't the first time she'd incurred the wrath of a Bullet Catcher. "It'll pass. He understands family obligations."

Dan snorted. "Better than anyone. He's also just as taken with her."

"He's under cover," she volleyed back. "He knows the job. No one gets involved with the principal."

"Tell that to Alex and Max."

But the women they had protected and fallen in love with were not her niece. "Different situations."

"How's that?"

"*Who's* that, is what I want to know." She zeroed in on the older man leaving his seat to greet Sage with a warm hug.

Dan had his cell phone out in under a second, almost as fast as he drew a gun. He hit one button and she saw Johnny flip his own phone instantly.

"You got a visual on her?" Dan asked.

Johnny didn't appear to be looking at Sage, but Lucy knew he was.

"Who's the bald guy?" Dan listened for a minute, then whispered to Lucy, "The doctor he asked you to check out, Garron."

The doctor had checked out clean. But his hand lingered on Sage's shoulder and something in his body language bothered Lucy. "He wants something from her," she said to Dan, mentally reviewing the benign report on Dr. Garron that she'd e-mailed to Johnny.

"What do you *think* he wants from her?"

"Not sex. But something," Lucy said, her spy's instinct hard at work.

"You're blinded by your feelings for her," Dan said quietly to her, then he spoke into the phone: "Go get your woman, JC."

Johnny shot a dark look up to where they sat.

"Whoops," Dan said. "I mean your principal."

Johnny closed the phone, moving like liquid through the crowd toward Sage. In a moment he approached her, and Lucy watched the three talk, analyzing their body language. Was she really blinded by her feelings? Is that why she listened to her screaming gut now?

"Think Johnny likes this assignment?" Dan said with a little smile.

She had to agree, and the attraction obviously went both ways. Lucy could see the affection and admiration, sense the chemistry between them. But her attention shifted back to Garron, who hadn't taken his eyes off Sage. "I should dig deeper into that doctor," she said. "That report might not have been complete."

"You need a new assistant," Dan said.

"I'm working on it," Lucy said absently, watching as Johnny and Sage made their way to their seats.

Johnny put a casual hand on Sage's back, very professional. Of course, he knew he was under his boss's— and Sage's aunt's—scrutiny. They sat close to the court and Sage leaned into Johnny's side as if it were the one place on earth she wanted to be, giving Lucy a little tug of guilt. She certainly hadn't expected Sage to fall for Johnny. She hadn't meant to hurt Sage more with this.

The lights flickered once, twice, then the arena was awash in total darkness and a deafening cheer rose from the crowd. In a lightning flash of strobe, Lucy saw Sage turn to Johnny. A single drumbeat thumped from a hundred speakers. Someone from the crowd hollered and a cacophony of whistles followed, but Lucy watched her niece.

The strobe flashed in rapid succession, making Sage's movements jerk like an old movie reel as she reached up and put her hands on Johnny's face.

"Ladies and gentlemen of Boston, Massachusetts!"

The response was earsplitting, but still Lucy stayed locked on the blinking image of Sage and Johnny. Getting closer. Touching, looking, lost in each other.

"The New England Snow Bunnies have a message for you!"

Blinding brightness alternated with total darkness. In each flash, Sage pulled him closer, wrapped her hands around his neck, closed her eyes.

Then it was completely dark. Not a hint of light. Still, Lucy stared at the spot where she knew her Bullet Catcher and her niece sat. The pulse of the drum and noise of the crowd built to a crescendo as a singer screamed, "I want you!"

Suddenly, spotlights poured icy blue light over the court where twenty-some dancers appeared in white leather hot pants and halters and screamed, "To want me!"

The song blasted from the speakers, the cheerleaders exploded into motion, the spectators bellowed in approval, but Lucy ignored it all. Her attention stayed on the couple in the courtside seats where a young woman kissed a young man, looking at him with lust and longing and . . .

"Oh." The sound escaped Lucy's lips before she even realized it.

"Johnny's in deep, huh?" Dan asked.

"It's not Johnny I'm worried about."

The arena suddenly went pitch-black and Dan squeezed her hand. "She'll be okay."

All she'd wanted was to protect Sage. To guard and watch over her, like . . . well, like a mother would.

Again, they kissed. Long, slow, with aching familiarity.

Oh, Lord. What had she done? If Sage found out why Johnny was really there, the remote possibility of reconciliation would disappear forever.

The answer was simple. She could never, ever find out.

Sage thought of how she could shake Johnny, which, judging by the way he'd had a hand on her ever since he'd appeared out of nowhere to pull her away from Dr. Garron, wasn't going to be easy. She'd considered the truth, but he'd hate Glenda's insistence that Sage meet with LeTroy alone. And then he would follow her.

Adrien Fletcher slipped into an empty seat next to Johnny's in the last minutes of the game. He said something to Johnny that Sage didn't hear, and she leaned over to ask him if he would be waiting for Vivian at the back entrance.

"Johnny can show you where it is," she said. "I'm going back into the dressing room to finish interviewing a few of the girls."

Johnny glanced at her. "You're not done yet?"

She shook her head. "Just a few more minutes, then I'll be out with Vivian."

The Blizzard scored a three-pointer in the last five seconds, sending the crowd into a frenzy and the Snow Bunnies to the court for a victory dance to a sexy OutKast rap.

As the players disappeared, Sage stood, eager to get to LeTroy the minute he left the locker room. "Glenda said to be waiting the minute the game is over. I'm going to go. 'Bye." She already had one foot in the aisle when Johnny grabbed her hand tightly.

"Whoa, hang on, honey. I'll go with you."

"You have to show Fletch where the girls come out. You have to get to that exit by the outside, remember? You can't go where I'm going."

"I can go most of the way. C'mon, Fletch." Johnny tapped his friend's shoulder to pull his attention from the dancers. By the time they reached the outer band of the arena, hundreds of people were pouring out of the stands. Johnny moved Sage to his left side and kept a solid arm around her.

"Is this your good side?" she asked. "You always move me over here."

"So I can get my gun easier," he said, never taking his eyes from the passersby.

A strange, tingly sensation shot through her. Was he serious or was that a joke? He zoomed in on someone or something that caught his attention in the crowd. She started to follow his gaze, but he tightened his grip and pulled her into him, dropping an unexpected kiss on her head.

What didn't he want her to see? She peered past him to see into the crowd . . . then slowed her step and stared hard at a couple leaving the arena.

"Was that your friend Dan?" she asked.

Johnny barely glanced that way. "I don't know. Could have been. He's a fan."

"Does he date a tall blonde?"

"Tall, short, blond, brunette. The man's a machine." He threw a look at Fletch, who agreed with a laugh.

She didn't pursue it because straight ahead was a door marked NO ENTRANCE manned by an arena security guard.

"That's where I'm going," she announced. "I'll see you guys." She wanted Johnny gone when she announced herself, in case Glenda mentioned LeTroy.

"We'll wait until you get in," Johnny said.

"You know, in this crowd, it's going to take you a while to get all the way around the back of the arena. You better go so that Vivian and I don't have to wait for you."

Johnny held out his hand. "Give me your cell phone."

"Why?"

"Just give it to me."

She did, and he pressed a bunch of buttons and handed it back to her. "Press One and it will speed dial my cell phone. Your number's already in mine. Do not leave this building until we talk, okay? We'll be waiting for you and Vivian."

"Okay. Bye." She nudged him away.

"Hey, hey." He slid his hand under her hair and tipped her face toward his. "Be careful, 'kay?" He kissed her softly, a gesture so affectionate and natural that she felt even worse about lying. She'd make it up to him later. She kissed him again on the cheek. "I will. Bye."

As soon as he stepped away, she told the guard that Glenda was expecting her, and waited while he relayed her request into a radiophone. Johnny and Fletch lingered twenty feet away, still watching. She gave him a little finger wave, mouthing an insistent "Goodbye."

The door opened with a clunk and Sage did a double take at the sight of Julian Hewitt's icy eyes staring at her from behind thick, rimless glasses.

"Oh, hi." She stepped aside, assuming he was leaving. "Mr. Hewitt."

He indicated the corridor behind him with one hand. "We're going this way."

"We . . . we are." She'd been kept so far from the Snow Bunnies' business manager and Glenda Hewitt's husband that she was surprised he'd escort her to an interview. She glanced over her shoulder at Johnny, whose hard, dark glare bored through Julian.

Julian returned the look.

"I don't suppose you'd relent and let me bring my boyfriend to the interview?" Suddenly having Johnny with her seemed smarter than going into a dimly lit hallway alone with this guy.

"No, sorry. LeTroy would never allow it."

The guard closed the door, blocking out all the echoes of the arena.

"This way," Julian said, staying a step behind her.

"Great game, wasn't it?" she said, breaking the awkward silence. "LeTroy should be in an excellent mood for the interview."

"Yes, he should."

They continued their progress to the point where the hall split into a T. To the left, down a long corridor, past the dancers' dressing rooms, was the exit where Johnny and Fletch would be waiting. Should she go there and tell Vivian that, first?

"Is he ready to meet right now?" Sage asked. "Because I'd like to—"

"Do you have a camera?" Julian asked, ignoring the question.

"No."

They turned right, away from the dressing rooms, and continued to the end of the hallway to an unmarked door.

"Let me see your cell phone," he said.

Slowly, she pulled it out and held it in front of him. "Here it is. I'll turn it off, if I have to."

"That's a camera phone."

"I swear to God I won't take a picture of the guy." She could barely keep the exasperation out of her voice. "Honestly."

Julian shook his head. "You give me the phone or the interview's off."

"Are you serious?"

His expression left no doubt. "Quite."

Irritation shot through her as she opened her palm and he took the phone. "Fine."

He opened the next door and practically shoved her into the room. "Wait here for LeTroy." Then he left, slamming the door behind him.

Cursing him, and herself for giving him her phone, she glanced around the windowless room, sparsely furnished with a few vinyl chairs, a coffee table, and the New England Blizzard logo painted on one wall. On the table, two glasses were placed on napkins next to a pad of paper and several pencils.

She wanted out of there. She put her hand on the knob and turned, but it just clicked in her hand. Locked. "Oh, come on," she groaned. "What's going on?"

Cold air blew down from a duct in the ceiling, sending goose bumps down her body. Or was that because she was locked in a room alone, without her cell phone, and without anyone except creepy Julian Hewitt knowing where she was?

She dropped onto a chair, picked up a cup, and sniffed. The same lousy energy drink. Without taking a sip, she put it back on the table, giving into the funny sensation she'd had all night.

Why couldn't she shake the feeling that she was being watched?

CHAPTER
Eighteen

When Vivian Masters stepped into the beam of the security light and gave Johnny a surprised look, he cursed under his breath in Italian. How could he have been so stupid?

Fletch speared him with a look that echoed the thought.

"Where's Sage?" Johnny demanded of Vivian. "Is she still in the dressing room?"

She shook her head. "She didn't come in after the game. Sorry, I have no idea where she is."

The game had been over for half an hour. About twenty other girls had come through the exit. Fury and fear rocked Johnny right down to his feet. "Get her home," he said to Fletch, pulling out his cell phone and calling Sage's number for the second time in fifteen minutes. Voice mail. He pocketed the phone and walked up to the oversize security guard. "I need to go in there."

"I don't think so, bud." His glare had no doubt been honed over years as a nightclub bouncer.

"Listen," Johnny said. "My girlfriend is in there and she was supposed to come out fifteen minutes ago with her." He indicated Vivian. "She's not answering her cell."

The guard unclipped a comm radio from his belt. "Which one is she?"

"She's not a dancer. She's a reporter."

He lifted his eyebrows in surprise. "Let me have someone check the interview rooms. Hang on." As he talked into his radiophone, Johnny scanned the parking lot. He spotted the van in the far western corner, parked among Dumpsters and near the woods. He couldn't see if the bumper was hanging off, but the van looked really familiar.

As he considered his options, his cell phone rang Lucy's tone. "Oh, great."

Fletch grinned. "Busted."

Johnny put his hand on the phone but didn't open it. What the hell would he tell her? *I lost your niece?*

"Get it," Vivian urged. "It's probably Sage."

"No, it's someone else." He flipped the phone open. "Yo. Christiano here."

"Did she see me?" Lucy asked.

"Almost. I thought you guys were . . ." He glanced at Vivian, who listened to every word. "Never mind. What's up?"

"I just wanted to know if we were spotted. Johnny, don't blow your cover. For any reason. You understand? Call me later."

Shit. He'd never lied to Lucy. Not even a lie of omission, like this.

"Got it."

"Who was that?" Vivian asked, still watching him closely.

"Not Sage." He felt like the world's worst betrayer. Had Lucy backed off when he'd been asked to do the hardest thing a man could possibly do, kill someone he loved? No. Lucy had risked her own life, unselfishly and willingly, for Bella and for him. And now he was lying to her.

The radio squealed in the guard's hand and a man's voice announced, "That reporter's interviewing LeTroy and can't be disturbed."

How did that happen? "Where is she?" Johnny asked the guard.

The guard relayed the question, along with a look that said he was way too busy for this.

"Media one," the voice on the radio responded. "And the last two girls are on their way, Smitty. You can lock up then."

"Lock up?" Johnny demanded. "She's still in there."

"I'll take them to their cars and lock up." He re-clipped the radiophone with an air of self-importance. "Media one is an interview room at the other end of the arena. Go all the way around to the west lot entrance, there's a door like this one. Wait there."

The door opened and two more dancers and another guard stepped out into the light.

"Night, Ellie, night, Susannah," Vivian said.

"You got 'em, Smitty?" the escort asked the door guard.

"Yep. I'll take them to their cars." When the door

slammed closed, Mr. Self Important, the night watchman, put one hand on each of the dancer's backs. "You need to get out of here."

Fletch leaned closer to Johnny. "We can go over there with you, mate."

"No, thanks," Johnny said. Too much time with Fletch, especially chasing after a lost principal, and Vivian might figure out they weren't "gym rats" but trained security professionals. Even if they kept their cover intact, she might raise questions to Sage, and then how long until she put two and two together and came up with Aunt Lucy? "I'm good. I'll be there in five minutes and, trust me, I'll get in."

"Okay," Vivian said. "But can you call her again before we leave?"

He did, scoping the lot behind him again as it rang. A car, one of the dancers', he imagined, pulled out of a spot, and the security escort walked across the lot with the other woman. The guy was an idiot. It was like he made an effort to avoid the well-lit sections. Some muscle.

At the sound of Sage's recorded voice, he flipped the phone shut, and said goodbye to Fletch and Vivian. In his car, he backed out of his spot and caught one last glimpse of the security guard and the dancer. Why did she park so far away? He waited for Fletch to take off, then finished the three-point turn, heading him in the opposite direction of the guard and the dancer.

Who walked, he realized when he looked in the rearview mirror, directly to the only vehicle parked in that corner. The van.

He whipped the car around into the next lane to shine his headlights in that direction. He didn't hit them with the beam, but he could see the woman running, so he cut the car to the right and nailed them both with the light. The guard was chasing her.

Son of a bitch, what was going on? He slammed the gas, headed toward them, the noise and lights making both of them turn and freeze. The guard caught up with her, grabbed her, and dragged her the last five feet to the van. Johnny floored the Toyota and whipped through an empty slot between two parked cars, burning rubber.

But the guard was fast. He flipped open the back doors and tossed her inside. Just as Johnny's car reached them, the guard dived into the driver's seat and slammed the door. Johnny threw the Toyota directly in front of the van and leaped from the seat, his gun drawn.

At the rumble of the van's ignition, he cocked and aimed at the windshield. The van backed up and he lowered his weapon, shot the right front tire, then lifted it again. "Get out!" he shouted.

After a second, the driver's door opened very slowly and the guard stepped out with both hands up. "What the fuck?" he yelled. "She paid for it!"

Johnny took a few steps closer. "What are you doing?"

"My fuckin' job. She paid to get kidnapped and that's what I'm doing."

Johnny peered at him. This is what they hired to kidnap these women? This pudgy lowlife? "Get the hell out of here."

"Hey, man, I gotta job to do."

"You did it."

He didn't move. "They won't pay me, asshole. Let me take her to the right spot. Then you can rescue her. Trust me, you got the better gig tonight."

Inside the van, a woman screamed, "Hey!" and pounded on the back door. "What's going on?"

Johnny raised the gun, aimed it at his face. "Go."

The guard swore softly, turned, and ran into the darkness of the lot. Johnny jogged to the back of the van, kicked the falling bumper, and opened the door.

"Who are you?" she asked.

"Your rescuer," he said dryly, reaching for her. "Let's go, fast. I got another job."

She looked dismayed but climbed out. "Already? Isn't this part supposed to last longer?"

He closed his eyes in disgust. "Where are you parked?"

She pointed to a car closer to the entrance. "This sucks," she grumbled, pulling keys from her bag. "I thought I got a lot more for Glenda's two grand."

Glenda's? "She paid for this?"

"You think we can afford this? At ninety dollars a game?" She blew out an annoyed breath and pointed her remote toward a Honda Civic. "This is her idea of building squad spirit. I didn't really want to do it anyway. Julian's right."

"About what?"

She pushed some hair out of her face. "That this is really Glenda's way of getting all of us to act like whores and ruin our self-respect."

No shit. But one word stuck in his brain as he opened the driver's door for her. "Did he use that word? *Whore?*"

"Hell yes. He called me one tonight."

"So he knows who's getting kidnapped? And when and where?"

"Duh, they *are* married." She swept him with a long, slow look and gave him a sultry smile. "Sure you won't change your mind? I didn't see you on the website, but you're really cute."

"Then Julian would be right, wouldn't he?"

Surprise flashed in her eyes, which still had clumps of mascara around the edges. "Hey, it fuels his fantasies."

"How do you mean?"

She made a distasteful face. "He's torn. Part of him wants to be protective; the other part wants to fuck every one of us."

Really. He guided her into the front seat of her car. "Here you go, sweetheart. Be good, now."

"Like any of us would do that geek," she continued, an adrenaline rush obviously making her talkative. "He's a very sad man. He was so mad at Keisha when she did the kidnapping, I swear he was actually happy when she died."

Johnny froze in the act of closing the door. "What?"

She nodded, her mouth moving way faster than her brain. "She was one of the dancers. She died. Suicide. Oh, he had it so bad for Keisha. He followed her all the time, called her into his office for no reason, just totally wanted her. He was so pissed when she signed up. *So* pissed. I can't imagine what he'll say to me when he finds out."

"Has he ever hurt any of the girls?"

"*He* doesn't," she said. "But Glenda pays those guards plenty to keep us in line."

He didn't have time to put this puzzle together, but one thing was sure: He had to get Sage away from where Glenda or Julian or any of their well-paid security guards were. He eased the woman into the driver's seat and tugged at the seat belt for her. "Good night."

She gave him a pout of pure disappointment. "It still could be a good night if you want to come with me."

"Not tonight, babe." He closed her door, turned, and ran to the opposite side of the building. He had to get Sage out of there.

It didn't take a trained journalist to know that LeTroy Burgess wanted to be anywhere else in the world but this interview. He arrived alone, didn't even say hello, and refused to make eye contact with Sage. He folded his seven feet of self into a chair, plopped size-20 shoes on the coffee table, took one sip of the energy drink and spit it back into the glass, and glowered straight ahead.

"You got three questions," he said as though he were talking to the door. "One about the game. One about my career. One about my family. Anything else goes to my publicist, who should be here but is in L.A. And nothing about that third foul in the last period." He lifted his left arm, waved a diamond Rolex, and said, "Go."

"How well did you know Keisha Kingston?"

He whipped toward her, his near-black eyes on fire. "What the fuck do you care?"

"My name is Sage Valentine. Does that mean anything to you?"

He searched her face, his bushy black eyebrows drawn. "No."

"I was Keisha's roommate. I shared her Beacon Hill apartment with her."

He scowled at her. "If this is going to turn into some fuckin' Kobe Bryant rape charge, you can stop right there."

Sage took a deep breath and settled her hands on her lap, hoping he'd notice there was no recorder, no notebook, no pencil. "I'm trying to figure out why she killed herself." She paused and leaned an inch forward. "*If* she killed herself."

She saw him struggle to swallow. "I want my lawyer."

Sage drew back. "Why?"

" 'Cause you just rapped me, bitch. I did not kill her." He snarled the words, leaning closer. "I did not rape her. I did not kill her. I did not do anything wrong. You understand? Damn." The last word was muttered on a snort of frustration.

"I know that you were her friend, LeTroy." She purposely lowered her voice. "I know that she talked to you, and trusted you. I remember her mentioning your name and telling me the press was wrong about you."

His expression morphed into something unreadable. "She's gone, and that's really too bad. She was a good kid. A sweet girl."

"Did you get her pregnant?"

Closing his eyes, he stood, towering over her like a skyscraper. "Interview's done."

"Please, LeTroy. I'm not trying to place blame. I'm just trying to figure out what happened."

He looked down at her for a long time. "It don't matter what happened. She's gone. I miss her, too. 'Nuff said."

"Then why did you agree to do this interview?" she asked.

"Because Glenda asked me."

"Do you do whatever Glenda says?"

He shrugged, attempting for casual, but missing. "She's got some dirt on me and we keep things cool this way, 'kay? You got a problem with that?"

"I have a problem with not knowing what happened to my roommate."

He closed his eyes for a second. "I don't know what happened to her. I know what happened to *us*. I told her the first time, I wasn't never leavin' my wife. Keisha, she thought . . ." He shook his head. "Shit happens, okay? And shit happened with us, you hear me?"

She heard him. "Was she pregnant?"

"She mighta been. We weren't talkin' there at the end." He slumped down. "The first time . . . we were on the road. In Salt Lake. Not much to do in Utah, you know? So we were talking, late into the night. And one thing led to another."

"Okay." Sage didn't want to pass judgment or stop his confession.

"Well, that was it." He waited a beat before adding,

"We hooked up a few more times. But then I got all scared and shit."

It seemed monumental for a man of his size to admit to fear. "Did you think she'd go public with the affair?"

"No." He let out a slow breath of resignation. "I got scared 'cause she . . . she—"

"She what, LeTroy?"

"She was cool. Like she could take me or not. But I started to get, like, I couldn't think, couldn't play, couldn't do nothin', unless I could be with her."

A shiver worked its way up Sage's back. Could he have killed Keisha? Could she have been a threat to his reputation, his marriage? Because he'd fallen in love with her? "So what did you do?"

"Nothin'," he said quickly. "She didn't return my calls and I figured she'd moved on."

"Are you sure?"

"A fine woman like that? Who wouldn't want her?" He shoved his hands into his pockets. "But you know, I was wondering . . . I was hoping— I just didn't want to be the reason she killed herself."

As he jingled his keys, the top of a cell phone peeked out of his pocket. His cell phone, and the tip of a pen.

"Does anyone else know about your relationship with her?"

His eyes sparked like black diamonds. "No. And you ain't about to tell anybody 'cause I will deny it."

"Because it would ruin your reputation?"

"Because it would ruin hers."

Sage reached for her notebook. She just had to see one more thing. "Thanks for your time, LeTroy. Would you be kind enough to give me your autograph or do you just sell those for profit?"

"You want my autograph?"

"Please." She reached out, offering him an empty page. But no pen.

Automatically, he dipped into his pocket and brought out something he probably kept on him at all times. A signing pen. A thick, black marker.

Whores must die.

He signed it, then handed her the notebook. "She liked you a lot," he said quietly.

"Yeah," Sage said. "I liked her a lot, too."

With a quick nod, he was gone.

As his footsteps disappeared down the hall, another set came closer, running fast. One of the guards popped his head in the open doorway.

"Are you Sage Valentine?" he asked, a little out of breath.

"Yes."

"You better get outside. Your boyfriend Rambo has a gun, and he's seriously not afraid to use it."

Julian Hewitt read every name and number in Sage's cell phone address book. Then he read her text messages. Then he examined her call history.

And still he knew very little about her.

What he did know, he didn't like. She was nosy. She was relentless. And she was getting too close for comfort. Glenda didn't seem at all worried about her, but

Glenda wasn't doing anything wrong, just getting the girls to have some fun. There was nothing illegal about working out a cut with the guy who owned the website. Still, she was smart to keep Sage occupied with LeTroy Burgess while Susannah headed off for her fun and games.

White-hot anger shot through him. If only Glenda had come up with some other way to make the money. The girls were whores, and if it weren't for a drunken, drugged-up whore who plowed her truck into his little girl seven years ago, they wouldn't be in this situation—desperate for money to keep Emily alive.

The phone in his hand rang and he jerked out of his thoughts. The caller ID showed the same number that had called four times in the last half hour; probably her boyfriend. He let it ring. He'd give her five more minutes; enough time to make sure that Susannah's fantasy was fulfilled. Then he'd go pick up the van and . . . maybe stop at Susannah's house to leave her a message. It wouldn't hurt to make sure she didn't do it again. And just the act of scrawling his message over their faces, of reminding them what had happened to Keisha, made him feel better. It made him feel like he was doing something other than sending them off for . . . money.

Glenda would never believe that the whole thing made him sick with guilt. After all, he'd hacked the firewall and made it possible for her to get into the system, for her to work her deals and build their bank account. And she'd done that amazingly well for the past eight months. For the first time in years, they could relax. Emily could stay at the facility that kept her alive. And that was all that mattered to him.

Until Keisha. Then, the way they were making money made him sick, because she reminded him of Emily. Certainly not because of her ebony skin and sleek black hair. His daughter was pale, curly haired, and gentle. But before the accident, Emily had that same something that Keisha Kingston had. Confidence. Vitality. Life.

And now she was gone.

Just like Emily soon would be. But until she was, there was hope. After seven sad years, he still harbored hope. And that was why he let Glenda do what she did best: control things. Except she couldn't control Emily's life. Any day, any minute, the call from the facility would come. Then he'd have no more hope.

As though on cue, the phone clipped to his belt rang, and he answered it immediately.

"Mr. Hewitt, this is the security guard at the West End."

Not the one they'd paid to help with the abduction, he thought quickly. Still, it wasn't good that one of the guards would call him. "What's the problem?"

"Some guy out here is looking for a reporter, and he says you took her in. We think she's with LeTroy in Media one."

"And?"

"And he's pointing a gun at me and says he wants to see you. Now."

A bead of sweat trickled down Julian's back. He

knew that girl was trouble, but Glenda was so sure she could handle anything. "I'll be out in a minute."

But first, he had to be sure the van was gone with Susannah in it. Still holding both cell phones, he slipped into the hall and headed for the east exit through the passageway only the players used, bypassing the interview rooms. He shoved the door hard and peered across the dark parking lot.

The van was still there. Swearing softly, he looked around. Where was the guard who was supposed to take her? Where was Susannah? Were they in the van? What were they *doing*?

A screw-up could cost a lot of money. Thousands and thousands. Months of care for Emily, months of hope.

Drawing in a breath, he stepped into the parking lot and started toward the van. There was no movement anywhere, no sound except his loafers against the pavement, picking up speed to match his pulse.

When he reached the van, he saw the flat tire. He pivoted, looking for the Honda Susannah usually parked in the first row by the door. It was gone. Could she have aided in her own kidnapping?

Then his cell phone rang. He almost ignored it, but then he pulled it out and checked the blue digital readout.

And felt his heart literally stop.

LAND'S END CRITICAL CARE.

There was no reason for them to call at this hour, except the inevitable.

Anger, regret, and the blackest of furies swamped his brain and he flung the phone as hard and far as he could. He heard it clunk against a windshield as he doubled over in pain.

Bright white lights bathed him, brakes screamed to a stop, and the sight of a cold, hard gun in his face was something of a relief.

"Get up, Hewitt." The man was gruff, impatient.

Julian blinkied at the gun, seeing the reporter's boyfriend on the other end of it. "What do you want?"

"Just get up."

Julian shifted his focus to the woman next to the gunman. She reminded him of Emily, too. Same bright look in her eyes. But Emily's eyes were closed forever now.

He sat down on the cold cement to weep, and finally confess what he'd done.

CHAPTER
Nineteen

As the door of the police station closed behind them, Sage let out a sigh of frustration. "So, now we know that Julian has a hang-up about bad girls and decided to vandalize some homes to let them know they shouldn't do nasty things. Big deal."

Johnny didn't respond, so she tugged his arm as they turned the corner to the side street where he'd parked the Toyota so many hours ago.

"Doesn't it bother you?" she asked.

What bothered him was that he'd lied to Lucy. What bothered him was that he'd lost his mind when he thought Sage was in danger, and that moment of insanity had nothing to do with who she was—a principal or his boss's niece. He was crazed because he cared, and that was all kinds of dangerous.

"No, Sage," he answered. "It doesn't bother me, because the only crime committed was vandalism and he confessed to it."

She yanked his arm again. "Hello? Keisha is dead.

Did you forget the elevator at the library? The note? What if she was murdered?"

"Julian has an airtight alibi. Plus, the guy's not a killer. You could see that. He may not be the right guy to manage a bunch of good-looking dancers, but it seems like his wife is really in charge of that end of the business. I'm not ready to dismiss her, though. Something's not right there."

"I know." Her fingers threaded through his, trusting and tight, made his chest hurt.

"I'm sorry you still don't have your original question answered," he said, opening the car door. "But it's three in the morning, so let's go home."

She raised her hand to his cheek. "And where exactly is that for you?" she asked softly, rubbing the whiskers that had grown since he'd last shaved. "You don't live in that hotel." Her eyes were full of honesty and desire. "I want you to take me home. To your real home. I want to see where you live, how you live. I want to know who you are."

"No, you don't," he said gruffly, stepping out of her touch. "And I do live at that hotel. And we can go there if you want, or to your house. Wherever we can——"

All that honesty and desire evaporated.

"Sleep," he finished.

"Just take me to my apartment." She dropped into the seat and slammed the door.

Nice work, JC. Now she was pissed, so he'd have to come up with some new and *creative* way to stay at her apartment, or spend a damned uncomfortable night of surveillance in his car.

They drove to her place in silence and she said, "Just drop me off at the door."

"I'm going up with you."

"Johnny—"

"I'm going to make sure you're safe."

The moment he pulled into the spot, she flung open the door and was out in one move.

Son of a bitch. He'd forgotten how fast she was. He took off after her, but she got to her door twenty seconds before he did. Then she realized he had her keys.

"What are you doing?" he asked, climbing the three stairs to reach her. "I'm not going to stay. I just want to check the place out."

She turned, hands on hips, that determined fire burning in her eyes. "Who *are* you?"

Oh, man. "It's late, Sage." He moved around her, put the key in the door, and turned it. "I don't want to talk."

"You never want to talk. You want to eat or sleep or screw or . . . *protect* me, but you never want to talk."

"Which pretty much makes me a guy."

"But what kind of guy?"

"Tired. Uncomplicated. Italian. Pick one." He brushed by her, did a complete security check, and found her back in the living room waiting at the door, a blank, hard expression on her face.

"Give me back my keys," she said, palm out-stretched.

He unclipped her house key from the rental-car ring. "Here you go."

They looked at each other for a second, and a little

light of hope flickered in his chest. God, he wanted to stay. And not just because he didn't want to spend the next few hours in the car. "Sure you don't want me to stay, Sage?"

She closed her eyes. "Now he remembers my name. Just in time for the break-up."

"I never forget your name. And we aren't breaking up." Not until Lucy called and told him to leave. Sometimes it was a bitch to be so freaking dedicated.

"Then help me out here, Johnny. You drop into my life out of nowhere, you care about me, you worry about me, you feed me and give me insane pleasure. But you won't tell me anything about *you*—not where you live, what makes you tick. Why? Is it so hard to understand that I need to know this before you spend the night again? Before I lose myself with you again?"

He took her face in his hand. Her pulse hammered under his fingertips, her lips separated to let out a quick breath. She opened her mouth to say something, but he covered it with a hard, fast kiss.

"Honestly, sweetheart, you don't want to know."

She jerked out of his touch. "And you haven't been paying attention, if you think I can't find out what I want to know."

She would never find out about Lucy. He'd sworn that to his boss, just like he'd sworn a lifetime of loyalty in exchange for the life Lucy had saved. "I've been paying attention. That's just the problem. I've been paying too much attention." He considered saying he would call her, but didn't want to risk yet another lie. His phone could ring at any minute and he'd disappear in the same mysterious way he arrived. And now he knew that would hurt her.

And him.

She tapped his shoulder to push him out the door. "*Ciao*, Italian boy."

That made him smile. "*Ciao, mia cara.*"

Behind him, the door closed and the dead bolt snapped into place. He stood on the step for a minute, staring at a gaslight through the spring leaves, hoping she'd flip the latch with a change of heart.

But there was no flip, no change, and no hope tonight.

He jogged back to the Camry, where he had a clear shot of her front door and bedroom window. In five minutes he saw the light go out in that window, and he stared at the dark square, imagining her in bed. Remembering her sweet skin, her tender mouth, her warm woman's body.

An hour later the bedroom light came on again, and ten minutes after that the front door opened and he saw the gleam of her blond ponytail just as a cab pulled up to her door. What the hell?

He sat up straight. Where the hell was she going at this hour? When the cabbie pulled out on Charles Street, he was three car lengths behind. The cab headed toward Back Bay, making every light on the yellow and forcing Johnny to slide in under the red.

In less than ten minutes the cab pulled under the awning of The Eliot Hotel and a warm rush of something close to joy and even closer to arousal blasted through him.

She was going to him.

He parked the car illegally and hung back as she paid the cabbie and entered the hotel. A minute later, he dashed up the stairs and saw her standing at his door.

He approached without making a sound. "Looking for someone special?" he whispered, unable to take the smile out of his voice or off his face.

She whipped around, eyes blazing and just a little too bright. "I know."

She knew?

"I know who you are."

He froze, biting back a curse. "I told you it wasn't pretty." But just how ugly it was, remained to be seen.

"And I told you I'm very handy at getting information."

He nodded and took a cautious step forward. "And so you came here to, what? Confront me? Hear a denial? What do you want?"

She leaned her head against the doorjamb. "I want you to know that I don't care who your uncle is, Johnny. I wish you had trusted me with this. You wouldn't have had to be so secretive."

Johnny just stood there, running through his options. Denial. Humor. Sex. Hell, he could make her happy and *talk* his way through this. At least she didn't know about Lucy.

"How'd you find out?" he asked, pulling out the hotel key.

"I searched your nona's last name. Cardinale. Achilles Cardinale is your mother's brother, isn't he?"

"Yep." He led her inside.

"And I read about your sister, how she died."

"Don't believe everything you read online, sugar," he said as he turned on a lamp in the living room and sat on the armrest of the sofa, crossing his arms against the questions he knew she was winding up to pitch.

She didn't even take a second to warm up. "Is it true that your uncle . . ." Her voice faded. "Did he have your sister killed?"

He swallowed. Twice. If he told her even one word of the real story—one word—he would be breaking a promise to Lucy and putting Bella's life on the line again. "Not exactly."

"What happened?" Her voice was soft, but he saw the intensity in her eyes, the unstoppable will to discover the truth.

"Sage, honey, I can't tell you that."

"I'm not going to tell anyone."

"It's not because I don't trust you. It's because it's too big a risk to take for you."

"Johnny." She reached out and touched his hand. "I'll take that risk. That's the connection that matters to me. That's what makes this . . ." she indicated the two of them with a wave of her hand, "more than sex."

He closed his eyes. "I've never told anyone. Ever."

"Please."

Part of it. He could tell her part of the story. "I was given the job to . . ." No, he'd have to go further back.

"I told you my mother married an Italian businessman. It was her escape from the family. She met my dad, saw an out, and took it, moving to Tuscany with him, living happily and having two children—me and Bella. When they were in the accident—"

"Was it an accident?"

He gave her a humorless smile. "We'll never know, but Achilles never had a son and he wanted one. A nephew was the closest he could get, and when my parents died, he got me. My little sister was sent to live with distant Christiano relatives and I went to New York to be raised by my nona Cardinale and learn the ways of the family."

"Did you?"

"Some of them. But there was a man, an FBI agent working undercover, although I didn't know that, and he . . . he sort of took a liking to me." He ran a hand through his hair, blowing out a breath. This was hard. Made even harder by the fact that even though he was breaking his personal code to tell her the truth about Bella, he couldn't slip and reveal the true "orchestrater" of his fate: Lucy Sharpe.

"Anyway, about seven years ago, the word was out that my sister wanted to avenge my parents' death and was going to turn evidence over to the FBI against Achilles. He ordered her to be killed."

She closed her eyes in horror.

"And he wanted me to do it."

They opened in more horror. "No."

"Yes. But I didn't, Sage. She's my baby sister." He

tried to swallow. "The FBI agent had some incredible connections with some international power brokers. Bella was saved, given a new life and a new name. She lives in what we would call the witness protection program, in Italy."

"So she's not dead?"

He shook his head. "No. Though as far as anyone in the world except for a handful of people know, Bella Christiano was killed." But Natalia Allesandro lived in a cozy house in Lake Como, alive and well. Thanks to Lucy and Dan Gallagher.

"And what happened to you?"

"My uncle thought I'd done the deed. Then I gave the FBI everything they needed to put him away for life."

"But did he know you'd turned him in? How did you get out?" She narrowed her eyes. "You did get out, didn't you?"

He nodded. "Those same powers negotiated with my uncle. He got life in exchange for a release of several family members who wanted out permanently."

"I didn't know you *could* get out."

With Lucy pulling the strings, anything was possible. "I have some friends in high places."

She studied him, no doubt reassessing her attraction. "Do you see her?"

For a moment he thought she meant Lucy, then he realized she meant Bella. "Every once in a while I sneak in under the radar and get a day or two with her." He smiled, thinking of Bella's infectious laugh, her long black hair, her black-olive eyes.

"I'd like to meet her," she said softly.

He shook his head. "No." That would be a level of trust he'd never feel for any woman, ever.

"And I guess I understand why you carry a gun."

"Yeah." Let her think it was habit and self-preservation.

He waited for the next barrage: *What did you do? How rough was it? How many people did you whack?*

But she surprised him by stepping into his arms and sliding her hands up his neck. "Here's the thing, Johnny."

A smile pulled at his lips. "What's the thing, Sage?"

"I understand, better than anyone else in the world, that you can't pick your relatives. Believe me, I know firsthand the horrific impact an uncle—or in my case, an aunt—can make on your life."

His stomach turned when he realized where she was going.

"You can't choose these people; you are born to them. But you absolutely mustn't let them control your life."

"I don't."

"No? You live in fear that someone you care about will find this out."

"Not exactly fear." But, to some extent, she was right.

"Well, I found out and it doesn't make me like you any less. On the contrary, it makes you pretty heroic, the way you saved your sister."

He couldn't let her think that, even if she despised the real hero. "I had help."

"And you turned your back on your uncle. I respect that."

"I had help," he repeated, knowing that if he said the name of his help, all that sympathy and empathy would disappear in a heartbeat.

She threaded her fingers into his hair. "You're too modest," she said. "I like that in a guy."

His lips curled up in a mirthless smile. "You do?"

"In fact," she said, "I like everything about you."

"I'm starting to get that impression."

She laid her palm on his chest. "Especially the fact that your heart's pounding like mad. It's sweet."

He hadn't even noticed. But his heart was slamming against his ribs, and his blood was thrumming through his veins. He opened his mouth to say, *That's what you do to me, sweetheart,* but closed it again. He was so sick of lies. His heart wasn't beating because of her; it was beating because she'd just forgiven his worst sins, and still he had to hide more from her. He hated that.

When she looked up at him, he said, "It makes me sick to talk about that family, that's why. I hate this subject."

"Then change it." She rose to kiss him.

Instantly, his body warmed with a natural response. No chance he could fight this, and he didn't want to anyway. He ran his hands over the tight muscles of her back, to the bare skin exposed between her top and smooth, fitted workout pants. "Sage," he whispered, emotion squeezing his throat. "Now you know that you're too good for me."

A little moan escaped her throat. "Not true," she said, nibbling at his jaw.

He closed his eyes on a sigh and she must have taken it as a signal, kissing him again. He felt a shudder run through him as his hands rounded her waist and closed over her breasts, and he instinctively rocked into her.

"Listen to me, Johnny," she said. "As long as you're honest, you're worthy."

Honest? He was still lying through his teeth. Lucy held the cards, and the cards said, lie. Or at least, be vague and distracting. Charming. Clever. Persuasive. Protective.

"I have more secrets, Sage." At least he'd told her something. He mentally braced for the demand that he tell her, but she merely rubbed against him, caressing his back and rear, pulling him into her.

"Tell me tomorrow." She nuzzled his neck. "You know what I love?"

He grazed his fingertips over her collarbone, down the neat little tank top she wore, settling into her delicate cleavage. "I know what I love. This spot."

"I love it when you call me Sage."

She loved it because it was honest and real. Like she was.

"Sage," he whispered as he kissed her throat, dipping lower to taste that sweet crease. "That's one of my favorite ingredients in the world, you know that?"

"You have good taste." She took his hand and led him through the French doors to the bedroom. "Have some more in here."

She pulled him onto the mountain of decorative pillows, turned on the soft bedside lamp, then knelt on the bed as he removed his gun and kicked off his shoes. He ran a hand over his eighteen-hour stubble. "Want me to shave?"

"I want you to watch." With one finger, she inched up the hem of her cropped tank top, revealing the luscious, round bottoms of her breasts. "I want you to forget everything else right now but me."

"I can do that." For now, anyway.

She slowly raised the top. His body jolted when her breasts popped free and her dark, ripe nipples hardened. Sliding off the top, she pulled her ponytail out and shook her hair down over her shoulders in a dead sexy move.

"Tell me something," she said.

"Anything." Anything she'd want to hear, at least.

"What do you like best?" She dipped her thumbs into the low band around her hips, pushing it just low enough to reveal the feminine angle of her hip bones and that sweet, tight skin just below her navel.

He managed a wink. "Is this another one of those interviews?"

"This can be anything you want it to be." She turned to the side, giving him a profile of her rear end. She slowly slid the material over her round curves, bending over as she stripped the cotton down her thighs. Silky blond hair draped over the bedspread. Blood surged south, punching him to a rock-hard erection as he rose to reach for her.

"Tell me what you want, Johnny," she said again.

Sweat beaded on his neck, and his mouth went bone dry. He wanted this fiery, sexy, understanding woman who offered her body so willingly. "I want . . ." Something lasting. Something meaningful. With her. But he'd never get that. "To taste Sage."

He grasped her hips from the back, and dropped a hot, slow, wet kiss on the dip above her rump and the twin to its left, moaning at the smoothness of her skin.

She lifted herself, offering him access between her legs. He licked her there, tasting her moisture, sliding his tongue inside. She tensed, and he felt the bedspread shift as her fingers balled the fabric and her knees widened to let him underneath.

He dropped flat on the bed, turned over, and slid between her legs to fill his mouth with her. Taking her thighs in his hands, he feasted on her hot, delicious, tangy, sweet womanhood.

She rocked with an orgasm, panting his name, shuddering out of control. She fell back on the bed, undressing him with shaky hands. He sped the process, and throbbing with the need to get inside her.

Sage closed her fist over his shaft, lowering her head to reciprocate, but he stopped her and grabbed for the stash of condoms in the nightstand. "No, no. I want you."

Understanding, she lay back and opened herself to him. He wanted to say something tender. He wanted to touch her lovingly, to kiss her mouth and breasts with delicate feather touches. He wanted to tell her that this was real, and that it mattered, and that he was so damn sorry he'd lied from the beginning.

But he couldn't even look in her eyes as he sheathed himself.

He'd lied from the beginning and he'd lie to the end, because his loyalty belonged to someone else. Still needing her to the point of insanity, he plunged into her.

She pulled his face to hers for a kiss, but he buried his mouth near her ear, in her hair, letting the pillow muffle his groans.

All he wanted was comfort and release and forgiveness.

Biting his lip so hard he tasted blood, he took two out of three, feeling lucky to get those from a woman who, by all rights, should hate him.

The New England Snow Bunnies were dancing to an old Beatles' song, doing the H formation with Keisha Kingston in the center spot. Her skin glistened like semisweet chocolate, and, unlike all the other girls in white, she wore black shorts and a one-shouldered tank top. All around the arena, men in masks held AK-47s, aimed at the girls, waiting for the order to fire. At the far end of the arena a woman directed the music with a conductor's baton, her black hair flowing down to her knees, with a single bloodred streak down the front.

The chorus screamed through the speakers and the girls sang, but they weren't singing words. They were singing beeps, like an electronic organ. *Be be be be beeeeep be bee bee.*

Keisha was the only one singing the words.

Lucy in the sky with diamonds. Her lips moved, her black eyes sparkled, her smile melted every heart in the audience.

Lucy in the . . .

Light and consciousness slammed Sage as she pulled out of the dream, and she saw Johnny, naked and desperately digging for his pants under the bedspread on the floor.

"Is that your phone ringing?" she asked, rubbing her eyes. She hadn't heard that melody ring before.

He plucked the device from his pants pocket and gave her a look between horror and hope. "I'm going to take this in there." Leaving no room for argument, he disappeared into the living room, closing the French doors with a click.

He'd locked her in the bedroom?

She snuggled into the pillow and sniffed the warm spot he'd left. Oh, the man was too much. Too sexy, too good, too charming. So his uncle had a rap sheet as long as her arm. So he had a sordid past. Did he really think she'd shun him because his family was involved with the mob?

Everyone had some skeletons in their closet. That could just bring them closer, couldn't it? She could help him heal, and he . . . he . . . She closed her eyes and saw the vivid image of Keisha in her dream.

He could help her get over this, too. Even if she never got the answers she wanted, he could help her accept this death. And possibly the deeper wound her mother had left years ago. For some reason, this man, this fascinating, sweet, funny man, just might be the—

The French doors popped open and Johnny stood there, naked and magnificent. He looked like a Roman centurion, carved from stone with broad shoulders and rippling muscles, his manhood a breath away from erect, lying perfectly against his corded thigh.

She had to restrain herself from throwing over the covers and demanding more. More rough sex. More sweet sex. More slow sex. More great sex.

"Keisha did not have an abortion. In fact, her autopsy showed that she was menstruating at the time of death."

The announcement drenched her like an icy shower. "What?" She pushed up on one elbow. "How do you know?"

"I have sources."

"Are you sure?"

"Absolutely." He tossed the phone onto the dresser. "That's not all."

"What?"

"There is no connection between takemetonight.com and either Glenda or Julian Hewitt. The head of the company has never heard of either one, nor have any of the employees. Hewitt was lying to the cops."

Ice trickled into her veins. "What? How do you know?" She sounded like a pathetic parrot repeating herself. "Was that Cervaris on the phone?"

"No. It was a very trusted source." At her look, he added, "Trusted and classified."

"*Classified*? Are you hiding a military background, too?"

He waved a hand. "Whatever you media types call it."

Now she was a "media type"? A big demotion from the "queen of delight" she'd been last night. "We media types generally call sources that refuse to be named 'confidential' or 'anonymous.' Whatever you call them, they are the least reliable." She sat up and brushed hair from her face. "Are you absolutely positive about this? Do you know what it—"

"Yes. I'm positive."

His tone was harsh, his expression matching. He disappeared into the bathroom, closing the door with a thump that echoed hers when she dropped onto the pillows.

"Sheez," she whispered, bewildered by the message and the messenger.

Her gaze shifted from the bathroom door to the dresser, where his cell phone lay. A reliable and classified source. Who could that be? Who would be able to find out whether Keisha had an abortion and what was in her autopsy report *and* what kind of business relationship the Hewitts had with Fantasy Adventures?

A worm of apprehension slithered up her spine. She stared at the phone, running through a mental list of possibilities until her brain hit one so hard, it actually hurt.

No. *No.* Was it possible? The question came as a whisper at first, a nudge to her conscious, as distant as the notes of a song that had awakened her.

Lucy in the sky . . .

Oh, God. Her heart plummeted into her stomach. She tried to swallow, but couldn't. No. Oh, please, *no.*

She threw the cover back and crossed the room in purposeful strides. She had to destroy the sickening thought that had just taken hold. She'd do whatever was necessary to assure herself that this was impossible. She'd do anything—

And so would her aunt.

The phone was still warm from his hand. She flipped it open and pressed a menu key. CALL HISTORY. INCOMING CALLS. UNKNOWN NUMBER. She pressed Talk, then held the phone to her ear. One ring. Two.

"Lucy Sharpe's office."

Betrayal rose like bile in her throat as she snapped the phone closed and dropped it like it had burned her. All this time, all this *time* . . .

He was her eyes. Her ears. Her watchdog. Her puppet. And Lucy was in the background, sneaking, conniving, manipulating. *Controlling.*

She closed her eyes and gripped the side of the dresser. Behind the bathroom door, she heard running water and the tap of a razor against the sink.

"You know what I think?" he called.

In one move, she scooped up her clothes from the floor. "What?" she replied, forcing calm into the single syllable.

"I think we have to look harder at Glenda. She's the one who told you about the abortion in the first place."

She yanked on her top, then pulled the pants on one shaky leg at a time. "Yeah." *Just stay in there, Johnny.* "Maybe."

The water shut off. "I have a plan," he said.

Or Lucy does. She grabbed her shoes and ran into the living room, slipped her purse and jacket under her arm, and made it to the door just as the digital song sang again.

"I'll get that!" he hollered gruffly.

But she was halfway down the hall and never heard him answer Lucy's private ring.

CHAPTER
Twenty

"I have to fire that girl." Lucy hugged one of the citron-green silk pillows that dotted the Ambassador Suite of the Four Seasons Hotel, staring out the fourth-floor window at the tops of the trees.

Dan snorted. Across the room, he was draped over a matching sofa, long legs sprawled in front of him. "She sure isn't Raquel Durant. But those are big shoes to fill."

She pulled her attention from the window to meet a pair of eyes as green as the spring willows surrounding the park outside.

"It doesn't take a mental giant to realize you don't call someone working undercover from my line."

"True, but she was following your orders. You told her to call him immediately with the reports and she must have been sitting at your desk, hung up with you, then dialed him."

"And Sage figured it all out." She studied the carved mahogany crown molding. "How could I have underestimated Lydia's child?"

"I've never seen you like this, Lucy," he said.

No, even he didn't know about the dark days. She absently brushed a strand of white hair from her cheek, the constant reminder of the cost of loving and losing.

"I wanted so much to protect her. I knew she'd go digging for information and answers, and my gut told me it could be dangerous." She stood and walked to the window, her high heels making no sound on the luxurious carpet. "But she would never have let me help her."

"Why didn't you tell Johnny the truth?"

"I didn't want him to know this was so personal. I wanted him to treat her like any Bullet Catcher assignment." She pushed aside the heavy damask drape and studied the pedestrians on the sidewalk below. "He should be here by now."

"Maybe he took a detour to Beacon Hill," Dan suggested.

"And flat-out defy my instructions? Not the Johnny Christiano I know."

"The guy I saw at that basketball game last night . . ." Dan stood and joined her at the window. "He wasn't the Johnny Christiano I know, either. And I've known him for a lot of years. Since he was a kid on the streets, a wiseguy, and ready to be made."

But he hadn't been "made." Lucy and Dan had stepped in and changed Johnny's life, and in return, she'd been rewarded with a fiercely devoted Bullet Catcher who'd performed every assignment with signature style and near perfection.

"That wasn't your run-of-the-mill lust I saw at that basketball game."

Lucy gave Dan a knowing smile. "I told him to be charming and creative to stay in cover. He was taught by a master of the game."

Dan acknowledged the compliment just as Johnny rapped lightly on the door. "See that? He got right into this building and you didn't even see him. He's good."

"I didn't say he wasn't," she said, crossing the room to let Johnny in. When she did, she knew instantly that he was in more misery than she was.

He brushed by her, nodded to Dan, and went straight to the long granite bar for coffee. "She didn't go home."

Dan and Lucy shared a look. So he had gone to Beacon Hill first.

"What are the other possibilities?" Lucy asked. "A close friend? An office?"

"If I know Sage, she won't stop just because you're involved, or I'm not. She is single-minded and determined, and finding out that Julian Hewitt was leaving notes on the posters of the girls who'd done the kidnappings just made her more resolved to get answers. My guess is she's off investigating. I'd go straight to Glenda Hewitt, and so will she."

Lucy nodded. "Here's what we think, Johnny. Glenda and Julian have been hacking into takeme-tonite.com. That's how they know when and where these kidnappings take place. Not through any relationship with the site, but they know, and I think I know why." At his interested look, she explained, "Evidently, they have a daughter who was hit by a drunk driver and has been in a vegetative state for seven years.

They need lots of money to keep her alive at a high-end facility. Much more money than they make running an NBA dance team. They're doing something that's allowing them to send twenty thousand a month to Land's End Critical Care. And Julian was wrong when you trapped him in the parking lot. His daughter is still alive."

Johnny frowned. "So where's the kickback for the kidnapping?"

"That's what we haven't figured out yet. Some of the dancers apparently sign up and have the full kidnapping experience. According to the website, others have canceled, yet they think they've been kidnapped. They've all been put into the same dark van, but don't necessarily remember or share anything after that."

"Whatever they're doing," Johnny said, "it sounds like Keisha found out, and they had to get rid of her. Possibly Ashley, too?"

Dan eased onto the sofa. "You know, there are twenty-some damn near flawless women, together all the time. It's like some kind of bizarre sociology experiment."

"They're like a pack of perfect specimens." Johnny put his coffee cup down, thinking hard. "Vivian said the guy didn't want her because she was a 'mutt'—she thought he meant a mixed race."

Lucy's cell phone rang and she glanced at it, then looked at Johnny. "It's my assistant. Shall I kill her for you?"

He met her gaze straight on. "I take full responsibility for being the bigger of two morons. I shouldn't have left my phone on the dresser and Sage in the room."

No, he shouldn't have. Nor should he take all the blame for this. Lucy had to shoulder her share, and she would—as soon as she had this situation in hand. She left to talk to Nancy in another room, and when she returned, Johnny was leaning over the dining table, poring over some of the reports that she'd accumulated on the case. "You didn't tell me Glenda Hewitt is a patient of Alonzo Garron's," he said.

"And guess who Nancy just connected me to on that call?"

"Garron?" Johnny asked.

"The CEO of Massachusetts General, who happens to be a friend of a friend. And Garron's former boss."

Johnny looked up from the papers. "What?"

"It seems Dr. Garron didn't leave his position at the hospital just because he was a whistle-blower for Sage's insurance-scam story, as he'd like everyone to believe." Lucy put her elbows on the counter. "Evidently he lost two patients having routine D-and-Cs, and while nothing at all was proven, rumors were rampant. Some patients were reportedly uncomfortable with him. My contact wouldn't say why, since he's already breached ethical boundaries to give me this much."

Johnny's body tensed as he stood, straightening the papers. "One of the few people Sage would ask for help is Alonzo Garron. She trusts that guy, a lot."

"Dan and I will pay Glenda Hewitt a visit," Lucy said. "You go find Garron."

"I'll get my jacket and gear," Dan said. "Back in five minutes."

When the door closed behind him, Lucy took a deep breath and asked the question that troubled her most: "Why aren't you tearing into me for keeping you in the dark, Johnny?"

"Because."

She laughed softly. "Because I'm the boss? Because you are the most dedicated employee in the world? Because you understand my motives? Because *why*?"

His smile was so sweet, it broke her heart. "Because I got to know her, and she's the most amazing woman I've ever met."

Oh, no. He had it worse than she'd thought. "Then I'm jealous," she admitted. "Because I'd really like to know her, too."

"I hate to break it to you, Luce, but that isn't going to happen in this lifetime. She's not about to forgive you for what you did, and what happened to her mother. And I doubt she'll ever forgive me for lying to her."

Lucy swallowed the hard lump in her throat. She'd long ago become accustomed to the bitterness that rose with the false accusations, and the fact that she was protecting her niece from the real truth about what had happened. Sage had already lost her mother; there was no reason to steal her father from her, as well. "You lied because I asked you to, Johnny."

"Yeah. You tell her that next time you see her, 'cause I figure I'm pretty much on her permanent shit list."

She hated that she'd helped put that much hurt in his voice. "I'm sorry. But I couldn't have trusted her with a better Bullet Catcher."

"I slept with her," he said simply. "We were intimate on every imaginable level. I know your policy about bodyguards and principals."

She appreciated the admission, but it came as no surprise. "I told you to be creative and charming. These were extenuating circumstances. I'm certain that you merely did what needed to be done to protect her and maintain your cover."

"Then you'd be dead wrong." He turned to the door just as his cell phone rang. He swiftly read the ID, his shoulders dropping in disappointment. "It's Detective Cervaris."

She watched him as he listened, his frown deepening, his body tensing, then he snapped the phone closed. "Ashley McCafferty's body was just dredged up from the Charles River."

"Any clues?"

"Her stomach was slashed and all of her female organs were removed."

Fear shot through Lucy. "Find that doctor, Johnny."

"I'm on it."

This must be what Charlie felt like on his endless train ride on Boston's MBTA.

Sage fingered the Charlie Ticket she'd used a few dozen times that day. In the hours since she'd left The Eliot Hotel, she'd taken the Green Line four times from Lechmere out to Riverside. She transferred to the Blue Line and meandered up the north shore near Revere.

The realization that Lucy Sharpe had sent Johnny Christiano as some kind of . . . of watchdog folded her spirit so badly, Sage had her pity party on the T, as it crawled back and forth like an injured snake over the tracks of Boston's public transportation system.

With her phone turned off, the day grew darker, just like her mood, and she met her only goal for the afternoon: She avoided going home.

Because she had no doubt who'd be sitting on her front step, or even in her living room since he was so damn good at infiltrating things. Like her apartment. Her bedroom. Her body. Her heart.

She turned in her seat, checking the car for the twentieth time to see if he was following her. Then she leaned her head against the cool glass of the train window and inhaled the rancid smell of sweat and oil and humanity and truth that she'd become accustomed to today.

She closed her eyes to ward off the next wave of tears. How in God's name could she have been so blind? So stupid? So willing not to see the obvious? How could she have ever forgotten the power of Lucy Sharpe?

John Anthony Christiano—or whoever the hell he was—had been no "rescuer" for a fantasy-abduction site. He'd been no male prostitute. He'd been no lover, no partner, no nothing. He was a liar, a con, a spy. A puppet. A gun-carrying, crime-scene-sniffing, bad-guy-fighting professional Bullet Catcher.

There were so many clues—how could she have missed them? She stifled a groan. And the gym rats! God, she'd been played like a complete fool.

But why? His job, she was certain, was to follow Lucy Sharpe's orders, and he was no doubt richly rewarded. But why did Lucy care what happened to her?

What did it matter to that coldhearted bitch who'd turned on her sister, and her sister's family, thirteen years ago?

It was nearly five in the afternoon when the train rolled into the elevated stop at Charles Street. Should she chance going home? Yes. Because no lame excuses or pan-fried delicacies or brain-rattling sex would work this time.

And he shouldn't have the power to keep her from home, from finding out what happened to Keisha. She'd do whatever it took to get those answers, even face that charming smile.

Getting the answers might require another kidnapping, because she didn't trust any of the information they'd gotten from Lucy. Who knew what her agenda really was? Next time, her fantasy abduction wouldn't be interrupted by Lucy and her band of merry men. She'd register tonight.

Her stomach rumbled, reminding her of the many hours since she'd eaten. Maybe she should get something to eat, so that when she arrived, he couldn't tempt her. With food, anyway.

At the bottom of the station steps, she rounded the corner, opening her bag to tuck her Charlie Ticket into its pocket. As she did, a strong hand gripped her elbow from behind. She gasped, then froze. "Is this your idea of showing me how much I need a thug to protect me?"

"No, this is my idea of a pleasant surprise."

She turned around at the lilted voice. "Alonzo! What are you doing here?"

"You think I am too snobby to take a train?"

Relief fluttered through her. "I'm just glad to see you."

That made his gray eyes twinkle. "I dropped my daughter off." He ran a hand over his wet, bald head. "But her train was delayed and I didn't bring an umbrella."

He did look like he'd been there awhile. "I don't have one either, I'm afraid. I didn't even realize it had started raining."

He put a friendly, casual arm around her and led her away from the crowd. "And where have you been all day and all night?"

She drew back. "All night?"

"I saw you with your young chef at the arena last night, remember? And don't forget my business, Sage. I know women. And you . . ." he touched her chin, raw from a night of friction with Johnny's beard, "have the appearance of a woman who has been well and thoroughly attended to."

The intimacy of the comment sent a frisson of discomfort up her spine. "More like well and thoroughly kicked in the gut."

His eyes darkened to the color of the rainy Boston sky. "Do I have to kill this Johnny character? Or at least pull his résumé from the Ritz?"

Oh, God. She'd had him *interview* for a job. She'd forgotten that.

"Well?" He studied her expression for a moment. "Seriously, Sage, are you all right?"

"I'm fine, but it's nice to see a friend right now."

She normally wouldn't have been so bold as to call him a friend, but at the moment it seemed appropriate. "I've got some problems."

He continued to guide her away from the station to a small commuters' parking lot. "This sounds like more than man trouble. Why don't we go somewhere dry and talk?"

"I don't know. I'm not such good company right now." How could she explain to him the mess she was in and the answers she needed? But then she remembered that he might have one of those answers—and maybe his information was different from what Johnny got from Lucy. At the thought, she felt emboldened. "Were you ever able to find out that information I needed about my roommate?"

"As a matter of fact, something came in late yesterday, but I didn't open it because I didn't want to miss the Blizzard tip-off. Would you like to go check it out now?"

"Yes," she said without hesitation. Not only did it beat going home to find the trash on her doorstep, it was action in the right direction.

He gave her a smile of enormous satisfaction. "And you can see my new offices."

As she climbed into his cherry-red Mercedes, she couldn't help but check the side mirror to see if anyone was around.

He glanced her way as he slid in behind the wheel. "Are you looking for someone, Sage?"

She slipped into a sad smile. "Not anymore." She searched her mind for an appropriate change of subject. "I thought you didn't have any children."

"My daughter is from my first marriage. Perhaps you remember me mentioning that Alicia couldn't conceive. In fact, that's what got me so interested in infertility treatment." He gave her the strangest smile. "Women's fertility is such a fascinating miracle, don't you think?"

"I guess." She laughed. "Unless you're trying to avoid it."

"Of course, you wouldn't want a baby yet."

"Not yet." At the rate she was going, not ever.

"When was your last period?"

She drew back in surprise. "Excuse me?"

"I'm a gynecologist, Sage. That's like asking 'how are you' in my business."

Still. "Uh, about, I don't know . . ." She did some mental calculations. "Ten or twelve days ago, I guess."

He held her eyes for a moment, his own bright and clear. "Let's go get that paper for you and have a talk, okay?"

She didn't answer, but plucked at the collar of her jacket, warmth prickling her skin.

He followed Charles Street, passing her apartment on Chestnut. Unable to resist, she glanced at the front steps.

"Did you expect him to be waiting?" Alonzo asked.

"No," she said, averting her eyes from the building. "And it's better this way."

"He was smothering? Is that why you made the 'thug' comment?"

"Exactly." That was the easiest way to explain it. "Too . . . controlling."

He looped onto Storrow Drive, following the river north toward the medical offices that dotted the neighborhood around Mass General. Traffic was always jammed at this point, but today it seemed worse than usual, especially for a Sunday.

"I wonder what the problem is," she said, peering into the misty, darkening evening. As he rounded the bend, the problem became clear. A dozen police cars and ambulances blocked the side of the road that bordered the river.

"I know a back way," he said, whipping into a side street and tooling through some one-way roads toward the hospital. In a few minutes, he pulled into an alley separating a large brick office and a much smaller one-story building.

He indicated the more humble facility with an apologetic smile. "It's not the glamour of Mass General," he admitted, "but I own the whole thing. Come on, I'd love for you to see what I've done with it."

She waited, glancing around the abandoned alley and side street, while he pulled out a key ring, opened three locks, and stepped into a cool, dark hallway that was obviously the back of a medical facility.

"Wait here while I disarm the security system."

She held the door with her shoulder as he took a few steps in and touched a keypad. In the shadows, she saw a typical doctor's office with a hallway of closed doors, a nurse's station, and a frosted glass door at the end, which she assumed led to the lobby.

"All right, we're in." He opened the first door on the left, to a spacious, well-appointed office. Despite the darkness, she could see a large, uncluttered desk, a darkened computer screen, and a long, leather couch under an impressive array of diplomas and awards.

"The building may be smaller than Mass General," she said, "but this is a much bigger office."

"It is that. Have a seat. I'll get the report. In the meantime, how about something to drink. A soda? Water? Something stronger? I have wine."

She sat on the edge of the couch. "You give your patients wine?"

"I give my *guests* wine," he corrected.

"I really don't need anything. Just that information." For some reason she couldn't quite understand, she just wanted to get out of the dark, empty building.

"Wait here a moment," he instructed, then left. She put her purse down and wandered around the room, glancing at the wall of honors, then the pictures on his credenza. She'd met Alicia Garron once, but where was this daughter he'd mentioned? Why wasn't there a picture of her?

Unable to see in the shadows, she reached for the window blinds and twisted the plastic rod, giving her a view of his car just as a dark sedan pulled into the same alley. In a moment, a woman emerged, pushing blond hair from her sharp features and squaring narrow shoulders as she marched directly to the door through which Sage had just entered. Glenda Hewitt. What was she doing here?

Spinning around, Sage sidestepped the large desk and rushed to the door, half expecting to come face-to-face with the woman she'd left in the police station paying bail for her husband fifteen hours earlier. But the hall was empty, with no sign of Alonzo or Glenda. The back door clicked, as though it had just been locked.

Sage dived for it, twisting the knob with a fruitless jerk. Had Glenda locked it from the outside?

She swore under her breath, then headed for the lobby at the other end of the hall. "Alonzo!" she called, looking left and right. "Dr. Garron?"

The door to the lobby was locked. She called out again, an eerie chill meandering up from the base of her spine. Back in the hall, she started pushing doors open, but they all led to examination rooms, the beds all covered with fresh paper, the stirrups suspended in air waiting for tomorrow morning's patients. The rooms smelled like antiseptic and alcohol, and the emptiness just increased her fear.

But fear gave way to anger. "Dr. Garron!" she hollered, as loudly as she could. "Where are you?" She shoved another door open but stopped when she saw it was a stairwell. Leading where? To a basement? Above the door, a tiny green sign read EXIT.

But she didn't want to go down there, even if it promised an exit. She wanted to go out. "Alonzo!" she screamed so hard it hurt her throat. "Where are you?"

Surprised at how much she was trembling with adrenaline and frustration, Sage jogged to the back door again and pounded on it. She grabbed the handle and gave it a good jerk, gasping when the door opened and she stumbled through the opening.

Had she only imagined it was locked? Had she just panicked for no good reason? She took one step forward, then remembered her purse. But what if the door locked again when she closed it?

She kept her foot in the doorjamb, searching for

something to hold the door open. Stretching as far as she could, she swiped a clipboard from the nurse's counter, slid it between the door and the jamb, and went back into his office for her purse, then checked to make sure she had her phone. But who should she call?

Johnny. The temptation was powerful. Wasn't her phone programmed to his cell phone? She squeezed her eyes shut. No, she couldn't turn to that untrustworthy liar in her time of need.

She flipped the bag over her shoulder and headed back into the hall, a whimper of frustration escaping when she saw that the clipboard had somehow slipped out and the door, she soon discovered, was locked tight again.

"What the hell is going on?" She stared at the tiny exit sign about the stairwell. Did she have any choice at this point? "Alonzo!" Her call just echoed down the tile floor. As she approached the door, she reached into her bag and pulled out her cell phone, holding the Talk button until it beeped softly.

She stared at the phone, running through her options. Had Alonzo gotten an emergency call? Or was he just in another part of the building and her imagination had gone wild? She took one step toward the stairwell, then stopped.

She might be mad, a little scared, and a lot confused, but she wasn't stupid. She pressed 1 and it didn't ring even half a time before he answered.

"Sage!" Johnny's voice almost brought life back to her numb, cold fingertips. "Listen to me. Please. I—"

"I don't want your explanations. I don't want your lies or excuses. You work for my aunt as a spy or a watchdog or whatever. I hate her, so by extension I hate you."

"Sage, please, this is imp—"

"I know you were doing your job, but I sure as hell don't know why she sent you. And I don't care," she said quickly before he could interrupt. "Because I'm only calling to tell you—"

"Whatever you do, don't talk to Alonzo Garron."

"What?"

"He's the connection, Sage. To Glenda and the kidnappings. Probably to Keisha. They're taking the girls for some reason, we don't know why. Please stay away from that man."

"I'm in his office."

He groaned. "I've been there ten times today," he said. "The place has been deserted all day."

"He said he was here before he took his daughter to the T."

"He doesn't have a daughter."

She closed her eyes. "He has a daughter from his first marriage."

"He's lying. About everything. About why he left the hospital, at the very least. Maybe more. Please don't trust him, Sage."

She scanned the deserted office hall. "I don't know who to trust anymore."

"Oh, baby, I'm so sorry—"

"Don't, Johnny. Not now. Not . . . ever. I have to go.

I have to get out of here. I'm locked in and I'm alone."
And scared. But she refused to admit that to him.

"I'll be there in fifteen minutes, twenty at the most.
I'm in Chestnut Hill, circling his mansion."

"I don't want to wait," she said, a shiver running
through her. "Plus, it'll take you longer than that.
There's a ton of traffic on Storrow Drive, an accident or
something."

"That's no accident, Sage."

Something in his voice terrified her. "What do you
mean?"

"They're dredging up Ashley McCafferty's body.
She's been . . . brutalized."

"Oh." Her body sank in shock.

"Sage, listen to me. Don't go anywhere with Garron. You can scream, holler, and kill me later if you
want, but please, baby, please don't go anywhere with
him."

"I'm just going to try to get out of here. But I
wanted somebody to know where I am."

"Sage." His voice was so soft, she could imagine the
warmth of his breath as he said her name. And here she
was, in some abandoned stairwell, letting that voice
permeate her veins, her head, her heart. Why?

"I know, I know—don't leave with him."

"Don't. And listen to me, okay? Nothing, not one
minute of time with you, wasn't real. Or perfect. Or
amazing. I love being with you. I love—"

"Stop." She squeezed her eyes against tears. "You
lied about everything, Johnny. You lay there in bed
and let me spill my guts about my aunt and never even

blinked." Her voice hitched. "You, who think betrayal is the worst crime of all."

"Everyone's motives were good, Sage. She only wanted to be sure you were safe. She loves you. Honestly. Lucy loves you and, Sage, I—"

She snapped the phone shut.

With her eyes on the exit sign, she thrust open the door and entered the stairwell. In one step, the door behind her closed and everything was pitch black.

She took baby steps until she was on the stairs, then started down, reaching for a handrail that wasn't there. It was like a tomb, silent, dark, and terrifying.

What if Johnny was right? What if Alonzo was a connection to Keisha's death? Had he been waiting for her at the T? Why had he asked her personal questions and brought her here, only to disappear?

"Alonzo?" she called again, the echo even more pronounced down here. She got to the bottom step, touched the wall, her fingers scraping over concrete until they reached metal. Thank God, a door. There was no knob or handle, so she just leaned against it, and, miraculously, it opened. But still she was entombed in blackness.

She blinked, forcing her eyes to see anything, but the darkness was total, nothing even resembling a shadow. She put her hands on the cold, damp concrete, feeling her way until she finally reached another door. This one had a handle. And it was unlocked.

She pushed it in and was rewarded with the dim, milky light of a single bulb, revealing another hallway, lined with several doors.

She tried the first door and it swung open to a tiny

room. She couldn't find a light on the wall, but she could see two small cots with white sheets and an empty bookshelf. She left and moved to the next one. Locked. There were two doors at the very end of the hall. A dim light peeked out from under one. *Please, God. An exit.*

The knob turned easily but it took all her weight to push the thick, industrial steel. As soon as she opened it, she squeezed her eyes shut against intense, white light.

"There you are, Sage."

She swallowed a loud gasp, squinting to avoid a blinding beam of light. "Alonzo?" Eyes stinging, she managed to escape the glare and make out the shape of the man who'd brought her here.

He was dressed for surgery in dark green scrubs, a hairnet, and a protective mask. Beside him, a medical bed appeared ready for a patient.

"What's going on?" Sage barely got the words out.

"You have something I want, Sage." Alonzo came closer and Sage backed up. "Something I want for my own. The others were for profit. But you have something very few women have."

Heat and blood sang in her head. "What?"

"Brains and beauty. And something . . . special. Drive. Dogged will. I like those qualities in a woman. I'd like them in my daughter."

The daughter thing, again. "What are you doing down here?"

"Welcome to my infertility lab. Look what excellent company you are in."

He stepped to one side and Sage stared at the wall

behind him, at the poster she'd seen a hundred times on Keisha's wall.

Neon-yellow index cards covered many of the faces, with notes on each. Dates and checks and slashes. Her eyes went immediately to Keisha's face, but instead of yellow, her card was the familiar chartreuse index card with one word on it: *Deceased.* Her heart sank into her stomach when she saw a matching card over Ashley McCafferty's face, bearing the same single word.

"Sometimes things don't go exactly as planned," he said. "And sometimes"—he tilted his head to her and lifted the hypodermic needle he held—"we find a young woman with such valuable eggs that my customers will pay top dollar. But I don't want yours on that dreary gray market, Sage. I want yours for my poor, infertile wife."

The words left her reeling. "You're stealing eggs? And selling them?"

He lifted one shoulder. "A healthy Caucasian, athletic and beautiful, can demand nearly seventy thousand dollars on the underground market. But not yours, dear. I promise."

She swallowed, stuck on one word. *Caucasian.* "And a non-Caucasian?"

"Of no use to me."

"Is that what happened to Keisha?"

He snorted derisively. "There's a market for black eggs like Keisha's, not that mulatto with the yellow eyes. I don't know why she brought the Masters woman to me."

She? "What happened to Keisha? She didn't commit suicide, did she?"

"She was pregnant. Only a few weeks, but of no use to me. It just seemed cleaner to aspirate the pregnancy so it appeared she was menstruating. Then I gave her the ephedra." He lifted the needle. "All right now, Sage. This is simple, and painless."

And insane. But he was a big man, with a needle. Could she fight him? Hold him off long enough for Johnny to get here? Maybe she could talk him out of it.

"Dr. Garron, did you know I'm part Asian? My great-grandmother was born in Micronesia. You don't want me."

"Sage, I don't care what you are. I'm not selling your eggs; I'm going to plant them in my wife and fertilize them. I told you, I want a daughter just like you. I knew it the first day you interviewed me, all spit and vinegar trying to get your story. A daughter I could be so proud of."

"Why didn't you just ask me?"

"What would you have said?"

"That you're crazy." She regretted the words the minute they were out, seeing a flash of something mean and deadly in his eyes. She stepped back, but behind her, the door clunked open and Sage whipped around. Johnny!

The sight of Glenda Hewitt kicked her in the stomach with disappointment.

"You have to leave!" she shouted at Alonzo, not even looking at Sage. "They found Ashley's body. Some

Amazon woman with a stripe in her hair is all over this. We have to run. We have to get out of here."

An Amazon woman with a . . . *Lucy*.

"Please wash and get scrubs on, Glen. We have work to do," Alonzo said slowly, pointedly.

Glenda spared Sage a disgusted glance. "You have no idea if she's ready. She never drank anything I gave her. Get rid of her."

Sage lunged toward the door, but Alonzo grabbed one arm and Glenda got the other one.

She fought his grip, and Glenda pushed her back, holding her in place with a surprisingly strong grasp for such a slight woman. "We can't exactly drive her into the Charles River with half of the Boston PD out there," she said, immobilizing Sage from the front. "Any ideas?"

Sage jerked at the burst of fiery heat in her neck, the warmth spreading like flames through her veins, instantly numbing her upper body.

"Yes, I have an idea." Alonzo's voice was already garbled and distant as the drug infiltrated her body. "But I have to do one last thing before we leave."

"You don't have time to operate."

"Do you want to die with her, Glen? Then shut up."

CHAPTER
Twenty-one

Johnny drove like a maniac, weaving in and out of traffic as adeptly as the pathetic little Camry would let him. The sound of Sage's voice rang in his head, and his own desperate words. He'd almost said he loved her.

He gripped the steering wheel, swore viciously at another driver, and swooped around the car in front of him. The crowded side streets east of the Charles and south of Mass General were a mess of narrow one-ways, truly mapped out by the cows that roamed the town hundreds of years earlier. He ignored an indignant horn and barreled the wrong way down Philips. Finally, he reached the tiny white building with a brass plate on the front: ALONZO GARRON. OBSTETRICS, GYNECOLOGY, INFERTILITY.

It had been seventeen minutes. Was she still in there? He double parked in the middle of the street and ran to the entrance to pound on the glass. "Sage!"

Inside, it was completely dark. To get to the back of

the building, he'd have to run to the end of the block and down the alley in the back. Which would be faster than driving in circles on one-way streets. He took off for the corner, turning it just as a dark car screamed toward him. He jumped away, scraping brick and barely saving himself. By the time he got on his feet, the asshole was gone. He continued his run to the back, making it down the alley in less than a minute.

Garron's red Mercedes was the only car parked there. At least she hadn't left with him. But had she gotten out, or was she still locked inside? As he started toward the back door, pulling out his gun and ready to shoot anyone or anything that stopped him, he heard a deep rumble under the ground. Then the entire building ruptured in a deafening blast of smoke, fire, and concrete, sending him sailing ten feet backward and slamming him so hard into a brick wall, he was sure he was dead.

But he could still hear. An alarm, another powerful boom, windows popping and glass shattering, a scream in the distance. And the acrid, bitter smell of dynamite and destruction.

"Sage!" The gun still in his hand, he wiped soot and grime from his eyes to clear his vision. His heart collapsed at the destruction of the building where Sage had been. Bright orange flames started to lick what was left of the little facility, as a siren wailed and people shouted.

His cell phone buzzed against his hip. He managed to reach into his pocket, flip it open, praying for a miracle. If there was anything in the world he wanted to hear, it was Sage saying, *I'm home, Johnny.*

"Did you find her?"

He managed not to swear at Dan. "I think so." He stared at the rubble, imagining her rising from the ashes and running to him like in the movies. But only strangers poured out of the nearby buildings, drawn to the disaster.

Johnny knew too much about a bomb in a building like that. No one had survived that blast.

"What's all the noise?" Dan asked.

Black smoke billowed toward him. "Are you with Lucy?"

"Yeah."

How could he tell her? How could he admit that he was the first Bullet Catcher to lose a principal, and that principal was the niece she loved?

"Is everything okay?" Dan asked. "Are you okay?"

He lied, again. "Yeah." Another siren wailed.

"Where's Sage?"

"I don't know." More lies.

"Listen to me," Dan said. "If you haven't found the doctor, you need to go after Glenda. Lucy planted a GPS tracker on Glenda's car this afternoon. We think the doctor and Glenda are together, and that may lead us to Sage."

Johnny looked in the direction where the dark sedan had almost creamed him, and grabbed the tendril of hope with everything he had. "Let's get her."

Every bone and muscle in her body hurt. Her throat was so dry, it felt like she'd tear flesh if she tried to make a sound. But even if she could blink, move, or swallow, she wouldn't dare. Her survival instinct screamed at her to be still and act dead.

Or else she'd *be* dead.

Sage knew that the minute she woke up in a car trunk, bound and choking on a rag that smelled of formaldehyde and alcohol. She couldn't reach the trunk release, and wouldn't survive a jump even if she had been able to knee the thing open. So, for God knew how long, she forced herself to wake up, to think, to try to imagine where these two lunatics were taking her and what her best chance at escape was.

As they rumbled along at highway speed, Sage concentrated on breathing slowly, relaxing into the pain that racked her body, and replaying the answers she finally had.

They were stealing eggs. No wonder Glenda knew when every dancer was having her period. Glenda was arranging these kidnappings, and then down in the bowels of his office, Garron was taking their eggs. And when Keisha's turn came up . . . she was already pregnant with LeTroy's baby. So they killed it, and her.

Breathe, Sage. Breathe. And think about something good. Something to live for. Something to fight for.

She closed her eyes, and all she could see was one man. What if she was murdered tonight and she never saw Johnny Christiano again? Her heart pummeled against her knees and she curled her head down into the fetal postion they'd bound her in, her hands tied tightly behind her, crushed between the weight of her body and something sharp and hard.

A wave of terror threatened, so she breathed through her nose as slowly and deeply as she could, focusing on the sound of the engine changing gears, realizing they were slowing down. They rumbled over cinders or stones, and her weight shifted as the car headed uphill. A very steep hill. Where in God's name were they taking her?

And who would ever find her?

Johnny. She practically whimpered his name. She hadn't even given him a chance to finish his sentence. She could still hear his voice.

Nothing, not one minute of time with you, wasn't real. Or perfect. Or amazing. I love being with you. I love . . .

The car stopped on the hill, rolling her closer to the back, then the engine died. If Garron thought she'd come out of her hypodermic haze, he'd stab her again. Or worse.

She steeled herself in raw determination. She could act unconscious, play dead, find the right time to run. She could do whatever it took to stay alive.

Glenda made a shrill demand, but all Sage understood was the tone of desperation. Alonzo didn't respond. In a minute, the trunk popped open. She instantly sank into her role.

But blood rushed in her head, thrumming through her veins, singing in her ears. If the doctor took her pulse now, he'd know she was wide awake. But she fought every instinct, so still not even an eyelash fluttered. They lifted her, clunking her knees against the car, but she didn't even flinch. She let her head and limbs go completely slack, while Alonzo dragged her over gravel.

Then she heard the sound of water, a rushing powerful swell of surf pounding against rocks. Hadn't he mentioned a home on Marblehead Neck? She tried to visualize the pricey peninsula connected to Boston's North Shore. That had to be where she was. Even with the rag in her mouth, she could smell the salt water of New England's coast, could imagine the black Atlantic Ocean far below a ragged, rocky cliff.

"Upstairs," Alonzo said, pulling Sage into somewhere even darker, chillier. A garage.

"Can't we use a downstairs bedroom?" Glenda asked.

"I need equipment," he said gruffly. "An aspirator. The right needle. She'll need ten more milligrams of Versed, stat. What I gave her is going to wear off any minute."

Sage let her head drop forward, concentrating on staying limp. With her face down, she risked a tiny peek under her lashes, but saw only a gray floor and her own feet. They dragged her up carpeted stairs, then up a narrow wooden set. She tried to picture her surroundings, find an escape route. She imagined herself being taken to an attic.

"Put her there," he ordered.

Glenda flung her onto something high and hard, like the examining tables at his office. "Hurry," Glenda insisted. "Get the Versed before she wakes up."

"I can't make a mistake. She hasn't taken hormones. I'll be lucky to get one egg."

"Why is this so important?" Glenda's voice shot up an octave. "This isn't why we do this. There's no profit in this."

"Sometimes there are more important things than profit. Isn't that why you first came to me? You wanted another child. Or have you gotten so wrapped up in the money that you forget I have the power to do what God can't? To make babies where there wasn't ever going to be one?

"I want a baby. Why do you think I got rid of my first wife and married someone half my age?" He snorted. "An *infertile* someone half my age. But Sage's eggs could make the child I want to have. Surely you, of all people, understand that."

Metal clanged, like surgical tools being taken out of a drawer.

"Just hurry up," Glenda finally whispered. "It'll be my job to get rid of her just like Keisha and Ashley, so let's get this over with before she wakes up."

"It doesn't matter if she wakes up, because no one's going to come for her. They'll find her purse in the rubble in my office and pronounce her blown to bits."

It took everything Sage had not to let a whimper escape her lips. He'd set an explosion in his office! Johnny would assume she was dead.

She felt her last shred of hope shrivel and die. This one time, Johnny hadn't followed her, like she'd secretly imagined. He wasn't coming for her. She'd have to get herself out of this on her own. Or die.

"Help me undress her," he ordered, already tugging at one shoe, then the other, dropping them to the floor. He grabbed the waistband of her yoga pants and pulled them down, the air chilling her bare skin. Sage held her breath to keep her stomach from clenching and revealing her as awake.

One of them got her pants off and she heard the material fall to the floor.

"You don't have to stare at her," Glenda said sharply. "You've seen a million naked women."

Creepy chills threatened. *Oh, God, no goose bumps.* He'd know she was awake and listening.

"Some women," Garron said slowly, "are more beautiful than others."

She braced herself for his touch, for a hot hand that would make her flinch. But there was none.

"I'm going downstairs to get my bag from the car," he said, his voice gruff.

In a moment, a door opened and closed. This was it. He had to go down two flights of stairs and into the driveway. Sage clenched her teeth to keep them from chattering. This was her only chance. She heard a sound to her right, and from under her lashes she saw Glenda, her back turned. Sage didn't even take a minute to think. She just popped up and flung her arm around Glenda's neck, yanking it back as hard as she could.

Glenda stabbed a powerful elbow into Sage's rib but Sage tightened her stranglehold, her eyes darting madly in search of a weapon. On the counter, she grabbed the sharpest, longest blade she could find, fighting Glenda's vicious struggle with nothing but sheer determination. With a grunt, Sage shoved the point into Glenda's side, the knife making a sickening rubbery sound as it slid through flesh.

Glenda jerked and threw herself forward, but Sage held on. She wrenched the knife out and stabbed again, warm, wet blood squirting all over her bare legs as Glenda's cry of pain faded into a growl as she lost the fight. Sage pushed her to the door and managed to open it and shove her outside. She yanked the door and locked it with a dead bolt, her breath strangled, her heart still galloping. What did that buy her? Five minutes? Two? Nothing?

She heard Glenda call out a low, long plea for help.

For the first time, she looked around the room, her vision blurred from the drugs and the fight, her body quaking with adrenaline and fear. Three of the walls were windows. Not an attic. A lookout, maybe under a widow's walk like on so many Marblehead homes. Without taking an extra second she scooped up her pants, held them between her teeth, and lunged to a windowsill. Tugging the cord of a flimsy blind in a frenzy, she patted the edges of the window with desperate hands.

She found a lock and pushed it to the side, just as she heard footsteps. "Come on!" she pleaded, shoving at the window frame, the paint stuck like glue. Should she try another window? With superhuman strength, she pried the bottom pane open, pushing it wide in one mighty thrust. She scrambled out to the roof but couldn't get her footing and went sliding down a slope of shingles that tore and scraped her bare legs and bottom.

Crying softly, she thunked onto a flat overhang, landing on her knees and barely hanging on to the flat metal roof. She risked a glance up to the window, gasping for breath. Any minute he'd be after her. With a knife, a gun, a *needle*. Wincing at her cuts, she shimmied into her pants to protect her mangled skin, and looked at where she was.

Oh, hell. She was twenty feet over a cement patio, and everything in the moonless night was black. Black water, black cliffs, black night. Squinting, she tried to make out the edges of the lawn, but it appeared to be completely enclosed by a high brick wall. She'd climb it if she had to. She'd scale the cliffs and risk drowning. But she wasn't going to sacrifice her life for that monster who'd killed Keisha and would kill her.

A thud and a holler told her he'd gotten in. She scrambled to the side of the overhang, deciding between a fall, a perilous jump to an oak tree branch, or testing her weight on the gutterspout that ran to the ground. Grabbing hold of the gutter, she eased her trembling body over the edge of the roof and wrapped her legs around the downspout. It groaned and one metal strap popped out of a tenuous screw, but it held. More screws poked her bare feet and her fingers burned as she held on and dropped inch by agonizing inch. Ten feet from the ground, she let go and hit the concrete so hard, the impact cracked her teeth together. But she was down, and alive.

She spun around, in search of a gate or a tree tall enough to climb over the wall, but there was nothing but ominous shadows. Over her rushing pulse, she heard the sound of waves crashing against the cliffs and rocks and offering her only escape . . . or instant death. She had no idea how far down it was. Too damn far to jump, that was for sure.

Maybe she could hide, or scale the cliff? Running toward the sound of the water, she stumbled down a few stone steps and then reached damp, cold grass. She risked one quick glance at the lighted window, saw nothing, and kept running to a low wooden fence that edged the cliffs. She could step right through that fence and face whatever was on the other side. Over the sound of the waves, she heard a door slam. He was outside now.

She pushed herself through a wide opening in the fence, inched toward the edge, and peered straight down at what had to be a thirty-foot drop of solid, sheered rock. She looked left, right, and straight ahead. There were no boats, no beam of light from a lighthouse.

"Go ahead, Sage. Jump." She spun around at the sound of Alonzo's voice, making out his shape moving closer to her. "That's exactly how my first wife died."

He approached slowly enough for her to see the needle in his hand. She took a step back, her bare feet hitting the first edge of rock. She was inches from death . . . and a few feet from sleep that would mean death.

Now, only the fence separated them. "I don't want you to die, Sage. I only want your egg, your child. I really do. I've been so fond of you from the moment I met you. You reminded me of a daughter . . . a daughter I haven't had. Yet."

She had nowhere to go but down. "Okay," she said quietly. "But isn't there a better way than this to ensure you get what you want? If I cooperated, it would be better, wouldn't it?"

"You were supposed to drink the hormone stimulator, but I understand you were too busy interviewing and investigating." He climbed over the fence in one move, and her heel slid, making her gasp as she righted herself. "You've always been willful. I like that in a person. I'd like that in my child." He reached out to her. "Come on, Sage. Come back to the house. I don't want you to die."

Maybe not like this, but he *did* want her to die.

She moved to a more secure spot, digging her toes into the grass as she reached toward his extended hand. She let him come to her—one step, then another.

The moment his hand closed over hers, she whipped around, yanking him toward the edge. The needle went flying and he stumbled to the ground, bringing her down with him.

He rolled them both over, almost to the edge. "You'll die with me," he vowed.

"No," she gasped as she fought, taking them both perilously closer to the cliff.

He managed to roll on top of her. "You don't want to die, Sage," he said raggedly. "I can keep you alive. I have the power to do that."

"So . . . *Do* . . . I!" She flipped him all the way over her. Now they were at the edge, locked in each other's grasp.

"One more move and we're both dead," he growled.

"Just you." She gave a hard kick to his ribs that sent his legs over the edge. As he fell, he managed to snag her ankle. Her fingers dug into wet dirt and grass, desperate for a hold as she slid partially over the cliff.

He must have found a foothold below, because they both stopped, suspended between dirt and death. If he fell, she knew he was taking her with him.

"Don't do this, Sage," he rasped out, pulling her so hard that rocks stabbed into her hands as she clung for life.

"*You* did it," she insisted. "You're the one who wants to play God!" She managed to pull back her right knee and slam it full force into his nose, hearing the bone crack and his pained grunt.

Swearing viciously, he reached for her but she managed to swing in the other direction. Her fingers sunk deeper into the wet earth at the edge of the cliff, but she knew it could give way at any moment. With a growl of fury, she arched her back and fired her knee into his head again, and he howled and freed her leg.

"Bastard!" If she risked another shot she might lose her hold; then she'd die.

"Sage!"

The sound was barely audible, but she heard it. The sound injected her with one last blast of power and adrenaline. With a sob of fury, she crashed her knee one last time into Alonzo's face, and he let go. His scream echoed into the night as he plunged into a free fall, then disappeared into a crashing wave.

Her arms burned and her fingers ached and her body felt much too heavy for the wet earth that was keeping her from falling, too. Was his final cry loud enough for someone to hear?

"Sage!"

"Johnny!" Her voice was lost in the wind, drowned out by the pounding surf. If she could just pull herself up, she would hold him and love him and never let him go. "Johnny!"

Her fingers slipped an inch and she squeezed her eyes closed with an agonized cry. She pulled and kicked, and below her, vicious waves crashed against the deadly rocks.

She had nothing left. Her strength was gone. "Johnny!" She'd die now, his name the last thing on her lips. But she couldn't stand the pain anymore. She had . . . to let . . . go.

Two powerful hands closed over her wrists and squeezed with determination. "I'm here, baby. Hang on."

In one shockingly swift move, he jerked her up onto the grass, so hard she fell on top of him. His arms wrapped around her, strong and safe and pulsing with life and warmth.

"Sage, Sage." He pressed his lips to her hair, her temples, her face. "Oh my God, I thought I lost you."

She managed a whimper, unable to speak or breathe, her body quaking. He kissed her hair, her face, her tears, cooing her name, holding her against his pounding heart. "I don't know how you did that, baby. I don't know how you hung on."

"She does whatever it takes, just like her mother," a woman said.

Sage lifted her face as floodlights electrified the scene. A six-foot silhouette of a woman stood in a gun-fighter's stance, a menacing black weapon in one hand. Her waist-length hair blew in the gust of the North Atlantic wind, one thin white strand lifting like a flag of surrender.

Johnny kissed her again and again, until Sage dropped her head to his shoulder, finally giving up her fight.

CHAPTER
Twenty-two

The image of Lydia Sharpe, her arm around a gap-toothed Sage, yanked a ragged breath from Lucy's lips. She'd found the picture in a cracked porcelain frame, against the side of a cardboard moving box full of knickknacks from Sage's living room bookshelf. She hadn't meant to pry, but Sage was keeping her waiting a good long time, and naturally, being a former spy, she searched the half-packed room for clues about exactly who her niece had become.

She heard a man's low chuckle, and Sage's lighter laugh in echo.

In the weeks that had passed since they'd stormed the house on Marblehead Neck to save Sage, Lucy had realized that Johnny's temporary hiatus from work had nothing to do with lack of dedication or a loss of passion for his job, but everything to do with Sage. She left them alone, holding tightly to the brief conversation she'd had with her niece after they'd all met with Detective Cervaris. Sage had simply thanked her for saving her life, and kept the cool distance they'd maintained for the last thirteen years.

A distance Lucy ached to close. She tightened her fingers around the two envelopes in her hand, praying she was doing the right thing. At the sound of Sage's footsteps behind her, she dropped the picture back into the box and turned to meet her niece's cool gaze.

"That was taken at Disney World," Sage said, glancing at the box.

"I remember when you went," Lucy said. "Your mother was morally opposed to all things Disney, but she gave in because you wouldn't stop begging to go on Mr. Toad's Wild Ride."

"And after all that, I hated it. Things kept jumping out of the dark and scaring the life out of me."

Lucy crossed her arms, then shifted her weight from one stiletto to the other. "I suppose you wonder why I'm here."

"Johnny said you wanted to talk to me about Dr. Garron."

Among other things. "Yes. Here." She handed Sage the less combustible of the two manila envelopes. "I was able to locate and destroy almost all of the eggs stolen from the dancers, as well as those of a network of college students he had infiltrated. A few have already been used for fertilization and one has resulted in a child. I'll let you decide if you'd like to tell the biological mother."

Sage took the envelope. "Thank you." The note of appreciation was genuine. "I'll speak to each of the dancers."

"Have you finished the cover story you're doing?"

"I have one more interview with the DA, now that Glenda's out of the hospital and both the Hewitts are in custody. I've spoken to the doctors about their daughter, who is still alive though gravely ill." She turned the envelope in her hand and looked expectantly at Lucy. "Is that it?"

No, that was not it. The urge to reach out and fold Sage in her arms squeezed the breath out of her. She'd already suffered the worst loss a mother could, and nothing would ever bring that child back. But this woman, her niece, stood two feet away . . . and yet it might have been a thousand miles.

Lucy took a slow, deep breath. She'd made her decision out there on the cliffs of Marblehead Neck. And once Lucy made a decision, she never second-guessed it. "About that trip to Disney World."

Sage looked surprised. "What about it?"

"You may recall that your father didn't go."

Sage nodded. "He had to work. He had a case go to trial."

Lucy swallowed. "No, he didn't." The envelope felt heavy with the weight of what she had to tell Sage. She turned it over very slowly, showing the CIA seal and the stamp of STRICTLY CONFIDENTIAL to Sage. "Not as an in-house attorney for a consumer products company, anyway."

She held the envelope out in the space between them. "Your father worked for the CIA, Sage. His role was quite high level and confidential. As a matter of fact, he was my boss. I introduced him to my sister, and was overjoyed when they married."

Sage looked more stunned with each word.

"It was your father who learned of the story Lydia planned to write on the CIA, and your father who discovered how damning it could be. Not to a covert operation, as you have been led to believe, but to the public reputation of the Agency. The American lives at risk were not citizens living overseas. They were agents. Very high-level agents, and what was in jeopardy was their jobs."

"Whatever was in jeopardy, you killed the story, Lucy." She reached for the envelope, her fingers quivering. "And with that, you killed my mother."

"I did manage to stop the story from publication," she conceded. "It was one of my first assignments with the Agency."

"And you managed to ruin my mother's professional reputation in the process."

Lucy closed he eyes, hating that she had to do this. "At the time, we lived in a different world. And it was a different organization. Things were changing faster than many people could understand. There were those who manipulated others to maintain control and secrecy."

"You must have fit right in."

Lucy ignored the dig. "There were those," she continued, "who believed that a top-level spy married to an investigative reporter was a very bad mix for the Agency."

Sage just listened, but a hint of color began to seep from her cheeks.

"Those people are gone," Lucy assured her. "Long gone. They've paid the price for their shortsightedness."

"What are you saying?" Sage insisted. "That my mother's suicide was somehow orchestrated by the CIA?" Her voice rose in a little panic.

"Not by me."

The implication was obvious. "By my father?"

"Not by his own hand," she said. "Perhaps by his lack of it. We'll never know, because the answer lies in his lost memory."

Sage dropped onto the sofa, stricken. "He killed her."

Lucy fell to her knees in front of her. "No, no—I don't think he did. He might not have known. I didn't learn the truth until a few years after. I left the Agency immediately." Her voice cracked and she dug for composure. "By then, your father was already very sick."

Sage stared at her, then reached up and touched the white streak of hair that fell over Lucy's cheek. "Is that what caused this?"

"No," she said. "But I have spent every day aching for the sister I lost, and the niece."

"What's in this?" Sage tapped the envelope Lucy held.

"Some top-secret files that I managed to get. Your father's name is never mentioned. No one's is. But there is some closure here, I think."

Sage thought for a moment. "Why did you let him blame you all these years? Why did you let me hate you?"

"Because you'd already lost your mother. I didn't want you to lose your father, too."

"I have one last question." Sage took the envelope, fingered the seal, closed her eyes. "Why are you telling me now?"

"Because," Lucy said, putting her hands on Sage's knees, "I love you. Just as your mother did. And your father. I love you and I don't want our lives to be separate anymore. We are all the family we've got, you and me."

Johnny entered the living room then and sat next to Sage, his protective arm immediately around her shoulders. "You okay, babe?"

She nodded.

"Read the report, Sage," Lucy said, standing to her full height. "Draw your own conclusions and place the blame where you think it belongs. And please." She waited until Sage finally met her gaze. "Don't ever stop doing whatever it takes to find the truth. That's what she would have wanted most."

"I know that." Her voice tightened and she laid her head on Johnny's shoulder. "I've always known that."

Lucy left the apartment, heading straight to the limousine waiting outside, wishing she had a shoulder to lean on, someone who could dry the tears she was about to shed.

Sage did, now—and that gave her bone-deep satisfaction.

Johnny skipped "Volare" and "When You're Smiling" and went straight for the heart of his Dean Martin file on Sage's iPod: "That's Amoré."

Whistling, he crossed the bridge and paused to watch the late summer sunshine dancing on the pond in the Boston Public Garden. A swan boat with picture-snapping tourists slipped under the arch, their laughter floating on the breeze.

Leaning against the stone, he scanned the paths of the Garden until he found a familiar swinging blond pony-tail, the rhythmic sway of her hips magically matching the music in his ears. That was *amoré*, all right. His *amoré*.

They'd been coming to the Public Garden every single day all summer. Ever since Sage had returned from a brief visit to Vermont, where she'd confronted a man who wasn't able to confirm or deny his own name, let alone his dark secrets, she'd needed to run.

So Sage ran and he watched her, sometimes running with her. But not today. He knew she was getting an important call and wanted her to be alone when she received it. Then she could tell him her decision, unin-fluenced by his presence.

In the shade of a willow tree across the water, he watched her slow down, then reach for her cell phone. He hit the Pause button on the music so he could study her body language without distraction. She nod-ded, played with her hair, stretched her legs, rested on the grass, and even laughed once. Every move shot a little hope to his heart.

But mostly she listened . . . while Lucy talked. The conversation continued long enough for Johnny to get way too optimistic about his wild idea, seized on by Lucy.

Sage finally flipped the phone closed, so he crossed

the bridge and headed to the bench where he always met her after her run. In a few minutes, she jogged toward him, ponytail flying, smile beaming, as sleek and graceful and alluring as the first time he'd seen her, running straight into danger in the middle of the night.

Now their troubles were behind them, and they'd found consolation, acceptance, and love in each other's arms. But the respite had to end eventually. He had to go back to work, and then . . .

That's where his plan came in.

"Hey, gorgeous," she called as she reached him, then swooped down on the bench with an exhale. She popped an earbud out and kissed him on the cheek. "Whatchya listenin' to?"

"Two guesses."

She rolled her eyes. "We're going to have to get you into some twenty-first-century tunes, baby."

Was she not even going to mention the call? He lifted her ponytail and blew softly on her neck. "You're sweating."

She winked. "The way you like me best."

"I like you any way best, and you know it." He slipped an arm around her and resisted the urge to tug away her phone and see if it really was Lucy who had called. "How was your run?"

"Okay. I got distracted." She fanned herself with both hands and leaned back on the bench. "And now I'm starved. What are you making me for dinner?"

"Dinner?" He couldn't keep the surprise out of his voice. Lucy had just called with a life-changing offer, and she was worried about food?

"Yeah, you know, that meal we have between late-afternoon Limoncello and midnight cannolis? You make it, I eat it."

He laughed. "All you ever think about is food, Sage."

"And the sex that comes after the food." She nudged him.

Wasn't she even going to tell him that Lucy had called? "What about the future? Your work? Life? Don't you ever think about that?"

Her smile was slow, but she kept her eyes on the swan boat that passed. "Sure I do. Whenever we're not eating or making love. Which doesn't leave a lot of time, you may have noticed."

"Yeah." She hated the idea. That had to be it. She still thought Lucy was the dark angel of death, and that this was a fling that would end as soon as the hot weather did. "When you run, do you think about the future?"

"Sometimes." She pointed and flexed her toes. "Today I did."

Finally. "What did you think about?"

A swan boat floated by, two rollerbladers passed, and an endless minute dragged on.

"I think," she said slowly, "that the future . . ." Every pause was killing him. "Looks bright."

"Sage, come on." He let out an exasperated breath. "Did she call or not? Are you taking the job or not? Are you moving to Upstate New York or not? Will you—" He cut himself off and took her hands. "I need to know, baby."

She threaded her fingers in his and lifted his hands to her mouth. "Yes." She kissed his right knuckles. "Yes." She kissed his left knuckles. "Yes." She opened his hand and kissed his palm. "Now, what was the last question? Will I what, let you be my boyfriend while I work as Lucy's assistant?"

He smiled, the sun as warm on his face as the love in his heart. "No, that wasn't my question. So you're going to do it? You're going to take the job with the Bullet Catchers?"

She narrowed one eye at him. "Think I can do it?"

"In a heartbeat." He tapped his chest.

That earned him a smile and a kiss. "Thanks for the recommendation. I understand you live up there between assignments."

"Usually in a hotel, but I've had my eye on a house on the river. It has a big kitchen with a gas stove and a huge master bedroom—"

"The important stuff."

"And lots of room for . . ." *Kids.* "Us."

She inched closer to him. "You've been thinking a lot about the future beyond dinner, haven't you?"

"Sage." He leaned his forehead against hers. "That's all I've been thinking about. I love you and I want to spend every minute I can with you, and I want to cook for you and make love to you and share my messy past and spotty present and anything beyond that with you, and I—"

"Shhhh." She put her finger on his lips. "I love you, too. You are my boyfriend. I promise."

He half smiled. "I don't want to be your boyfriend, and you know it." He took her hand in his, his heart galloping as he looked into her eyes. "I want to be your husband."

She drew in a soft breath.

"I want it all. I want to take you to Italy to meet my sister, I want to marry you on the soil where I was born, and I want to spend every day of the rest of my life next to you."

"Sweetheart," she said softly, "you had me at the first rescue."

"I hate to break it to you, but you rescued *me*. Here." He put her hand over his heart. "You saved me from a lonely life of hotels and regret and hiding who I am."

"Oh, Johnny." Her eyes welled with tears, and she smiled. "I love who you were, who you are, and who you will be—and I will do whatever it takes to spend the rest of my life with you."

He briefly closed his eyes in relief. "Whatever it takes?" he asked.

"Whatever it takes."

He laughed softly, slipped the tiny white speaker into her ear, then pressed the Play button on the iPod. "Sometimes, it takes this."

Together they soaked up the sun, dreamed of the future, and listened to Dino sing about love.

Welcome to the exciting world
of the Bullet Catchers!

Turn the page to meet

ALEX ROMERO from *Kill Me Twice,*

AND

MAX ROPER from *Thrill Me to Death*!

Kill Me Twice

Jasmine Adams didn't bother to knock at her sister's door; she just slid the key in and opened it. She started to call out Jessica's name, but the pitch blackness of the apartment stopped her. Her sister was obviously not home.

Jazz blinked into the darkness, then flattened her hand against the wall to find a light switch. Remembering the alarm, she turned around looking for the key pad, but didn't see anything.

She pushed the door wider to allow the hallway light into the apartment, but the door was suddenly yanked from her hand and slammed closed with a rush of air that sent the hair on her neck to a full stand. Terror punched her stomach and every muscle in her body seized up for a fight. "What the—?"

From behind her, a hand slapped over her mouth so hard she choked on a gasp. She could feel the heat of a man against her back; a solid, sizable man who'd pinned her right arm with a paralyzing grip. Hot breath warmed her ear, the smell of raw masculinity filled her nostrils.

"That was stupid." His voice was low, almost a lilting growl that vibrated from his chest through her body.

No. Leaving her gun at home was stupid.

Her teeth snapped over his palm and she slammed her left elbow into his solar plexus with a resounding *thwumpf.*

Sucking in a surprised breath, Alex almost laughed at his mistake. He'd intended his warning to be gentle, but her free fist flew up at his nose, barely giving him a millisecond to stop it. He grabbed her forearm and saved his face, but she managed to get a handful of hair and yank for all she was worth.

The newscaster could fight.

He tightened his hold, squeezing her body against his, and

wrapping one leg around her calves. "Let go," he warned, shaking his head to loosen her grip on his long hair.

She pulled harder then smashed a boot heel into the top of his foot and crunched his toes.

Swearing at the unexpected pain, he swiped the foot she was balanced on and knocked her to her knees, going right to the floor with her. He used his right hand to break their fall, covering her body with his as they grappled to the carpet. He finally managed to free his hair from her death grip. Her butt jutted into his stomach as she grunted.

He immediately slid his hand over her mouth, again, to silence the inevitable scream. She obviously knew the basics of self-defense, which would make his job easier. As soon as she stopped practicing on him.

"I'm not going to hurt you."

She kicked a leg and grunted furiously, and he cupped his hand to avoid the bite this time. He pinned her legs under his. Her limbs stopped flailing but she kept pushing her rear end into his crotch. He'd have to train her not to dilute her excellent self-defense skills by offering her ass to an attacker.

His groin tightened as she slammed her round backside into him one more time. *Carajo!* She'd never stop fighting if she felt a boner in her back.

"Hold still," he insisted, raising his body to lessen the contact that had suddenly become more arousing than aggressive. "I only wanted to show you how vulnerable you are."

She froze at that. *"Mmm-what?"* The word was muffled by his hand, but her indignation came through loud and clear.

"Sometimes a good scare can help you take a threat more seriously."

All the tension and steely defense eased out of her muscles as he felt her go limp under him. Was that a trick? Could she be that good? It took years of training to learn how to stop the adrenaline dump and appear to drop your guard so your opponent did the same.

He didn't fall for it, but eased his hold on her.

"Listen to me," he whispered, surprised that his breath had quickened from that little bit of wrestling. "Someone who wants to hurt you could glide right by the so-called guard downstairs, pick your lock, use the last four numbers of your social to disarm the alarm, and have a knife at your neck in a matter of minutes."

He could feel her rapid heartbeat, and fast breaths warmed his hand. Sex demons teased him again as he imagined those responses caused by an encounter of a different kind.

He eased back, removing his hand from her mouth, but ready for her to flip and fight again. "It only took me about six minutes to get in here," he added. "Of course, I'm a professional. We don't know if your stalker is."

"What . . . are you talking about?" She turned her head toward him.

"I'm talking about your personal security liabilities." He slowly inched to her right and his eyes adjusted to the darkness enough to begin to make out her features. "In your situation, you need to listen. And look. And get the doorman to escort you up here instead of sitting on his rear end reading *El Nuevo Herald.* And, for God's sake, get a little creative on your alarm code."

Silver eyes flashed at him, giving him just enough warning to flatten his arm over her before she launched herself up. Instantly, all of the steel returned to her well-toned muscles, but he held her in place.

"Get off me," she ground out.

"Have you learned your lesson?"

"Yes," she whispered, her voice strained with effort as she tightened under his arm.

"And you believe I won't hurt you?"

"Yes," she insisted. "Let me up, damn it."

"Will you scream and attack me again?"

"Attack *you*?" She nearly choked at that.

"I'm demonstrating a point. You, on the other hand, are attempting to rip out my hair and shatter my foot."

"Excuse me, but you jumped me, asshole."

Good, she wasn't afraid anymore. Just mad. That made her a little safer. He eased off her and stood. She stayed on the floor, her head turned to watch him warily.

"I'll get the light," he said, sidestepping toward the living room without taking his eyes off her.

He knew exactly where the lamp was. He'd already scoured every inch of the apartment, searching for security flaws and learning even more about his principal. He knew that she was absurdly neat, had expensive taste in everything from clothes to art, and planned on marinated steak for dinner. He hoped he could change her opinion of him before she cooked it and refused to share.

As the light bathed the room and she stood, he took his first long look at the newscaster.

The picture had not done her justice. It hadn't captured her . . . energy. There was something so alive about her; she seemed to glisten with vitality. Her eyes were like polished platinum, sparking at him. Her slanted cheekbones flushed as much from anger as a graze with the carpet. He'd smeared her lipstick with his palm, leaving her full lips stained and parted as she stared back at him and drew shallow breaths, a dangerous combination of threatened and pissed off.

She placed her hands on her hips in a classic confrontational pose that accentuated the feminine but defined shape of her bare arms, and revealed the rise and fall of her chest.

His gaze dropped over her ribbed, strappy top just long enough to confirm his boss's assertion. They *were* real. He could tell by the softness of the flesh and the natural shape of her cleavage. He was, after all, an expert.

But something didn't fit. It was the clothes. He'd just searched her closets and drawers, looking for more letters from her stalker, but also getting to know his principal. Nowhere had he seen evidence that she'd wear a cotton undershirt and camos. Where had she been, dressed like that? Certainly not in front of the cameras, trilling about a bank robbery.

"Who the hell are you?" she demanded.

"Alex Romero. Mr. Parrish hired me."

She opened her mouth, and then closed it again.

"You did meet with Kimball Parrish today?" he prompted.

She shrugged and nodded, a mixture of such non-commitment that he almost laughed. "Briefly," she said.

It seemed a little silly after they'd had full horizontal body contact, but he reached out his hand to shake hers. She took a step backward, her expression still dubious. "Alex Romero." She said his name slowly, as though flipping through a memory bank.

"Your bodyguard."

"My—*what*?"

Son of a bitch. The idiot hadn't told her. He dropped his hand. "Mr. Parrish has arranged for personal security for you. Evidently he believes there is validity to the threats you've been receiving."

"Threats?"

Jesus, was she so immersed in her job that she didn't even consider the letters threatening? Doubtful, after that near pounding he just took. "Obviously, you've bothered to learn a thing or two about self-defense already."

"Who hired you again?"

"Mr. Parrish."

No light of recognition, no response to the mention of her boss—who also happened to be one of the most powerful men in her business.

"Which threats are you referring to, exactly?" she asked, shoving her hands into the back pockets of her pants. A move that did nothing to lessen the impact of the skintight tank top.

"I'm referring to the letters you've received from a fan. Six, as far as I know. And several untraceable e-mails."

Her frown deepened. "How do I know *you're* not a stalker? And that's why you know all this? Not to mention your rather bizarre idea of a welcome."

"Good point," he conceded. "Mr. Parrish was supposed to have told you his decision to hire security."

Still she didn't move. He waited for her to take control of her environment, to waltz past him and wrap herself in the familiarity of her home. She remained . . . cautious.

"As a matter of fact, he didn't tell me," she said. "And until I have that conversation with him, you'll have to leave."

"I'm afraid I can't do that."

She managed a tight smile. "Yes, you can. And it should be much simpler getting out than all the trouble you went merely to scare the shit out of me and *make a point*."

She stepped to the door, but he stopped her with a look. "I'm not leaving, Miss Adams."

"Excuse me?"

"Would you prefer I call you Jessica?"

She pointed to the door. "I'd prefer you get the hell out of here. Then I can call Kendall Parrish and discuss this with him."

Kendall. Her error set off a full warning bell in his head. He took a step closer and her shoulders tensed visibly.

"Why don't you call him while I wait?" he suggested.

"I'll call him later. Then we can discuss this tomorrow."

"Please call him now, Miss Adams. This could be a matter of life and death."

"Can the drama. I'm perfectly safe here . . ." Her voice faded into uncertainty. "Okay. I'll call him." She bent to retrieve her purse that she'd dropped, but as she lifted the shoulder strap, the top opened, spewing out papers, makeup, a mirror, and roll of mints.

He crouched down and flipped his cell phone open in front of her. "Use mine."

She rose from the disarray and gave him another suspicious look, then studied the keypad as she punched in a number.

Why hadn't she just picked up her own cordless phone sitting ten feet away on the living-room table?

She pressed his cell phone to her ear and looked away. "Hi. This is me . . . Jessica. I need to talk to you. It's very important. Call me. On my cell." She snapped the phone with finality and handed it back to him. "If you leave me a number where I can reach you, I'll call you after I've heard back from him. I'm sure you understand my reluctance to have a complete stranger in my home."

Nothing added up right. There was no way, no matter how on guard she was, this woman would have called her boss by the wrong name. And she hadn't known where to find the alarm pad when she'd walked in. His gaze dropped once more over her revealing top, down to the black boots surrounded by the chaos that was her handbag. Something was most definitely wrong with this picture.

"Let me try him myself," he said as he flipped the phone again. "I have his private line."

He faked thumbing a phone number, but simply pressed redial. Unlike her, he was able to hold her gaze and added his most charming smile while he listened to the taped message:

Hi. This is Jessica Adams. Please leave a message and I'll get right back to you.

"Well, what do you know," he said, dipping his head so close to hers he could almost kiss the smeared lipstick from her mouth. "I jumped the wrong Miss Adams."

Thrill Me to Death

From the top of the stairs, a shadow eclipsed the glittering party lights. Caroline looked up and swayed a little. God in heaven, it *was* Max. "What are you doing here?"

"I'm with the Bullet Catchers. Lucy Sharpe sent me."

His gaze never wavered from Caroline, slicing her with those black-diamond eyes that refused to reveal any emotion. An expensive sports jacket covered what she knew to be a Herculean chest, and in that chest pounded a heart that she'd once considered her most treasured possession. Long ago.

"There must be a mistake," she said. "I arranged for a bodyguard, not a DEA hunting dog."

The corner of his mouth quirked—for Max Roper, a full-blown grin. He reached out a hand for a formal shake. "Max Roper, here to offer you unparalleled personal security."

She backed away. "She sent *you* to protect *me?*"

"I suppose there's some irony in that, but Lucy has her reasons and we rarely question them, Mrs. Peyton." The emphasis on Caroline's married name wasn't lost on her. Of course, he'd believe what everyone else did: Caroline had married an older man for his money and won the lottery when he died in their bed, leaving her an heiress to a two-billion-dollar estate and controlling interest in Peyton Enterprises.

"I'll call Lucy and make other arrangements. Obviously she doesn't realize we have . . ." Her voice trailed off.

"A history?"

Her mind flashed with the memory of soul-flattening kisses and heart-cracking tears and gut-wrenching accusations, all delivered in a dingy hallway of a hundred-year-old building in Chicago. Yeah, that was certainly *history.*

"A conflict of interest," she concluded.

"That assumes . . . interest." His eyes glittered, but of course he didn't smile.

"I have no intention of playing word games with you." She'd lose. "If you don't call your boss, I will. You're not . . . what I had in mind." Now there was an understatement.

He pulled out a cell phone and held it toward her. "Just press one. It's programmed to her private line."

He was a world-class bluff caller. She remembered that from the nights she'd played poker with him and her father and a couple of other DEA agents. Max loved nothing more than tempting her into higher bets, his impassive expression never revealing his cards. Or his feelings.

She had bet everything on him and lost.

She took the phone as she regarded him. He really hadn't changed at all. If he'd spent the last eight years chasing evil drug lords, the job hadn't ravaged his handsome face; if anything, he looked better. Older. Wiser. Scarier. His dark hair was just as thick as it had been back in the days when Caroline's fingers explored it endlessly, although he'd grown it longer, letting it touch his collar and fall over one ominous-looking brow. A brow that still knotted at the sight of her, as though he could never figure her out but refused to stop trying.

"Are you going to call or just stare at me?" he asked.

Max was the bluntest human being she'd ever met. The bluntest, brashest, coldest human being, who once brought her to orgasm using nothing but . . .

She almost choked on the memory. "I just can't believe you're here."

"I understand." He crossed his arms, pulling the fabric of his sports jacket across that endless chest. "I've had some time to get used to the idea."

"You knew who I was when you accepted this assignment?"

"The whole world knows who Caroline Peyton is." He

dipped his head closer to her. "And, by the way, my deepest sympathies on the loss of your husband."

There was no indictment in his voice. None of the veiled resentment at her fortune. In fact, she heard that underlying gentleness he loved to hide, and her heart just about stopped. Max could always get her with softness. No matter how big and tough and mean and bad he was, when he turned soft, it killed her.

No, she reminded herself sharply, it killed her *father*.

She opened the skinny silver phone and pressed the talk button. As the screen lit up, she asked, "Did you say press one?"

He flipped the phone closed. "I'm the best she's got, Caroline."

She looked up and met his gaze. "I understand the whole Bullet Catchers force is the cream of the security crop. I'm sure we can find a suitable replacement."

He reached for the phone, but she tugged it toward her chest.

He relented and let her have it. "Before you call, why don't you tell me exactly what the problem is," he suggested. "Then I can help Lucy pick the right bodyguard for you."

A shatter of glass and metal reverberated from the patio. In one split second, Max whirled around, blocked Caroline with his massive body, and whipped out a handgun.

"I just want to talk to her." The strident voice echoed across the lawn, loud enough to hush two hundred inquisitive guests who peered at the scene from around the pavilion and on every balcony. "I don't need a fucking invitation to my own house."

Oh, God. *Billy.*

"Don't shoot him, Max," Caroline said, stepping away from the human wall he'd made. "He's my stepson. And that's"—she added with a quiet sigh—"precisely what the problem is."

Billy Peyton ambled across the expanse of the lawn, drawing every eye. Caroline knew the cellular buzz from South Beach to Coral Gables tomorrow would be that Billy Peyton was wasted. But that wasn't exactly news.

She squared her shoulders, bracing for the worst. She'd become adept at acting as though his behavior was normal, a trick she'd used to keep William from getting enraged over the antics of his only son. "I'm right here, Billy."

As she took the steps to the upper lawn to meet him, she sensed Max right behind her.

Billy stumbled as he approached her and she reached out to steady him. "What do you want?" she asked.

He leaned back and even in the dim party light, she could see his enlarged pupils and pink-rimmed eyes. What was it tonight? Weed? Coke? Ecstasy?

Those battered eyes swept over her. "That's a pretty stupid question, *Mom.*"

Disgust roiled through her, but she kept her tone modulated. "I received the papers, and my attorney will contact yours. There's really nothing else to discuss. Especially not tonight. This is a critical fund-raiser for the Foundation. Please. Do me a favor . . . and leave."

He dropped his head in a bull-like gesture that might have been threatening if he wasn't just this side of throwing up and his floppy surfer locks didn't ruin the whole effect. "I don't want to discuss shit and I couldn't give a rat's ass about your Foundation. Where's the bar?"

"It's closed."

"Open it."

"I would very much like you to leave," she said through gritted teeth, vaguely aware that Max had moved from behind her to behind Billy. "Without making a scene."

He opened his mouth to continue the argument, but before a sound came out, Max seized him into a headlock. Billy lunged away, but Max overpowered him, effectively paralyzing him with one unyielding hand.

The other hand rose slowly, holding a sleek black gun.

"Holy fuck—" Billy's eyes widened in terror and he jerked again, but Max immobilized every muscle with one squeeze.

"Watch your language around the lady," Max growled, pointing the gun straight up. Caroline's limbs grew numb as she stared at the pistol, but she forced herself to look at the horrified expression on Billy's contorted face.

"Who the hell are you?" Billy grunted, twisting his head to see Max. "Get your fu—"

Max yanked tighter. "I said, watch your language around the lady."

Caroline took a step toward them. "Billy, I've hired a bodyguard. And you know exactly why I've done that. I will not be intimidated or threatened by you or your sluglike friends."

He snorted. "You are swimming in delusions of grandeur, Caro. No one is trying to hurt you. I just want what is mine. Just because you got flat on your back for—"

Max wrenched his neck, maybe a little harder than necessary. "The lady wants you to leave, Mr. Peyton."

Fury flashed in Billy's pale blue eyes and he tried to shake his head. "This is my house and I'm—"

Max cocked the gun. "Let's take a walk."

Billy stared at the weapon, beads of sweat forming over his upper lip.

"Is there another way out besides the front?" Max asked Caroline.

She indicated the north lawn. "You can take him around there to the gatehouse."

Billy narrowed his eyes at her and all she could see was the blackness of his dilated pupils. "Whore." He mouthed the word at her so Max didn't hear it.

"He shouldn't drive," she said quietly. "I'll meet you in the front and get a cab for him."

"I'll take care of him," Max said, walking away with Billy tightly in his grasp. "Billy and I are going to have a little talk."

Caroline watched them disappear in the shadows and stared into the darkness. What would he do? What would they talk about? Billy hated her, but Max wouldn't believe his lies.

Would he?

Maybe Lucy Sharpe did have someone else just as good in her stable of bodyguards, but there was a certain comfort in knowing it was Max Roper responsible for her life.

After all—who owed her more than Max?